D1525586

ABOUT THE AUTHOR

From an early age, Martin was enchanted with old movies from Hollywood's golden era—from the dawn of the talkies in the late 1920s to the close of the studio system in the late 1950s—and has spent many a happy hour watching the likes of Garland, Gable, Crawford, Garbo, Grant, Miller, Kelly, Astaire, Rogers, Turner, and Welles go through their paces. It feels inevitable that he would someday end up writing about them.

Originally from Melbourne, Australia, Martin moved to Los Angeles in the mid-90s where he now works as a writer, blogger, webmaster, and tour guide.

www.MartinTurnbull.com

This book is dedicated to

Bob Molinari

with whom everything is possible,
without whom nothing is worthwhile.

ISBN-13: 978-1466218956
ISBN-10: 1466218959

THE GARDEN ON SUNSET

a novel

by

Martin Turnbull

Book One in the Hollywood's Garden of Allah novels

CHAPTER 1

When the Hollywood Red Car lurched to a stop, Marcus Adler pulled open his eyes to find a wheezing old conductor staring right at him.

Marcus looked around. He was the only passenger left. "Where are we?"

The conductor jerked his head toward the door. "End of the line."

"Don't suppose you know where 8152 Sunset Boulevard is?"

"What do I look like? A street map?"

Marcus took that for a no, picked up his cardboard suitcase, and climbed down to the street. A line of rickety stores huddled on the south side of Sunset Boulevard up to where the asphalt ended; a sign near the curb read LOS ANGELES CITY LIMIT. Past the sign, west of Crescent Heights Boulevard, Sunset disintegrated into a wandering dirt road. A knot of horses stood in the shade of a tree with thin, dusty leaves Marcus had never seen back in Pennsylvania. One of the horses raised its head to study him for a moment, then returned to grazing.

"Hey!" The conductor hung from the streetcar's doorway. "8152 Sunset? Try thataway." He pointed toward the horses.

Eighty-one fifty-two Sunset Boulevard, Hollywood, California. It was an address Marcus had repeated over and over to himself since that time when he was eleven years old, swollen grotesquely with diphtheria in the hospital. His parents had written Madame Alla Nazimova a letter at his request, never thinking that a motion picture star so unspeakably exotic, so stupefyingly glamorous would respond. But she did. And she came to call on him, a diaphanous vision in lavender tulle. How kind she was, and so humble. Surely she would remember him. How many bedside visits had she made to children inflated with diphtheria in the middle of Pennsylvania? How many did she look in the eye and say, "If you ever come to Hollywood, I want you to come visit me. My house is very large, and I have plenty of room for you. I live at 8152 Sunset Boulevard, Hollywood, California."

And now he was almost there.

Marcus crossed the deserted intersection and headed toward a nest of two-story bungalows that loomed behind a tall white wall. They were freshly painted; the sheen caught the light of the setting sun as it descended into the dirt track.

As he made his way along the wall, an unbroken trumpet note sliced the still air. What will Nazimova say when she answers the door? he wondered.

The trumpet player ran out of steam and a thunderclap of applause erupted. Maybe this wasn't a good time. He peeked around the corner and looked up at a twelve-foot-high sign.

GARDEN OF ALLAH HOTEL
8152 Sunset Boulevard

Marcus set his suitcase down in the dust and stared at the gold letters of *Allah*. He didn't expect Sunset Boulevard to be a dirt track and he certainly didn't expect to find a hotel sign out front of Alla Nazimova's movie star mansion.

He peered at the hotel past the sign. It was painted the same cream as the garden wall, with tall, arched windows and dark brown shutters. It looked like the California missions he'd studied in high school.

He pulled out a handkerchief and swiped his broad forehead, round cheeks and the back of his neck. It was hard to believe this was January. Back home, they'd be shoveling the driveway, but here there wasn't even a cool breeze. He picked up his suitcase and made his way past a long bed of pale roses and into the white hotel.

The murky foyer had paneled walls and octagonal avocado-green tiles the size of dinner plates. The reception desk would have been hard to spot without the lamp casting a pool of amber light on it. Its stained-glass shade was a kitschy pyramid with a sphinx and a clump of palm trees. There was no one in sight.

Marcus rang the bell. Laughter and clinking glasses wafted through the double doors that opened onto a wide brick path to a swimming pool curved like a grand piano at the far end. A crowd too large to count was scattered around it in knots of fours and fives; a hundred, two hundred people maybe. Shiny tuxedos, sparkling diamonds, ropes of pearls, patent leather shoes.

Marcus gaped at a clutch of women dancing the Black Bottom. Their short hair, high hemlines and cigarettes were a far cry from the Pennsylvania Dutch girls he'd grown up with. A girl Marcus had known in McKeesport had turned up at a St. Stephen's tea dance social with her hair bobbed like Louise Brooks and her stockings rolled down below her knees; she hadn't lasted ten minutes, and Marcus had never seen her again. Maybe she'd been run out of town too.

Six days, three trains, a bus and two streetcars later, the sting of his father's last words still jabbed at Marcus' heart. "You get out of my town and get as far as you can go, and don't come back." On the night train to Chicago, he'd stared into the darkness and wondered where to go. Eighty-one fifty-two Sunset Boulevard was the only address outside of McKeesport he knew, so when his train pulled into Chicago, he took the next one heading west.

There wasn't a Pickford curl in sight at this party. It was all crisp bangs, bright rouge and red lipstick, ivory cigarette holders and cream bowties on outrageous three-inch heels. Oriental butlers circulated with silver cocktail trays and virtually every girl had a martini in her hand. So much for seven years of Prohibition. There was a lively, frantic quality to this crowd Marcus had never witnessed before. Everyone seemed to be having such a riot that he had to wonder: What was so bad about booze if this was the result?

A troupe of musicians decked out like Spanish matadors made their way to the pool and lined up at the far end. They brought their Continental spin on "Ain't She Sweet" to a close and started counting backwards from ten. When they shouted "ONE!" the trumpeter blew a long note and paper lanterns in orange, blue, green and red strung throughout the maple trees lit up, transforming the garden into a fairytale wonderland with their gentle glow. The crowd sighed and clapped. It looks like the set of *Camille*, thought Marcus, where Nazimova wore that shimmering cloak with the white camellias. How luminous she'd been, falling in love with Valentino.

The matadors merged into the crowd playing "Five Foot Two, Eyes of Blue" and the chatter swelled again.

"You look a little lost."

The voice belonged to a tall man with a long, narrow face. It took Marcus a moment to realize he was staring into the eyes of Francis X. Bushman. Marcus had seen *Ben-Hur* twelve times when it came to McKeesport; he'd thought Bushman was stupendously hateful as Massala, the villain. Tonight he wore a tuxedo that looked twice as expensive as Marcus' entire wardrobe. His first movie star!

"I . . . ah . . ." The words dried up on Marcus' tongue like August dirt.

Bushman peered down at Marcus' cardboard suitcase and his eyes lit up. "Good gravy! You're here to check in!" Bushman lifted his hand to his mouth. "Hey! Brophy!" The actor's voice carried easily over the commotion.

A wide-faced man with a Cheshire cat smile turned around and raised his eyebrows. Bushman grabbed Marcus' suitcase out of his hand and lifted it high. "You have a guest!"

Brophy cut through the crowd with the eagerness of a groundhog in February. "Is that right, son? You want to check in? To the hotel?"

Marcus scanned the crowd. He couldn't see Alla Nazimova anywhere. "This is 8152 Sunset Boulevard, isn't it?"

"Sure is."

Marcus felt stupid asking if Madame Nazimova still lived there. This is a hotel, you big nincompoop, he told himself. Clearly she isn't here any more. "I guess I do need a room," he conceded.

Brophy stepped up onto the diving board and let out a whistle that slashed through the crowd and stopped the band.

"Everybody!" Brophy announced. "I have an exciting announcement to make. I would like to introduce you all to a most important person." He pulled Marcus up alongside him on the diving board and out of the side of his mouth murmured, "What's your name, kid?"

"Marcus Adler."

"Ladies and gentlemen, I would like to present the Garden of Allah Hotel's very first guest, Mister Marcus Adler, Esquire!" The crowd, easy to impress on bathtub gin, let out a collective "Oooohh!" and burst into a thunderclap of applause. "Mister Adler hails from the great city of . . ." He nudged Marcus.

"McKeesport, Pennsylvania."

" . . . Of McKeesport, Pennsylvania!" Brophy spun around in surprise. "McKeesport? Ain't that where the first nickelodeon opened up?"

Marcus nodded. It was McKeesport's sole claim to fame. Thin, to be sure, but eagerly brought up in conversation with every visiting relative and Fuller Brush man passing through town.

"Seems to me," Brophy beamed, "that our Mr. Adler here is bringing the coals back to Newcastle, which I think qualifies him to an extra-special rate. What do you say, friends?"

A loud cheer erupted. It dropped off quickly, though; the crowd was keen to get back to its gin. Brophy swept Marcus off the diving board, grabbed up his suitcase and led him back into the gloomy foyer. He opened the first page of the hotel register, swung it around toward Marcus and handed him a fountain pen.

"You on the level about being from McKeesport?"

Marcus nodded.

"Well, if that don't beat all. You planning on staying long with us, Mr. Adler?"

Marcus looked up from the blank page and summoned up a fistful of courage. "Does Alla Nazimova still live here?"

CHAPTER 2

The Garden of Allah Hotel's opening night party was only just starting to wind down when Marcus peered out of his tiny room late the next morning. All he could see was a couple of pretty girls in ginger-brown muslin, their velvet headbands slipped down around their necks. The shorter one had lost something and they were searching in the bushes of one of the villas.

Marcus saw the silhouette of a woman pull back the villa's heavy lace curtain to watch the girls fumble around in the flower beds. The figure remained disturbingly still until the girl with a long, bedraggled mess of peroxided hair held up the missing shoe and departed with her pal. The curtain fell, then was suddenly pulled back again. Had she seen him looking at her?

Marcus stepped away from his window and sat on the bed. "Okay," he said out loud. "So now what?"

Not once in the six days it had taken to get to Hollywood had it occurred to him that Alla Nazimova might no longer live in her Sunset Boulevard mansion. He'd expected that she might not recall her visit to his sick bed, but what sort of dunderhead crosses the entire country without an alternate plan?

He looked around his room. It wasn't very expensive, nor was it very big. There was barely enough room for a bedside table, and it was dark even during the day. Why was he sitting inside this cramped and dim hotel room instead of reveling in the boundless California sunshine? Surely the Pacific Ocean was easy enough to find.

* * *

Marcus had taken a wrong turn inside the hotel and ended up on the far side of the pool, where a handful of people in chaises lounged, none of them too chatty or sociable. The grounds looked a lot bigger today without a couple of hundred smartly dressed partygoers in varying stages of sobriety and subsequent disarray. The garden was thick with broad-leaved ferns, pink rhododendrons, yellow lantana and profusions of purple bougainvillea; villas spread to the east and west sides of the property. Marcus kept his eye on the one he could see from his room, but the curtain was drawn.

The California sun, which Marcus had traveled like a pack mule to feel on his face, had burned away the last of the morning haze. He tilted his face toward it and soaked up the warmth. He couldn't help but smile; the poor folks back home wouldn't get to feel this for another four months.

When he opened his eyes, a slim woman with bony shoulders had stretched out on a chaise lounge on the other side of the pool. He gasped and looked away — she looked like Greta Garbo. She also looked nude. He snuck another peek and took in the fawnish brown bathing suit that hugged her lean body and matched her legs. He had to know if it was her.

He wandered closer to the pool's edge and dropped to one knee to retie his shoelace. He snuck a sideways glance, squinting to see more clearly; it sure looked like Garbo. While he was messing around with the double knot, somebody's knee smacked him right in the forehead and sent him tumbling ass over chin into the pool. His hand hit the water with a thwack and the cold sucked the air out of his lungs. He groped at the water like a terrified octopus until his hand connected with something soft and fleshy. It moved like it was trying to shrug him free.

He broke through the surface and gulped air, shaking the water from his face. When he opened his eyes, a girl with startling white skin and hazel eyes was frowning at him, her forehead pinched. Dark brown hair draped across her narrow face like seaweed.

"Are you trying to drown me?" she demanded. "Can't you swim?"

"Pennsylvania state champion," Marcus snapped back. It wasn't entirely accurate, but this girl wouldn't know that. She made for the nearest edge, doing a one-armed side stroke, and Marcus followed her.

"I'm so sorry," the girl whispered. "I didn't see you. I got distracted by . . ." She glanced at the woman in the fawn bathing suit. They were a mere seven feet from her now.

"Is that who I think it is?" he murmured.

The girl smiled but didn't take her eyes off the woman. "I think so."

Marcus had seen Greta Garbo in *Flesh and the Devil* just a few months ago. It was the last movie he and Dwight Brewster had seen together. Marcus wondered for a moment how Dwight was. And then he wondered where Dwight was. Did he get run out of town too? Would he ever see Dwight again?

"Are you two drowned?" The voice was deep and possibly foreign but, Marcus asked himself, who knew how Greta Garbo sounded when she spoke?

"We're fine," the girl replied.

"Do you need a towel?"

"No, no," the girl called out, "we're okay. But thank you." She pushed off for the far side of the pool and motioned for Marcus to follow her.

They hoisted themselves out of the water and sat with their feet paddling the water. "I'm really sorry about all that," she said, and offered her hand. "My name is Kathryn," she said. "Kathryn Massey."

CHAPTER 3

Kathryn Massey smoothed her cotton sundress across the palm of her left hand. "See?" she said to the guy she'd knocked into the hotel pool right in front of someone who may or may not have been Greta Garbo. "This is almost dry already." She nodded toward their shoes. "They won't take too long."

"I hope not," he replied seriously. "They're the only ones I've got."

Kathryn studied the guy a little more closely. With his round, corn-fed face, apple cheeks and sandy blonde hair, he didn't seem the down-and-out type. "You've only got one pair of shoes?"

"I sort of left home in a hurry," Marcus said. His face shaded with something Kathryn couldn't quite identify. "You just check in?" he asked. She nodded. "Rooms are kind of small, huh?"

"There's barely room to swing a dead duck in mine." She shrugged. "Still, they're cheap, so what can you expect?" She stared at the villas. "I wonder how much they cost."

"Do you see the woman in the window?" he asked.

Kathryn followed Marcus' gaze to villa twenty-four. There was definitely someone standing there, holding the curtain back, unnervingly still.

"I noticed her from my window this morning," Marcus said. "I was thinking maybe it was Alla Nazimova."

"The movie star?"

"This used to be her home. I asked the manager if she still lives here, but he said he'd heard she had a place in New York."

"Would you stick around if someone got the bright idea to turn your home into a hotel?"

Marcus smiled a quiet sort of smile, more to himself than anything else. His teeth were big and white, and a couple were slightly snaggletoothed, which gave him a quiet sort of charm. Thank God you don't have one of those thousand watt smiles, Kathryn thought. I'm so tired of the ones designed to mesmerize casting agents and costars.

"You a big fan?" she asked.

Marcus hesitated, weighing something in his mind, and then nodded. "I've got this uncle and aunt in Pittsburgh. They took me to see her in *A Doll's House* when I was ten. I was completely captivated. Then I came down with diphtheria and my folks asked her to come see me. Nobody could believe it when she turned up. Before she left, she looked me right in the eye and said, 'If you ever come to Hollywood, I want you to visit me.' So last week when—"

He stopped himself and looked away, fixing his gaze on the woman in the fawn bathing suit. "So last week when I left town, there was only one address I could think of." He sighed. "I'm embarrassed to say that I'd expected Nazimova herself to be standing at the front gate beckoning me. 'Come in! I have been expecting you!'" He forced a smile. "What about you? From back east, too?"

"Sort of. About nine blocks east of here."

"Nine blocks? Why even bother?"

Oh lord, Kathryn thought. Where do I start? She pictured her mother perched like a gargoyle on the letterbox, waiting to hear where she'd gone. "I suspect that I left home like you left town." She watched Marcus' smile wilt.

"In that case, you have my condolences." His gaze drifted back to the window in villa twenty-four, but the woman had disappeared.

Kathryn decided this conversation needed a change of topic. "Have you seen the Pacific yet?"

"No, I haven't. Is it far?"

"Not at all. We can take the Red Car down to Santa Monica."

"You have your own automobile?"

"No, no, the streetcar. Takes about forty-five minutes. Want to go now?"

Marcus hesitated.

"You got something better to do? I'll even pay the nickel fare for you. It's the least I can do." Kathryn smiled. "Look," she said, "you're in a town full of strangers now. You're going to have to start trusting some of us sooner or later."

"It's not that. I was thinking that maybe we should invite her along."

He pointed to a girl who stood at the hotel's double doors. She couldn't have been over seventeen, but she was tall and held herself like a doe: all eyes and skittish alertness. Kathryn let out a silent sigh. There was always going to be another girl more beautiful than the last, wasn't there? But this one needed help.

The girl's eyes darted around the Garden while three men lingered around her like buzzards, each twice her age, three times her waist size, and sporting four-day growths.

Kathryn got to her feet. "Come on," she said to Marcus. "The trick is to never stop talking."

They jammed on their damp shoes and strode up to the girl. "There you are!" Kathryn exclaimed. Up close she was even more striking. Look at that skin, Kathryn thought. It's really quite perfect, isn't it? And I bet that rose in your cheeks isn't even rouge. The girl's jaw would have been mannishly square had it not reached a pixie-point chin and culminated in the subtlest of dimples. Her hair was a light honey in a messy flapper bob that she may have done herself.

The girl looked at Kathryn with wide eyes the color of holly leaves and allowed her to grab hold of her hands. "I thought we arranged to meet in the foyer," Kathryn continued. "Or are we late? I put my wristwatch down someplace, but do you think I can remember where?" The creeps pulled back a step. Kathryn turned to Marcus and nodded toward the girl. "You two know each other, don't you? Oh, of course you do. You must have met a hundred times by now. Well, we're off to a bit of a late start now, but at this point we'll only be fashionably late."

She pulled the girl through the front door of the Garden of Allah and didn't stop moving until they reached the rose bushes.

"Who are—do I know you?" the girl stammered.

"You looked like you needed rescuing. I'm Marcus and this here is Kathryn."

"You don't mind, do you?" Kathryn asked the girl.

"Oh, heavens no, I'm so terribly grateful. Those three men pert near stuck to me like cotton candy in August. I could not get rid of them."

The girl had the comeliest southern accent Kathryn had ever heard. Of course you do, Kathryn thought. Because you're just not charming enough. Kathryn decided she was going to have to do something about that because the men in this town would eat her alive once they got an earful of it.

"My name is Miss Gwendolyn Brick," the girl said, offering her hand. "But it's just the most awful name, so I'm going to change it. So pleased to meet you both. Grateful to meet you both, in fact. I've just arrived. Checked in this very morning."

"From where?" Marcus asked.

"Hollywood."

"What a coincidence," Marcus said. "Kathryn's just come nine blocks, too."

"Oh, no," Gwendolyn laughed a musical, tinkling sort of laugh. "I'm from the other Hollywood."

"There are two?"

"Hollywood, Florida. Took me a streetcar, then two buses, then two trains and another streetcar to get here, but I made it."

"We're heading out to Santa Monica Beach. You want to come along?"

Gwendolyn bit into a pair of plump lips. "I'd love to, but I have something here in my purse that I probably shouldn't take to the beach."

"What is it?"

When Gwendolyn hesitated, Marcus said, "You're in a town full of strangers now. You're going to have to start trusting some of us sooner or later." He flickered a smile over to Kathryn.

Gwendolyn opened her purse. It was a dark cherry red that almost matched the brick-red stripes of her dress. She pulled out a brown leather wallet with stitching that was starting to come loose. "A fella who sat next to me out of Dallas left it behind," she said.

"It looks awfully thick. What's in it?"

"Four thousand dollars."

CHAPTER 4

Gwendolyn stood at the front gate of 1239½ Fountain Ave and wondered if her cockamamie idea of coming to the other Hollywood to become a movie star had been such a smart idea. Maybe I should just keep the four grand in my purse and call it a day, she thought. For pert near my whole life I've been hankering to come to Hollywood, California so bad I've been fixin' to be–

Gwendolyn mentally slapped herself in the face. Kathryn had patiently explained that to the men in this town, a southern belle accent like hers was like a lame muskrat to an alligator. 'If you want to be taken seriously in this town, and not just taken advantage of, my advice is to lose the southern fried accent.'

She took a moment to study the little bungalow in front of her. She thought it was a dear little place, in a "we just got married and this is all we can afford for now" sort of way, and a fresh coat of paint would perk it up to no end. The clumps of geraniums and pansies wilting in the flower beds looked like they'd not been watered since before Valentino died, but it was all easily fixable. Clearly, Mr. Eugene Hammerschmidt was a bachelor.

Gwendolyn reached into the genuine leather handbag that Kathryn had lent her and pulled out the ratty wallet. Four thousand dollars was enough to live on for at least a couple of years. More than enough time for a movie studio to discover her. Do I really have to give it back? she wondered.

"With any luck, he won't be home. Or it'll be the wrong address," Marcus said. He and Kathryn stood behind her. "You're here to do the right thing because you're a good person. And if he's not home, or nobody here has heard of him, then you can walk away with a clear conscience."

Gwendolyn knew Marcus was right. She had to at least try and return the money. Her mama hadn't done much of a job bringing up her children, but she did teach them what was right and what wasn't.

"We'll be sitting in that park across the street watching you," Kathryn said. "So if anything happens, we're close by."

Gwendolyn stepped onto the front porch and banged on the front door with a hand-shaped brass doorknocker that could have done with a good scrubbing. She let a minute crawl by before she knocked a second time. Still nothing. Okay, she thought, I'll give it one more—

The door swung open and Gwendolyn's heart fell a little. It was the guy from the train, all right; she'd know those mudflap ears anywhere.

"What the hell do you want?"

"Mr. Hammerschmidt," Gwendolyn ventured, "You probably won't remem–"

"You're that girl from the train with all the questions about the studios. Look, honey, now isn't a good time."

Gwendolyn held up the wallet. "You left this on the train. There's an awful lot of money in it, so I thought—"

"Keep it."

"What?"

"You heard me." Hammerschmidt slammed the door shut.

Gwendolyn gasped. Who could afford to give away four thousand dollars just like that? Maybe the streets of Hollywood, California really were paved with gold.

She turned around and met Marcus and Kathryn halfway down the gravel path. "What did he say?" Marcus asked.

"I showed him his wallet and he told me to get lost."

"He didn't want the money?"

Gwendolyn shook her head.

Something caught Kathryn's attention and her eyes darted behind Gwendolyn. "Look out," she murmured.

Hammerschmidt stood at the top of his porch steps, his hairy-knuckled hands on his hips and his face pressed into a grimace. "Where the hell did you two come from?"

"We're with her," Kathryn said.

He sized the three of them up. "Get in here," he said, and jutted his head toward his open front door.

They followed him into a living room that smelled like it had never been opened. "You working for Zwillman?" the guy asked when the door was shut behind them. He swiped a porthole in the filthy window and peered into the street.

"We don't know any Zwillman," Gwendolyn told him. She opened up the wallet and pulled out a yellow slip of paper. "You left your laundry receipt in your wallet. Wong's All Nite Laundry."

That made him turn around. His brown eyes widened when he saw the receipt. "So you came here of your own accord? Just to give me back my four grand?"

"You're not making it easy, I must say."

Gwendolyn placed the wallet on a small table by the door. Hammerschmidt stared at it like a hungry dog at a suspicious bone, but he didn't touch it. Behind him stood a cardboard suitcase, the kind Woolworth's sold for a buck fifty. Tied around it was a brown belt as used and frayed as his wallet.

Hammerschmidt started pacing back and forth, chewing the inside of his cheek. Gwendolyn winced as he cracked his knuckles.

"I meant for you to find the wallet and keep the cash," he said. "You were going to Hollywood to try your luck. Figured you could do with it more than me."

Gwendolyn peered around the shadowy room. "Looks to me like you could do with four thousand dollars. For starters, you could paint your house."

"When I left that money on my seat, I wasn't going for no drink. Was gonna throw myself off the train when we crossed the river at the New Mexico border. Only my timing was screwy. I missed the goddamned bridge and fell onto a hillside covered with the softest goddamned green grass you ever saw. I walked away without a scratch, if you can believe that."

"So you're in trouble . . . ?" It was Kathryn. She stepped closer to him.

"That four thousand there," Hammerschmidt said, "used to be eight. It wasn't mine to play with, but I like the track too much. The boss won't be happy to learn that his eight grand's been on a reducing diet." He turned back to the window. "God *damn* it." Hammerschmidt began to pace. "I'm dead meat. I'm dead meat." He stopped and squinted at Gwendolyn. "Are you really an actress? Or just a pretty girl?"

Gwendolyn looked at the front door, then back at Hammerschmidt. "What do y'all have in mind?"

He hurried to a grimy desk in the corner and pulled a small white card out of a drawer. He gave it to Gwendolyn. It was a business card, embossed with the Warner Brothers logo, *Bill Brockton, Casting Department*, and an address on Sunset Boulevard. Gwendolyn's heart started beating.

"Make like you're my girlfriend to whoever knocks on that door. You're mad as blazes because you haven't heard from me in a week."

There was a rat-a-tat-tat of sharp knocks on the door.

"You call Bill. He's a way in to Warner that ten thousand girls just like you would give their last square meal for." Hammerschmidt swiped the wallet off the table, grabbed his suitcase, and disappeared through the kitchen door. "Thanks, toots."

Gwendolyn looked at Kathryn, her eyes pleading.

Kathryn glanced toward the kitchen and looked at Gwendolyn. "Remember when we met at the Garden of Allah? You go on the defensive and you don't stop talking."

Another three knocks pounded the musty air.

Gwendolyn felt like there was no air left in her lungs. "But I . . . I just . . ."

Kathryn lay her hand on the tarnished door knob. "Sweetie, if you want to make it here in Hollywood, this is how it's done," she said, and yanked open the door. A couple of guys, dark suits, dark ties, and dark hair filled the doorway. A somber blue Packard waited in the street behind them, its engine running.

"Where the hell is he?" Kathryn snapped. They lurched back a couple of inches. "So help me, sweet Jesus, you two had better have come here to tell me that Mr. Eugene Hammerschmidt has gone to meet his maker. Because I swear to God, boys, if he's still drawing breath it's only because he hasn't got the guts to come back here and face me like a man. A whole lousy week and I ain't heard a peep out of that bum? So?" She crossed her arms and glared at them. "Where is he?"

The guy on the right with the tennis court tan held out his hand. "Whoa, sister. Calm down, will ya? We came to find out where The Hammer is."

The Hammer? Gwendolyn thought. Oh, that's cute. He's a big puffball, if anything.

"You mean you've lost him?" Kathryn demanded. "You people just slay me. So even Zwillman doesn't know? I thought he knew everything."

The men frowned and looked at each other. Gwendolyn's heart leapt. Had Kathryn gone too far? The way Hammerschmidt talked, Zwillman was the number one guy. Did Kathryn know something she didn't?

"What's The Hammer said about Zwillman?"

"It's just a name I've heard mentioned around here quite a lot lately." Kathryn made a big Pola Negri shrug. "All you lugheads need to do is tell The Hammer he's blown it and I won't be here when he gets back."

Kathryn stepped back into the gloom like Norma Talmadge in *Secrets* and slammed the door shut.

The three of them listened as the footsteps receded down the gravel path. Gwendolyn waited a few moments then called out to Eugene. When there was no reply, they picked their way through the shadows and opened the door onto a bright kitchen. It was all yellows and greens and looked like it had barely been used. On the kitchen table was a scrawled note.

Don't forget! We need more cookies!

Gwendolyn picked it up. "What in the name of Satan's pantry is this supposed to mean?"

Marcus looked around the kitchen and spotted a cookie jar in the shape of a bunch of carrots. "Cookies," he said. He went over to it and pulled the top off. Inside was another note, which Marcus extracted and read out loud. "When you call Bill Brockton at WB, tell him I said 'TARNISH.' He'll know you're legit. Good luck—and thanks."

Marcus looked inside the cookie jar again and pulled out Hammer's wallet, still stuffed with cash. He handed it to Gwendolyn. When she was done counting, she leaned against the counter and let out a long, slow whistle.

CHAPTER 5

Marcus hunted around for the men's room but couldn't see it.

Gwendolyn and Kathryn pulled up beside him. "I don't know," Gwendolyn said. "It wasn't as though he was talking through the *whole* picture."

"But when he did, didn't you think it was impressive?" Kathryn asked. "We really heard him talking. That was Al Jolson's actual voice. I don't think pictures will ever be the same again."

Gwendolyn shrugged and pulled on her velvet cloche. "But it's not like he's any great shakes as a singer. It's called *The Jazz Singer*—shouldn't they have cast someone who can sing? I cannot believe Al Jolson is the biggest thing in vaudeville."

A couple of girls in cheap fox furs pushed past them, their cigar-smoking boyfriends trailing them. One of the men sang out, "Mammy! Mammy! How I love you, how I love you!" in a voice that grated down Marcus' back. The girls erupted into giggles. "I ain't your Mammy!" one of them said over her shoulder.

"Is something wrong?" Kathryn asked. "You're awfully quiet."

"I need the men's room," Marcus said as a woman in a ridiculous hat moved aside. The explosion of baby pink feathers arching over its brim had hidden the men's room sign. "I'll be right back."

He barreled through the crowd, shouldered open the door, and dashed across the black and white tiles, and into the first cubicle he came to. He shot the bolt across. When metal slammed into metal, it sounded like the air gun the boys back home shot owls with. Marcus threw his fedora onto the hook, yanked off a couple of feet of toilet paper, and bunched the whole thing into a wad. He pressed it to his face as the first groan bubbled up from his throat and burst out of his mouth.

He held his breath, but a second groan, as deep and painful as the first, welled up from the pit of his stomach. He felt it rise and push against the sides of his chest, then squeeze up through his throat, and force its way into his mouth. It tasted like old cabbage. Marcus pressed the wad of toilet paper against his mouth and screwed his eyes so tight it hurt, then released the groan. He could see the words exactly as they had appeared on the screen.

Remember, Jakie, a son is a son, no matter if his papa throws him out a hundred times.

It felt like a brick to the chest—unforgiving and brutal. Another bubble of pain started to rise like toxic porridge from deep in his chest. He pressed his forehead against the cool metal partition of the cubicle. It was soothing. The first tears seeped between his lids and trickled down his cheeks into the tissue. He took as deep a breath as he could muster, but it wobbled and the tears started to flow again.

Remember, Jakie, a son is a son, no matter if his papa throws him out a hundred times.

"Oh, Father," he whispered, "Another half hour and you'd never have known. You wouldn't have seen me with Dwight."

He squeezed his eyes shut so hard he could see geometric patterns flash like fireworks. The pyrotechnics faded and in their place was his father.

Roland Adler's face was long and narrow and pinched from years of frowning. His hair was thick but had long gone gray, the color of garbage can lids and gun powder. Marcus could see his father's flinty blue eyes as he gave his son a final shove into the train. "And don't come back here until you've—"

But Marcus never heard the rest. The steam whistle lopped off the end of the commandment and the train slowly pulled out of the station. Marcus stood in the doorway and shouted, "Don't come back until I've *what?*" but his father didn't hear him.

In the bathroom stall of the Warner Brothers Theater on Hollywood Boulevard one month and two thousand miles later, Marcus repeated the question: Don't come back until I've *what?*

* * *

"There you are!"

"Sorry, girls." Marcus avoided looking at his new friends lest they spot his bloodshot eyes. He faced the curved staircase that enveloped the tallest indoor fountain Marcus had ever seen. "Let's go get some coffee."

The ten o'clock session had already begun, so the foyer was fairly deserted. It was all decked out in black and white marble that ran the length and breadth of the entrance and a good dozen feet up the walls to a gold-leafed ceiling and a pair of crystal chandeliers ten feet tall. There was certainly nothing like this back home.

How ironic, he thought. I spent my whole childhood feeling like I didn't fit in, like I didn't belong in that no-account backwater. How many nights did I lay in bed thinking surely, surely, *surely* I was destined for bigger things in brighter places? And yet now that I'm gone, all I can think of is how deeply I miss it.

"Are you okay?" Kathryn asked, frowning.

"Bad dinner. All gone now. Better out than in."

They were on the sidewalk in front of a huge poster for the movie they'd just seen, a drawing of Al Jolson in blackface and a white bow-tie. His white-gloved hands were outstretched and begging for acceptance. Marcus let his gaze wander back into the theater's foyer. A small woman in dark purple lace and a matching hat was gazing up at the poster for *Love,* the new Greta Garbo/John Gilbert movie. She looked vaguely familiar.

"The truth is, I'm having a fairly strong reaction to that movie," he said.

"Half the country is," Gwendolyn added, but in a tone that indicated she really didn't understand why.

"I think I know what it is," Kathryn said. The electric light from inside lit up Kathryn's pale face. She didn't sport the Californian tan he'd noticed on nearly every other girl here, but her dark chocolate hair and bold red lipstick made her look striking. "I had the same thought."

"You did?" he asked.

She nodded. "When I heard Al Jolson speak on screen for the first time, I thought, So that's how he sounds? But then I thought, Somebody's got to have written those lines. With pictures being silent, nobody really cared what the actors were saying. But if talking pictures take off—"

"They'll never take off," Gwendolyn cut in. "I think that movie columnist in the *Examiner*, Louella somebody-or-other, I think she's right. It's just a gimmick."

"But if they do take off, somebody's got to write the words the actors say. Just like in a stage play," Kathryn said.

"You've got a point," Marcus allowed. He looked back at the woman in the purple lace. Where had he seen her before?

"I *knew* we'd had the same thought!"

"Which was?" Gwendolyn asked.

Yes, Marcus wondered. Just what is this same thought we've both had?

Kathryn smiled and poked him in the chest. "That's what you should do. Write plays for the talking pictures."

"You're a writer?" Gwendolyn asked.

He looked at Kathryn, startled. How the hell had she seen his stories? When his father had given him fifteen minutes to pack, they were the first things he'd shoved into his suitcase. Those stories he'd spent summers upon summers scribbling down in his room when his father thought he should be out hunting owls were the last things he wanted to leave behind and the first things his father would've set fire to. But he hadn't told anyone here about them.

"I like to write short stories," he allowed.

"Ha! I knew it!" Kathryn said. "I can recognize a fellow writer when I meet one. You're so well mannered and reserved. All the quiet boys I've ever met have been writers."

"You write, too?" Gwendolyn asked Kathryn. "I had no idea I was in the company of such talented folks."

"I plan on being a journalist, like Nellie Bly," Kathryn said. "But you —" she poked Marcus in the chest again, "you've got 'picture play writer' written all over you." Then she frowned. "Now that pictures can talk, they're going to have to come up with a better title than 'picture play writer.'"

Marcus nodded and looked back for the woman in lace, but she had disappeared.

CHAPTER 6

Kathryn's money was running low. For the past couple of years she'd been squirreling it away as she plotted her escape from the motherland, but it wasn't going to last much longer.

She absently turned another page of the *Los Angeles Examiner* and stared across her patio table at the Black Sea-shaped pool, letting her mind wander to Marcus. She'd only told him to become a picture play writer because he'd looked so stricken and woeful, and had found herself prattling on and on about talking pictures and plays and dialogue and vocabulary. "I should have kept my mouth shut," she murmured to herself. "How about you stick to the problem of your own career?"

It was all very well to want to be a courageous girl reporter, but by the age of twenty-five, Nellie Bly had published an exposé on life inside a women's lunatic asylum and made it around the world faster than Phileas Fogg in *Around the World in Eighty Days*. But all Kathryn had done was get dragged by her mother from dance class to acting class to one useless audition after another. She wasn't pretty enough to play the romantic lead, or kooky enough to play the best friend, or cute enough to play the kid sister. She wasn't even ugly enough to play the enemy. For seven years she'd had to follow her mother to every studio in Hollywood and had never gotten a bite. It was a colossal waste of a childhood.

But no more! Kathryn had staged her exit. She would never go back to her mother's termite-infested apartment. Her hotel room may be darker than midnight in hell's basement, but it was hers and hers alone. Still, she'd have to get a job soon.

But the newspaper business was such an old boys' club. Elbowing her way in would be tantamount to breaking into First National Bank in broad daylight with a cowbell tied around her neck.

"Holy crap!"

Kathryn watched as a woman's hand lowered an enormous martini glass to the patio table. There was a chip in the rim that looked like it could do some damage. An alarmingly pale woman with half-closed eyes plunked herself down next to Kathryn. Her dark hair was parted at the top of her head and flopped down around a long face with a pointed chin. She made a grand to-do of prying open her eyelids and moaning as though she bled from every pore.

"Darling, please do me the *greatest* favor and reassure me that it is well past the cocktail hour."

"It's not quite one o'clock yet."

"I'm talking Greenwich Mean Time, naturally." The woman cast a bleary glance over the newspapers. "Good lord, if these are the Saturday papers, I can't imagine how thick the Sunday ones will be."

"These *are* the Sunday papers."

The woman took a long sip of her martini. "Tell me, how does one procure the Sunday papers on a Saturday?"

"This is Sunday."

The woman reared back. "But what happened to Saturday?"

"That was yesterday."

The woman paused to consider that she'd missed an entire day, then shrugged. "Not the first time that's happened. Tell me darling, what's your name?"

"Kathryn Massey."

"I'm positively charmed to meet you. The name is Tallulah."

"Oh!" Kathryn exclaimed. "Tallulah Bankhead!"

Miss Bankhead reached into an enormous aubergine shoulder bag that matched what was left of her nail polish and pulled out a silver cigarette case. It caught the afternoon sun and reflected into Kathryn's eyes as she flipped it open and offered up a row of slim white cigarettes.

Kathryn smiled and took one. "I enjoyed you in *The Trap*."

Tallulah seemed startled. "Good heavens, even I'd forgotten about that one." She reached back into her bag for a fat wad of envelopes bound with a length of pink lace that looked like it had been torn from a French negligee. She tossed it onto the table. "Thank you. That was very kind of you to say. If perhaps unlikely."

"You out here to make a picture?" Kathryn asked.

Miss Bankhead pulled the lace off the bundle of envelopes and started flipping through them. She sucked her cigarette down to its tip and slurped at her martini. "No, no, just checking the lay of the land, so to speak. I was at one of Eva LeGallienne's parties back in New York and I met a theater director there. Sweet man. George Cukor. Heard of him? No, I hadn't either. At any rate, he pressed me to come out here and snoop around for work."

"Any luck?"

"To be honest, I've hardly seen the light of day. The gin out here is simply too marvelous for words. Takes the edge off the cocaine which, I'm sorry to say, is disappointingly average." She pushed the letters across the table and let out a low sigh. "Fan mail. So tedious."

"You get fan mail?" Kathryn asked.

"I'm Tallulah Bankhead, my pet, not Lady Fucking Macbeth."

"What I meant was that they pass your fan mail on to you?"

"Nobody else wants it. Hell, I don't even want it, but these little darlings . . ." She waved her talons across the scattered pile of letters. "They did take the time to commit pen to paper." She gave a half-hearted cough.

Kathryn picked up the nearest letter. The envelope was tinted a light lavender color and smelled of some sort of flowery perfume.

"Violets," Tallulah explained. "Every other one positively reeks of violet water."

Kathryn stared thoughtfully at the letters. "Do you answer them?"

"The odd one, perhaps. Far fewer than I really should. Oh, what I wouldn't give for someone to answer them for me."

"How much would you give, exactly?" Kathryn asked, her wheels turning.

Tallulah let out a deep belch. "The absolute earth! What a burden that would lift from my slender shoulders. Don't get me wrong: without fans, how would someone like me earn her way in Russian caviar and Hungarian water crackers? But dear God in heaven, so many. And so frequently. This is just the start."

"I can do it for you," Kathryn said.

"Can you type?"

"Up to fifty words a minute."

Just don't ask me why I can type so fast, Kathryn thought. She didn't want to admit the hours she'd spent typing out every Nellie Bly article she could find, pretending she'd written them herself.

Tallulah slapped both hands on the patio table. "How does thirty dollars a week sound?

Kathryn barely kept her mouth from falling open. She was going to ask for twenty. "That'll be just fine."

"Just one more question, if I may?"

"Shoot."

Tallulah Bankhead lifted her enormous chipped glass. "How are you in the martini-making department, darling?"

CHAPTER 7

Bill Brockton turned out to be the sort of guy that people want to race to the nearest restaurant and fill up with potatoes and sour cream, fluffy biscuits awash in gravy, a mountain of fresh corn and a whopping slice of chocolate cake. The veins on the guy's hand stuck out like drizzled strawberry sauce and his cheeks looked like they'd been hollowed out with an ice cream scoop.

He smiled weakly at Gwendolyn and held his business card between his fingertips like he was afraid to touch it. He studied it longer than Gwendolyn ever had, then studied Gwendolyn even longer. "Come with me," he murmured.

He didn't say another word until they were deep within a cavernous warehouse on the Warner Brothers lot. It was a good fifty feet tall and more than two hundred feet long, with a concrete floor and a single barn door to let in light. It was empty except for a team of workmen at the far end securing mattresses to the walls.

Gwendolyn and Brockton watched the men struggle with a mattress. "Now that we seem to be in the business of making talkies," he said, "we have to soundproof all our production stages, or the microphone will pick up every sneeze and hiccup in a three-block radius. Where did you get my card?"

When Gwendolyn said the name 'Eugene Hammerschmidt,' Brockton winced.

"Is he . . . still alive?"

"As far as I know."

"Exactly what do you know?" Once Gwendolyn was through explaining how she met Eugene, he asked, "And the money?"

She considered her options. Should she confess that Eugene had only taken five hundred bucks and left her with thirty-five hundred? And if she did, would he demand she give it back? A girl's got to eat, she decided. "Money . . . ?"

Brockton sighed.

He took her elbow and guided her back outside. A troupe of Middle Eastern slave girls glided past, their skirts slit all the way up to their hipbones. When they were thirty feet from the studio gate, Brockton said, "I want to thank you for taking the time to come down here and tell me that The Hammer's okay."

Gwendolyn could smell another brush-off coming her way. "He told me to tell you *tarnish*. I suppose that's some sort of code word?"

Brockton smiled. "Yeah. A few years ago, we made a Ronald Colman picture here called *Tarnish*. It was about all sorts of people getting into all sorts of trouble. It became our in-joke for 'Oh boy, am I in a jam!' We figured we needed a code word once we started running bootleg around here, so we agreed on *tarnish*. At any rate, thanks again for dropping by."

He started to lead her back toward the gate, but Gwendolyn didn't move. Brockton wrinkled his brow and shifted his weight onto the other foot.

Gwendolyn crossed her arms knowing full well how much it lifted her bust. "Eugene promised me that if I were to contact you, and present you with your business card, and tell you the word *tarnish*, that you would get me a screen test."

"He knew better than to promise something like that."

"His bootlegging bosses — *your* bootlegging bosses — were knocking on his front door. I was the only one there who could stall them while he snuck out the back. He said that if I lied to his bosses, he would make it worth my while. He promised me you could arrange a screen test."

Brockton interlaced his fingers and pressed his palms to the top of his red hair. "You're a very pretty girl, and I wish I could get you a screen test, honey, I really do. But you might as well ask me to crown you the queen of England."

"Eugene promised on his mother's life."

"God damn it! If I was so important around here, do you think I'd be one of the schmucks hauling the bootleg? I'm just a lackey."

Behind Brockton a studio security guard waved through a dark blue automobile. It was longer than most and gleamed in the Hollywood sun. Gwendolyn had no idea if it was the same vehicle parked out front of Eugene's house—the good lord knew she was no expert on anything with wheels—but as it drove past them, a last-ditch opportunity conjured itself like a genie.

She pulled her lips into what she hoped was a knowing smile and pointed. "Do you see that there car?" she asked Brockton. By the time he turned around, it was no longer in sight. "It was the one parked out front of Eugene's house that day." Gwendolyn gave Brockton a once-over and marched after the car.

"Where do you think you're going?" Brockton demanded. The tremor in his voice was all she needed to hear. God only knew what she would've said to the inhabitants of that car if he let her get that far. She was almost relieved when he grabbed her wrist and spun her around. She shot him her best Gloria Swanson glare.

"Jesus!" he exclaimed under his breath. "Could you just—okay, okay. You girls don't ever make it easy on a guy, do you?"

"I took The Hammer for his word when he promised—"

"All right, all right already! Here's what I can do. And this really is the best I can do, take it or leave it. We're gonna be holding a closed open call. That's when we ask talent scouts to send along anyone they feel might have potential, but who is currently unsigned and not represented by any agent. I'm going to give you the name of a talent scout— Beau Gussington. Can you remember that?"

"Of course! How do I contact him?"

"No need to do that. I'm going to put you on the list. You just be sure to show up at the front gate, ten o'clock, February thirteenth. And do not be late."

It was more than Gwendolyn had dared hope for. She softened her face into a smile and offered her hand.

He took it, and shook it limply. "You look mighty fine in that dress, by the way. It's as good a choice as any to wear to the call."

Gwendolyn considered telling him that she had made the dress herself and had finished it that morning, but decided against it. Us movie stars, she told herself, must maintain an aura of mystery.

She waved to the guard on her way out of the studio. Just an hour ago, she'd been a nobody with a cheap business card. And now? A little voice inside her head, sounding suspiciously like Mama's, told her that she wasn't nothing but a scheming actress who wasn't above an ugly bluff. There was no telling what she'd do when she got in front of the cameras.

CHAPTER 8

It wasn't until after Marcus had enrolled in a one-week
intensive course at the Melrose School for Efficient
Typewriting that it occurred to him that maybe Kathryn had
only been kidding about his becoming a picture play writer.
She'd taken him by surprise, but the more he thought about
it, the more he liked the idea. Imagine his father's reaction
when he saw his son's name up on the movie screen:
WORDS BY MARCUS ADLER. Would that be enough to
change his mind?

He pulled open the door of Classroom B to find the room
almost full. The teacher's sullen gray suit matched the paint
on the walls. She stood at the front of the class with the
posture of a ballerina in a back brace and turned around
dramatically to look at the clock on the wall behind her. It
was less than a minute till one.

"As I was saying," the teacher projected like a midway
barker, "it is essential that you are seated at your
typewriting machine *before* this clock strikes the hour."

* * *

By six P.M., Marcus' shoulders, elbows and knuckles were a
twinge away from seizing up altogether. All day long, AAA,
SSS, LLL, KKK—they'd learned twelve letters in five hours.
When the clock chimed six times, Mrs. Frobisher ended the
day with a curt instruction to be ready at one P.M.
tomorrow, *sharp*.

It had been chilly inside, despite the sun that shone through the narrow skylights. The gray walls didn't help much; they were the gray of battleships and jail cells. If the place had more bars over the windows and fewer typewriting machines, it could've been the lone jail cell in the McKeesport police station. Marcus looked out the window, instead of Melrose Avenue he saw his high school stadium, all lit up like it was the night his father and the mayor had caught him with Dwight. He pushed the memory out of his mind as he held the door open for the last of the girls in the class when he heard a voice behind him.

"I'm so glad you waited for me."

Marcus turned and met a smiling young man with a full face with soft corners, a brown fedora jammed onto his head. Marcus smiled back. They headed up the corridor together.

"I was so relieved when you showed up," the guy said. He looked to be in his mid-twenties, a couple of years older than Marcus. "I did *not* want to be the only guy in that class. Let me guess: a writer?"

"Aspiring," Marcus said.

"Novelist? Playwright?"

"I want to write for the pictures now that they can talk."

"Me too!" The guy gave Marcus a friendly punch to the shoulder. "The name's Hugo Marr. Hey, you got somewhere you need to be? How's about we get a bite to eat?"

Marcus hesitated. His funds were dissolving at an alarming rate. Every dime counted until he could get a job, but a couple of the writers at the Garden of Allah told him that no studio would hire him until he could type.

"My treat!" Hugo said. "Come on, I know a great diner just off La Brea. The Fog Cutter. You'll think the mashed potatoes were whipped in heaven by angels."

* * *

By the time Marcus knew Hugo Marr wasn't lying about the potatoes — they were fluffier than the cotton candy at the Pennsylvania State Fair — he'd learned that Hugo was the son of Edwin Marr, a cinematic genius worthy of being mentioned in the same breath as D. W. Griffith and Cecil B. DeMille, if Hugo was to be believed.

"He doesn't go in for this talkies stuff." Hugo held up a bunched fist. "'Ruination! Ruination!' That's his favorite word right now. He spends a lot of time running around proclaiming, 'Talking pictures will be the ruination of the art form!'" Hugo laughed gently. "I don't agree with him, though. I think talkies are the future of pictures. You've seen *The Jazz Singer*, right? Sensational, right? I can't wait to hear what John Barrymore sounds like. And Greta Garbo. And Norma Talmadge. And Billie Dove! She's one of my favorites. I can't wait to hear what *she* sounds like. Hell, I can't wait to hear what they all sound like!" He swiped up the last of his meatloaf's tomato sauce with a piece of bread and popped it into his mouth. "And with any luck, they'll be saying *my* words. Hey! And yours too, huh?"

Marcus felt like a phony. He looked across the table at the son of a big-time Hollywood director. Who am I to think I could write anything worthy of John Barrymore or Norma Talmadge? Just because I spent my teenage summers scribbling stories in five-and-dime notebooks? This town is probably chock full of real writers, ones with published novels and plays on Broadway. Exactly how many gallons of gall were flowing through my veins when I decided I'd be a writer for the talking pictures?

"Maybe they will," Marcus replied. "But in the meanwhile, I need a job."

"I know how that feels," Hugo said.

"You? But isn't your father . . . ?"

"My dad's way of doing things is the old way. Which is to say, the hard way. No help. No leg up."

Sounds familiar, Marcus thought. "Strict, huh?"

"On a good day. The only thing he ever gave me was advice. He said to me, 'Nobody takes a writer seriously if he can't type.' So here we are."

"Do you have a regular job?" Marcus asked.

Hugo opened his dark leather satchel and drew out a copy of the *Los Angeles Times*. He turned to the Entertainment section, folded it in half and then in half again, and dropped it in front of Marcus. He pointed to an ad for *The Road to Romance* featuring a photograph of Ramon Novarro in profile with his dark hair slicked back and his mouth curled up in a knowing smile. He was even more handsome than he had been in *Ben-Hur.*

"You heard of Grauman's Chinese Theater, right? Down on Hollywood Boulevard?"

"No, I don't think so."

"It opened up a few months ago. Talk about a movie palace. All decked out oriental-style. You've never seen anything like it. I just got a job there. Head usher. What a shame we didn't meet a week ago! I coulda got you a job, too."

Marcus had seen *Ben-Hur* dozens of times. He couldn't get enough of Ramon Novarro up there on the screen. He managed to pull his eyes off the ad and let them wander down the page. A familiar logo caught his eye above the words "NOW HIRING."

CHAPTER 9

Kathryn rearranged Tallulah Bankhead's fan mail on the dining room table. It had to look just right.

"Are you fiddling with all that stuff again?" Gwendolyn asked from the doorway of the bedroom of the villa they now shared.

"I want it to look like it's a lot of work."

"It *is* a lot of work. Tallulah Bankhead gets a ton of fan mail. Extraordinary, really, considering she hasn't made a picture in ten years."

"These letters aren't from movie fans," Kathryn said. "Most of these people saw her onstage." She combined a couple of stacks of letters into one tall pile and shifted her typewriter to face the front door.

Gwendolyn picked up one of the letters. "Why are so many of them on lavender note paper?"

Kathryn eyed her seventeen-year-old roommate. This wasn't the time to explain about lavender and women who preferred the company of other women. Her mother would be here in a few minutes, and she had a big impression to make. Kathryn watched the clock skip another minute closer to twelve. "Gwendolyn, honey, I don't want to throw you out of your own home, but you did promise . . . ?" She pointed to the clock.

Gwendolyn apologized, dropped the letter and picked up her handbag. "The new dress turned out well, even if I say so myself."

It had been two weeks since Kathryn had approached Gwendolyn with the suggestion they pool their resources and move into a villa together. They'd both been locked away in their tiny hotel rooms that seemed as dingy and suffocating as possible. If they opened their doors for air, they were met with a procession of peering gents, their brows greasy with anticipation.

It was Gwendolyn who had suggested that she could pay a little less rent by sewing a new dress for Kathryn each month. She displayed her wardrobe as proof of her skill; she had made pretty much everything in it. The girl's handiwork was top-notch so Kathryn agreed to a sixty-forty split of the rent. By the end of the first week, a dressmaker's dummy had appeared in the kitchen and a brand new dress — the rose-quartz one she wore today — was ready a week after that. Turns out that sewing wasn't the only thing Gwendolyn could do; she was a heck of a good cook as well, which suited Kathryn just fine. She'd left school before domestic arts classes came in, which left her bereft of the skills most girls were proficient at by the time they were Kathryn's age. Watching Gwendolyn stitch up a new suit made Kathryn feel woefully inadequate until she reminded herself that she was a working girl at heart, and had never been able to muster much enthusiasm for cooking succotash or attaching Peter Pan collars.

Gwendolyn hadn't been gone a minute when there was a knock on the door.

Kathryn hadn't expected that specific smile on her mother's face. Francine only wore that smile when she had secured an audition over the discarded body of a potential rival. Seeing it now threw her.

"Kathryn, darling," Francine greeted her grandly. "Come here and let me give my daughter a kiss."

When Kathryn wavered, Francine stepped through the doorway and embraced her, pressing their cheeks together. She let go and swept into the villa. "Why, this is . . . charming." The pause before the word 'charming' said everything Kathryn needed to know. Francine made straight for the bedroom and looked at the two single beds with a nightstand between them. "May I ask who lives here?"

"I do, mother." Where were the reprimands for the months of silence? Where were the teary demands of how she could treat her poor mother so heartlessly? Where were the remonstrations for walking out without a backward glance?

"Alone?"

"I live with a friend."

"Friend?"

Francine had tried to teach her daughter that any girl within a seven year radius of Kathryn was to be considered The Enemy. Any one of them could pluck from her grasp the chance at stardom that they had worked and schemed and chiseled and scrimped for all these years. They must be regarded as the snakes they would surely reveal themselves to be.

"I've made lots of new friends since I arrived here. My roommate's name is Gwendolyn."

"Gwendolyn? Is she as lovely as her name?"

Kathryn thought of Gwendolyn's enviably creamy skin, her charm school posture, her impressive bosom and of the way her gentle green eyes looked at someone like they were the only person south of Canada who mattered. In the aspiring movie star department, Gwendolyn was everything that Kathryn wasn't, and Francine would hate her for it. "Yes, she is."

"Fresh off the bus, I expect. A head full of dreams and no clue—" Francine cut herself off. "Would some tea be too much to ask?"

While the water boiled, Kathryn made a show of moving all the letters and papers to the far side of the table and onto the two spare seats, but Francine failed to ask about them. In the afternoon sunlight, Kathryn could see that her mother had tried too hard with her makeup. It was slathered on thick, the circles of rouge painted on like dolls' cheeks. Her lipstick was a shade darker than her dress and she'd missed the edge of her lips by an embarrassing margin. Tiny globs of too much mascara had bound her eyelashes together like baby spiders caught in their own webs. Mother and daughter sat down to tea and shortbread; it was a minute or two before either spoke.

"This is all very lovely," Francine said, "but it's time you came home."

Kathryn braced herself. "I *am* home, Mother."

"I fought tooth and nail to secure that audition for you at Paramount. They didn't want to see you; told me they had seen enough girls."

"Because they probably had."

Kathryn had risen on the morning of the Paramount audition and gone through the ritual of every other audition morning. She showered and dressed in just the right outfit, set her hair in just the right way, and headed out to the streetcar stop. But when the Red Car came rattling up Hollywood Boulevard, she found herself cemented to the sidewalk.

When the streetcar was out of sight, Kathryn wandered to the Top Hat Café up on Sunset. She'd passed it a million times, but that day she went in on the trail of a dead ringer for Theda Bara. Kathryn followed the woman inside and ordered a chocolate malted milk for cover, sneaking glances until she was sure it wasn't Theda Bara after all.

By the time she was halfway through the malt, she'd decided that she loved chocolate malts more than she loved acting, and she proceeded to have not one but two—and a slice of lemon meringue pie, the devil be damned. She walked into her mother's apartment to announce that she'd skipped the Paramount audition. A doozie of an argument erupted–Francine's fury was cutting and cruel and took even Kathryn by surprise–so she packed two suitcases and headed west, past where the pavement ended, and checked into the first hotel she came to: the Garden of Allah.

"Kathryn, my darling, what's going on? What was all that talk about not wanting to be an actress? Of course you do. We both do. It's what we've been working and slaving for all these years. How can you throw it all away?"

"Throw what away? What do we have to show for seven years of trudging from studio to studio, office to office, agent to agent? Nothing, Mother. Nothing! I've never won any audition or booked any job. And that's because I'm no good."

Francine was incredulous. "Are you drunk? Is that it? Because I passed a rather motley rabble near one of those bungalows out there, and they were clearly drunk as lords."

Kathryn leaned in. "Mother! I never wanted it in the first place. All that came from you. I have other things I want to do. Like get a real job. Lead a normal life."

"You've never had a job. What are you going to do with yourself?" Francine made a dismissive shrug.

"I have a job." Kathryn swept her hand across the mounds of mauve papers. "I manage all of Tallulah Bankhead's correspondence."

"Tallulah Bankhead? That actress who's always drunk, and running around saying the most scandalous things? And anyway, how could you do such a job? You can't even use one of those." Francine flicked her wrist toward the typewriting machine.

"Fifty words a minute," Kathryn said.

Francine stared at the typewriter as though she'd never seen one before. Kathryn leaned back in her chair to let the news sink in. Kathryn let several moments tick by before she said in a voice, carefully calibrated for maximum impact, "I'm very happy now. I have a good job with decent pay. I have a lovely roommate and a very nice place to live."

An eruption of male laughter burst through the kitchen window. "And then, and then," one of them said, barely able to catch his breath from laughing so hard, "the dame set fire to the guy's trousers while he was still in 'em! He never saw her again!" The men — likely the drunken lords — were close to choking on their laughter.

Francine looked from the typewriter to the fan letters to her daughter, confused. "All this looks like a lot of work. It must take up a lot of time. When will you find time to go on auditions?

CHAPTER 10

Gwendolyn stopped twenty feet down Sunset Boulevard from the main gate of Warner Brothers studios. Kathryn's T-straps looked much better with her new daffodil-yellow dress than either pair of her own pumps, but they were half a size too small, which made walking like a glamour girl an acting lesson in itself. She gave her feet a minute's rest before she presented herself to the guard.

"Your name?" he asked.

"Gwendolyn Brick."

He ran his finger down a list of fifty or sixty names twice. "You're not on the list," he told her.

"I must be. Please check again."

"I got no Gwendolyn and I got no Brick. If you're not on, then you're not in."

"In that case, I need to speak to Bill Brockton. If you could—"

"Brockton no longer works here."

"But I—"

"You need to step aside." He motioned for her to make way for a couple of arresting redheads who'd appeared behind her. Gwendolyn watched as they gave their names and the guard directed them to soundstage number six, then she tried to approach the guard again. "Don't make me be rude, toots," he told her. "Just run along."

Gwendolyn backed off along the sidewalk and leaned against the twelve-foot wall that encircled the studio like a prison barricade. Bill Brockton was her only way in, and if he was no longer working there, she was out.

She watched a gorgeous brunette in a brown pinstripe alight from the Red Car and be waved through the gate. Gwendolyn was about to give up and head home when a pack of sailors rounded the corner. They strolled past her, shooting her appreciative smiles. She smiled at each one, hoping some girl in some faraway port would do the same for her brother. Gwendolyn hadn't put up a fight when he'd asked her to forge Mama's signature on his navy papers the day after the funeral; it was all he'd ever wanted to do, for as long as she could remember. She watched the sailors make a right turn into the studio lot. "Oh for goodness sakes," Gwendolyn muttered, "they're not sailors at all; just a bunch of extras in costume."

Gwendolyn began to miss her brother, Seaman First Class Montgomery Brick. Tall, gangly Monty with his silly grin and his sillier cowlick that wouldn't stay down for love nor Brilliantine. He'd make her see the bright side of missing an audition with a Hollywood studio for the second time in two months. He'd have her laughing before she could say "swab the decks."

Wait! Just hold on a cotton-pickin' second. Where the heck did those extras come from? Gwendolyn walked to the corner and looked up the street. Halfway up the block was a sign over a doorway. She hurried toward it.

COSTUMES - MAKE-UP – HAIR
Studio Employees Only.
All others proceed to main gate on Sunset Boulevard.

She tried the doorknob, but of course it was locked. She knocked and a pretend policeman opened up. Another extra.

"Locked yourself out, huh?" he asked with a crooked smile.

Gwendolyn blinked her biggest moo-moo eyes and walked into a leafy courtyard. Over to the left was a group of men dressed like New York cops who were slapping wooden batons into their palms. She strode past them into a long corridor lined with sewing rooms and make-up studios and walked through a pair of double doors at the end. Outside again, tall studio warehouses loomed on both sides of the street. A stream of young beauties caught her eye; she recognized the redheads. She followed them inside sound stage six, where nearly a hundred girls her age milled about. Nearly every one turned around when Gwendolyn walked through the door. They all looked her up and down, making the split second assessment of how much competition she represented, then went back to checking their lipstick or the seams in their stockings.

The warehouse was sparingly lit. Large round lights forty feet overhead poured light onto the girls and made slivers of shadows. Gwendolyn headed for a shadow. She felt like she was being watched and looked around until she noticed a statuesque blonde staring right at her. Gwendolyn ducked behind a clique of girls talking about Wallace Beery, but the stranger followed her. Could this girl be onto her? Had she followed her through the side door? Gwendolyn braced herself and turned to face her stalker.

"It's really quite remarkable, isn't it?" the stranger said. The girl looked just like her. "You could be my sister. Maybe even my twin."

They could have been separated at birth. They had the same shade of blonde hair, gently curled and shaped to bring out their large green eyes and fine cheekbones. Their chins came to the same soft point, their necks both long and slender. And, Gwendolyn noted, the girl carried the same full bosom as she did. It wasn't able to conform to the flatness of the flapper look any more than hers could. Did she also ache for the day the flat-chested look got escorted to the door?

She thrust her hand toward Gwendolyn. "My name is Alice Moore," she said. "And that's my real name, too."

"Gwendolyn Brick." She shook Alice's hand. "That's my real name but I don't care for it much, so I plan on changing it."

"To what?"

"Right now, I'm thinking Gwendolyn Day."

"Gwendolyn Day," Alice said. "I like it. I can see it up in lights." She looked around the studio. "So, what do you think our chances are? There are some mighty pretty girls here, don't you think?"

Gwendolyn looked around the vast room and started to take the other girls in. The redheads were talking to a couple of homely blondes who, she decided, didn't seem all that much to look at.

"You want to know the scoop?" Alice whispered. She drew her head closer to Gwendolyn's. "I've been told they're going to do the usual Door A and Door B routine."

"A and B?"

"Oh, you know, one of them is the good door and one of them is the bad one. 'Bad' meaning 'Thanks for your time, now scram because we don't want to see your ugly puss around here no more.'"

"But which door is which?"

Alice shrugged. "So, who was your talent scout? It wasn't Cap Cooney, was it? Cap found me at the Argyle Tea Room. You been there? It's a fun place for girls like us."

Gwendolyn wondered what kind of girl Alice thought she was.

"At first I thought he was a phony. Talent scout? Uh-huh, yeah, sure you are, buddy. 'Cause, you know, getting into the studios is much easier and faster if you've got a talent agent going to bat for you. So when this joker lays it on me that he really is a talent agent and then mentions this dog and pony show, I realized he was on the level. I couldn't believe my luck. So, what number did you get?"

Gwendolyn noticed for the first time that each girl held a wooden disk. Alice held hers up; she had number fourteen.

Five men filed through a door at the far end of the stage and made their way to a long table. Four took their seats and the fifth remained standing. He called all the girls to gather closer, but Gwendolyn held back. The man explained the rules. Easy as pie, he assured them. They'd call the numbers out at random so pay attention.

Gwendolyn tried not to panic. She'd lost her disk? She wasn't given a disk? Someone stole her disk? Nothing plausible came to mind.

She fixated on the cream-colored outfit of the girl standing in front of her. It was a lovely blend of ivory and vanilla, quite calming. Gwendolyn was wondering where she could find material like that when the girl started to shudder. Her shoulders caved in and her head wobbled around like someone had loosened the screws.

Gwendolyn touched her arm. "You okay, honey?"

The girl turned to look at Gwendolyn. Her face was cadaver white, her upper lip slick with sweat. "I can't do this. This is too much. I could never . . ."

"Number fourteen!"

Alice called out, "That's me!" Gwendolyn watched as Alice strode back and forth in front of the casting men with the confidence of a tiger in the gazelle cage. The pale girl shook her head from side to side and started to back away.

"Are you sure?" Gwendolyn asked the girl. "It don't look too hard."

The girl shook her head. She raised her hand to reveal a disk with the number forty-two stenciled on it in black. "What should I do with this?"

* * *

Kathryn's high heels still hurt like hell, but Gwendolyn knew they looked swell with her daffodil dress. When she was back at her starting point at the far end of the table, the executive in the middle asked for the name of her talent scout.

"Beau Gussington."

"Thank you," he said. "Door A, please."

Gwendolyn thanked the gentlemen for their precious time and headed toward the door marked with a large A. She pushed it open and encountered a sign that said, "Exit to street." She froze in the doorway and stared at it for a moment, then stepped back inside and approached the nearest man. "I was to go through door B, right?"

The guy looked at her. His face showed no sign of life. "No, sweetie. Door A."

Gwendolyn felt her throat go dry. Everyone was looking at her now. In a swift, smooth movement, the guy rose from his chair, collected her right arm and swept her into a dark corner of the stage. Her protest died before it reached her lips.

"The talent agent who put you up for this, what exactly did he look like?" His smile was part condescending, part sympathetic. Gwendolyn couldn't reply. "Did Bill Brockton give you Gussington's name?"

"Uh-huh."

"Honey, Beau Gussington doesn't exist. It's a code word we use."

"You boys and your code words! What are you, frustrated spies?

The guy smiled, more condescending this time. "Beau Gussington," he repeated. "Beau Guss. Bogus. Get it?"

Gwendolyn closed her eyes and let out a defeated breath. "It's the code you use to make a girl think she stands a chance, when all you really want to do is get her out of your office. Am I close?"

When she opened her eyes, the guy was gone.

CHAPTER 11

Kathryn hadn't thought anything of Gwendolyn's invitation to go with her to some place called the Argyle Tea Room on the corner of Argyle and Hollywood Boulevard. Gwendolyn hadn't wanted to go alone, nor did Kathryn want her sweet, trusting roommate to wander into some Hollywood joint by herself, so she agreed to come along.

They hadn't been inside two minutes before Kathryn figured it out. "Gwendolyn, tell me again why we're here."

"I met this girl, Alice, at that Warner Brothers cattle call, and she asked me if I'd ever been here."

Gwendolyn studied the room a bit more. "Oh, I get it!" she exclaimed, and pointed to the wallpaper on the far wall. It was a diamond pattern of pale red and even paler pink squares with an overlapping gray stripe. "We're on Argyle Avenue and that's an argyle pattern on the wallpaper. Oh! And look at the lamps on the tables up there: they've got the exact same pattern. Ain't that divine?!"

Handsome people smoked and drank from teacups at tall tables on the lower level, and two steps up, couples sat at tiny cocktail tables. A waiter with a waxed moustache and a long white apron–he could have walked straight off the set of a von Stroheim picture–carried an ornate teapot and four matching cups that Francine would have ached to own; the scent it trailed through the room confirmed Kathryn's suspicions.

She turned to her friend and lowered her voice. "Sweetie, this isn't a tea room."

"But the sign . . ."

"They probably do serve tea here, but did you smell the tea that waiter was carrying?"

"Why, yes I did. Strong, wasn't it?"

"That wasn't tea, honey. That was brandy."

Gwendolyn let out a quiet "Oh!" and pressed her fingers to her mouth. "I've brought us to a *speakeasy*!"

"Gwendolyn? Is that you?"

The girls turned around to find the spitting image of Gwendolyn waving at them. It was alarming. Their hair was the same shade of blonde, their eyes the same green, and the two girls stood at the same height. They grinned at each other like sisters.

"Alice!" Gwendolyn greeted the girl.

"I thought you said you never come here." The girl had the smile of a wayward driver stopped by a cop.

Gwendolyn was one of those girls who don't need to be taught how to carry themselves or dress well, but she didn't know it. She swore she came from the poor end of the wrong side of the tracks of the Other Hollywood, but nobody would know it from her gorgeous dresses and subtle makeup.

Alice, on the other hand, was her opposite. She had Gwendolyn's height, her figure, and her hairstyle, but she'd been thrown together in a hurry with the emphasis on the wrong things. Where Gwendolyn's short blonde hair was natural, Alice's was clearly dyed at home. Where Gwendolyn's clothes were perfectly tailored, Alice's dress was probably off the rack at Woolworth's five-and-dime, dressed up with a costume brooch that only emphasized its cheapness. Even her lipstick was too much, too red.

"Why don't you join us?" Alice pointed to three girls clustered around a tall table on the lower floor. With their eagerly painted faces and coats just starting to fray at the sleeves, each girl sported a variation on the look that Kathryn knew well: chorus girl on the make.

The smell of brandy hovered over the chorines like a dirigible. Alice waved Gustav over and ordered another pot of "ahem tea" for the table. When Gwendolyn asked if they had any other sort of tea, Gustav hesitated.

"What did you have in mind?" Kathryn asked Gwendolyn.

"I was hoping for Earl Grey," Gwendolyn replied. Alice's friends let out a peal of high-pitched giggles rarely heard outside of a Girl Scout meeting.

Kathryn looked around the split-level room and saw only two sorts of people: pretty girls and older men. Oh, great. "If you have it, I'll take some, too," she told the waiter. On the odd occasion that Kathryn had tried brandy, she'd rather enjoyed it. But it was one thing to sip a Brandy Stinger at some party at the Garden of Allah, but buying illegal booze in a pick-up joint like this didn't seem right.

"Oh, Alice, no!" one of the girls exclaimed. Her babydoll voice was for the benefit of the graying bachelor within earshot. "Don't show them *that*. At least not until we've had a go first!"

But Alice had already started to pull a sheet of paper from her purse. "There's enough for everybody, dearie." She unfolded the paper and handed it to Gwendolyn. "This here is a list of the fifty most eligible bachelors in California. *With* their addresses."

"Have you heard of any of these men?" Kathryn asked.

"Oh gosh, yes," said Baby Doll. "At least three quarters. It's a quality list."

"And it's doing the rounds, I'm sure," Alice added. "So we can't be too slow off the mark. Do any of these guys appeal?"

Kathryn examined Alice's face as Gwendolyn read through the list. It had a veneer of casual amusement but there was a steeliness to Alice's eyes that wasn't too hard to miss.

I get it, Kathryn thought. Gwendolyn looks just like you, only she's classier, nicer, and more put-together than you'll ever be, so your best course of action is to remove her from the competition altogether.

"What do you think?" Alice pressed.

Gwendolyn laughed. "I have no intention of getting married. My career is far more important to me." She let out an angelic sigh. "All those silly men have been ogling me since the day I strapped on my first brassiere. But not one of them has ever stopped to ask me if I even wanted a boyfriend, let alone a husband." She pushed the list back to Alice.

"Oh you sweet, sweet thing," said one of the other girls, "Nobody said anything about marrying any of these fellas!"

With the deliberation of a cobra, Alice slid the list back. "Oh, come on, now," she said. "Surely there's somebody on this list that takes your fancy?"

CHAPTER 12

Marcus peeled off his Western Union jacket and flopped onto his bed. It had been a busy Saturday, which meant lots of tips. Nickels and dimes, mainly, but the odd quarter if the telegram he delivered bore good news. He counted out the morning's haul; three dollars and thirty-five cents. Not bad.

He kicked off his shoes and settled in with the *L.A. Times*, looking for the movie listings. He still hadn't seen *The Lights of New York*, the first all-talking motion picture, and if he was going to write talking pictures, he needed to see every single one.

An ad for the new Lon Chaney–*West of Zanzibar*–caught his eye. Marcus always thought of his mom when he saw Chaney's name. He was a favorite of hers. She cried so hard at the end of *Phantom of the Opera* that his dad had to help her from the theater. It was one of his favorite childhood memories.

Marcus sighed. He'd been missing his mom a lot lately. What did she think about him just up and leaving town? What had Father told her when he got home that night? Did she believe whatever story he'd invented? Did she wonder where he was and how he was doing? Three or four times he'd started a letter to her but he hadn't finished any of them. If his father intercepted it, there might be hell to pay and that was the last thing he wanted to put his mom through.

He forced his eyes to move further down the page.

A large ad caught his eye. *AUCTION*, it said in large capital letters. *Home Furnishings and Art Collection.* Marcus' eyes widened. He looked at his watch, grabbed his wallet, and flew out the door.

* * *

Van Keuren Galleries was a stark, two-story white stucco building with large windows along the front and sides. Glorious midsummer sunlight filled a breezy mint-green gallery heavy with dark, somber furniture. A mahogany headboard was propped against a towering wardrobe inlaid with diamond-shaped panels of pewter gray quartz, its top a baroque crown of carved leaves and thorns. Next to it stood a six-foot-tall lamp with an enormous dark purple velvet shade. There were three aisles of this stuff, all of it smelling of closed-up rooms and dead flowers.

"She sure had old-fashioned taste, didn't she?" Kathryn asked. "Do you think she's dead?"

Marcus felt a prickle of sweat collect in his underarms. The ad hadn't explained why Alla Nazimova's personal effects were being auctioned off. At some point in the last year, he'd given up hope that he'd bump into her at a party in the Garden of Allah, or in the hotel's restaurant. When he saw the ad, he thought, If I can't meet her, perhaps I could buy something that belonged to her. The thought hadn't occurred to him that she might be dead.

"That's a darned shame," Gwendolyn said. She picked up a porcelain figurine of three women who were either ballerinas or nuns. Its cobalt glaze was faded but their white headdresses were still bright. "I would like to have met her. *Salome* was the very first picture Mama took me to. Remember how she looked in that?"

Marcus nodded. He'd been to see *Salome* too, but not with his mother. She was too Pennsylvania Dutch practical to waste her weekly movie dime on something that outlandish and indulgent, even if it had starred the actress who came to visit her sickly son. Lon Chaney was one thing, but Alla Nazimova was another.

So he'd snuck away after church one Sunday to see it by himself. Alla was a glimmering vision in that movie, all draped clothes and striking poses. And that wig she wore — what was it? Baby roses? Marcus ran his hand along the goosebumps raised on his arm.

He wandered down an aisle stacked with oriental rugs, silver tea services, huge sets of china and glassware, a pair of matching sideboards, an array of porcelain dancers, exotic birds, and abstract sculptures. Even Alla's enormous Steinway was for sale. He looked back toward the bright windows at the front of the gallery. Despite the sunshine, everything had a sad, dank air. Alla's belongings seemed like orphans, left behind and forgotten.

At the back of the gallery, a small woman in a black velvet dress held something in her hands. It was an odd dress for July, Marcus thought, unless she was in mourning. Marcus' shoulders drooped as he realized he must have missed Alla's funeral.

He watched the woman set something down on the piano and caught her eye as she glanced down the aisle. It was the woman from villa twenty-four, the one who peeked through her window, and who he saw at *The Jazz Singer*.

She disappeared around the corner and Marcus went to see what she had been holding. It was a wooden rocking horse, ten inches high and painted in blues and reds worn away over years of handling. It reminded him of his father's rocking horse. As far back as he could recall, it had always been there, sitting in the corner, calling Marcus for a ride. What happy hours he'd spent astride Rocky the Rocking Horse. This toy version that sat now in his hands looked just like it.

A deep voice announced the beginning of the auction, and around twenty people assembled at the rear of the gallery. Marcus took a seat beside Kathryn and Gwendolyn and picked up his bidding paddle. He looked for the woman in velvet and found her on the far side of the room, scowling next to a woman with a thin face and a long gray braid. Her dark hair, streaked with silver, was pulled back in a snug bun over the high collar of her blouse. There was much head shaking, pursing of lips, and whispered sniping back and forth between the two.

"Isn't that our mysterious neighbor?" Kathryn asked. "From twenty-four?"

Marcus nodded. "I'd begun to think she had no friends at all."

"I found out her name!" Gwendolyn whispered. "I had a strange encounter with her the other day. I was down in the restaurant dining room cutting out a dress pattern and she wandered in. I looked up and she was standing there staring at me. We got to talking—or rather, I did. She didn't say much. But then she asked me, 'Do you have someone, a close confidante to whom you can run when life overwhelms?' She was all frightfully serious about it. I told her, sure, I have my good friends Kathryn and Marcus. She looked relieved and said, 'That is good. Keep them close.'

"So I asked her if she had someone like that, and she said, 'Oh yes, I have Arzner.' as though I was supposed to know who that was. Do you suppose that disapproving old biddy with the hairbun is Arzner?"

Marcus and Kathryn shrugged. "What else did she say?"

"That was pretty much it. She left and I went back to my sewing. A little while later, Brophy came in and I asked him who she was. Apparently her name is Mariam Leventon."

The auctioneer was a gentleman in his sixties who looked like he was born to play British butlers. He stepped onto a platform at the front of the gallery and commenced the auction. Tiffany lamps and Louis Quatorze tables, Turkish tapestries and oriental rugs went under the hammer one by one. The collection was extraordinary in size and scope, and fetched what seemed to Marcus handsome sums.

Then the rocking horse appeared on the bidding table. The auctioneer described it as "an exquisite example of handicraft from the Crimea, the birthplace of Madame Nazimova, cherished by Madame herself as one of the few tokens of remembrance of her beloved father, who carved this enchanting piece for her."

A lump formed in Marcus' throat. Go as high as ten dollars, he told himself. Ten dollars was a whole week's worth of tips. It took a lot of bicycling around the often unpaved streets of Hollywood to earn that kind of money, but he'd never wanted anything so badly in his life.

"Do I hear fifty cents?"

Marcus raised his paddle.

"Thank you, sir. Do I hear seventy-five cents?"

Out of the corner of his eye, Marcus saw a paddle rise on the other side of the room.

"Thank you, ma'am. Do I hear one dollar?"

Marcus raised his paddle.

"You'd pay a whole dollar for that?" Kathryn whispered.

"Thank you, sir. Do I hear one dollar and fifty cents?"

A gentleman in a brown suit a couple of rows ahead raised his paddle. Before Marcus or the woman in black velvet could raise the bid, a woman in a moss-green cape raised her paddle.

When the bidding reached five dollars, Marcus felt Kathryn's hand on his arm. "Five dollars is a lot to spend on a toy horse." The lump in Marcus' throat had grown to the size of a golf ball. Even if he had wanted to explain, he couldn't have pushed the words out.

Gwendolyn leaned in. "Not for something that belonged to Alla Nazimova, right?"

Marcus had never told Gwendolyn about Alla coming to his sickbed; perhaps Kathryn had told her. He nodded, smiled, and raised his paddle.

"Five dollars and fifty cents. Do I hear six dollars?"

The man in the brown suit quit at seven dollars and the woman with the cape bailed at eight-fifty. At nine dollars, it was back to Marcus and Miss Leventon. At nine-fifty, the bid was against Marcus. His heart beat against his ribs so hard he was afraid it would break loose and bounce right out of his chest. He just *had* to have that horse. Marcus raised his paddle once more.

"Nine dollars and fifty cents. Thank you, sir."

"Ma'am?"

Leventon hesitated. Her friend with the braid whispered at her, barely able to contain her anger. Leventon waved her hand dismissively and shook her head in short jabs, but didn't raise her paddle.

Keep it down, Miss Leventon, Marcus thought. Keep your paddle right where it is.

"Ma'am, the bid is yours. It stands at nine dollars fifty. Do I hear ten dollars?"

Keep it down. Keep it down.

"All right, then. Going once. Going twice."

Marcus' heart lurched as he saw the woman raise her paddle.

CHAPTER 13

Gwendolyn and Marcus alighted from the Red Car at the corner of Hollywood and Vine and headed south.

"Gwennie, honey, where are we going, and why is it such a mystery?"

Gwendolyn pointed to a building just ahead.

"The Brown Derby?" Marcus asked.

The Brown Derby had become one of the most famous restaurants in Hollywood. Not just because radio stations broadcast to national audiences from the same corner, but also because it was a quick drive from Paramount Studios, RKO, Columbia and Warner Brothers. It was the in-place for the in-crowd, and star spotting there was already legendary.

Marcus groaned. "Please tell me you didn't haul me all the way here to keep you company while you stand out front waiting to be discovered."

"I've got a much better plan than that," Gwendolyn told him. Honestly, when would people stop underestimating her? She smoothed down her new dark caramel dress. "Come on." She led Marcus past the passel of autograph hounds gathered out front and up to the maitre d's podium.

"Table for two, Brick, eight o'clock."

The maitre d' checked his pocket watch. "You're twenty minutes early, but we'll probably be able to seat you soon."

The restaurant looked exactly as it had in *Photoplay* magazine. The dining room was lined with booths that were raised slightly for improved see-and-be-seen-ing. That's where the stars and the big guns — studio bosses, producers, directors — sat. Hangers-on positioned further down the Hollywood ladder were seated at square tables arranged in a diamond pattern in the center of the room. Gwendolyn wondered whether talent agents were high enough on the food chain to warrant a booth.

Marcus' blue eyes were wide with panic. "Dinner for two here can be four, maybe even five dollars. That's more than a week's pay. Too rich for my blood."

"Who said you were paying? This is my treat."

"You're a girl!" Marcus spluttered. "I can't let you pay. I'll look like a gigolo." He shook his head. "This is crazy. Let's go to Al Levy's across the street. I delivered a telegram there a few weeks ago; they do a swell dinner for seventy-five cents. Please, Gwendolyn, let's get out of here."

He grabbed her by the elbow but she didn't budge. Instead she held up three fingers and folded them down as she listed each name. "Louis B. Mayer. Cecil B. DeMille. David O. Selznick."

"What about them?"

"Mayer is in the booth directly across from us. DeMille is four booths to his right. And Mr. Selznick is sitting in the corner booth to your left. He's with his brother Myron, who is one of *the* most powerful talent agents in Hollywood."

Marcus pulled back half a step, shifting from panic to surprise. "You took all that in with a quick sweep of the room?"

Now will he take me more seriously? Gwendolyn wondered. Now does he get that I know what I'm doing?

The article she'd read in *Photoplay* last week was about some henna-rinsed sparrow with large eyes and no waist who was fortunate enough to be seated across from Selznick, recently moved from Paramount to head of production at RKO. By the following morning, the big-eyed sparrow was filming a screen test.

All of a sudden, as if by a signal only dogs could hear, every woman in the restaurant put on her hat and every man pulled out his wallet. Everyone started to stand.

"What's happening?" Marcus asked. "Where are they all going?"

Gwendolyn watched as Selznick strode past her without so much as a sideways glance. Several yards behind him was DeMille, equally disinterested in how lovely she looked in her caramel dress.

"To the fights."

Gwendolyn turned to the tuxedoed gentleman with a walking stick and white whiskers who was standing next to her. "What fights?"

"Next door. The Hollywood Legion Stadium. They hold boxing matches every Friday night. It's all the rage these days. This crowd," he rolled his eyes in the direction of the exiting masses, "comes early so they're out of here before eight." Gwendolyn's heart sank as she watched the well-heeled crowd file past her. "In ten minutes they'll all have left, and you'll be able to hear yourself think, thank the heavens."

Gwendolyn didn't want to hear herself think. She wanted the bigwigs to watch her parade around the room. How was she to know she was competing with grown men punching each other silly?

"Brick, party of two," the maitre d' called out. "I can seat you now."

Marcus looked at Gwendolyn with a sad smile. "Why don't we save this for some other day?"

Gwendolyn sighed and looked around. A few minutes ago the Brown Derby was buzzing with the most famous people in the country, and now it looked like any other joint on a slow night. She'd been preparing for this evening all week. If she went home without having dined at the Brown Derby, she'd feel like a failure.

"No," she replied, "we're staying. I have a Plan B."

The maitre d' led them to a booth with a view of the whole restaurant. They had barely settled in when a young waiter, who was skinnier than spaghetti, took their orders for ginger beer. Gwendolyn peeked over the top of her menu and scanned the room. Not one famous face to be seen.

A few minutes later, the skinny waiter reappeared without their ginger beers and offered them an embarrassed smile. "I'm sorry, but I'm going to have to move you. A regular has just arrived, and this is his favorite booth."

"I don't suppose it's anyone famous," Gwendolyn said ruefully, gathering her gloves and purse.

The waiter ducked his head and whispered, "As a matter of fact, it's Douglas Fairbanks Junior. So if you could follow me?"

"Is he here with his new wife?"

"Joan Crawford?" The young man smiled. "No, not tonight."

"Could we meet him?" Gwendolyn asked. "Surely it would be the courteous thing to do if he wants our table."

The waiter shook his head. "Oh, no, no, no. It's never done that way. You simply move tables. If you catch his eye, he'll probably nod, and you can nod back."

Gwendolyn shook her curls. "I'm sorry," she peered at the etched name plate pinned to his lapel, "Ritchie from Oklahoma, but you're going to have to go back there and tell Mr. Douglas Fairbanks Junior that if he wants our table, the polite thing to do is come over here and ask for it himself."

Ritchie from Oklahoma stared at Gwendolyn as though she'd just skewered him with a javelin. He leaned in. "This is supposed to have been a surprise, but Mr. Fairbanks intends to pay your check as a way of showing his gratitude."

Marcus shot to his feet. "That's it," he said, "we're moving."

They settled at their new table and consulted the menu but most of it was in French. What the heck was *Petite Marmite a la Française*? Or *Escargots Bourguignon*? They decided instead to simply order the most expensive things they could see. Ritchie from Oklahoma took down their order with a hint of a good-for-you smile and disappeared.

"So," Marcus said, "you have a Plan B?"

Gwendolyn flagged down a busboy and asked for a bowl of matchbooks, then reached into her purse for an ink pad and a rubber stamp. When the busboy returned, she took a matchbook off the top and whispered to Marcus, "Watch this." She surreptitiously pressed her stamp inside the cover and gave it to Marcus.

Ritchie appeared at the table with the escargots. "Enjoy." When they peered into the dish they were none the wiser, but everything smelled deliciously loaded with garlic and butter. They grabbed forks and stabbed at the soft, buttery lumps.

Marcus studied the matchbook. "What's this supposed to mean?"

Gwendolyn handed over the stamp she'd ordered at the stationer's after yet another ego-crushing cattle call at Mack Sennett's studio. "It's my secret publicity campaign."

GWENDOLYN

WAS

HERE

She took another matchbook from the bowl and stamped it in her lap, then another. "My plan is that everywhere I go — cafés, restaurants, speakeasies — I'll stamp the menus, the matchbooks, the coasters, the napkins, with *Gwendolyn Was Here*. After a while, people are going to see me pop up all over the place and they're going to wonder, 'Who in the great tarnation *is* this Gwendolyn person?' And then perhaps they'll meet me at a party or an audition and they'll ask, 'Are *you* that Gwendolyn we keep hearing so much about?'"

Gwendolyn fought to keep herself from wincing as Marcus chewed his garlicky ball of something-or-other. It had sounded wonderfully clever until she said it out loud. Now she wondered if it was just a delusion dreamed up by a naïve little girl from a two-horse backwater that nobody would've heard of except that it shared its name with the most famous town in the country. She felt such a kinship with Marcus. Kathryn was used to the real Hollywood, but dear, sweet Marcus was from a two-horse backwater, too.

He never talked about home but there were times when she'd catch him staring off into the distance. His face would take on such a sad, forlorn look–she'd seen the very same look at that auction when Kathryn had wondered out loud if Nazimova was dead–that Gwendolyn had to wonder if he ever suffered from homesickness. It seemed that going back home was not an option for him. As steep the uphill climb here might sometimes feel, returning home wasn't an option for her either. There was nobody to return home to.

"How does that sound?" she ventured.

Marcus swallowed and said, "That would have to be the god-damndest smartest, wiliest, most ingenious scheme I think I've ever heard. Kudos to you, Miss Gwendolyn."

Gwendolyn didn't know what a kudos was, but the smile on Marcus' face told her that it was a good thing. She let out a breath of relief.

"Here's something else you can stamp," Marcus said. He reached down to the empty chair next to him and brought up a copy of the *Examiner* and held out his hand. "Allow me, if you will?" He surveyed the front page and pressed the stamp against a photograph of an enormous airship.

"Oh look!" Marcus exclaimed. "That mysterious Gwendolyn has even been seen on the *Graf Zeppelin*."

CHAPTER 14

When Gwendolyn and Marcus told Kathryn that they were going down to Mine's Field to watch the *Graf Zeppelin* land, she decided to go along. Newspaper magnate William Randolph Hearst had made sure that everybody in America knew of its round-the-world voyage, and its arrival in Los Angeles dominated conversations from Beverly Hills dining rooms to the Woolworth's lunch counter.

Gwendolyn had concocted a plan to maneuver herself in front of the Movietone cameras that would be there. She'd read how one starlet got her break when someone at Fox had seen her on a newsreel and tracked her down. Never mind the fact that it was probably just a studio-generated publicity stunt and the girl would most likely get dropped as soon as that particular Movietone was no longer in circulation. Still, Kathryn admired Gwennie's initiative. She wasn't as wild about the *Gwendolyn Was Here* scheme as Marcus had been — it sounded like a plot out of some loopy Mabel Normand picture — but Gwennie was doing everything she could to jumpstart her career.

Kathryn had been working for Tallulah Bankhead for eighteen months. Her fan mail job had evolved into a nebulous mélange of personal-secretary-companion-chaperone-nursemaid-bartender. She was now handling all of Ms. Bankhead's affairs: fan mail, business transactions, appointments, the lot.

A while back, the Garden of Allah acquired a new tenant: Robert Benchley, a genial New Yorker with an obscenely lucrative contract at Paramount. He was a big, kindhearted man and Kathryn adored him, but he swallowed bootleg on a scale Kathryn hadn't suspected humanly possible. As with most people in Los Angeles, the fact that Prohibition had been in place for ten years seemed to not have registered on his horizon. When he heard what Kathryn did for Tallulah, he roped her into doing the same for him. Benchley was paying her generously, but now it had been a year and a half since Kathryn had set out to become an ace reporter, and she had yet to interview for a single newspaper. The *Graf Zeppelin*'s arrival was the perfect subject for a sample article, so she had arrived at Mine's Field today with a notebook and sharpened pencils. She hadn't counted on the forty thousand people crowded around the airstrip, though. "We're not going to get anywhere near it," she moaned.

They threaded their way through throngs of people for ages without making any progress toward the center. Then they heard a man's voice call out over the din. "Gwendolyn! Oh, Gwendolyn! Over here!"

Kathryn saw an uncommonly tall, thin young man with a jumble of brown hair that was flapping in the hot breeze. He waved and pressed toward them. "Who's that?" she asked.

"Is that our waiter from the Brown Derby?" Marcus said. "What was his name?"

"Ritchie from Oklahoma?" Gwendolyn asked. "Heavens above, I do believe you're right."

Ritchie stepped past a couple of geisha girls in kimonos intricately embroidered with storks. He was so tall and gangly that he reminded Kathryn of a stork himself. "I've been keeping an eye out for you." His smile was as big as a dirigible.

"How did you know we'd be down here?" Gwendolyn asked.

"People forget waiters have ears. I heard you two talking about this, and I thought it was a grand idea. I didn't think I'd actually see you, what with the size of this crowd and all, but here we are!"

"This is our friend Kathryn," Gwendolyn said.

Kathryn shook Ritchie's hand.

"I've been here since five this morning, so I've got a spot up near the front. You all want to join me?"

They picked their way past families on picnic blankets, workers in overalls, Great War veterans corseted into their uniforms, marines with bayonets and a tidy German family armed with bratwurst and bread rolls. After what seemed more like a trek across the Rockies than a walk through a field a stone's throw from Venice Beach, they arrived at Ritchie's oasis.

Ritchie's friends were fellow waiters who'd called in sick too. Ritchie pointed through the crowd at the perimeter the authorities had erected; his site was about a dozen feet away. Given that the *Graf Zeppelin* was seven hundred feet long, the two-hundred-foot perimeter struck Kathryn as more symbolic than safe.

"You see that?" Ritchie pointed to a low platform made of milk crates. On top of it sat a camera with the Movietone News logo painted on its side. A cameraman in a tartan beret was tilting the camera to the sky, moving it slowly to the ground, then back up again.

"You could tell them you're a soda heiress from Chicago," Ritchie suggested. "Those Movietone guys love that sort of stuff. Do you think you could dance the Charleston in those heels?"

"In this dirt? Honey, I could dance the Charleston if you blindfolded me, put me on stilts and shoved me into Lake Okeechobee."

Kathryn watched Gwendolyn and Ritchie squeeze their way closer to the camera, then looked at the people around her. Folks from all walks of life had gathered to witness a miracle of the modern age. How anybody could build something so large and fly it around the world in less than a month was beyond her. She pulled out her notebook and started recording her impressions. She took in the lines on people's faces, the light in their eyes as they scrutinized the skies, hoping to be the first one to spot the approaching airship.

A man in a dark, tailored suit caught her eye. He looked satisfied with himself, like he'd just had a close shave and a hot towel facial. He stood there with his hands in his pockets, his serene expression angled up to the sky.

Kathryn nudged one of Ritchie's friends and pointed out the guy in the suit. "Don't suppose you know who that is."

The waiter only needed a glance. "That's Billy Wilkerson. He's at the Derby a few times a month."

"Does he work for one of the studios?"

"Bootlegger, I think. Or a gambler. Throws his money around like he is. Always leaves a big tip. Left me ten bucks once. But he's going legit."

"Doing what?"

"I overheard him telling some studio big shot that he's starting a newspaper. Going to call it the *Hollywood Reporter.*"

"LOOK!" a woman screamed. "I think I see it! Is that it? There!"

Forty thousand heads turned as one toward the ocean. With the grace of a swan, the airship emerged from a cloud and headed toward them. The crowd let out a cheer that startled a hoard of seagulls into the air and sent them screeching toward the water.

The massive vessel was about a mile away now, and moved so smoothly and quietly that even when the crowd hushed, it couldn't be heard. When the sun broke through the clouds, it lit up the gray zeppelin and made it gleam like molten silver. The crowd erupted in applause.

Kathryn stole a glance at Billy Wilkerson. He wasn't waving any flags; he wasn't even watching the airship. He was looking at the people around him, almost as though he were a camera himself. She broke away from Marcus and threaded a path the long way around until she was standing next to Wilkerson. He was a tall chap with the posture of a tango dancer and black hair that was starting to recede. His clothes were crisp and probably put together by a valet.

"I don't know which is more incredible," Kathryn declared. "The sight of this magnificent zeppelin or the sight of this crowd coming together as one. I've never seen anything quite like it." Wilkerson smiled and nodded, but kept his eyes on the crowd. She went on. "I hope the newspaper reports are able to capture the feeling of what it's like to be here." He smiled and nodded again. She decided to take a risk. "I think I know you. Wilkerson, isn't it?"

He finally looked down at her. "Yes, that's right."

"We shared a blackjack table on the *Rex*."

California law prohibited games of chance for three miles off the coast, but a few casino boats had cast anchor just outside the grasp of the Los Angeles vice squad. The *Rex* was the best-known of the lot.

"Was it recently?" Wilkerson asked.

Kathryn was poised to launch into an unlikely tale when the crowd let out a gasp. The *Graf Zeppelin* was barely ten feet from the restraining mast when a gust of wind blew up from the east and barreled over the field. It hit the airship along its flank and swept the ship over the heads of the southern section of the crowd.

"It's supposed to resist a wind like that," Wilkerson murmured.

The crowd scattered like startled deer. The zeppelin was still a good hundred feet above them, but standing below a whale-sized vessel filled with flammable gas suddenly seemed like a bad idea. People started shoving their way out, ignoring the chief of police's commands for calm and order over the loud speaker system.

Kathryn turned to Wilkerson, but he was gone. By the time she'd rejoined Marcus the airship had righted itself and was inching its way to the mast amid a round of applause.

"God love her," Marcus said. His eyes were on Gwendolyn, who was Charlestoning for the camera like a woman possessed. "Even when the zeppelin lost its bearings, she kept dancing." He let out a chuckle. "You know that she's going to insist we go to every theater in Hollywood until we see her up on the screen."

Kathryn nodded, but she barely saw Gwendolyn. A new daily trade paper! To fill a whole newspaper every day, they were going to need reporters, and lots of them.

CHAPTER 15

The sound of rain always reminded Marcus of home. The way the fat drops splattered onto the rooftop, light at first and then pounding against the shingles. It was a comforting sound that made him feel safe, even through the spiteful Pennsylvania winters

Marcus hadn't heard rain in nearly a year. So when he woke one Sunday morning and heard it beating against the window, he was flooded with memories. He thought of the elm tree in his parents' front yard, how its leaves must be turning red and gold and starting to fall. The backyard pumpkin patch would be on its way to Halloween fullness, and his father would be checking the snow shovel's blade.

Still half asleep, Marcus indulged in an early morning fantasy of what he might be doing right now if his father and the mayor had walked into the town's jail an hour later than they had that night. He'd probably be roaming the creek on the far side of town with Dwight, the way they used to. Or maybe he'd be romping inside the Adler's back door and his mom would be offering to make waffles. Oh boy, her waffles were the cat's meow. He sighed into his pillow and pushed thoughts of his mom out of his mind. He'd come to learn that dwelling on her for too long invariably led to excessive amounts of bootleg.

When the rain had spent itself against his small window pane, it was past nine o'clock. He slid out of bed, pulled on his robe and opened the door to retrieve the Sunday *Times*. Instead, he found Jake, the Garden of Allah's middle-aged bellboy crouching outside his door with a cardboard box in his hands.

Jake squeezed his eyes shut like it would make him invisible. "Damn," he said. "You weren't supposed to see me here."

"What have you got there?"

Jake's knees cracked as he stood up. He looked from the box in his hands to Marcus, and handed it over. Marcus lifted the flap and peered inside; it was the toy rocking horse he'd bid on at Alla Nazimova's auction over a year ago.

"Where did this come from?" Marcus asked.

"Can't you just pretend you never saw me? I kinda promised . . ."

"I've got some real gin in my room."

Jake's mouth curled into a grin.

* * *

Marcus reached the door of villa twenty-four and rapped three times with the brass knocker. He waited half a minute and rapped again, a little louder this time. He leaned over to the left to look through the window. The cheap lace curtain wasn't enough to hide the figure silhouetted in the lamplight.

"Miss Leventon?" Marcus called. "It's Marcus Adler. I came to thank you for the rocking horse."

The front door slowly opened. Mariam Leventon's face was starting to line with age, but her smile was warm. Her hair was gathered in a loose bun at the nape of her neck, as though it were too much work to keep it neatly in place.

"Either you are the world's greatest sleuth, or Jake the bellboy cannot keep a promise." She sounded vaguely European.

"It might be worth remembering," Marcus said, "that Jake the bellboy is a pushover for gin." Her laugh was deep and throaty. "I wanted to thank you for the rocking horse."

Miss Leventon opened her door a little wider. "I'm making orange blossom tea. Would you like some?"

"I don't believe I've ever had it, but it sounds delicious."

Miss Leventon's villa was as full of shadow as Kathryn and Gwendolyn's was full of light. Where the girls had a full dining set, Miss Leventon had two chairs tucked into a small parlor table. The girls' living room held two sofas, an armchair, and a coffee table, but here a small sofa and mismatched chair huddled around an upended beer barrel that had been painted a desperately cheery red. Her walls were bare, the tables were empty.

She kept her back to him as she poured boiling water into a delicate red and white teapot. "I'm glad you like the rocking horse. I've regretted bidding against you that day, but at the very last minute, I found I could not part with it. My father was not a kind man, but he carved and painted that horse for me when I was a child."

"Your . . . father?"

"My friend, Glesca, was so very angry with me at the auction. Kept telling me to let go of the past. I thought I had, thought I could. But I'd forgotten about Papa's rocking horse and found it was one thing I could not surrender. I saw your face when you picked it up and it has haunted me ever since. Today I woke up in a nostalgic mood and thought to myself, Enough! Give the boy the rocking horse."

Marcus felt his face flush as he found his voice. "I thought you were—"

Alla Nazimova turned around and smiled at him, letting him see the violet eyes he'd remembered a thousand times.

"Dead?" Madame Nazimova gave a soft laugh. "No, just closer to broke than I ever thought I would be."

Marcus could hardly breathe. "I'm sorry to hear you're in such financial difficulty," he managed. He stepped up to the counter between them. "You won't remember this, but about a dozen years ago—"

"Diphtheria. I remember you. Very clearly."

Marcus could feel the color drain from his face. He needed to sit down. Alla seemed not to notice, though. She shrugged and pulled her face into a frown. "I never should have let them talk me into turning my home into a hotel. But we are all geniuses when we look backwards, no?" She set the teapot and two exquisite teacups on matching saucers onto a pewter tray–the only touch of luxury Marcus had seen–and gestured to Marcus to follow her into the living room. She settled into her armchair underneath a floor lamp with a faded crimson shade. In its suffused pink light, she looked angelic.

"You must miss living in the big house," Marcus said.

"Houses. They come, they go." Nazimova's violet eyes pierced him. "What I miss is my 8080 Club. You heard of this, yes?"

He shook his head.

"It was a little bit . . . ," her eyes narrowed slyly, "notorious." She cut the word loose and let it float between them like a soap bubble. "It was a group of *interesting* people. Mae Murray, Lilyan Tashman, the Talmadge sisters. And of course, marvelous June Mathis."

"June Mathis?" Marcus asked. "The woman who wrote *Ben-Hur*?"

"Ah, you know your writers. Madame is impressed. She wrote *The Four Horsemen of the Apocalypse*. That is how I met her. She wrote it for Valentino who was Armand Duval to my Camille. Hollywood was a very small town then. Everyone would gather in my living room to talk of important things — culture, the arts, philosophy. And of course . . . ," she paused for half a second, "about sexuality. Endlessly we would talk!"

"You mean a salon, like they have in Paris? Gertrude Stein and that whole crowd?"

Madame Nazimova smiled her cat-with-cream smile and clapped her hands together. "Gertrude Stein! *Exactement!* And of course we discussed poetry. Ah, such passion for the poets. Do you like poetry, *monsieur*?"

"Some," Marcus replied.

"What about Sappho? Have you read anything by Sappho?"

Marcus had never read a poem in his life. He shook his head and wondered when he would stop feeling like a rube.

"No?" Nazimova pulled her face into a frown. "Tsk, tsk." She sounded like Marcus' mother when a scolding wasn't far away. "Sappho was the greatest poet of her age. She lived on the Greek island of Lesbos. You have heard of Lesbos, n'est-ce pas?"

Marcus lowered his teacup to the delicate saucer on his lap. "My Greek geography isn't really up to snuff."

"Sappho wrote great poems about the special sort of love that exists between one woman and another."

Madame Nazimova watched Marcus' face with interest and amusement as he licked the orange-flavored sweetness from his dry lips. She had steered the conversation into an area Marcus had never wandered before. Not out loud, anyway. Same sex love. How could that ever be an appropriate conversation in public? He could hear the sound of a clock he couldn't see anywhere. Tick-tick. Tick-tick. Tick-tick. He looked at his hands and found them drained of color. He could feel her violet eyes boring into him.

Same sex love was the whole reason why he was tossed out of town by his own father. It'd been two whole years now but the memory of that night still gutted him. Maybe some day I'll be able to say those words out loud, he decided, but not today.

"Is there any more tea?" he asked.

Nazimova reached over and poured them both some more orange blossom tea. The spicy-sweet aroma filled the lonely room. "I always see you with that girl with the pale skin and chestnut hair."

Marcus nodded, relieved. "Her name is Kathryn."

"I see much when I look out my window," Madame Nazimova said. "And I look out of my window a lot. I like to see what goes on in my own backyard." She lifted a shoulder and made a self-deprecating chuckle. "Used to be my backyard. But your Kathryn, she is very smart, yes? And the pretty one she lives with. Tall with the blonde hair. The dressmaker. You are all very good friends."

"Yes, we are. I'm very thankful—"

"It is important to have good friends. Especially when you are so far from home." Nazimova offered him another enigmatic smile. "So, what do you do for a living, Mister Marcus Adler?"

"I deliver telegrams for Western Union."

"Do you enjoy this work?"

"It's a job. But it takes a lot out of you."

"I can imagine."

"All that pedaling around. It'll be easier when they get around to paving all the streets. Most times I get home so exhausted that I barely have the energy to write. That's what I really want to do."

"So you are a writer. Madame is not surprised to hear this. Tell me now, Monsieur Marcus, what have you written?"

Marcus' first attempts at writing had been the literary equivalent of playing hopscotch in the dark. They were horribly trite, but he'd persisted until he wrote a story he liked. It was about a stage hand in a Broadway theater who planted himself in the wings every night and dreamed of standing in the spotlight.

"And what do your friends think of it?" Nazimova asked.

"I haven't had the courage to show it to anyone."

"The artist cannot fear rejection! Fear of rejection is a fire-breathing dragon. We must fight until all the air is sucked from our lungs." She leaned forward and fixed him with a stare. "These people, they are your friends?"

Marcus nodded.

"Go to them. Tell them, 'I am a writer and this is my story.' How will you know if your work is good if you do not give anyone a chance to reject it?" She looked at him softly. "True friends must be honest with each other. If you are not honest about who you are, how can you expect anyone to love you?"

CHAPTER 16

Gwendolyn gazed up at the mammoth billboard and wondered if it was too late to back out. It had sounded like an exciting adventure when she'd said yes, and God knows it was the only work she'd secured that was even remotely connected with the movie business in the whole two years she'd been in Hollywood. But now it seemed like an exercise in madness.

"It's taller than I'd expected," said the girl next to her. She looked even paler than the white sailor suit they all wore. She fingered the red, white, and blue feathered hat in her hand.

"Never mind that," Gwendolyn said. "Take a look at that platform. I hope it's wider than it seems."

Gwendolyn's soda-heiress story hadn't fooled the Movietone cameraman, but he was impressed enough to hook her up with his pal at MGM, who needed "ambitious, outgoing, fun-loving girls" for a brand-new endeavor. It sounded terrific on paper, especially the 175 smackers for seven nights of work. If they were willing to pay her to stand on a platform and do a little dance routine that hadn't taken but ten minutes to learn, Gwendolyn couldn't see any reason not to. Especially with The Hammer's money starting to dwindle the way it was. At least she was working for MGM.

Gwendolyn noticed Alice standing next to her, gazing up at the looming billboard. When they'd bumped into each other at the rehearsal, Alice had seemed cooler than she had at the Argyle, but tonight she was back to her usual wise-cracking self. She put her hands on her hips and scoffed. "Oh, come on, girls, where's your gumption? This'll be fun. A lark! Something to tell your grandchildren."

"If we live long enough to have grandchildren," the pale girl said.

Alice surveyed the crowd gathering on the corners of Hollywood Boulevard and Highland Avenue. "Look at all these people!" she said. "They've come to see us!"

"Don't kid yourself," said one of the other girls. "These people have come to see one of us fall off. And they say there's no such thing as bad publicity. Yeah well, phooey on that, is what I say."

That girl's right, Gwendolyn decided. None of these people were here to see the lighting of the largest billboard ever constructed in Los Angeles. Publicity was publicity, but a human billboard had to be the craziest scheme any studio had ever dreamed up.

MGM had poured a small fortune into their new picture, *The Hollywood Revue of 1929*. Almost every major star on their roster — John Gilbert, Norma Shearer, Joan Crawford, Buster Keaton, Billy Haines — had been thrown into a string of all-singing, all-dancing, all-talking, all-star songs and acts. As if that wasn't enough, some bright spark in publicity had decided that Hollywood's Biggest Picture needed Hollywood's Biggest Billboard. And then some other wisenheimer had dreamed up an even wilder idea — to put real people on it. Of course, by 'real people' they meant 'pretty chorines.'

Two huge words had been painted onto the billboard: HOLLYWOOD and REVUE, twelve feet high, and ringed with red electric bulbs.

Below each word a platform jutted out; neither of them looked terribly wide from down on the street. When they'd climbed the ladder and tottered out on their allotted position, they seemed even narrower.

The pale girl sighed. "How's about them mattresses they promised, huh?" The choreographer, a dark-haired, serious fellow named Busby, had guaranteed them that the sidewalk would be covered with thick, bouncy mattresses, but neither the mattresses nor Busby had appeared.

"Who cares?" Alice said. "I just heard one of the assistants tell the Metronome Newsreel guy that he wants a photograph of every girl because the head of casting at MGM is here tonight.

A flashbulb popped inside Gwendolyn's head. At the Brown Derby that night, she'd asked Ritchie who the dapper gent with the "I'm very important around here" air was. Ritchie had smirked, "He's the busiest casting couch in the West. That's Mr. Metro-Goldwyn-Snare." Gwendolyn peered down from her perch three stories up, trying to pick him out of the crowd. Oh Lordy, she thought, the head of casting for MGM could be watching me right this very minute.

* * *

The view from the top almost made the climb worthwhile. Gwendolyn could see over the red roof of the sprawling Hollywood Hotel on the opposite corner. The onlookers were the size of poppies, but their wolf-whistles and cat calls reached the chorus girls all the way up above the twelve-foot-tall letters of HOLLYWOOD. Gwendolyn clung to the rope banister over the Y and wondered if Mr. MGM was more likely to be watching the girls on the ends.

The pale girl stood to Gwendolyn's left and let out a soft groan. "That dance routine has completely flown out of my head."

"It's easy!" Alice called from Gwendolyn's right. "Right kick, left kick, right kick, left kick, clap above your head then thrice in front—" She danced on the two-foot deep platform just the same as she had on the pine floor at the Vine Street Dance Academy. Gwendolyn admired the nerve of her look-alike. Alice might be a little on the cheap side, and perhaps a mite pushier than need be, but here, with the winds of the Pacific blowing in her face, she was an inspiration.

"GIRLS!" The MGM supervisor's voice boomed up at them through his megaphone. "Your attention, please. The lights go on in two minutes. The music will start two minutes after that. Count to thirty-two and start dancing. Every newspaper and newsreel in Los Angeles is here. You are making history!"

"In other words, don't screw it up," Alice said wryly. The girls laughed, relieved to break the tension. "Look out! We're on!"

One of the assistants pumped his fist into the air. "Five . . . four . . . three . . . two . . . one . . ."

Four enormous klieg lights burst into life, flooding the billboard with blinding light. The crowd, the traffic, the streetcars, even the Hollywood Hotel disappeared. All Gwendolyn could see were her feet at the edge of the platform. Beyond that? Nothing.

Hundreds of globes flickered to life around the words HOLLYWOOD REVUE. A candy cane red glow enveloped them. The jaunty opening strains of the picture's big finale number–"Singin' in the Rain"–started up, but Gwendolyn missed the count and started to panic. "Is anybody counting?" she called out.

"Twenty-two, twenty-three, twenty-four . . ." Alice counted out loud to thirty-two. "And GO! Right kick, left kick, right kick, left kick, clap above your head then thrice in front . . ."

Had Busby included a spin or a turn, the masses below would have been treated to a cascade of showgirls before the end of the first sixteen bars, but his choreography was largely looping arms and feathered caps.

Gwendolyn's shoulders started to relax after a couple of verses. Twenty-six chorus girls kicked and waved and hoped and dreamed in perfect sync, praying that this would be their big break.

The song ended in a flourish of white caps and red, white and blue feathers. Gwendolyn's eyes followed a stray feather toward the ground and her heart lurched. She grabbed at the rope banister and missed the count on the next song.

"Alice!" she called toward the curtain of light. "Are you counting?"

"Nine, ten, eleven, twelve, am-I-the-only-one-who-can-count-here? Fifteen, sixteen . . ."

By the time Alice reached the count of thirty-two, Gwendolyn was frozen to the platform.

"Come on, Brick, what are you waiting for? And left kick, clap above your head then thrice in front."

Gwendolyn knew that if she just stood there like a dead clam, the casting guy really would notice her, and not in the way she hoped. With her heart pounding in her ears, she forced herself to start moving but struggled to keep up with the routine. Out of the corner of her eye, she could see that even Alice was out of step now, and drifting closer to Gwendolyn.

Right on the last line–"In the ra-a-a-a-in!"–Gwendolyn let go of the rope to grab her hat for the final flourish. At the last second, she saw the feathers on Alice's cap arcing around and heading straight for her. Their wrists connected and Alice cried out, "OH!"

She let go of her cap and Gwendolyn ducked, but it hit her squarely on the ear. She lost her balance, her right knee gave way, and she stumbled to the wooden platform as her own cap flew into the sea of light. Her right hand burned as it slid along the rope, and she let go. Her fingernails scraped the edge of the platform and she felt a rush of cool air. She looked down at the space between her and the ground and wondered if the cameras were getting all of this.

CHAPTER 17

Kathryn came out of the bathroom drying her hair with a towel.

"What did you say, dear?"

"It's just so quiet!" Gwendolyn said from the sofa. Her ankle, still so swollen and bruised, was bandaged and propped up on a pillow. She let the *Examiner* fall into her lap. "I'd gotten used to all the noise around here. All the parties, the drinking, the laughing, the music. Even all those guys banging away at their typewriters. But now it's like God's reached across the Garden and turned off the radio."

Kathryn pointed to the front page. "Well, if that won't hush things up, I don't know what will."

STOCK MARKET CRASHES FURTHER
DAILY LOSSES EXCEED 10% PER DAY
Bankers Seen Leaping from Manhattan Skyscrapers

The raucous almost-nightly parties around the Garden had evaporated within a week. Everyone had retreated into their villas to hibernate until the acorns grew back. But, Kathryn wondered, how long would this financial winter last?

Gwendolyn adjusted her ankle on the pillows. "I think this is one of the times where you can say it's not so bad being poor. Having no money in the first place means not losing any when everything comes busting apart."

There was a loud knock on the door. "Miss Massey. It's Jake. You got a telephone call in the lobby. Your mother — sounds plenty upset."

The girls raised their eyebrows at each other and Kathryn slipped on her shoes.

* * *

When Kathryn returned, Gwendolyn was balancing on one foot at the kitchen sink, attempting to fill the kettle. "Is your mama okay?"

Kathryn took the kettle and shooed her friend back to the sofa. "Really, Gwennie, you're lucky you came away from that awful fall with just a badly sprained ankle. You were incredibly lucky you landed on the roof of that convertible."

"I was lucky that convertible had its roof up."

"Exactly. So don't go making it worse by ignoring the doctor's orders."

"But what about your mama?"

"My mother has more melodrama than Norma Talmadge. She was all teary and barking on about some sort of calamity."

"Why? What's happened?"

"I don't know, but we're about to find out. She's on her way over." Kathryn struck a long match and lit the burner. "Don't get sucked in by her act."

"How do you know it's an act?"

Kathryn looked into Gwendolyn's big, trusting green eyes. "It's always an act."

"You'll want me to go, then, and give you some privacy," Gwendolyn said, hobbling to her feet again.

"You sit your pert little behind back down on that sofa, missy. I want you right here so you can witness firsthand what I have to put up with."

Francine must have splurged on a taxicab because she was knocking on the front door before the water boiled.

Kathryn opened the door to find her mother in a shapeless dress of the drabbest mud-brown imaginable. She hadn't worn it since their most threadbare time, when they lived on day-old bread and that vile, watery onion and black bean soup. The fact that Francine had dragged out this dress gave Kathryn reason to pause.

"Kathryn, darling, you have no idea the calamity — oh! Gwendolyn. You're here."

"She does live here, Mother."

"Whatever have you done to your ankle?"

"Took a bad fall," Gwendolyn said.

Francine nodded as though in sympathy but Kathryn could tell that her mother was more than happy to have an audience. Kathryn pointed her mother to a loveseat and sat down in the armchair. "So, what's going on that you had to rush all the way over here?"

Francine intertwined her fingers and squeezed her hands together so tightly her fingernails turned white. She sucked in a full lung's worth of air, held it for a good five seconds, and then cried out, "I'm destitute!"

Ah, Kathryn thought, so the resurfaced frumpy brown dress is a costume in which to play the Penniless Mother. Kathryn shot Gwendolyn a withering look, and then turned back to her mother. "What do you mean, you're destitute?"

"Don't tell me you haven't heard the news? The stock market! It's collapsed! Everybody is in ruins!"

"Mother, the only people who are in ruins are the investors who had money in the stock market."

"But that's the whole problem. I had all my money tied up in it."

"Oh, Mother, really. All your money tied up in the stock market? What did you have, four dollars of Woolworth stock?

Francine was working herself up into hysterics. "I have a friend whose brother owns a pawn shop. He gave me a very good price for my wedding ring." Kathryn glanced at her mother's empty left hand and was surprised to see it bare. What's the bet, she thought, it's stashed in her handbag? "I needed money and my friend is very good with it. So he took what I got for my ring and invested it in the stock market." Francine shot her daughter a sharp look. "I had to do *something* once you'd deserted me. It wasn't much to begin with, but this fellow was a wizard with money. My tiny nest egg grew and grew and grew. It was astonishing."

Kathryn watched her mother take a handkerchief stashed up her sleeve and dab her eyes. "And now?"

"And now it's all gone. All of it! Every spare dollar I had. I am utterly broke."

"Exactly how much money are we talking here?" Kathryn asked.

"What does that matter?" Francine snapped. "The point is that it's all gone, and I cannot afford the rent. You're just going to have to move back home with me."

"I'm *what*?" Kathryn realized they'd commenced the third act of today's performance.

"If you don't come home, I'll be thrown out. I'll be on the streets. Homeless!" She turned to Gwendolyn with tears in her eyes, careful not to let them tip over the bottom lids and spill down her cheeks. It was more dramatic that way, and Francine ought to know: it was Francine who taught her that just before an audition for DeMille. "Gwendolyn, my dear, what sort of daughter would allow her mother to be tossed into the gutter like yesterday's garbage?"

Gwendolyn's eyes were wide as she tried to think of an answer.

"Mother!" Kathryn said. "Look at me."

Francine drew her imploring gaze slowly back to her daughter.

"My entire life, you've never had more than twenty dollars in the bank. And now you expect me to believe that the stock market crash has reduced you to penury? Oh, Mother."

Francine opened her handbag. "I know someone in the costume department of Warner Brothers," she said. "Her son works at the Ambassador Hotel."

"So?"

"So her son mentioned last week that the hotel's nightclub needs a new cigarette girl. You know, the Cocoanut Grove? They have the palm trees they used in that Valentino movie, *The Sheik*."

"Everybody's heard of the Cocoanut Grove, mother. What about it?"

"Their last cigarette girl was discovered by a talent scout from Universal." She pulled a folded piece of paper out of her handbag and waved it at Kathryn. "You should call him right away."

"What for?"

Francine pulled a face as though Kathryn had just dumped sour cream in her coffee. "This silly fan mail job you're doing for Tallulah Bankhead isn't going to get you anywhere. But a job at the Cocoanut Grove?"

Kathryn thought of the article she wrote about the landing of the *Graf* Zeppelin. It was pretty damn good, even if she did say so herself. She hadn't heard back from Wilkerson yet, but that could only be a matter of time. She jutted her head forward. "Is that the best you think I can do? A cigarette girl in a night club?"

"You'll be right in front of every bigwig in the business. Kathryn, darling, think of what it might lead to! Sooner or later, someone is bound to notice you. Look where it got the last girl. Universal Studios!"

"MOTHER!" Kathryn exploded. "How many times do I need to say this? I. Do. Not. Want. To. Be. An. Actress. I'm doing fine here. Just *fine*. If you need help covering your rent, I can lend you next month's. But I will *not* be moving back in with you."

Francine sniffed. "They say that this stock market thing is going to lead to the most awful recession imaginable." She lay the address on the coffee table. "I think a steady paycheck will be hard to come by."

"You're probably right," Kathryn agreed. She strode to the front door and yanked it open. "So you'll need to start looking for a job before all the good ones are taken, won't you? I hear there's something going at the Cocoanut Grove."

Francine rose to her feet as though she were Queen Victoria. "I cannot believe my own daughter is throwing me out into the street."

"I'm not throwing you anywhere, Mother."

Francine stopped at the door and turned to Gwendolyn. "I know you wouldn't treat your mother like this," she said, all *grande dame*. "You're too much of a lady. I hope your ankle heals quickly, dear." She turned and marched out.

Kathryn slammed the door shut with a whump. "Am I the world's worst daughter?" she moaned.

"That depends on whether or not your mother was telling you the truth."

"I can guarantee you she was doing nothing of the sort."

"In that case, you've done a very brave thing. You've just declared yourself an independent woman of the world who had to make it clear to her mother that things have changed."

Kathryn stepped outside and watched her mother trot along the path and disappear into the shadows of the Garden of Allah Hotel. Or, she thought, one who pushed her mother out to starve to death in the street.

CHAPTER 18

Gwendolyn stood outside the double doors of the Cocoanut Grove and hoisted up her cleavage, wishing she had worn her own clothes. The silky midnight blue cocktail dress fit perfectly around the waist, but her neighbor's bust was much fuller than hers. Their neighbor, Bessie Love, had assured Gwendolyn that if she wore her lucky dress, she wouldn't have to worry about a thing, but right that minute, Gwendolyn had serious doubts about both Bessie's luck and her bosom. She gave it another push and opened the etched glass doors.

Inside, the nightclub was lit strictly for daytime business. A half dozen bare bulbs burned as the cleaners scrubbed away the sins committed in the bootlegged blur of last night's Charleston contest. In the stark light, the dark floral carpet and the velvet drapes seemed worn out, and the papier-mâché trees looked cheap and flimsy.

"Hello?" Gwendolyn called out.

"You must be Kathryn Massey."

A doughy man with the face of a midway bouncer appeared by a palm tree.

"As a matter of fact, I don't go by that name anymore."

The man sucked on the fat cigar that hung from the side of his mouth like a gangplank. "Of course you don't." He beckoned her to follow him into his office.

After two years of shoestring budgeting, Gwendolyn was down to three hundred Eugene Hammerschmidt dollars. With all this talk of a deep recession filling the pages of every newspaper these days, Gwendolyn had come to the hard conclusion that she was going to have to get a job until Hollywood's fickle gods found her. Francine's cigarette girl tip was just the ticket. She tried to walk as though her sprained ankle no longer hurt like the dickens, although she needn't have bothered. The guy didn't seem to be paying her much attention.

"Lawrence Grainger," the man said, revealing teeth yellowed by too many Havanas. "What's your name this week, toots?"

"Gwendolyn Brick," she replied, and wished she hadn't. Lord, how she hated that name. She'd gone off 'Gwendolyn Day' and now thought 'Gwendolyn Reed' had a nice ring to it. But good ol' Gwendolyn Brick kept popping out before she could stop it.

Grainger was hunting through papers, menus and seating charts for something on his desk. "So," he said without bothering to look up, "cigarette girl. You know what the job entails, don'cha?"

"Selling cigars and cigarettes to patrons of the nightclub."

Grainger grunted and shook his head. "No, sweetheart," he said. "The job is to sell sex." He watched her for a response.

Gwendolyn was startled but amused. "Really?" she smiled. "I thought that was the work of madams and pimps."

Grainger's smile was genuine this time. "Sassy," he said, nodding, "sassy is good. No, tootsie, what I mean is this: Nightclubs are in the same business Hollywood's in. We sell glamour, fun, excitement, anticipation—all of which are just foreplay to the main event."

"Sex," she repeated, now that she realized he was serious.

"The *promise* of sex. You saw what that nightclub looked like out there, didn't you? The renowned Cocoanut Grove nightclub at the glamorous Ambassador Hotel. Playground of the famously infamous and the infamously famous. Not what you were expecting, huh? Pretty awful, right? But turn off those stark overheads, and turn on the table lamps and the starlights in the ceiling, add an orchestra with a classy torch singer out front, and what have you got now?" He shimmied his hands like a minstrel. "A place reeking with the anticipation of sex." He pulled the cigar from his drooly mouth and flicked ash into an ashtray shaped like a palm tree. "And when there's the possibility of sex, people will hand over everything in their wallets. That's why the cigarette girl is a real important part of what we're selling here."

They stared at each other for a moment. Grainger heaved himself out of his chair and walked around his desk to park his generous behind on its edge. When he looked down at her, his three chins folded up like a concertina. She could smell his aftershave balm; it was musky and old-fashioned, and reminded her of her grandpa.

"My last cigarette girl left because she got a contract at Universal. One of those full seven-year ones. They don't come along every day."

Gwendolyn smiled. "They most certainly do not."

"You'd be seen by all the big kahunas in the industry."

"I imagine I would."

He cleared his throat and adjusted his egg-stained tie. "So, don't you think that's worth a little something?"

Gwendolyn forced herself not to blink.

So much for the clever speech about selling the possibility of sex and the cigarette girl's importance to the team. It came down to *I have what you want but do you want it badly enough to give me what I want?* She should have seen Grainger as the lowlife sleazeball that he was, but his nifty spiel about selling sex had blindsided her. She had less than one minute to consider her options.

Gwendolyn held the guy's gaze and wondered if he realized that she was the type of girl who wasn't completely above trading favors. After all, this was the nineteen twenties—women could vote now, they could smoke in public, go to college, even have a career. In other words they could behave exactly like men if they wanted. The question, Gwendolyn decided, wasn't whether or not to consent, but if consenting was worth the reward.

She thought about the dusty palm trees and the brandy stains on the carpet, her sprained ankle and her cozy villa, the interminable ride from Florida, her growing list of last names and her odds of making it to the silver screen. Gwendolyn adjusted her neckline and stood up. She bunched her right hand into a fist, pulled back and swiped the nightclub manager with a mean right hook, just the way her brother had taught her.

"Hey!" Grainger cried out, covering his cheek. "That was pretty good for a dame."

Gwendolyn grabbed her purse and sneered at him. "Damn right it is, you big creep."

The putz suddenly broke into a genial smile and laughed a little. "Congrats, toots, you can relax now."

"Congratulations?" Gwendolyn's heart was racing and her knuckles ached.

"Sit down." He gave her a nudge firm enough to land her back in the chair. "If you work here, you'll have to handle every sort of pass mankind has ever dreamed up. The crude, the subtle, the squeezes, the sleazes—it's a jungle out there, and you gotta be ready. You just proved that you can. You're on the list, sweetheart."

"There's a list?"

He threw her an understanding look. "Don't worry. None of them ever stay for long. You'll move up fast. But hey, at least you're on the list. Every girl I've put the make on who says yes, they don't even get on the list. You did good, sugarpuss." He picked up his cigar and jammed it back into his mouth. A pocket of drool collected at the edge of his lips. "You're okay showing yourself out, aren't you?"

Gwendolyn nodded. Outside Grainger's cluttered office, she gazed around at the papier-mâché trees and stuffed monkeys and chuckled. "I'm at the bottom of a list."

CHAPTER 19

When John G. Bullock announced he was building a new department store on Wilshire Boulevard, people looked at each other over hands of gin rummy and asked who on earth was going to trek all the way down Wilshire to go shopping? All the good stores were downtown.

When Bullock announced that he was going to face his store's entrance toward the parking lot, people were ready to call the nut house. No street entrance? Valet parking for a department store?

But when John G. Bullock opened his art deco temple on that half-deserted stretch of Wilshire Boulevard, people had to agree that the nutty guy had built a gorgeous building. The soaring fourteen-story tower was sheathed in copper that was already tarnishing a delightful shade of green, and the decorative panels were stunning. And wasn't it so terribly convenient the way the parking attendant would give you a numbered card and deliver your packages to your car while you shopped?

Kathryn Massey stood under Bullock's porte-cochere admiring the hand-painted geometric mural named *The Spirit of Transportation.* It was as art deco as art deco gets: an ocean liner, the figure of Mercury, and a trio of biplanes escorting the *Graf Zeppelin,* all with a patina of emerald green and sky blue and sunset orange.

She gazed up at the dirigible and thought, So, the three of us meet again.

Kathryn had sent three sample articles to Mr. Wilkerson in the past few months, but she hadn't heard a word from him which was disappointing because she believed they were all damn fine articles. One was about Britain's Chancellor of the Exchequer, Winston Churchill, and his recent speech at MGM, the second was about Douglas Fairbanks Junior's marriage to Joan Crawford, and the other covered the banning of Norma Shearer's new movie *The Trial of Mary Dugan* by the stiff-necked bluenoses. She'd been to his office twice to try and talk her way into an interview, but the guy proved as slippery as soap in the rain.

When she discovered that Robert Benchley and Wilkerson shared the same bootlegger, she learned he drove a kelly green Pontiac Landaulette with silver-white trim. Through a series of lucky coincidences enabled by the reliably soused residents of the Garden of Allah—this on-going recession hadn't killed the Garden of Allah party for long—Kathryn learned that Billy Wilkerson took his wife to Bullock's new store every Thursday for supper in the tea room on the top floor.

"Are you still waiting for your automobile, ma'am?" A valet offered her one of those concerned professional smiles.

"Oh no," she said, "I'm waiting for a friend."

The attendant nodded and withdrew, leaving her to feel conspicuously out of place. The only other people lingering around the store's porte-cochere were swells still rich enough to afford the top-drawer prices at Bullock's Wilshire.

Kathryn glanced at her wristwatch. It was nearly six P.M.; Wilkerson and his wife were nearly half an hour late. Out of the corner of her eye, she could see the attendant watching her. Perhaps she should wait inside.

Just then, a shiny green Landaulette pulled into the parking lot.

Kathryn stepped into a shaded corner and watched Mr. and Mrs. Wilkerson climb out of their car and walk into the store. She followed closely and strolled past them as Wilkerson kissed his wife by the fox furs and headed for the hat department.

Wilkerson browsed his way through bowlers, panamas, top hats and straw boaters. When he wandered over to an ornate display of felt fedoras, Kathryn decided to make her move. Her heart rate ratcheted up a notch or two.

A couple of skinny guys in faintly shiny suits in different shades of gray strode past her and straight for Wilkerson. They both sported the pallor of people who spent too much time indoors, which made them more than conspicuous in the rarified atmosphere of the leisure class.

Wilkerson swung around with his back to the hat display and acknowledged them with a curt nod. Kathryn made her way around the curved display case and stood with her back pressed against a column.

"In the market for a hat?" a shiny suit asked.

"You know what I'm in the market for." Wilkerson sounded terse.

"The captain of the *Montfalcone* wants you to know that this meeting has no bearing on your reputation, good, bad or otherwise."

"Nor," added the second suit, "does it mean he doesn't consider you the type to welsh on your debts."

"That situation at the Colony Club, it was a one-time thing," Wilkerson retorted. "A misunderstanding that got out of hand."

"He just needs to ensure the quality of his passengers."

"I get it. One bad apple and all that. So am I in?"

"It ain't up to us."

"So when will I hear?"

"We just needed to meet ya first, is all. In person, like. Expect a telegram in due course."

Kathryn peered through the fedora stands to see the men's shiny backs retreat toward the entrance. She turned to follow Wilkerson but couldn't move. She tugged again. She reached behind her back and touched cool metal. Her coat was caught on something that wouldn't give.

"I wouldn't do that if I were you," said a husky European voice.

Kathryn twisted inside her coat to look over her shoulder at a slim woman enveloped in an enormous mink coat. "You should not move," she said. "You have become caught on a fire extinguisher. If you pull it the wrong way, you will cover all those lovely fedoras with foam." She began to untangle Kathryn. "I have seen you at the Garden of Allah, yes?"

"Do you live there, too?"

The woman gave Kathryn's coat a tug. "I like to go there when I am feeling . . . ensnared. The first time I saw you was right after the opening. You tripped over a man with hair the color of sand and a round face. He was tying his shoelaces. You collided and fell into the pool. Ah! Voila!"

Freed from the claws of the fire extinguisher, Kathryn turned around to find Greta Garbo exactly as she looked onscreen. Her face was perfectly symmetrical, her skin as smooth and unblemished as a Swedish snowfall.

"Oh!" Kathryn could feel herself blush. "You saw that, huh?"

Garbo allowed herself a cool smile and shrugged. "I am a keen observer of people. I endeavor to remember everything I see. At the Garden of Allah, I am left alone to watch and witness."

"Well, thank you for saving me from myself."

Garbo shook her head. "Think nothing of it. If our positions had been reversed, I would like to think that you'd have paid me the same courtesy. But may I ask upon whom were you spying?"

Kathryn stared at Garbo and considered the actress' notorious wariness of the press. How would she react to Kathryn's story of stalking someone who was about to start up a new trade newspaper? She'd probably wish she had left Kathryn hanging off the fire extinguisher.

"I overheard some men talking about the *Montfalcone*," Kathryn said. "Do you know what that is?"

Garbo smiled her famously enigmatic smile. "It is one of those floating casinos anchored beyond the reach of the vice squad."

"You mean like the *Rex*. Have you been there? Is it classy?"

Garbo laughed easily. "They probably think that it is. But nothing compares to Monte Carlo."

CHAPTER 20

The color didn't suit her, the shoulder pads were an inch too wide, and the cigarette tray weighed more than she'd expected, but the Cocoanut Grove had lost three girls in two weeks and telegrammed the day before New Year's Eve. Gwendolyn showed up early.

"How does it fit?" Grainger asked through the door. "Hopefully good, 'cause it's the only one we got."

"It's good enough," Gwendolyn answered. The purple and emerald panels and fine gold braid wouldn't have been her first choice, but it wasn't awful. She emerged from the storeroom.

Her new boss nodded his approval. "Okay, so here are the rules. Firstly: No drinking with customers. Ever. Secondly, flirting is acceptable, but only for the purposes of increasing tips. You can smile, wink, laugh, giggle and wiggle all you want, but no kissing, no dancing, and definitely no fucking. Tips are fine, but only in cash. No jewelry, no furs, no clothes, no flowers, no nothing. If I catch wind of you breaking the rules, I'll can your ass faster than you can say 'Chesterfields or Camels.' Any questions?"

"What if someone asks me for something I don't have in my tray?"

"If the jerk is real particular, there's a tobacconist in the foyer. His name is Bobo. He's got everything—and I mean everything. Bobo is your new best friend."

Grainger motioned to a stoic-looking guy with dark eyes and a deeply dimpled chin. "Chuck," said Grainger, "I want you to meet Gwendolyn, our new cigarette girl."

Chuck did a double take. "What happened to — ? Oh, the Chaplin thing?"

"Keep an eye on this one for me, will you?" He turned to Gwendolyn. "Chuck here is our bartender. Not that the Cocoanut Grove has a bar that needs tending, you understand?" He winked. "Good luck, kiddo."

That night, the Cocoanut Grove looked nothing like the shabby barn she had seen a couple of months ago. Tuxedoed gentlemen and their rhinestoned dates negotiated the huge dance floor while a brunette stood in a shaft of light onstage, her white dress shimmering with crystal beads that must have weighed a ton. She sang "Button up Your Overcoat" in front of Paul Whiteman's orchestra of nearly thirty. A few revelers hurled balled-up napkins at the stuffed monkeys in the papier mâché palm forest.

By eight-thirty, the place was packed with hedonists determined to send out the twenties with a bang. By ten, she knew the prices of every brand of tobacco in her tray and by eleven she figured she had enough tips to buy more comfortable shoes at a place Chuck recommended. The crowd grew louder as the night wore on, but nobody made any passes, or attempted to pinch her behind. This was just a fun crowd which happened to be liberally sprinkled with some of the world's most famous faces. She wasn't quite prepared, however, when a burly grizzly bear of a man appeared. He cornered her, leering like a drunken Viking.

"Havanas," he said, breathing whiskey on her.

Gwendolyn maintained her smile and held up the two brands she carried. "I have Old Q and Hall's Panatela."

He didn't break his stare. "Gimme six of the Old Q."

His eyes wandered over her cleavage as he extracted his wallet from his tuxedo jacket. The black satin lapel had a dime-sized stain on it and he was missing a cufflink. He pulled out a fifty dollar bill and let it flutter into her tray. "Keep the change."

"This is a fifty, sir. The cigars only come to nine dollars."

"I know what I got in my wallet," he said, raising his voice.

Gwendolyn felt heads turn in their direction. He took the cigars in one hand and opened his mouth, but Gwendolyn cut him off with a *thank-you-very-very-much-sir-and-enjoy-your-cigars* and pressed past him. She didn't look back.

The half hour leading up to midnight was busy. The more people drank, the more they smoked, and on New Year's Eve they smoked like Prohibition for tobacco was taking effect at midnight.

Paul Whiteman took the microphone and led the countdown to midnight. Everyone was on their feet, roaring out each second and waving paper poppers. When the clock struck midnight, the dance floor became a fountain of bright streamers, and the orchestra struck up a fast, noisy Charleston. Gwendolyn supplied the crowd with a steady stream of Chesterfields, Kools, and Camels, but she was feeling the pinch of her three-inch pumps. They showed off her legs very nicely but they were not the shoe of choice for a working girl on her feet most of the night.

At around one-thirty, a large, spirited party made a grand entrance. On the way to their table next to the dance floor, the men plopped into the laps of the most matronly ladies around and tweaked their noses. The ladies squealed and the dancers spun around to see what the fuss was. Gwendolyn caught Harpo Marx's eye and winked their secret wink.

He'd moved into the Garden of Allah just before the release of *The Cocoanuts,* the Marx Brothers' first picture, and had settled quite happily into life in the upstairs apartment of his villa. But his downstairs neighbor didn't appreciate his marathon piano playing as much as Gwendolyn and Kathryn did.

When Harpo played, the neighbor banged on the ceiling incessantly. Harpo's solution was to play Rachmaninoff's Piano Concerto Number One as loud as he could, over and over and over, ignoring his neighbor's pleas to stop. In the end, the downstairs neighbor couldn't stand it any longer and moved out. Gwendolyn was there when someone from the next villa told a triumphant Harpo that his neighbor had been Sergei Rachmaninoff himself, and that the only reason he'd complained was that Harpo played his concerto so badly. Poor Harpo was mortified and begged Gwendolyn not to mention it to anyone. She hadn't heard a note of the piece since then but now, whenever they passed each other around the Garden, they shared a Rachmaninoff wink.

Harpo broke into his cheeky grin when she approached his table, and introduced her to his brothers and their dates. Groucho was checking out her cigars when he reared back and stared just beyond her with bugged eyes.

"I want more cigars."

"You've landed yourself a whopper," Groucho said without moving his lips.

Gwendolyn turned reluctantly around to find the grizzly bear behind her, motioning for her to come closer. His top half wavered as though a gale was blowing through the club. His jacket was unbuttoned and his hair was coming unstuck. There was a bleariness to his eyes that wasn't there before and a harder edge to his smile. "Six m-more cigars."

"Would you like me to get this gorilla turfed out?" Harpo asked over her shoulder.

Gwendolyn shook her head and stepped forward until she was just out of reach of his paws. "You've gone through those six cigars already? My, you must be a real aficionado."

He grunted and lunged forward.

Oh god, Gwendolyn realized. I'm going to have to do something. She thought of Kathryn's bravado with The Hammer's gangster friends, raised her throbbing right foot, and landed her kick dead on.

The guy dropped to the carpet like a sack of cannon balls, his hands clutching at his crotch. As he did, it revealed Chuck the bartender standing with his arms outstretched. "I was going to come to your rescue, but I can see you don't need my help."

* * *

It was past four in the morning when Gwendolyn walked out across the parking lot toward the stand for the night bus. Her smile muscles hurt, her back hurt more, and her feet hurt the most. But it was nothing a better pair of shoes and some practice couldn't fix. She passed a grove of palm trees–real ones that shot thirty feet into the air–when the silhouette of a large man stepped out from the shadows. She recognized the gorilla at once and panicked. Forgetting the bone-deep ache in her feet, she broke into a run across the parking lot.

She made it to Sixth Street behind the hotel and had started to head for Normandie Avenue–a wider street with more traffic and street lights–when she felt him gaining on her. "Will you just hold your horses a moment?" he called out. "I need to apologize to you."

Gwendolyn didn't stop until she was under a street lamp. She grabbed it and leaned against it to catch her breath "Keep your distance," she warned him.

He took a step back to the outer edge of the street lamp's pool of light. "I'm so sorry for my behavior," he told her. "My mother would be ashamed of me." A hairy-knuckled bulldozer like this wasn't the sort that Gwendolyn would think of as having any sort of mother, let alone one whose approval he needed. "I got some real bad news this afternoon, and I did the only thing I could think of — get rotten, stinkin' drunk. I've had a whole pitcher of water and three strong coffees since you kicked me in the — since you kicked me."

The guy didn't seem like a grizzly bear any longer; more like a raggedy old teddy bear. "I'm sober now." He reached inside his jacket and pulled out a square box covered in red velvet. "By way of apology?" He offered the box to her but when she wouldn't take it from him, he opened it.

Gwendolyn's mouth dropped open. It was a diamond brooch. Before she could think twice, she took it from the velvet box and held it in her hands. The center was a diamond, about the size of a robin's egg, and from it shot a dozen silver stems, each of them ending in a smaller, but equally perfect diamond.

The gorilla said, "It's from Harry Winston. They call it *Egyptian Starburst*. I want you to have it."

The words were a faceful of ice water. "Thank you, but I am unable to accept any gifts."

"Says who?"

"House rules. Very strict."

"But you're not in the house now. And you're not on company time."

Gwendolyn looked at the diamond brooch. If it blazed this gorgeously from the light of a street lamp, what would it look like in daylight? The guy had a point, didn't he? She was off the clock, wasn't she? Not even on hotel property. When did an employee become a private citizen? Grainger hadn't bothered to clarify that. "I don't want you to get into no trouble," the guy said, "but a simple verbal apology don't seem no where near enough."

Gwendolyn looked him in the eye. "You always in the habit of carrying around absurdly breathtaking jewelry everywhere you go?"

"This," his eyes had settled on the brooch still in her hands, "was part of the bad news I got this afternoon. I don't want it no more. It would give me great joy if you would accept it."

CHAPTER 21

Marcus could have been anywhere when the job came in. The sender could have paid for general delivery. His boss could have given it to anyone.

It was fate.

Marcus pedaled up to the grand front gates of MGM and got off his bicycle. He approached the graying guard at the pedestrian entrance and held up the sealed envelope. "I'm from Western Union," he said. "I have a hand delivery for Mr. Ramon Novarro."

The guard held his hand out. "You can give that to me, son. I'll see to it that Mr. Novarro gets it."

Marcus pulled the envelope to his chest and pointed to the "Hand Delivery Only" stamp on the front. "The senders of this telegram paid extra to have it delivered into Mr. Novarro's hands and nobody else's."

The guard eyeballed him. "Wait right there." He retreated into his booth and picked up the telephone. Hand deliveries to movie stars were El Dorado for Western Union boys. You got to meet a movie star, and movie stars tipped big–Wallace Beery had once tipped twenty bucks. But Marcus didn't care about that. The thought of being close enough to touch his favorite movie idol was enough to suck the air clean out of his lungs.

Ben-Hur only had a four-week run at the Bijou in McKeesport, but Marcus saw it twelve times. His family kidded that he wasn't going to be happy until he *was* Ben-Hur. Novarro's scowling courage, the way he'd toss his black hair, and the chariot race had hypnotized Marcus. Oh! That chariot race! Every time Francis X. Bushman pounded his razor-edged wheels against Novarro's chariot, Marcus held his breath.

The guard approached him again and handed Marcus a card. "See this pass? That's the time you gotta be off the lot, or I will come find you. Trust me, son, you don't want that. Mr. Novarro is shooting on stage fourteen." He jabbed a finger into Marcus' face. "If you go in while the red light above the door is flashing, you'll spoil the take so they will shoot you on sight. And if they don't, I will."

* * *

Marcus walked out onto a road flanked with warehouse-sized sound stages. A guy in fatigues led a half-dozen camels past a mob of Canadian Mounties buttoned tightly into red jackets with gold buttons. They fanned themselves with their hats while a stagehand hauled a rack of raccoon coats down the street.

The number 14 was emblazoned in thick brown paint on the soundstage's cream walls; the red light above its door wasn't flashing. Marcus slipped inside and headed toward the set, a stark, stylized bar with a shiny floor and cocktail tables with white tablecloths and small black lamps. The black chairs and glasses stood out against the white wall in the background. Marcus was stunned.

A pair of workers adjusted the furniture and glassware, moving things a fraction of an inch to the left and right. Someone on a very tall ladder was fiddling with a microphone attached to a long pole.

When Ramon Novarro walked onto stage left pulling at his cuffs, Marcus could barely breathe. A woman with a tape measure slung around her neck followed closely behind him. "I think we've fixed it now," she called out, nodding. They laughed over something about a falcon. Marcus pulled the telegram from his jacket pocket and took a couple of steps closer.

"Where the hell have you been?"

Marcus turned around to find a guy in a homemade sleeveless sweater glowering at him. "How hard can it be to find — never mind. We've lost enough time already this morning. Follow me."

Marcus followed the guy toward the set when Novarro looked up and saw Marcus for the first time. Marcus was struck by his strong jaw, his lustrous hair, his expressive eyes. A blaze of lights exploded over his head, and Marcus slammed into a cocktail table.

"Watch it," the guy in the sweater told him, then lifted his hand to his eyes and yelled, "The kid is good to go!"

"Let's do a take, then."

The workers scurried off the set, leaving Marcus to refocus on Ramon Novarro's deep brown unblinking eyes. *Nice to meet you* they seemed to say. Or was that just wishful thinking? Marcus tried to speak but the words evaporated in the heat of the spotlights.

Someone behind Marcus said, "Mr. Novarro, we are rolling so commence when you're ready."

"Who the hell is THAT?"

Marcus looked around to find another guy in a sleeveless sweater standing next to a kid about half Marcus' age, dressed in a uniform almost exactly the same as his own. Everyone around the periphery of the set turned to look at them.

Novarro's smile widened and a HA! of a laugh flew out of his mouth. "Don't tell me you are a real Western Union messenger?" His voice filled Marcus' ears with honey.

Marcus nodded and held out the telegram.

The first sleeveless sweater strode onto the set, his face redder than lava. "You idiot!" he screamed. "Why didn't you tell me you were here to deliver a goddamned telegram?"

"Calm down," Ramon said. "No harm is done. It is not his fault you assumed he was an actor."

The guy turned on Ramon. "We only had enough film left in the can for one more take. Now we have to change the can, which means exceeding our daily budget by a percentage—"

Ramon waved away the man's anger. "It was a simple mistake. And a funny one, you must admit." He turned his attention to Marcus. Marcus had never seen a person with such liquid eyes. "This is for me?"

* * *

When Marcus stepped outside again, the sunlight blinded him. He squeezed his eyes closed to let them adjust, and Ramon Novarro's smiling face quivered into view. His eyes flew open when he felt a hand grip his upper arm.

"What the hell did you do?" It was the guard.

"What do you mean?" Marcus tried to pull away, but the old coot held firm.

"You caused a ruckus. You ruined a take. What did I tell you?"

"That wasn't my fault!" Marcus protested.

The guard marched Marcus toward the gate. "I don't need no pansy assistant directors screaming at me for letting in a telegram boy who runs around impersonating bit-part actors just so he can meet pretty-boy movie stars."

"That's not the way—"

But the guard had just been bawled out by a snarky assistant director and wasn't interested in explanations. At the gate, he grabbed Marcus by the shoulders and made a big show of jabbing at Marcus' name plate. "Marcus Adler, huh? You are hereby banned from the MGM lot. I'm an elephant, son. Don't even bother trying to get past me in the future. You got that, Marcus Adler from Western Union?"

Marcus nodded and headed for the sidewalk. He didn't care he'd been stiffed for a tip or that he'd been banned from the biggest studio in Hollywood because when Ramon Novarro signed for his telegram, their hands had touched.

The man had the smoothest hands Marcus Adler had ever felt.

CHAPTER 22

Marcus leaned over and whispered into Kathryn's ear. "Is this even legal?"

Kathryn glanced at Hugo and his little tart of a date, then back at Marcus. "Bob Benchley tells me it's perfectly legal," she said, "in a loophole sort of way."

For a while now, Marcus and Hugo had been meeting up for weekly booster sessions at the Top Hat Café, where they spitballed story ideas over coffee and a shared slice of pineapple upside-down cake. It was Hugo who told Marcus that the fastest way to a screenwriter contract was to get a few short stories printed in magazines, preferably the classier ones like *Vanity Fair, Saturday Evening Post*, or *The New Yorker*, but anything was better than nothing. It was all too clear to everyone in Hollywood that these new-fangled talkies weren't just the gimmicky fad that the moguls and theater owners hoped they would be. The public was clamoring for more, and all the studios were now converting to sound and, Hugo pointed out, the pair of them were in the right place in the right time to get in on the action from the start.

Much to his own surprise, Marcus found he had a knack for coming up with story ideas. They seemed to bubble up out of him like a water fountain.

However, it didn't take him long to realize that while getting a great story idea was one thing, turning it into a great story was something else again. It was hard for him not to be envious of Hugo: he'd had two stories placed already but he encouraged Marcus to stick at it, and reminded him that the main difference between being unpublished and published was 'not quitting.'

Last week, when Hugo started talking about a story set on the *Montfalcone*, Marcus sat up straight. He'd heard Ramon Novarro mention that boat to his seamstress. Hugo's father was chummy with the casino boss, who could get them aboard to research the story, so Hugo suggested they both bring dates and make a night of it. When Marcus asked Kathryn; her eyes lit up like jack-o-lanterns.

* * *

As the motorboat pulled up to the Santa Monica pier to shuttle the foursome to the *Montfalcone*, Kathryn fingered the diamond brooch pinned to her lapel. She had protested when Gwendolyn tried to loan it to her, but Gwendolyn was firm. "Nobody will question your right to be there if you wear this."

Hugo's date nearly toppled into the Pacific when her heel caught on a slice of rotten wood halfway down the gangplank. They made it the rest of the way without falling into the drink and were ushered onboard by an old sailor in a uniform that couldn't have seen action since the Great War. The casino ran nearly the length of the ship. It was jammed with a motley collection of second hand roulette, blackjack, and poker tables crowded with people determined to lose as much money as possible in as short a time as possible.

The guys went to rustle up some drinks, leaving Kathryn to watch Kitty chew her gum. "So Hugo tells me you work for Tallulah Bankhead."

"Yes, that's right." Kathryn surveyed the room for Billy Wilkerson.

"Is it true that she's a lesbian?"

Tallulah Bankhead probably slept with anyone who'd ever raised an eyebrow in her direction, but Kathryn answered, "She's never made a pass at me."

"Are you a lesbian?"

Kathryn turned to look at Kitty's cud-chomping mouth. "No, I'm not."

"So, you and Marcus . . . ?"

"We're just real good friends."

Kitty winked and chomped. "Gotcha. So's Hugo. He's a swell writer, didya know that? He lets me read his stories before he sends 'em out to magazines and stuff. Does Marcus do that with you?"

"Oh sure," she said, scanning the poker tables over Kitty's shoulder. Marcus had only recently started showing her his stories. She wasn't terribly impressed at first but his output had been remarkable. Lately they'd shown noticeable improvement so she was glad for him that he was persisting.

"It's amazing where these guys get their ideas, ain't it? Hugo's working on a ripper right now. It's about this guy and this girl, see, and they wake up in bed, right? Only they don't know who the other one is, and they don't know how they got there. But there's a piece of string tying their wrists together. What a setup, huh?"

"It's only a good setup if he can match it with a good resolution."

Kathryn spotted Wilkerson's Brylcreemed profile at a table in the far corner.

"Reso-what? Oh, you mean a boffo ending? I think it's a knockout of an idea. Don't you?"

Reluctantly Kathryn pulled her eyes away from Wilkerson's poker table. "I'm sorry. What?"

"I said, don't you think that's a terrific idea for a story?"

"Oh, look," Kathryn muttered, "the boys found us some drinks after all."

* * *

"How much money you got on you?" Marcus asked Kathryn.

She gave him a look. As they left the Garden of Allah, Kathryn insisted they make a pact: Under no circumstances were they to allow each other to gamble. Both of them were barely getting by as it was.

"I doubt I've got five dollars in my purse," Kathryn replied.

Marcus' stomach churned. Ramon Novarro was playing blackjack at a ten dollar table, and he only had nine dollars. The look in Kathryn's eyes said, Don't ask, but the pythons squeezing his heart screamed louder.

"Will you let me have it?"

Kathryn's eyes widened.

"Ten bucks ain't going to get you anywhere," Hugo announced from behind them. He reached into his tuxedo jacket and pulled out his wallet. "Will a hundred get things rolling for you?"

* * *

A roar surged like a geyser around Wilkerson. Kathryn arrived at his roulette table in time to see the croupier push towers of black and red chips in his direction. She leaned on the high edge around the wheel and stroked Gwendolyn's diamond brooch. She had noticed women eyeing it. "So," she whispered to herself, "this is how it feels to be the envy of people like you."

Wilkerson studied the roulette table and placed several large bets, then the croupier shot the ball into the wheel's groove. Kathryn thought she'd approach him at the first opportunity, but when the ball landed on red five and another whoop flew out of Wilkerson's mouth, she changed her mind. The crowd applauded as he boxed the air. She wouldn't be the one to break his winning streak.

* * *

When a barrel-shaped man vacated his seat at Novarro's blackjack table, Marcus sat down. By the time he heard the second whoop from one of the roulette tables, Marcus was ahead sixty dollars. In half an hour, he was up three hundred. A little voice that sounded suspiciously like Kathryn's nagged at him to pick up one of those hundreds and shove it into the tux he'd borrowed from Ronald Colman, his newest neighbor at the Garden of Allah. But his lucky streak had attracted Ramon's attention. They had exchanged a number of *'Well played!'* looks.

When the man between them slapped his cards down, Ramon moved into his seat. Marcus' arm now lay parallel to Ramon's; it tingled from his shoulder to his wrist.

"You are an excellent player of blackjack," Ramon said. "Perhaps some of your skill will rub off onto me."

All Marcus could manage was a smile and a tiny nod. Fuzzy clouds drifted through his mind.

The dealer called for bets and Marcus flung out a hundred and seventy-five dollars. It was more money than he made in six months and if he lost it, he couldn't pay Hugo back. Marcus was horrified at himself, but was helpless to stop.

"You have stronger nerves than I," Ramon said. He raised his right hand and extended it toward Marcus. "Allow me to congratulate you on your courage."

Marcus took Ramon's hand and forgot how to breathe.

* * *

Kathryn had never seen anyone gamble the way Billy Wilkerson did. Stacks of cash flowed in and out of his hands like tissue paper. His winning streak was long, but when he lost a thousand dollars in one hand, he pushed away from the table.

Kathryn followed him through a morass of fur coats and opera capes, and saw him escape through an exit at the end of the hall. She yanked the heavy wooden door open and peered into the cool night. Wilkerson was standing under a string of orange Japanese lanterns that went a long way to pretty up the old tub. He gazed across the sea at the lights dotting the Santa Monica shore and breathed out a plume of cigarette smoke. He was pensive and–more importantly–alone.

Kathryn stepped onto the deck and the door slammed closed behind her. Wilkerson looked in her direction, but couldn't see her smile in the dim light. She waved hesitantly and tried to compose a pithy line about roulette being a fickle mistress. All of a sudden, they were plunged into darkness and a woman screamed, "FIRE! FIRE!" A siren blared and everyone ran for the decks.

* * *

Marcus wondered if he was nuts. He couldn't afford to gamble like this. He looked down at the last hundred dollars on the table, thinking that if he had any sense, he'd scoop it up and walk away. He'd made his impression.

"All or nothing!" he said, and pushed his chips next to Novarro's last fifty.

The dealer revealed a pair of queens, beating Novarro's ten and nine of clubs and Marcus' Jack and eight of hearts.

"Oh well," Novarro shrugged. "This is why they call it gambling." He looked down at the five-dollar chip in front of him. "It is nights like this that remind me I ought to save my money for my Valentino collection."

"Your what?"

"I collect Rudolph Valentino's belongings," Ramon confided. "His autographs, letters, costumes. I have his headdress from *The Sheik*, the one he wears in the poster." He winked. "I stole it from the costume department at MGM. Tell no one!"

"My lips are sealed. Did you know him?"

Novarro nodded. "Slightly. I was an extra in *The Four Horsemen of the Apocalypse* and we met one day when there was a problem with the camera. He was a good man, a gentleman. I was heartbroken when he died. I started to collect his things soon afterwards."

Novarro stood and swiped the chip off the table. Say something, you dolt! Marcus told himself. Something! Anything! "Do you have very many of his things?"

Novarro smiled. "It's okay but nothing like the collector I know in New York. She's a wealthy widow, Fifth Avenue society, his number one fan. Her collection takes up most of her apartment. Someone told her about my *Sheik* headdress, and she's been after me to sell it to her. I am not that desperate, but a few more nights here, and maybe I will be forced to reconsider." He extended his hand toward Marcus. "Friend," he said, "it has been a pleasure playing with you."

Marcus went to take Novarro's smooth, gentle hand again, but suddenly the room was plunged into darkness. A woman screamed, "FIRE! FIRE!" and a glare of orange light flared at the far end of the boat. Fire tore up the wall and everyone started shoving toward the exits. A woman with an enormous bosom knocked him out of her way and he fell to his knees. By the time he was back on his feet, Ramon was nowhere in sight. Nor was Kathryn.

Panicked gamblers surged toward the closest door, but nobody was going to get out any time soon. He made for the far door and broke into the frosty night air.

"The fore lifeboats are full," he heard someone say. "Let's head aft."

He followed them down the side of the boat, looking for Kathryn. She was a sensible girl, he told himself. Surely she'd already headed for the lifeboats.

An explosion under the water rocked the *Montfalcone* from side to side. He spotted a lifeboat already off its hinges and filling up with tuxedos and furs. He ran over and was reaching out for it when he felt a light touch on his wrist. He spun around. "Ramon?" It was a woman with an enormous fur collar.

"Oh!" she exclaimed, "did you get here first? I didn't mean to push in."

As she gestured for him to get in, a sailor lit a hurricane lantern and Marcus met Greta Garbo's eyes. She smiled at him. "Your friend with the dark hair. I saw her on a lifeboat on the other side. Alas, it was full, and so I came here."

Marcus was at home the day Kathryn came back from stalking Billy Wilkerson at Bullock's Wilshire. Kathryn wasn't kidding, he thought. Your face is hypnotic.

"We only have one seat left," the sailor said. "Lady? Are you coming?"

Garbo shook her head. "You got here first," she told Marcus.

"But I am a Pennsylvania state long distance champion," Marcus said. It was a half-truth. He'd been a state champion in high school, in the four and eight hundred yard races. He could already see the headlines: "*ASPIRING SCREENWRITER SAVES GARBO AS FLOATING CASINO BURNS.*"

* * *

Kathryn lost Wilkerson when the underwater explosion knocked her off her feet. She saw a lifeboat filling up at the far end of the ship and dashed toward it, looking for Marcus. Last time she'd seen him, he was playing blackjack next to a Latino guy in an expensive tux. So much for their pact.

A weather-beaten sailor helped her into the lifeboat and pushed off from the ship as bright flames engulfed the *Montfalcone*. There was another explosion and the barkentine started to slip beneath the horizon. Kathryn scanned the other lifeboats hoping to see Marcus' face but the gloom of the night had all but swallowed them whole. A wind blew up, damp and chilly. She pulled her jacket tighter and realized for the first time that Gwendolyn's diamond brooch was missing.

CHAPTER 23

Gwendolyn stared at the bartender. "A birthday party? For a mouse?"

"You'd better not have that look on your face when you go out there," Chuck said, smoothing the sash on her cigarette tray. "This mouse has fan clubs."

Gwendolyn shook her head. "We are talking about grown men, aren't we?"

Chuck nodded. "Tonight's party is a very big deal. All the biggies will be here, so unless you want to sling tobacco for the rest of your life, you need to charm like you've never charmed before."

Hauling around the Cocoanut Grove's cigarette tray was easy work. The surroundings were plush — at least in the dark — and the clientele was good-looking, glamorous, and rich. Every now and then there a guy who felt entitled to a handful, or who suffered from matrimonial amnesia, but her reputation took care of things: Don't mess with the cigarette girl. One funny move and she'll deck you right in the rubber parts. Thank God she'd never seen that schmuck again; she could lose her job for accepting that brooch. The only people she'd told were Marcus and Kathryn.

Poor Kathryn. So pale, so stricken with guilt as she burst through their door the night the *Montfalcone* sank. And how shocked she'd looked when Gwendolyn's only reaction was to laugh.

Gwendolyn had never told her roommate she'd had the piece valued at three thousand dollars by a jeweler who made her an excellent copy for twenty bucks. It was the copy that she lent Kathryn and it was the real version that she later pulled out of the secret hidey-hole in their bedroom ceiling.

Gwendolyn hefted her cigarette tray and set out for the big kahunas gathering under a billboard-sized Happy Birthday banner emblazoned with Mickey Mouse's beaming face. She thought about the soup kitchen lines she passed on the way to work. It seemed like every day they grew a little bit longer and the people standing in them a little bit more disheveled. She was lucky she'd been able to hold onto her job, but surely the pile of dough they had splurged on this party could be better spent helping out the homeless and unemployed? Maybe these big kahunas know something I don't, she decided. Perhaps all this was going to turn around real soon.

She hit the MGM table first, headed up by Louis B. Mayer and his right-hand man, Irving Thalberg. Memorizing faces was the most important job of an aspiring actress, and Gwendolyn had done her homework. David O. Selznick, head of RKO, towered over a tableful of yes men. Mack Sennett arrived with Charlie Chaplin and a flock of feathered beauties. Jack Warner was flanked by assistants, each with a starlet on his arm. And every one of them smoked.

Someone lifted his hand to beckon her over but Gwendolyn didn't recognize him. He was handsome; not silver-screen handsome — his chin was too weak and ears stuck out, and he was prematurely gray — but he was striking enough.

As soon as he caught her attention, Gwendolyn knew he was going to pop The Question: *Are you, by any chance, an actress?* Gwendolyn wasn't as impressed with high-paid studio brass as she'd been a year before. She was still flattered, even hopeful, but they always acted like they were the first studio executive in the world to play the game.

Gwendolyn nodded and smiled her way to his tiny cocktail table. She pulled out pouches of tobacco when she spotted the pipe in his glass ashtray, but he waved them away. I see, Gwendolyn thought, you're just going to cut straight to The Question.

He pointed to the Cocoanut Grove's newest crooner who was singing a lovely new tune called "You Came to Me out of Nowhere" that Gwendolyn was growing to love. "I've been enjoying this singer immensely," the customer said, "but I didn't catch his name. I was hoping you could tell me what it is."

What? Gwendolyn thought. No popping of The Question? A miracle just happened at the Cocoanut Grove. Get Louella Parsons on the line. "His name is Bing Crosby," she replied.

She took a step backwards and hesitated before turning to go. That's when they usually popped The Question. *Oh, and, um, by the way* . . . But the man in the striped cravat and the nautical jacket was engrossed in the music, so she withdrew.

At exactly eight o'clock, Walt Disney made his entrance. Everyone rose and applauded. He waved happily and led his party to the table of honor on the far side of the dance floor. That meant the speeches would come later, when they were all a bit drunk. If Gwendolyn was going to make any sort of impression, she had to do it now.

David Selznick and Mack Sennett both took a second look when she thanked them for their tips, and Charlie Chaplin practically devoured her with his eyes, but he seemed incapable of resisting a skirt with a pulse so that didn't strike Gwendolyn as being much of an accomplishment. The MGM table must have come fully stocked with smokes; not one of them beckoned her over, no matter how she strolled and superdazzled past them. But she didn't worry — they were smoking like the Great Chicago Fire and were bound to run out sooner or later.

However, when she heard a familiar growl, her heart sank. She ducked behind a palm tree but knew the dodge wouldn't work. Everyone knew that cigarette girls had the keenest ears in the city.

"Hey! Cigettes!" he slurred. When Gwendolyn didn't respond, he yelled it. "Cigettes! You. Girl. I need cigettes."

Gwendolyn scanned a table of four for sympathy and found it in Marlene Dietrich, a German actress everyone had been talking about lately. Gwendolyn could see why; bathed in the glow of the table lamp, the woman's face was positively luminescent. The actress looked from Gwendolyn to the gorilla then back at Gwendolyn. Her eyes widened as Gwendolyn smelled whiskey.

"I give you a brooch worth a coupla G's, and now you're too good to talk to me?"

Gwendolyn steadied herself and turned around. "Oh, come now, don't be silly! It's a busy night. You can see for yourself that you're not the only smoker in the room."

He sneered and vacillated under the fake trees. He put up a hand against one of them for support, and it started to topple towards Marlene Dietrich's table. A guy who could very well have been William Haines stood up and raised his arms, but Broochie—that's what Kathryn and Gwendolyn had taken to calling him—caught it in time and righted the tree again.

Gwendolyn ventured a step closer and whispered, "Hey, you want to get me fired? Taking that brooch from you was a big no-no. If anyone hears you and reports it to the boss, I'll be out on my ever-lovin' hiney." She looked away and caught the eye of the question popper in the striped cravat, but he didn't look like he was about to rush gallantly to her rescue.

"I've thought about you every day since that night." The words dribbled out of Broochie's mouth and he reached for her hair, but she pulled away. He made another grab, but her tray was in the way. He almost fell sideways but somehow managed to right himself. The stink of liquor clung to him in a sour fog.

126

"I never got a chance to tell you. My brother-in-law. Do you know who he is?" Gwendolyn cast a quick glance around her; their little scene was attracting attention. Were they waiting to witness another one of her famous kicks to the groin? "He's the head of P.R. over at Paramount. One word from me and — " he botched an attempt to click his fingers, "you'll be in. Christ, you're gorgeous."

Gwendolyn tried to sidestep the drunken oaf but he caught her by the wrist. He towered over her and bent her arm behind her until it hurt. Any further and he might break it.

"I thought after I gave you that diamond brooch you'd be open to . . . you know."

"You haven't even been around here," Gwendolyn countered.

"Well, I'm here now." His breath sat hot in her ear. "And if you don't say yes, I'm going straight to your — "

Like a paper bag in a rain storm, Broochie crumpled to the floor. Gwendolyn looked up to see the question popper. "Did you do that?" she asked, pointing to the scruffy pile of expensive suit on the floor.

He smiled. "I hope you don't mind."

"Are you kidding?" Gwendolyn replied. "Thank you. I fear he was about to get — "

"Awkward . . . ?"

She nodded, embarrassed but relieved. He stepped over Broochie, took her gently by the arm and led her toward the safety of the bar, where he began to study the contents of her tray.

"Pipe tobacco, wasn't it?" she said, picking out pouches. "I have Prince Albert, Raleigh, and St. Bruno."

He smiled the serious smile of a man with something on his mind. He plucked a business card from his breast pocket and dropped it into her tray. "I'd like you to call me. Whenever it's convenient for you. Give your name as Corinne Grimes."

Gwendolyn looked at his card, then back at Anderson McRae, Head of Casting, RKO, as he headed for the door. Her head felt like the radio transmitter shooting lightning bolts on his card. She tucked it into her cleavage. I knew you were a question popper, she thought.

"Are you sleeping with him?" Chuck was suddenly behind her.

"Anderson McRae?" Gwendolyn asked. "I only just met him."

"I'm talking about that big oaf who just bit the deck."

"That guy? Please, Chuck, give me some credit."

"I'm glad to hear it. What did he offer you? Was it jewelry?" Hell's bells, he's onto me! Gwendolyn pleaded silently with Chuck to leave it alone. "That chump has some relative at Paramount. His M.O. is to use jewelry as a lure and the promise of a screen test to reel 'em in. Don't lie to me, Gwen. I saw the look on your face. I've seen it before on one or two of your predecessors."

Gwendolyn looked around; nobody appeared to be listening. "It was a diamond brooch. Oh my lord in heaven, Chuck, it was only *the* most gorgeous thing I've ever seen in my life!"

"Thank you for telling me the truth."

"You won't tell Grainger?"

Chuck took a drag on his cigarette and shook his head. "Of course not. We're pals, aren't we? But no more jewelry." A lady in green satin waved for cigarettes and Gwendolyn started off, but Chuck stopped her. "The guy next to Mayer and Thalberg is Eddie Mannix, the general manager. Third in line for the throne." He gave her a discreet swat. "Go get 'em."

* * *

As Gwendolyn made change for the lady in satin, Walt Disney took the stage. He delivered a humble and articulate speech about animation's important role in cinema, during which she rested her feet and waited for the MGM table to smoke its way through every cigarette and cigar they came in with.

It took several more swoops, but eventually Irving Thalberg waved her over. For someone with a reputation for being one of the industry's heavyweights, Gwendolyn found MGM's production chief surprisingly slight and pale, and extremely soft-spoken. She didn't mind leaning in to hear his request; it gave the other flunkies a chance to look her over.

Thalberg wanted a brand of French cigarette that Gwendolyn didn't have, but she assured him the Ambassador's tobacconist would. As she hurried off to see Bobo, she suddenly thought of her mother. Mama didn't come into her thoughts much these days but when she did, she left a tender spot of regret. *Can you believe it, Mama? I'm fetching cigarettes for Mr. Irving Thalberg of MGM.* She could hear Mama's voice now. *Be sure to smile for the man. Nobody enjoys the company of a sourpuss.*

When she returned with six packets of Gauloises, Louis B. Mayer called over to her. "Tell me, are you a professional cigarette girl, or do you do something else? Sing, or dance, or act, perhaps?"

Gwendolyn's heart heaved into her throat. Mayer wasn't just any old question popper; he was *the* question popper. She swallowed hard. *As a matter of fact, I do* was about to gush from her lips, when she saw Thalberg's neighbor roll his eyes. He had the hardened face of a day laborer. "Oh, sweet Jesus, it's that big lug," he muttered. "Whats-his-name, Paramount's brother-in-law."

Gwendolyn heard a rasping groan behind her, and held her breath.

"Hey, toots! You! Cigarette girlie. Gimme my brand. You know what I want." Broochie sounded like he was talking through a pillow.

She ignored him and counted out Thalberg's change. Thalberg tipped her ten dollars as Broochie called out again.

"CIGARETTE GIRL! Who you trying to impress?"

Gwendolyn had no choice but to straighten up and turn to face the hoary-eyed gorilla. His jacket was open and hanging off his shoulder. His mouth was curled up in a deep scowl. He held his freshened drink like it was a turkey leg.

"Why don't you follow me, sir?" Gwendolyn suggested and turned to lead Broochie away from the MGM table.

"Why don't you give me my jewelry back?" He spat out the words loud enough that most of the nearby tables heard him over Bing Crosby's "I've Got Rhythm." Gwendolyn scanned the room for help.

Broochie lunged at her. He stumbled but kept his whiskey level. His fingers brushed her sleeve and caught the loop of gold braid on her shoulder pad, spinning her around backwards. She reached out for Mr. Mayer's table, but grabbed at air.

The momentum spun her around full circle and she faced Broochie just in time to see the upward swoop of his cocktail hand. It hit the underside of her tray with a loud thwack and shot dozens of cigars and packets of cigarettes into the air. The tray slammed into her forehead. As it fell back down, the sash yanked at her neck and she tumbled forward under a hailstorm of tobacco. She toppled into Mr. Mayer's lap. Half of Broochie's whiskey smacked her in the face. She didn't want to know what the other half did to the most powerful man in movies.

CHAPTER 24

Kathryn rapped on her mother's front door as loudly as she could. "Mother! This silent treatment has gone on long enough." No answer. "Mother!" she called out again. "I still have my key."

Kathryn hadn't seen her mother in so many months she'd lost count. She regretted throwing Francine out of her villa that day, but, she had to remind herself, the melodrama was too much to take. Lost her fortune in the stock market crash, indeed.

After a couple of months without a word, though, Kathryn started to worry that she'd been too harsh. She dropped by from time to time when she was nearby on Gower, but her mother was never at home. Gwendolyn assured her that she must have found a job, and Kathryn started to leave lighthearted, sincere notes. When none drew a response, they became apologetic, then contrite, then exasperated and angry. In the end, Kathryn decided that she'd done all she could to mend the fences, and if Francine wanted to resume their relationship, the white flag had been raised. But when 1930 became 1931, Kathryn's patience ran out.

She pulled on the brown checked woolen overcoat Tallulah had given her for Christmas and marched to her mother's home. She stuck the key into the lock. "You give me no choice!" she called out. "I'm coming in now." But it refused to turn. It took Kathryn a couple of attempts to realize that her mother had changed the lock. She rounded the corner, took off her coat and jimmied the bathroom window in two minutes flat.

"Hello!" she called. No reply. She wandered up the hallway to her mother's room and pushed open the door. The room was neater than Kathryn had ever seen it, and the bed was covered with a new red, white, and blue paisley quilt. It was a huge improvement over the tatty swamp-green chenille bedspread it replaced. A delicate pink porcelain vase sat atop the bureau; that was new, too. It looked like Gwendolyn was right. Francine had found herself a good paying job — not easily done, now that they were calling the recession a "depression."

But when she studied the smiling couple in an antique silver frame, Kathryn's heart quickened. Who were these people? Francine Massey had no friends. She'd been so devoted to her daughter's career that she had never taken the time to cultivate her own friendships, and that had been part of the problem: neither could her daughter.

Kathryn put the picture down and picked up a small portrait of a woman in sparkling tulle just as the sun outside the window slipped behind a cloud. She opened the wardrobe and found lots of suits and trousers and neckties. She raced into the livingroom. It was freshly painted in very pale blue and over the fireplace hung a painting of Paris in the rain instead of the mirror with the crack, and brown spots staining the bottom corner.

"Good God. I'm in someone else's home."

She leaned against the doorway and gaped at Place de la Concorde, unable to move. Then she heard a man's laugh on the front step. "Sounds like the worst Christmas ever! I sure hope 1931 is better than that!"

Kathryn ran up the hallway to the bathroom as the front door opened. She was still only halfway through the window when she heard the man exclaim, "What the heck?!" Kathryn froze. "Get back in here!" he demanded. She eased herself backwards until she was standing on the john.

"Get down offa there, for crying out loud!" he ordered, and she turned around to face the man from the photos. He was older now, his eyes more crinkly and his hair largely a thing of the past. He frowned, puzzled at first, then it dawned on him. "Say, I know you!"

As gracefully as she could manage, Kathryn stepped down from the rim of the john. "No, I don't think so."

"You're the girl in the photographs, aren't you?"

"Are you in casting?"

He winced as though she had slugged him. "God, no. What are you doing crawling in my bathroom window?"

"Technically, I was climbing out–"

"Oh, wait, I get it now. You used to live here, didn't you?"

"Yes. But I didn't realize . . . I didn't know . . ."

His anger evaporated and he smiled at her. "Follow me."

He led her into her old bedroom. It was an office now with a desk and a row of metal filing cabinets. He crossed to a wardrobe in the corner, yanked open the door and grabbed an old May Company shirt box that Kathryn recognized immediately. "I don't know why I've kept this," he said, sliding off the top. He pulled out a photograph and handed it to Kathryn.

She nodded. "Yes, that's me. A million years ago." She was twelve in the photo, her hair set in long sausage curls. It had taken three laborious hours in the beauty parlor, and Kathryn couldn't believe that anyone, even Mary Pickford herself, would sit through that every day, even if she was earning five thousand a week.

"You're the one who wrote all those notes," he said, his face full of sympathy. Kathryn nodded up at him. "I'm sorry, young lady, but I don't know where your mother is."

"That's the problem. Neither do I."

CHAPTER 25

Marcus didn't just like his new necktie. He *loved* it.

It was Kathryn's Christmas present to him, and it was too beautiful to take it out of its Bullock's box and white tissue paper. He'd never seen this shade of purple before, deep and rich as a ripe plum, with a hint of lavender but vibrant as crimson. Pressed into the material was a light pattern of waves, hardly visible except close up, and even then you almost had to be touching it.

She shouldn't have gone and bought him anything for Christmas. God knows he hadn't gotten her anything. Western Union had cut his messenger pool from twelve to eight, and rumor was rife that it might soon go down to six. He was living on beans and rice, bread and Sanka until he knew whether he'd make the cut. His hopes of being hailed as Garbo's savior hadn't amounted to anything, either. Sure, the sinking of the *Montfalcone* had made all the papers and even sparked off a public furor over all the floating casinos lined up along the coastline, but there'd been no mention of Garbo in any of them. All he got for his trouble was a persistent ache deep in his bones from that grueling three-mile swim to shore. He was lucky the tide had been with him otherwise he might not have made it at all.

Tallulah hadn't cut Kathryn's wages yet, but it seemed like a matter of time before the Depression hit the movie stars, too. Kathryn shouldn't have bought him anything, and he told her so, but boy, oh boy, he loved that tie!

By the second Sunday in January, he couldn't wait any longer to wear it. He didn't have anything that matched it and a new suit wasn't on his sartorial horizon, but he dressed himself as smartly as he could in his best black flannel trousers and his tweed jacket from Kress. He took the Hollywood Boulevard Red Car downtown and got off a few blocks from the Biltmore Hotel. By the time he was within a block of Pershing Square, he'd given up trying to convince himself that a jolly Sunday promenade was all he was doing that day.

Marcus knew there had to be other men like him out there. So there had to be places he could meet them. He knew that his chances of meeting Ramon Novarro again were low-to-nonexistent, so it was time he looked further afield. Sure, he'd seen plenty of residents at the Garden scamper between villas late at night or early in the morning, but none of them had been men like him. Marcus didn't know where to go or who to talk to, but one thing was for damn sure: he wasn't going to meet anyone by sitting in his dark little room. It was time to take a chance.

On Sunday morning, the Pershing Square crowd was different from the workaday week crowd. The offices were all closed, but there were plenty of people around. A tall, thin guy about his own age did a double take when he saw Marcus' purple tie. His eyes flicked up and held Marcus' gaze until they'd passed each other.

Marcus didn't think much about it until the same thing happened half a block closer to Pershing Square. This time it was a much older gentleman with the rounded paunch and healthy gray beard of a doctor. He too spotted Marcus' necktie and lifted his eyes to meet Marcus', but hurried by without looking back. So Marcus headed for the square, a leafy park at the center of Los Angeles.

A pair of college students walked toward him with their shoulders and heads pressed together. They were smiling at him and murmuring out of the sides of their mouths. Their eyes kept flickering down to his tie and back up to his face. Marcus stopped and watched them walk past, wondering if they'd been laughing at him. One of them looked back, but when he saw Marcus staring at him, he swung around again and nudged his friend to walk faster.

On the way down the gravel path to the fountain in the center of the park, the same thing happened twice more. Each time, a single gent, all decked out in his Sunday best, stared at him as he walked by. The second one opened his mouth to speak, but changed his mind at the last moment.

Marcus stopped at the fountain and trailed his hand in the cold water for a moment. He felt someone watching him and glanced up into the eyes of a guy on a bench nearby. He wore a simple pair of dungarees, a white tee-shirt and a dark blue duffel coat. His wide open prairie-state face had nothing to hide. He was staring at Marcus in the same way the other men had, but didn't look away when Marcus looked back. Marcus shook the water off his hand and sat down next to him.

"I like your necktie," the guy said.

"It seems to be attracting more than its fair share of attention."

"I don't doubt that for a minute. That color. It's an interesting choice."

Marcus lifted the end of his necktie and angled it toward the late morning sun. Did it look different outside than in his shadowy room?

"You know," the guy said. "Purple." When Marcus looked at him blankly, the man's warm smile dimmed. "Purple," he repeated. "A purple necktie . . . ?"

Marcus felt suddenly awkward, like he had at a childhood party when he'd realized everyone was playing a game he'd never heard of. He could feel himself blushing.

The man's smile evaporated and in its place was a pair of thin lips pressed into a straight line. "Are you with the vice squad?"

Marcus wanted to laugh, but the man was quite serious. "I'm a telegram messenger with Western Union."

Warmth crept back into the man's smile. "The purple necktie," he said, "is a sort of code. Among a certain sort of people."

"What sort?

"The sort of men who are looking for . . ." He raised his eyebrows.

* * *

The hotel room at the Derbyshire Arms four blocks from Pershing Square was large and airy and smelled of wood polish. Marcus liked it. It had a low wooden bureau, moss green wall-to-wall carpeting, its own bathroom, and a four-poster bed.

"Do you live here?" Marcus asked.

The guy grinned and shook his head.

"It gets a lot of light."

"Not when I pull the blinds."

Marcus ran his hand down the post at the foot of the bed. "This is nice," he said. "You don't see four-poster beds in hotel rooms much anymore."

"Been in lots of hotel rooms, have you?"

A nervous laugh popped out of Marcus. "No, not really."

The guy took a couple of long strides. They were the same height. He was close enough now that Marcus could smell the salty tang of his tee-shirt.

"What's your name?" Marcus asked.

"My name? What the hell does that matter?"

"If we're going to . . . I thought it would be nice if we introduced ourselves."

The way the guy looked at him made Marcus feel like a fifteen-year-old debutante. "You can call me Zachary. Or Zach. Whichever you like." He reached up and pushed Marcus' tweed jacket open. It slipped down his back and landed in a jumble at his feet. When Marcus bent down to pick it up, Zachary told him to leave it there.

He loosened the purple necktie, pulled it over his head and tossed it onto the jacket. The smell of the ocean grew stronger as Zachary drew his hands around Marcus' waist and pulled their hips together. As he watched Zachary's mouth inch closer to his, he thought of Dwight, and his father's jail cell, and what happened last time he felt like this. Dear God, he thought, if there's any justice in the world, don't let the cops bust through that door.

Zachary forced his mouth against Marcus'. He slid his hand up until he palmed the back of Marcus' head and pressed their mouths even more firmly together. Marcus wrapped his arms around the man's body, so different from Dwight's. It was harder, firmer; he could feel each muscle in Zachary's back torque as Zachary crushed himself against Marcus. His tongue pushed into Marcus' mouth until the burn of chewing tobacco was all he could taste. He let his body melt into Zachary's, but suddenly Zachary pulled away.

"What is it?" Marcus gasped. "The cops?"

"You're a regular Mexican jumping bean, ain't you?" Zachary walked to the window and pulled down the blind. The room slid into half-darkness. A shaft of sunlight fought its way in and sliced a path between them. Marcus could only see Zachary in silhouette now.

"If you think the four posts are nice, wait till you try the mattress."

* * *

Marcus rolled over onto his back and stared up at a water stain that had been poorly whitewashed.

"For a while there, I thought this might've been your first time," Zachary said with a yawn. "But you took to that like a heifer at milking time, didn't you?"

Marcus was too embarrassed to admit that it had been his first time, so he kept his trap shut. Any doubts he may have harbored in the deepest, darkest corners of his mind about his feelings toward men had been wiped so clean that he could scarcely recall them. He felt unfettered and light-headed. In this moment, he was free of the shame and guilt that had yoked him for so many years. It was gone—swept away in less than an hour. He felt like an ex-con being let out of jail.

"I didn't hurt you, did I?" Zachary asked.

Hurt me? Marcus thought. On the contrary, you sent me to a corner of heaven I only ever suspected–hoped–might exist. He shook his head.

Zachary followed Marcus' eyes to the stain on the ceiling. "Sometimes I get carried away. The heat of the moment and all that. But for a guy like me, it can be a long time between drinks."

Marcus turned and stared at the mat of blonde hair that covered Zachary's chest. It was softer than he'd expected but the man's pecs were firm and tanned from years of outdoor work. He longed to feel Zachary's hands wander over his skin again and could feel the heat in his groin grow once more. Was it too soon to ask for another round?

Marcus reached up to run his fingers through Zachary's chest hair but the guy headed him off at the pass. In a smooth motion, he sat up and swung his feet around to the floor. "I don't suppose you know where I flung my shorts?"

Marcus looked at Zachary's back. It was wide at the shoulders and narrowed down into a taut waist. It was splattered with dark brown freckles; a patch of fuzz sat at the top of his butt cheeks. "When can I see you again?"

The naked man let out a laugh that seemed unnecessarily harsh. His back rippled; Marcus longed to lick it, press his face against it, feel the muscles twist under his fingers. The guy didn't turn around. "I'm a navy man. Never around. Besides, bucko, we're queers. We don't get to have dates any more than we get to have marriages or relationships or love. This is it, so learn to like it the way I have."

CHAPTER 26

Gwendolyn caught a single poppy seed in her fingernail and scraped it along the starched white tablecloth to the base of her fork. She picked out another and pushed it next to the first. Only forty-three seeds to go. She knew the exact number because she had just scraped each poppy seed, one at a time, to the base of her teaspoon. Ten seeds later, she checked her wristwatch. One-thirty. The waiter appeared with a sympathetic smile. "More bread?"

She smiled sadly. "I don't think he's coming. Do I owe you anything?"

The waiter shook his head. "He should have his head examined for standing up a tomato like you."

She smiled her thanks and shrugged her shoulders. Well, if that don't beat all, she thought. Here I am, a cigarette girl ready to outsmart a studio executive at his own game, and he doesn't even show.

She picked up her handbag and was standing up to leave when a voice behind her said, "Thank goodness you're still here." Anderson McRae appeared in front of her, windswept and out of breath. "My automobile clapped out on me all the way down past Wilcox. I am so sorry to have kept you waiting." He patted down his hair, called the waiter and smiled at Gwendolyn as he ordered two cups of London tea. His eyes began to wander around the room, taking in the details that Gwendolyn had studied for half an hour.

Lunch at the Montmartre Café was McRae's idea, and Gwendolyn was excited to meet him there. The Montmartre had been Hollywood's first nightclub a decade or so ago. Movie magazines eagerly reported whenever Rudolf Valentino won tango competitions or Joan Crawford out-Charlestoned everyone in the room. Such was its fame that Gwendolyn Brick in Hollywood, Florida, had known everything there was to know about the Montmartre Café long before her train pulled into the Southern Pacific station.

But as she waited for Mr. McRae to show, she realized that while McRae was half an hour late, she was five years too late. California's relentless sun had faded the burgundy velvet curtains framing the windows over Hollywood Boulevard. The tired lace sheers were the color of soured milk. Even the burgundy-flocked gold wallpaper was dowdy and old-fashioned now, as fussy and out of date as the chandeliers.

The waiter appeared with a matching pair of cups and saucers and took their orders; lobster salad with Roquefort dressing for him, cream cheese and tomato sandwiches with a side of coleslaw for her. McRae raised his teacup and said, "Here's to faded velvet."

Gwendolyn took a sip and immediately spat it out. "I thought you ordered tea!"

"I did."

"This is no tea! This tastes . . . like . . ."

"Gin. Beefeater, from London."

Gwendolyn pushed the cup and saucer away from her with a disapproving face. "If this is what gin tastes like then they were right to outlaw it."

McRae blushed so deeply that it was almost endearing. "I'm so very sorry," he stammered. "I assumed that a girl like you —"

"Like me?" She shot him a glare designed to hook him hard and make him squirm.

"What I mean is a girl who works where you work —"

"Prohibition is still on, last time I looked."

Gwendolyn had always been in two minds about Prohibition. The temperance movement was largely driven by women ground into perpetual poverty by their lousy husbands drinking away the contents of every pay packet. As the daughter of a hopeless lush, Gwendolyn couldn't help but sympathize. On the other hand she was enough of a realist to know that banning something like booze was a colossal waste of time and effort. But it wasn't in Gwendolyn's immediate interests for McRae to know that.

"Yes, yes, of course. I ought never have presumed." He called the waiter over and ordered Gwendolyn a lemonade.

"May we talk business now?" Gwendolyn said.

McRae broke out into that rarest Hollywood phenomena–a smile which didn't look like it was practiced in front of the mirror. "Not one for small talk, are you?"

"This is a business luncheon, is it not?"

"I guess you could say that."

Gwendolyn looked at Anderson McRae, in his meticulously pressed charcoal gray suit and his cobalt blue tie with matching pocket square. Had he guessed that she'd arrived at this luncheon fully prepared to comply with whatever overtures a man like him was bound to make? The trick was to make him think that *he* had painted *her* into a corner. She swiped away her poppy seeds. "Why did you tell me to give my name as Corinne Grimes? Why couldn't I give my actual name?"

"Sorry for the intrigue," McRae said. "I'm always on the lookout for new faces, and I give my card to a lot of people. I use a code to keep track of where I met them. Corinne Grimes tells me I saw you at the Cocoanut Grove. It's just a memory jogger."

"I see," Gwendolyn said, "I thought perhaps you'd already decided to change my name."

"I'd never do that. Gwendolyn is too lovely a name to lose, and it suits you perfectly. I'd fight tooth and nail any front office bonehead who thought we should change you from a Gwendolyn to a Corinne."

"How very gallant of you, Mr. McRae. I thank you."

Gwendolyn let fly with one of her giggly laughs that always seemed to impress guys, but it flew on right past McRae. He adjusted his perfect Windsor knot. "Let's not waste time playing games," he said, suddenly serious.

The waiter placed McRae's lobster salad in front of Gwendolyn. It reeked like a hamper full of gym socks. McRae swapped their plates and she stared at her sandwich for a moment. She came here to play the game the way the men play it. This is a business, she'd told herself on the Red Car the whole way up Hollywood Boulevard, and in business, people scratch each other's backs all the time. Nothing personal; just business. And besides, this McRae fella wasn't altogether repulsive. Far from it, in fact. He dressed well and had a decent haircut and a professional shave, so he was likely to have clean sheets on his bed. Plenty of girls have done a lot more for a lot less. But now that she was seated opposite him, and the moment had arrived for push to come to shove, she doubted that she had it in her. No! She scolded herself. You're a career girl. She put her sandwich down.

"So, this is the usual Hollywood back-scratching routine, right?" she said.

McRae swallowed a bite of lobster he hadn't finished chewing. "Excuse me?"

"You have what I want: entrée into a Hollywood studio. And I have what you want." She pushed her bosom his way and wondered what color his bed sheets were.

The man's eyes widened and his face blushed deep red. Tiny beads of sweat broke out along his hairline and they each caught the light of the grimy chandelier over Gwendolyn's left shoulder. Gwendolyn thought, Oh my goodness, have I just shoved my bust in the face of the only moral casting director in Hollywood?

McRae dropped his lobster fork into his salad. "You don't know who I am, do you?"

"You're head of casting at RKO."

"Yes, that is true. But my reputation usually precedes me." He pressed his forehead with his napkin; it came away blotted with sweat. "I thought everyone knew I'm the one guy in casting who girls like you are safe from."

Gwendolyn felt the heat from the blush blooming on her cheeks. So this guy was like Marcus. Not that she was sure Marcus was queer but in the four years she'd known him, she'd never seen him pursue a woman. "Oh. I see."

He offered her a relieved smile and dug into his salad again. "Good. I'm glad we got that out of the way. Now that we're on the level, there's something I need you to do for me."

Gwendolyn felt herself land back on square one with a thud. She couldn't imagine what kind of favors she'd have to do for guys who *didn't* want to sleep with her. "And what might that be?"

"I have a friend in need."

Of course you do, she thought ruefully.

"This is going to sound tacky, but I can assure you it's not. Well, perhaps it is. But there is no requirement for you to . . . how shall I put this?"

"Put out?"

"Exactly."

"So this is not a casting couch situation?"

"No, Miss Brick, I give you my word, it is not. My friend has discovered that his wife has been cheating on him since their honeymoon, and he wants to divorce her. His wife's family is old money, though. Blue Book, society. They're not about to admit that their golden daughter is at fault, so they're laying a bunch of cash on him to testify he's the one who strayed. But of course there must be proof that he's stepped outside the bonds of matrimony and—"

Gwendolyn held up her hand to stop him. "I get it. You need me to pose with your pal to make it look like he's being caught in the act."

He grinned sheepishly. "Something like that."

"And in return, you will . . . ?"

"I hold a key that opens all sorts of doors."

Gwendolyn gave McRae a tight smile and wondered if girls who wanted to break into the millinery business had to go through this hooey.

CHAPTER 27

Marcus knew that between the bank closings, job losses, and bread lines stretching from Culver City to Canada, 1932 had been pretty dismal, and he had been pretty lucky. He still had his job, a roof over his head, and enough to eat, which put him ahead of millions of Americans. All the same, he was depressed to end 1932 without publishing a single story. He believed the one about the stagehand would be the one to break him through the brick wall of Nope, but everyone had knocked it back, even the *Detroit Athletic Club News*. How fussy, he mused, could *they* choose to be?

His family had been on his mind lately, too. How were they faring? Five kids were a lot to feed. Did any of them wonder how he was getting on the same way he wondered about them?

Gwendolyn was working and Kathryn was at the new Rodeo Drive Brown Derby–she'd wrangled a one-night job so that she could stalk Billy Wilkerson some more–so Marcus found himself alone on New Year's Eve and decided to end the year with a quart of Portuguese gin and wake up in 1933.

Marcus was plunking ice cubes into a tumbler when Tallulah Bankhead rapped on his door. She swept into his room in a long gown of dark red silk and a double strand of pearls that reached her waist. "This is your lucky night!" she declared, tossing back her teak brown hair before it got caught up in her lipstick. "I need an escort for tonight, and I could think of nobody better than *vous*."

"I've kind of got plans—"

"Whatever they are, they won't be as much fun as the evening I've got in mind." She cast her gaze around his cramped room and landed on the bottle of bootleg. "Is that gin?" She grasped her pearls. "*Real* gin?"

"It had better be, for the price I paid." Marcus considered the full week's worth of tips he'd forked over to Bob Benchley's bootlegger was a sound investment in unconsciousness.

She grabbed the bottle like it was an oxygen tank at the bottom of the Pacific. "Oh, my darling man, this is gold!"

Marcus looked at Tallulah and wondered if Kathryn had sent her over knowing that he'd be spending the evening alone.

Tallulah couldn't pull her eyes from Marcus' bottle. "Whatever you paid for it, I'll repay you, plus five dollars and all your drinks at B.B.B.'s."

"Who is B.B.B.?"

Tallulah stared at Marcus slyly. "Oh, come now, Marcus, my darling, let us not be coy. We both know that I know that you know all about B.B.B.'s Cellar."

Marcus held Tallulah's eyes as long as he could, trying to decipher her meaning. He couldn't. "I really don't."

She tucked the bottle into the crook of one arm and wrapped the other around his neck. "In that case, you gorgeous, darling man, it's high time you did."

* * *

Like most speakeasies, B.B.B.'s Cellar didn't want to be found. There was no sign on the door, no window, no indication that it even existed.

Tallulah led Marcus down the shadowy concrete steps and opened a heavy door onto a packed, smoky room humming with boozed-up chatter. A thunderous WHACK! greeted them. Marcus jumped and Tallulah laughed throatily along with the crowd. "Your intention was to get hammered tonight, wasn't it?" Marcus looked around and saw small wooden hammers on every table.

"Yoohoo!" Tallulah called to a round-faced blond with his back against the wall.

His date was a pretty brunette whose jaw line, Marcus decided, must be the envy of every man in the place. Next to her sat a man with dark, slicked-back hair and an ill-fitting suit. He was handsome in a pale, underfed sort of way and was surveying the room the way a shark surveys a school of tuna. The blond guy beckoned them over.

As Tallulah and Marcus threaded their way to her friends, everyone picked up their hammers again. WHACK! A pair of heavyset women with cropped hair and unplucked eyebrows filled the doorway. This business with the hammers was unnerving.

Tallulah introduced Marcus to William Haines. Marcus raised his eyebrows and shook the man's hand appreciatively. Haines was a hugely popular actor who'd left MGM abruptly the year before and, despite the media uproar, no one was sure why. "You know Joan, don't you?" William said, introducing his date. Joan Crawford extended her hand and Marcus shook it gladly. Tallulah tucked in next to Joan and they put their heads together, chatting and laughing. William introduced the shark as Howard; he perused Marcus and returned to his school of tuna.

A waitress brought two more hammers and took their orders. Marcus turned his hammer over in his hands. This isn't the evening you had planned, he told himself, but it could be a whole lot better if you decide to enjoy yourself.

Haines leaned in so Marcus could hear him. "It's a B.B.B.'s tradition," he said. "Every time someone comes in, you bang it as loud as you can. It's awfully disconcerting when you're the one being hammered, but it's hysterical when you're not. And you're just in time to catch Karyl Norman," Haines added brightly, like he was imparting a delicious secret.

"Who's that?" Marcus asked.

"She's only the greatest entertainer of her generation," Haines said. "In her field. We're here tonight because I have the inside scoop that Karyl is going to do Joan in rain!"

Marcus wasn't sure what that meant, but Joan looked like she was having a good time. She sat back from the table and took long drags from her cigarette. Her hair was a shade Marcus had never seen before, somewhere between brown and black. It was bobbed and softly marcelled at the sides. Her mouth was wide and seemed to be permanently arranged in a furtive smile. Her gorgonzola-blue eyes were huge and unblinking, as though she didn't want to miss a moment.

A round of drinks arrived — something dry that resembled brandy, but not closely enough to make Marcus glad he'd sold Tallulah his gin. The lights dimmed and the crowd cheered as a pink spotlight lit the tiny two-foot-square stage. A tatty olive curtain parted for a creature the likes of which Marcus had never seen. She stepped into the light and the crowd greeted her with a deafening WHACK!

She was tall and commanding, more like a general than a speakeasy entertainer. She wore a knee-length black and white checked dress with large triangular lapels framing an impressive bosom. As the crowd drenched her in whoops and whistles, it occurred to Marcus that this Karyl Norman was dressed as Joan Crawford in her latest picture, *Rain*. Marcus didn't have the heart to look at Joan.

Karyl raised her arms, and the pianist pounded out the opening chords of that new Ethel Waters song Marcus had been hearing around the Garden lately, "Stormy Weather." The performer had a deep voice, quite powerful, and easily managed to fill the room. At the word "rainin'," the hammers walloped anew. The whole thing struck Marcus as a little cruel. The critics had blown *Rain* their collective raspberry and it had notoriously–and very publicly–flopped. He stole a look in Crawford's direction and was surprised that her smile was as broad as the Hollywoodland sign. Karyl followed "Stormy Weather" with "I Found a Million Dollar Baby in a Five and Ten Cent Store" and "I Need a Little Sugar in my Bowl," then left the stage to a raucous tidal wave of hammer blows.

As she was leaving, a group of swells in tuxedos entered the room and Marcus did a double take. One of them was Ramon Novarro.

It had been more than two years since that night on the *Montfalcone*. Marcus had managed to convince himself that he didn't mind that nothing had come of their fleeting encounters. It was enough to have met him, he told himself. But seeing him standing in the doorway, slim and dashing on New Year's Eve, made Marcus reassess all those furtive trysts with men whose names he'd learned not to ask, and whose faces he'd learned not to see. Who was he trying to fool? Admit it, he told himself, you've been dreaming for this moment. Marcus silently blessed Tallulah Bankhead and sat up straight in his seat.

"Look, there's Ben-Hur," Tallulah cried.

"Don't you mean Ben-*Her*?" Billy Haines asked.

Joan Crawford elbowed Haines in the side and he howled. "Must you be like that with everyone?" she asked. "I've met Ramon a whole bunch of times. We did that picture together, *Across to Singapore*, remember? He's very nice. Let's invite him over."

"Where's he going to sit, Joan?" Haines gestured around their packed table. "On your face?"

"I think he'd much prefer Marcus'," Tallulah said. Everyone laughed, including the shark, who hadn't said a word yet. "Oh, come on," Tallulah said, playfully slapping Marcus on the arm, "you wouldn't say no to an invitation like that, would you?"

Marcus felt the color drain from his face. This room was full of queers, he realized. Not all queers meet behind bushes and at the end of damp, dark alleys. They have their own speakeasies where they can be with their own kind. He felt like he was watching the Red Sea part. *How did I not know this?* He wiped the bathtub brandy from his chin and turned to Tallulah, pointing to the tiny stage. "That woman wasn't a woman, was she?"

Haines let out a gleeful yip and collapsed in giggles. Joan leaned forward and said, "Oh, Tallulah! You might have warned him."

"Darling," Tallulah said gently to Marcus, "are you trying to tell your Auntie Tallulah that you've never been to a joint like this?"

Marcus felt more like a rube than ever. He took a slug of his cocktail from his fake brandy and forced a nod.

Howard spoke up for the first time. "Then this calls for a celebration!" He reached up and clicked his fingers. "Waitress! Another round of whatever you've got brewing in your bathtub!"

"Yes, Mister Hughes." The waitress curtseyed, and disappeared into the back room.

Marcus' eyes widened and he pressed his head close to Tallulah's. "Howard Hughes is . . . ?"

She laughed and shook her head. "I've no idea. Not everybody here is. But, darling, what *are* we going to do about Mr. Ramon Novarro? He's been staring over here ever since he sat down."

Marcus looked up and caught Ramon looking right at him. It wasn't the intense *Valentino-Sheik-I-want-you* stare Marcus longed for, but a curious have-we-met gaze. He didn't break it when Marcus met his eye.

Ramon's friends were standing up and straightening their coats. One bent down to speak to Ramon, who maintained eye contact with Marcus. He nodded and they left.

"Well, now, look who's alone." Tallulah nudged Marcus.

Oh my god! Marcus panicked. Ramon Novarro is sitting in a queer bar staring at you. Isn't this what you've dreamed of? Marcus felt his stomach cave in. Hadn't 1932 been filled with enough disappointment? Did he really need to risk ending it with the sort of rejection that would hurt the most?

"May I say something?" Joan asked. She'd drained her glass and a curl fell over her eye. "If you want a life free of risk, I suggest you take the first bus back home."

It was exactly what Marcus needed to hear. He took a slug of Tallulah's drink and struggled to his feet.

"Atta girl," Billy Haines said.

The crammed tables in B.B.B.'s Cellar were like an obstacle course. By the time Marcus was halfway across the room, Ramon had stood up to leave. Marcus dodged left, but two hefty dykes pushed away from their table and formed a wall of hats and furs that blocked his view. Surely he can see me coming over there, Marcus thought. He's going to wait for me, isn't he?

But when the two women had squeezed out of his way, Ramon was nowhere to be seen. Marcus looked pleadingly back at Tallulah, who pointed at the door. Ramon Novarro had been waiting for Marcus to see him. He gave a friendly smile and a *sorry-but-I-have-to-go* shrug, then pointed to the table he had just left. When Marcus got there, he found a matchbook with two words inside the cover: *Western Union.*

CHAPTER 28

The matchbook was still in Marcus' pocket two months later when he dressed for the Garden of Allah's threes party. Tuesday would be March 3rd, 1933 — 3/3/33 — so the suggestion went around to throw a party with a "three" theme. Everyone agreed they all could do with a rollicking good bash. This Depression was dragging on and on, and although their new president, Franklin D. Roosevelt, had done some mighty high talking in his campaign, no one knew when the country would be back on its newspaper-soled feet. The consensus around the Garden of Allah was to scramble their pennies together and throw a humdinger.

Gwendolyn suggested they go as the three blind mice so she made tails out of brown velvet and belts, they found sunglasses at a pawn shop on Santa Monica Boulevard, and they scavenged walking sticks in the garden. Gwendolyn painted their whiskers on with kohl and they ventured outside.

More than one trio arrived as the three witches from *MacBeth*, but Clara Bow and her chorine friends were the best, in turquoise and silver costumes which could have come from Florenz Ziegfeld's storeroom. Although the 1920s had crystallized her as the quintessential Flapper, the talkies hadn't been kind to Clara; booze, scandals and legal battles had taken their toll. But God bless her, she was still up for a party.

Marlene Dietrich emerged from her villa in a diaphanous white caftan, joined by a chorus boy with beautifully thick hair the color of a moonless night, and an androgynous woman with a cross the size of a rifle: the Father, the Son and the Holy Ghost.

Robert Benchley's bootlegger spiked the sideways punch — "three cups of this and you'll see everyone sideways" — that Marcus was drinking when he wondered if anyone had invited Alla. She'd mentioned more than once that nobody thought to invite her to the parties thrown in what used to be her own back yard. "Not that I really wanted to go," she'd always add, "but the occasional invite would be nice."

He put down his punch glass and crossed the gardens to villa twenty-four. He was knocking for the second time when Brophy called, "She's gone."

Marcus turned around. "What do you mean, 'gone'?"

"Up and left in the middle of the night. Lock, stock, and barrel."

"I hadn't heard."

"Nobody had, which I assume was the point."

"Where did she go?"

"Dunno."

"No forwarding address?"

"Nope."

Marcus was frozen to the front step as Brophy left for the main house. Alla had left? Without saying goodbye? Not even to him? For three years of Saturdays, they had shared orange blossom tea and cookies and talked of everything from Will Rogers' latest observations (she usually laughed at them, he not so much) to President Roosevelt's New Deal (they were both big fans) to the pros and cons of Ernest Hemingway (he liked Hemingway's writing, she detested it.)

As the recession deepened into Depression, their afternoons together had become a precious escape from the grimy city. Homeless beggars and dustbowl refugees came to California in a tidal wave of flea-bitten, downtrodden humanity. He'd come to look upon Alla as his friend, his family, his favorite aunt, always there in her dark, spare villa with warm words, wise encouragement and another slice of shortbread. But she was gone without a word. He felt like someone had lopped off his arm with a machete.

"There you are," Gwendolyn said. "We've been looking for you. Tallulah has—what's the matter?" She put her hand on Marcus' arm and looked into his face with concern. He explained and she hugged him close, then squeezed his hand. "You look like you need another glass of sideways punch. Come on, let's get you a cup."

Marcus hesitated. He wanted to tell Gwendolyn that he felt like an orphan abandoned on the church steps, but he swallowed his words and followed her to the punch bowl. She talked the whole way about a friend Tallulah wanted him to meet.

They approached the pool and Tallulah Bankhead's voice carved through the crowd. She was pulling along a portly gentleman in his mid thirties who wore glasses and an uncertain smile. "Marcus, darling, there you are! I have someone I must introduce you to." She gestured to her friend. "George, this is Marcus Adler, one of my favorite neighbors. Marcus, this is George Cukor. He was my marvelous director on *Tarnished Lady* a couple of years back. Been lured out here from New York by the filthiest of Hollywood lucre."

Cukor gave off an easy laugh. "Well, that and the weather. New York may be New York, but this weather? Unbeatable."

Gwendolyn planted fresh cups of punch in their hands. "George here has just followed Selznick over to MGM. I'm afraid to ask what his salary is nowadays. Is it more than a thousand a week, George? Don't tell me—I don't want to know, or I shall have to open my veins with jealousy. At any rate, Marcus here is an aspiring screenwriter. I thought perhaps you could give him some pointers on how to break into the racket." Tallulah threw her hands into the air. "Holy crap! Is that Marlene? What *is* she wearing? Excuse me, boys!" She left Marcus and George in a cloud of scented cigarettes and Chanel No. 5.

When Cukor sipped his sideways punch, his head reared back. "Whoa, this stuff is potent! I've heard about the famous Garden of Allah parties, and now I see why."

"It's not always like this." Marcus looked around. It was barely past eight o'clock, and most everyone was buzzed up and halfway to screaming. "I take it back." He laughed. "It pretty much is." His gaze found Alla's villa. Where could she have gone? Why would she have left like that? And so suddenly. What could possibly have happened to–

"So you want to become a screenwriter with the studios?" Cukor asked. "You must be working hard on your submission."

"Submission?"

"For the screenplay competition. At MGM." Marcus was dumbfounded. Cukor was surprised. "The winner's script is picked up by MGM, and he gets a one-year contract at three hundred a week."

"Three hundred?" Marcus exclaimed. "When is the deadline?"

"The end of the month," Hugo answered. Marcus spun around to find Hugo behind them, dressed as an Egyptian mummy swathed in red, white and blue crepe paper. "You're talking about the MGM contest, right?"

Marcus wanted to kick himself. "Have you sent in anything?"

"Oh, God yes. Three."

"You've written three screenplays?"

"No! I've written fourteen screenplays in the last two years. I just took the best three, polished them as best I could and sent them off."

Marcus gaped at Hugo. All those booster sessions over coffee, week after week, endless discussions over plots and characters and concepts, and not a single mention of a single screenplay, let alone a screenplay contest.

"What're you looking at me like that for?" Hugo asked.

"I thought you were writing stories for magazines." Hugo had been published in *Colliers, American Mercury,* and *The Smart Set,* which rankled Marcus most because it put Hugo in the company of Willa Cather, Dorothy Parker, Sinclair Lewis, and Marcus' literary hero, F. Scott Fitzgerald.

"Well, yeah, sure. They start out as short stories, but that's just to get the plot down. Then I take that story and turn it into a screenplay. I thought you were doing that, too . . ." He finished his sentence with a shrug. Marcus swallowed the rest of his punch in a single throat-burning gulp. "Come on, Adler, old bean, you're the ideas guy. I've never met anyone with so many good ideas," Hugo said. "Cough up a few of your best and let's see which one you should tackle."

First Alla and now this, Marcus thought. Thank Christ the punch is spiked. He gave a noncommittal shrug. "I can't think of any right now."

Just then "Shadow Waltz" came on Benchley's radio and Kathryn grabbed Hugo's arm. "I love this song!" she exclaimed. "Hugo, dance with me." She dragged him onto the impromptu dancefloor by the pool.

As Marcus and George Cukor watched Kathryn and Hugo waltz, a man in creamy white gabardine strode down the path from the main house. A thrill shot through Marcus and he fingered the matchbook in his pocket. He watched as one of Clara Bow's Macbethian witches greeted Novarro with an extravagant hug.

It was asinine of him to assume that Ramon Novarro would–or even could–go to the trouble of tracking down a nameless stranger. You need to switch gears, he told himself. You have an MGM director standing right next to you. It's time to put your head in the game.

"As a matter of fact I do have some ideas," Marcus said. "But I've only got enough time to turn one of them into a screenplay. Could I possibly bounce some off you?"

"Original ideas are precious. What makes you think I can be trusted with yours?"

"Instinct?" Marcus smiled.

Cukor laughed. "Perfect answer. Shoot."

"My first idea," Marcus said, "is the story of the building of the White House. The way I figure it, right now, America needs a movie that would inspire loyalty to the president who will see us through this Depression. The White House is a symbol of the office we all hold in high esteem, and I think that its story — even if it's mostly made up — might make a good movie."

"Mmmm," Cukor replied, but his face was blank. "Idea number two?"

"A complete suck-up. I've been thinking about a story based on the life of Louis B. Mayer." In fact, his idea had been to write a story about Harold Ross, the legendary editor of the *New Yorker* to submit to that magazine but it wasn't hard to switch.

Cukor's left eyebrow couldn't help but raise itself.

"I'd change the setting to radio, or newspapers, or book publishing, perhaps. But it's the story of how a boy born in America to dirt-poor immigrant parents rises to the top of his profession in the way that someone like him can only achieve in America."

"And your third idea?"

Clara Bow and her witches let out a shriek. Marcus looked over at the commotion and was locked in Novarro's eyes. A frown flickered across Novarro's face as he looked over Marcus' costume. Marcus pushed his dark glasses over his eyes, and stretched out his tail. Novarro gave an approving nod and winked at him. Marcus almost dropped his empty punch glass, but managed to nod smoothly back.

"And your third idea?" Cukor asked again.

Marcus dragged his eyes back to Cukor. "I call it *The Making of Merry*. Merry is a mousy young girl who is the paid companion to a quartet of spinsters for whom she does everything. She has no life of her own, and even though she is thirty-five years younger than they are, she's already starting to look like them, and act like them. When she meets a guy who sees past her old maid façade, he encourages her to transform into a lively, pretty young thing. The old bats hate it—they want her to stay home with them with no life of her own. But everything works out in the end. The sisters discover he really is a good guy, and not just out to marry Merry because she's set to inherit everything they own. The lovers get married in the final reel with the spinsters' blessing."

Cukor granted him a smile. "There's no doubt which is the best story."

"The second one?"

"Good God, no. *The Making of Merry*. MGM can't get enough of that type of romantic balderdash. It's a story of love and hope and ducklings becoming swans, and audiences are going to lap it up in the middle of this Depression." He raised a finger. "Plus, prima donnas love those roles, and studios will buy anything to keep their stars happy."

Kathryn skipped happily off the dance floor. "Hugo never told me what a fine dancer he is!" she exclaimed, a little out of breath. She slapped her partner playfully on the arm. "You should have warned me!"

Out of the corner of his eye, Marcus could see a dashing figure in a gorgeous suit approach them.

"Good evening, everybody," Ramon Novarro said. "Would you recommend the punch tonight? I hear it's very strong."

"Strong enough to power a steam engine," Cukor said.

Ramon reached out and grabbed Cukor's hand. "We haven't met. I'm Ramon Novarro."

"George Cukor. Just starting at your old stomping ground."

"MGM?" Ramon's eye lit up. "Ah! I hope you shall be as happy there as I was. Well, mostly," he added and then turned to Kathryn. "And you are?"

"Kathryn Massey. I'm Tallulah Bankhead's secretary."

Ramon cocked a perfectly-shaped eyebrow. "*Si*? That must keep you very busy."

Kathryn smiled. "This is Hugo Marr, and Marcus Adler."

Ramon shook Hugo's hand next, saving Marcus' for last. He lay his left hand on top, pressing their hands together. His hands were as soft as Marcus had recalled. Marcus could feel his knees trembling

"I am very pleased to meet you, Mister Marcus Adler," Ramon said. He fixed Marcus with a knowing stare. Marcus watched the man's lips moving slightly. He wasn't entirely sure but it was possible he was repeating Marcus' name over and over.

Don't just stand there, Marcus thought. Say something!

Ramon broke their stare and turned to Kathryn. "You waltz very well, Miss Massey. Do you tango also?"

Marcus felt his heart plummet fourteen feet.

"As a matter of fact, I do," Kathryn said, beaming.

Ramon offered his arm and led Kathryn to the improvised dance floor, where he drew her close, wrapped his arms around her, and set off in a tight tango.

Marcus couldn't keep his eyes off them as they rounded the edges of the floor. Was it his imagination, or did Novarro keep looking back at him with hunger in his eyes? Oh Kathryn, Marcus thought, what I wouldn't give to be in your place.

At some point–Marcus hadn't noticed when–Cukor and Hugo wandered into other conversations and he found the Garden's bellboy standing next to him. "I've got a message for Kathryn, and a telegram for Gwendolyn," Jake said, "I've left the front desk unattended — can I leave these with you?" He handed Marcus a folded piece of paper and a telegram in a yellow Western Union envelope, then hurried back to the lobby. Marcus unfolded the paper; it read *505 Temple Street, Long Beach*. When Kathryn and Ramon came off the dance floor, he handed her the message.

"Mister Marcus Adler," Ramon said in a carefully clipped way that suggested he was trying hard to remember Marcus' name, "it was a pleasure to meet you." He offered his hand again. "I regret to say that I must depart. I have another engagement. It was a delight. Your friend is a very good dancer."

Ramon winked again and smiled a smile that made Marcus want to dive into his arms. There would be no sleep for him tonight. He watched Ramon Novarro retreat up the gravel path until he'd disappeared into the hotel, then slowly became aware that Kathryn was staring into space.

"I didn't know you knew anyone in Long Beach," he said.

"I've been socking away money for a private eye. He was awfully cheap so I didn't think he'd come up with anything, but it looks like he has."

"So whose address is that?"

"I think it's my mother's."

CHAPTER 29

Waves of heat emanated from white stucco walls as Gwendolyn ducked off Wilshire into a shaded walkway. She pushed open the heavy glass door of the Bryson Apartment Hotel. Someone had gone to a lot of trouble to match the iris blue carpet to four enormous Oriental pots that held miniature palm trees. The carpet and pots were all flecked with gold, as though some mad painter had come in and lost his marbles.

Ordinarily, Gwendolyn would have stopped to admire the effect, but this was no ordinary day. It had taken Anderson McRae several months to claim his favor. There had been a brief marital reconciliation, but when it fell apart, his friend needed her help after all. When McRae turned up at the Cocoanut Grove one night, serious and unsmiling, her heart sank. She'd been half hoping that she wouldn't hear from him. The whole thing sounded terribly tawdry, but she finally had the attention of a casting director, and that put her ahead of nearly every pretty girl in Hollywood. And the Bryson is one of the classiest addresses in town, she reminded herself. It's not like McRae has asked you to front up at some lowlife dive on the wrong side of town.

Gwendolyn approached the uniformed doorman. "I'm here to see Mr. Hank Hubbard."

The doorman, a heavy set guy in his fifties, let his bushy eyebrows rise. "Apartment 7-G. Seventh floor, west wing." He pointed to an elevator behind Gwendolyn.

Its brass doors were polished until they were practically mirrors. Gwendolyn pushed the call button and stared at herself. She looked a little washed-out and worried. She was so embarrassed by what she'd agreed to that she hadn't even told Kathryn about it. She could hear her roommate's voice in her head. *It's not too late to walk out of here.* A quiet bell dinged and the doors opened, splitting her reflection in two.

* * *

The door to apartment 7-G was like all the others along the bright corridor: dark wood with a chrome knocker in the shape of a seashell. The door opened promptly and she stepped back as though she'd been slapped. The man did the same. She took another step back into the hallway. "Mr. McRae didn't tell me it'd be you."

"And I didn't know the dish he'd lined up for me was going to be you." He shot his hand out toward her. She recoiled and felt the wall against her back. "Please. Don't go," he begged. "Really, I didn't know. I swear it."

The last time Gwendolyn had seen Broochie, he'd been drunker than a sailor on shore leave and had wrecked her chances of impressing the top brass of MGM. And all because of that damned diamond brooch. That damnably gorgeous diamond brooch which took her breath away whenever she slipped it out of its hidey-hole and drenched it in sunlight. But Broochie looked different. His bloated face had thinned down, making his chin more prominent and lending him a more dignified air. Dimples now emerged in his cheeks. He was almost handsome. Well, Gwendolyn decided, passably attractive, anyway.

"You have every reason to leave," he said rapidly. "I'd be the last person to blame you. But I want you to know I've given up the hooch." He shook his head. "Me and the hooch, we don't make a good combination. You know that better than anyone. Except for Mr. Mayer." He pulled a comical grimace. "You think he's got the stink of my whiskey out of his tux yet?"

They eyed each other for a long moment before he stepped to the side and swept his hand toward his apartment. "Please? I need you."

Inside, the carpet went all the way to the walls; Gwendolyn had never seen anything like it. Its pattern of pastel autumn leaves and flower petals was subtle but gave the place a palatial air. A pair of sofas in cream damask flanked a long matching coffee table. Gwendolyn took a seat and Broochie sat on the other sofa.

"Okay, so here's the situation," he said. "When I gave you that Harry Winston brooch, it was for my girlfriend who'd just broken up with me. But we got back together and I married her. Then I found out she'd been screwing every guy who crossed her path the whole time. But she comes from this big mucky-muck family — dear ol' dad's on the state supreme court — so a divorce naming her as the guilty party ain't in the cards." He gave his swank apartment a weary once-over. "So this here joint is my pay-off, as long as I play the villain."

Gwendolyn studied his sad smile. "And you say Mr. McRae had no idea of our history?"

"Andy's a good guy who's been keen to pay back a big favor I did for him when we was both at Paramount."

So life has laid a big stinky egg on the poor dope's head. If I pose for a couple of photos, it isn't such a bad deal for both the most beautiful brooch I'm ever likely to own, and the notice of RKO's casting department, is it? She cleared her throat. "Where's the photographer?"

"He's already here. He'll be taking photos through the window. It has to look authentic."

"Mr. Hubbard, we are seven stories up."

He pointed over Gwendolyn's shoulder. She turned and saw a slightly shriveled, balding man with a Clark Gable moustache looking down at her through the transom over Hubbard's bedroom door. "That's Lenny," Broochie said. Lenny lifted his camera for her to see.

"How do we do this, exactly?" Gwendolyn asked.

"I ain't gonna get you to go nude or nothing. Just down to your scanties. Maybe one of your bra straps off your shoulder? Could you do that? For authenticity's sake and all. But if you don't wanna, I'd understand, of course."

Gwendolyn nodded. "And you?"

"I'll get rumpled up, too. I thought we'd lie on this here sofa." He went to a teak cabinet carved in a geometric pattern and pulled open the lid. The sides swung open to reveal a fully stocked liquor cabinet. "I got props!" He lifted a bottle of Liberty Bell bourbon and two shot glasses and returned to the sofa. "Make it look like we're having a party."

As Gwendolyn stood up and let her camel skirt drop to the floor, Broochie said, "Gosh, you're an awful good sport."

"I'm doing this for Anderson McRae," she stated matter-of-factly. Broochie stripped down to his undershirt and blue-and-pink striped shorts, his expensive gray suit slung over the sofa like a snakeskin.

"I thought perhaps we oughta just pitch our stuff all over like we couldn't wait to get our duds off."

Gwendolyn scattered her things across the coffee table and stretched out on the white damask sofa. She glanced up at the transom; Lenny was lining up his shot.

Broochie knelt next to her in his undershorts and Gwendolyn could feel the sofa sag under his weight. He planted his knuckles on either side of her shoulders and lowered himself on top of her, pinning her down. He pulled his lips back in a smile that approached a leer. "Don't worry, Lenny's a pro." His casualness wasn't convincing. "He knows what these photos need to look like to sell them to the judge." He nodded at his pal peeking at them through the transom. "Ready!"

They went through a dozen contortions, the flash on Lenny's camera exploded each time with enough bright light to fill the room. But when Broochie buried his face between her breasts, Gwendolyn pushed him away. "I think that's quite enough!" She looked up at the transom for Lenny, but he was already opening the door, a folded-up step ladder in his hand. "The broad's right, Hank. We got plenty of good stuff." He left quickly, closing the front door behind him.

Sweat glistened on Broochie's forehead. "You can get off me now, Mr. Hubbard," she informed him. Broochie didn't move. "Mmm . . ." he moaned, lowering his mouth onto hers. She tasted egg salad and tried to scream, but he swallowed the syllable whole. Gwendolyn squirmed underneath him, but the sheer heft of the guy made it hard for her to breathe; he was squeezing the air out of her lungs. He grabbed her wrists and pressed them together with one meaty hand as the other slid up to her breast. He cupped it in his hand and pressed her nipple between his thumb and forefinger. Her heart just about caved in when she felt him swell against her thigh.

When he started to thrust against her, she yanked a hand free and groped for the lamp on the side table. Her fingertips scraped it, but she couldn't get a hold of it. "Come on, baby," he said, his voice low and hoarse. "I ain't so bad, huh?" He pressed his mouth against hers again before she could grunt her reply. She pushed on his shoulder with her free hand, but he didn't budge. Even thirty pounds lighter, he was still the size of a Black Angus. She groped the back of the sofa until her hand landed on his belt. She gripped the leather and yanked it toward her. The buckle caught on the edge of the sofa, then flipped over and came down hard on the small of Broochie's back. He winced.

"Awwww! What the hell?" He let go of Gwendolyn's hand and lifted his chest off her. She squirmed up the sofa a few inches and grabbed the glass lamp by the stem, then brought it down on the bastard's head. It hit his skull with a dead, cracking sound, and he slumped to the floor.

Gwendolyn scrambled off the sofa and grabbed her skirt. She pulled it over her slip and jammed her feet into her shoes as she scooped up the rest of her things. It wasn't until she was at the door that she glanced back at Broochie. A tremor shook her when she saw a scarlet pool of blood soaking into the carpet.

CHAPTER 30

Gwendolyn watched Kathryn fidget with the gold clasp on her handbag for the longest time before she asked, "You nervous, honey?" Kathryn seemed surprised. "You've been playing with that there clasp like you were knitting it into a sweater."

Kathryn lifted her hands away from her bag like it was suddenly two hundred degrees. "I guess so," she conceded and turned to gaze out the window. The streetcar rumbled down Western Avenue toward Long Beach.

If anyone's got something to be nervous about, it's me, Gwendolyn thought. It had been nearly a week since she'd left Broochie lying in a pool of his own blood at the Bryson Hotel. She'd never seen blood like that before. It was brighter than she ever imagined. She was so shaken that she threw the window open at the end of the hall and ran down the fire escape. She was back on Wilshire before she wondered if she should have checked to see if he was alive. What if she'd killed him? There was a photographer with a camera full of photos of her. And the doorman could identify her, too. Why hadn't she called the cops? Attempted rape is one thing, but it didn't stack up against murder. But she'd done nothing about it except run away and fret, barely sleeping the whole week.

"I haven't seen my mother in four years," Kathryn blurted out. "What sort of mother up and moves without telling her daughter where she is going? Maybe she doesn't want to be found. And if she doesn't want to be found, why the hell am I going all the way down to Long Beach to see her?" She paused. "Gwennie, what if she slams the door in my face?"

Gwendolyn pressed Kathryn's hands between her own. "Honey, she's still your mama. Nobody's going to be slamming no doors in no faces."

Kathryn's eyes were shiny with tears. "I hope you're right. But hey, what about you? You must be excited to see your brother again. How long's it been?"

The telegram that arrived for Gwendolyn during the threes party was from Monty, whose ship was in Long Beach for several days of drills. He'd told her to pick a place near the naval base and he'd spend his leave with her. She hadn't seen him since the day after they buried Mama, when he ran off to join the navy. For the last five hellish days, Gwendolyn had wondered if he'd have to come visit her in prison. The murder of a supreme court judge's son-in-law would send Hearst's tabloids into a froth-mouthed fit, but there was no mention of a murder at the Bryson Hotel in any of the papers. Maybe Broochie had only suffered a concussion, some blood loss and a badly bruised ego. Serves him right, the big heel. But, she told herself ruefully, you can kiss RKO goodbye.

"I haven't seen Monty in six years," Gwendolyn said. "The last time I saw him, he was just a tall, gangly fifteen-year-old who was lucky to pass for seventeen and to have a sister to forge his mother's signature. I'm glad you'll get to meet him. He's all the family I have."

Kathryn smiled and nodded sadly. Gwendolyn knew she was thinking that Francine was the only family she had, too.

* * *

The Making of Merry was starting to look a lot like *The Unmaking of Marcus Adler's Sanity*. If only he could figure out how to get Merry's love interest to impress the four batty spinsters that he's a good guy. But what would a guy with an allergy to horses be doing at a state fair? Maybe if he changed the allergy to a phobia? Or changed the state fair to a circus? Maybe relocated the whole thing to Coney Island, where the horses are made of wood?

The deadline was less than two weeks away, and Marcus had no idea what he was doing. He'd never written a screenplay before, and was still working out what happened when, where, and why. The deadline loomed like the long shadow of a firing squad at dawn.

And it didn't help that his new neighbors were newlyweds. They were at it morning, noon and night. The screams. The gasps. The groans. The endless thumping of the headboard against his wall. Didn't they ever get tired? Or sore?

"Enough already!" he yelled at the wall.

Thump-thump-thump-thump.

"This has got to stop!"

And then suddenly it did. "Thank you," Marcus muttered, and he returned to his typewriter. He hadn't typed a full sentence when there was a knock on the door. "This had better be an apology." He pulled open his door and reared back a step when he found Ramon Novarro filling his doorway.

"Oh!" Marcus said. "It's you! Wait—are you the guy next door?" He pointed to the honeymooners' room with his thumb.

Ramon looked up with blurry eyes and frowned. "No," he said. "Should I be?"

Marcus smelled bourbon. "What are you doing here?"

"I came to do this." Ramon reached out for Marcus with both hands, grabbed his head and pulled him close. Their lips touched, then pressed together. Marcus felt Ramon's tongue slip inside his mouth. They kissed deeply, wetly, hungrily. When Ramon pulled away, it was abrupt.

Marcus' eyes flew open. "What is it?" he asked, trying to keep his balance.

"I want more than just to kiss you."

"Me too," Marcus replied. He pulled at Ramon's hands. "Come inside."

Ramon wouldn't cross the threshold. "No, no. Not here. We must go where I can feel safe."

"It's safe here," Marcus whispered. He felt light-headed and breathless. After all these years of dreaming and fantasizing this very scene, Marcus found he wasn't quite as prepared as he assumed he'd be. He steadied himself on the doorknob and tried to pull Ramon inside, but Ramon moved into the hallway.

"I know a place," he said. "Grab your jacket. My automobile is parked outside."

* * *

Kathryn shook Gwendolyn's brother's huge paw of a hand. He half-crushed hers with his enthusiasm. "It looks like navy life agrees with you," she said.

"Yes, ma'am, it surely does!" Monty smiled that same smile Kathryn loved on Gwendolyn. With his thick crown of sun-bleached hair, his sailor's tan and the way his dark blue uniform hugged his lean body, Monty was as handsome as Gwendolyn was beautiful. Good lord, they sure do grow 'em good-looking in the Brick family, Kathryn thought.

"I'll leave you to it," Kathryn said. "You've got a lot of catching up to do."

"You ain't joinin' Googie and me?" Monty asked.

"Googie?" Kathryn asked with a smile.

Gwendolyn giggled and slapped her brother's shoulder. "I haven't heard that in years." She turned to Kathryn. "When Monty was growing up, my name was too long for him to pronounce. It came out 'Googie' and it kind of stuck. I was Googie and he was Mo-Mo. Kathryn here has some catching up of her own to do." She told her brother, then squeezed Kathryn's forearm. "I hope it all goes well. See you at home."

Kathryn headed east toward Temple Street. The nerves that had surfaced on the Red Car returned as a cold sweat. She dabbed her forehead with her gloves. Francine is your mother, she told herself. She won't slam the door in your face. She'll be glad to see you.

She stopped in front of a florist's shop. In the window was a pyramid of potted dahlias in ten different colors; shiny white, cinnamon red, saffron yellow, and at the top, an explosion of dark plum petals with edges dipped in guava. Kathryn heard her mother's voice as she had a thousand times: "If you ever bring me flowers, make them dahlias!"

She went inside to ask the price. The top plant was five dollars.

"For one plant?" Kathryn exclaimed.

"It's an Aurora's Kiss," the woman replied as though that were explanation enough.

Kathryn looked into her purse and totaled up her cash. "What have you got for two or three dollars?"

A man in a blue flannel shirt, dungarees and work boots walked in, and the florist greeted him. She turned back to Kathryn. "Our dahlias are upstairs. We have more than thirty varieties—feel free to take a look around."

The stairs at the rear of the shop led to a long room filled with dahlias of every imaginable color; greens greener than emeralds, pinks like cotton candy, oranges brighter than the sun. Every one was lovelier than the last.

When she got to the final table, however, the choice was easy. The Arabian Night's petals were dark pink on the periphery and graduated to a striking magenta in the center. It was every bit as eye-catching as the Aurora's Kiss, but only cost two-fifty. She put her handbag down and picked it up to inhale its fragrance; it smelled faintly of brine and reminded her of the Red Car rides to Santa Monica Beach with her mother when she was little.

A low rumble sounded on the street. Kathryn figured it was a big truck at first, but when it continued, she looked up and frowned. No, she thought, that's no truck.

The long windows overlooking the street began to rattle, then she heard a tile scrape down the roof and smash on the concrete sidewalk below. A second, third and fourth quickly followed, then another and another. The floor beneath her feet began to stir, rolling upwards as though something underground was rupturing to the surface. The rumble swelled to a loud thunder, and the walls shook and heaved. The plaster started to crumble, exposing bricks and splintering wood and breathing a cloud of dust into the room. An almighty crack cleaved the air and ripped a gash in the floorboards, throwing Kathryn off her feet. The wall in front of her crumbled like a slab of dry cheese and the building slumped to its side.

* * *

Navy life suited Monty and Gwendolyn told him so several times. Gone was that kid brother of hers, all elbows and kneecaps and hands that didn't know what to do with themselves. His shoulders were broad now, and his chest was strong, and she teased him about having a girl in every port. He didn't deny it, but he changed the subject.

"Are you a movie star yet?" Monty asked.

"Are you an admiral yet?" she countered.

"No," his voice serious, "but I plan to be."

All Monty had ever wanted to do was join the U.S. Navy. School didn't matter, college didn't matter, even his friends didn't matter much, because once he joined the navy, he'd never see them again. By the time he was twelve he could identify every ship in the navy's fleet, but Gwendolyn had never wondered what he wanted to do once he joined.

"Good for you, Mo-Mo!" she told him. "Aim for the top."

Monty slowly frowned. "But what about you, Googie?"

For a moment she saw the pool of blood seeping into Broochie's white carpet and wondered if her brother could see her guilt. "What about me?" she hedged.

He shrugged. "All I hear about Hollywood is about oversexed people indulging in wild parties with too much liquor and not enough morals."

"Why, Ensign Montgomery Horatio Brick!" Gwendolyn exclaimed. She sat up straight in the diner booth, opened her eyes wide, and slapped her hands on her hips. "Since when did you become such a bluenose?"

"Since my sister moved to the sin capital of America."

She swatted away Monty's concerns as though they were a sandfly. "I never figured my baby brother for the worrying type. You can put your ever-lovin' mind to rest. Hollywood is not all about wild parties and bootleg and orgies, or whatever you've been reading. You do not have to worry about me dissipating into any sort of tawdry life of fallen womanhood. I don't even drink."

"The boys on board told me that liquor was easy to come by in Hollywood."

"Oh, it is, it surely is. It's just that I don't want to . . ." she tore her donut in half and dunked a piece into her coffee. "Oh, you know. The way Mama was."

Monty looked at her with a sad light in his eyes. "But you're nothing like Mama."

"I wouldn't be so sure. If I lost my husband to the Spanish flu so young, I might turn to drink for comfort, too."

Monty let out a heartless laugh. "Oh, Googie, how can you spend so many years in a place like Hollywood and still be so naïve?"

"What's that supposed to mean?"

"Dear old Daddy didn't up and die o' no flu. And Mama sure as heck didn't turn to the booze because o' no lonely old heart."

An awkward silence fell between them. "What are you saying?"

"Mama's stories about Daddy. That's all they were: stories she made up so she didn't have to think about the truth."

Gwendolyn chewed on her bear claw; it suddenly seemed spongy and indigestible. "What truth?"

Monty sighed. "The long and short of it all was that Daddy went and died of syphilis."

"*Syphilis*?" All her life, Gwendolyn had sat through her mother's endless speechifying about the nobility of her father's death. How stoically he suffered! How rarely he complained! The indignities he endured!

"Old Doc Lewis reckons he knew what he had, but was too ashamed to admit it. Daddy let it go on for so long that by the time he landed himself in the doc's office, he was too far gone."

After a lifetime of thinking her father had died of the Spanish flu, Gwendolyn found it hard to switch over to syphilis. "But that's a venereal disease, isn't it?"

"Doc Lewis said that our daddy was the most notorious wildcat in all Broward County. It was just a matter of time before he picked up something. But you have to hand it to Mama. She didn't toss him out. She nursed him until he died."

"Of . . . syphilis." Maybe if I say the word often enough it eventually won't sound horrible.

"The Spanish flu was just a more socially acceptable way for Daddy to die. You know Mama." Monty's voice was more gentle now. "So proud to be born a Boyington. Raised to be a southern lady, all genteel-like, with nothing but magnolia blossoms and big floppy sun hats to fuss over. It wasn't her fault all that tobacco money ended up in the pockets of riverboat card sharks and Savannah madams. Life had to be one damned disappointment after another for her. No wonder she turned to the hooch."

Poor Mama, Gwendolyn thought. Gin for breakfast, gin for lunch, gin for dinner, always on that saggy old sofa with Grandma's lace doilies along the back to hide the rips and tears. "How come you know all of this and I don't?"

"Right after I signed up for the navy, I bumped into Doc Lewis. I told him I was going to be a sailor, and he frowned at me all serious-like. He said I was about to find myself in all sorts of situations all over the world, and he told me how to protect myself properly. He said, 'I'm telling you this because I don't want the same fate to befall you that befell your daddy.' Exactly what fate was that, I asked. And then he told me everything."

All too soon it was time for Monty to return to the ship. Gwendolyn walked him back to the naval base where they hugged for an extra long time. She felt ten years older than she had that morning. Monty extracted a promise to send him cakes and chocolates as often as she could–other guys' families sent care packages, the contents of which acted like currency on board ship. She watched Monty jog up the gangplank and turn around to wave before disappearing into the huge battleship.

As she wandered away from the base, she mentally tried to swat away the word 'syphilis' that bounced around her head like a rabid mosquito. What had she gained by learning that her daddy was a wildcat? Maybe it's a good thing, she thought with a silent sigh, that I live in a town that manufactures make-believe for a living.

Gwendolyn was window shopping at Baggenshue's when she saw a blood-red stiletto start to wobble. Within seconds, the window display toppled over and the sidewalk began to tremble. The trembles escalated to rapid shudders and pitched Gwendolyn sideways into a telephone pole. She hugged the pole and looked up, expecting thunderclouds to match the deafening noise, but the sky was clear, bright blue. A woman screamed inside Baggenshue's just before a shower of glass started to fall. Gwendolyn ducked and covered her head with her pocketbook as the telephone pole jolted, splintered, and plunged toward the store. Gwendolyn let go and tried to escape the glass and tile that crashed down to the pavement.

She started up the sidewalk, but it shook so hard she couldn't stand. She fell like she'd been punched and the concrete tore her palms and knees. A man screamed behind her, and she looked back in time to see a brick wall quiver like cardboard and the ground rise six inches into the air, then drop just as suddenly. The whole street shuddered and tilted toward her.

* * *

Ramon Novarro was in no shape to drive; the smell of rye liquor pervaded the insides of his black Pontiac. At the corner of Hollywood and Sunset, the set of *Intolerance,* Hollywood's first blockbuster, still towered. Ramon took the corner on two wheels. Marcus gave up counting the red lights they'd run somewhere around Aimee Semple McPherson's evangelical temple on the way into downtown.

"What's the hurry?" Marcus asked.

"We have waited too long for this moment, yes?"

Marcus nodded. But wouldn't it be nice to get there in one piece? he thought.

Ramon turned onto Fifth and lurched into a parking spot. Marcus looked across the street to the Derbyshire Arms where that sailor, Zachary, had told him queers don't get to have dates or marriage or relationships. The place was rattier than Marcus remembered.

"Is that where we're going?" Marcus asked.

Ramon's eyes followed Marcus' and he shot him a look that said, *Why would you even think that?* They got out of the car and Marcus followed Ramon to the top of Pershing Square and into the river of commuters entering the Subway Terminal, a huge, gray, four-pronged building. They descended two stories to a subway platform crammed with men anxious for the leafy outskirts of Pasadena.

Ramon led Marcus to the end of the platform and opened a door marked TRANSIT STAFF ONLY onto a corridor lit by bare bulbs every fifty feet or so. They rushed up a staircase and turned right at the fork onto a narrower corridor that smelled of wet concrete. Marcus ached to ask, Wouldn't my bed at the Garden of Allah have been more comfortable? but said nothing and followed Ramon through the next door. They walked into a wide, warm corridor. The air smelled inexplicably citrusy. Lemons? Pineapples? Marcus couldn't quite make it out.

Ramon took Marcus' hand and led him beneath a skylight made of thick, frosted glass, reinforced with wire. The light there was the gentle, forgiving light that movie stars favored. Did they drive all the way here so that Ramon could be well-lit for their romantic love scene? Marcus couldn't figure out if he was finally seeing Ramon Novarro for being the vain movie star he was, or was he marveling at Ramon's originality and ingenuity for finding such a perfect make out hideaway? I don't know what to think at this point, he told himself. You've got what you wanted, haven't you?

Ramon leaned against the wall and pulled Marcus to him. "Look up there." Marcus looked up at the soles of people's shoes walking along the street right above them. They listened to the metal tips of a girl's high heels hit the glass: clack-clack-clack-clack. "I love to come here," Ramon's voice echoed softly in the concrete hallway. "I watch the people walk past. I love that they are walking home from work, going to buy a newspaper, and just below them are two men making love. It gives me a thrill."

It dawned on Marcus that he wasn't the first guy Ramon Novarro had brought here. He searched himself and found that he wasn't jealous; he was flattered.

Ramon cupped his hands around Marcus' face and pulled their mouths together. Their tongues explored each other with a pent-up passion that Marcus' Pershing Square encounters lacked. He slid his arms around Ramon's waist and pulled him close until he could feel the heat of Ramon's body along the length of his own. Ramon's smooth hands wandered inside Marcus' shirt and down his trousers, melting his skin wherever he touched. Their trousers slid past their knees, and Marcus could feel the air of the underground corridor brush past his leg hair.

Two pairs of heels clattered across the glass slab a foot and a half above their heads. "I am close," Ramon whispered into Marcus' ear, "but we must not rush."

He reclaimed Marcus' mouth and they kissed again, long and hard. Ramon kneaded Marcus' ass and Marcus rode up and down Ramon's taut body, his climax rising inside him. He started to pant.

They froze when they heard the sound of steel girders scraping against each other. Someone stopped on the skylight and exclaimed, "What was that?" The wall that Ramon leaned against began to shudder, then jolt, and a deep crack snaked along the wall toward them. The thunder grew louder and louder and suddenly the corridor filled with dust. A skylight shook loose and a block of glass and wire slammed to the floor.

Ramon grabbed Marcus' hand and pulled him back the way they'd come. They had just reached the door when a violent jerk rocked them off their feet. Marcus yanked the door open as a load of bricks crashed down outside it.

CHAPTER 31

His name was Roy. It wasn't short for anything, and it hadn't been invented for a movie marquee. It suited him like his dungarees and sturdy boots did, and Kathryn liked it. This comforted her as she lay under Roy under the smashed second floor of Exotica Flowers and Bulbs amid plaster, glass, and a world-class selection of potted dahlias.

It was hard to know how long she had been out, but when she came to, the dead weight of a strange man was on top of her. He had been on the first floor and she on the second when the quake hit, so it wasn't clear how they ended up together, but there they were, head to head, toe to toe, groin to groin.

She assumed he was dead. She squirmed and writhed to get out from under his body but he was pinned to her by a heavy wooden beam. It was her squirming that brought him around. Her relief at discovering she wasn't buried underneath a cadaver was only short lived and quickly replaced by the discomfort of realizing that a fully conscious stranger was laying on top of her like a casual afternoon lover.

It seemed appropriate to introduce themselves before they struggled together again–*Hello Miss Kathryn Massey...Good afternoon Mr. Roy Quinn*–but they couldn't budge the beam an inch and quickly exhausted their strength. They called out for the florist. Kathryn closed her eyes. "She must be dead."

When Roy didn't reply, she opened her eyes and found him staring at her. "Your hair is absolutely gorgeous," he said, as though the quality of her hair was the most pressing problem facing them right at that moment. "My mother was a hairdresser, so I know more about hair than men ought to." He threw her a disarming smile that bunched his cheeks into the dreamiest dimples she'd ever seen. She blushed.

"Are you in pain?" he asked her. "Any bricks or broken beams jammed into your back?"

"No, nothing like that."

"And your legs? Your feet? They're not caught at an uncomfortable angle or anything?"

"My right ankle is throbbing a little," she admitted. "What about you?"

"I had a nice lady to break my fall."

They were screwing before the second aftershock. The first one was strong enough to disturb the rubble and shift the crossbeam from his thighs to his ankles, allowing him a greater range of motion. Straining against the beam did little other than drive Kathryn's orange sundress up to her hips. Roy said apologetically that he didn't think he could hold his head up for much longer, and would it be very forward of him to rest his forehead against hers.

Kathryn smiled to herself as she gazed along the curved driveway of the Long Beach Community Hospital, waiting for Roy to pick her up. *If I could just lay my forehead against yours . . .* Looking back now it was a wonder it took us a full ten minutes to start kissing. Was it because, by then, the sun had slipped away and we could hardly see each other? Kathryn laughed out loud. Sun or no sun, it was a hell of a way for a girl to lose her virginity.

A faded blue old Ford pick-up, rutted with dents and pockmarked with rust pulled up and Roy jumped out. His car suited him as well as his name did.

"Were you laughing at my truck?"

"Heavens, no," Kathryn said. She hooked her crutches under her arms. "You're a godsend for doing this for me."

A hundred and fifteen people were dead, thousands were homeless, and nearly everyone in Southern California had been injured by the great Long Beach earthquake. She'd even read a report about how it had interrupted filming of the "Shadow Waltz" a musical scene in a new Warner Brothers musical, *Gold Diggers of 1933*, nearly throwing choreographer Busby Berkeley from a camera boom, and rattling dancers on a thirty-foot-high platform. But somehow Kathryn and her sprained ankle scored a bed for the night. It wasn't until Roy headed west that the full impact of the earthquake hit her. Building after building lay in dusty piles of broken bricks and glass. Where a façade was shaken loose, the rest of a structure was exposed like a giant doll's house. That was the odd thing about earthquakes—one building could be reduced to a heap of dust while the one right next to it was undisturbed, as though nothing happened. Much like people, Kathryn reflected. She and Roy had survived relatively intact but that poor florist was probably laying in an awful, crowded morgue somewhere.

Roy turned north onto Temple and suddenly Kathryn imagined her mother's place in shambles. "Pull over!" she ordered. Roy looked surprised, but obeyed.

At the curb, Kathryn turned to him. "About what happened last night . . ." She wanted to say that she would never forget making love with him under such preposterous circumstances. Aside from the wrenched ankle and four-hour imprisonment under a mountain of bricks, she was so very glad to have spent that time with him, but she didn't want him to feel obligated to her. She wanted to say all that, but when she looked into his blue-gray eyes, the words evaporated like spit on a griddle. Instead, she was overwhelmed by the longing to slide into the strongest arms she'd ever seen. He read her mind and pulled her close.

"Please don't tell me you regret last night," he said into her hair. "I haven't stopped thinking about you since I left you at the hospital."

Talk to him, you big dummy, she told herself. This guy is so completely the opposite of all the slick Hollywood phoneys, pretty boys and sleaze balloons that the last thing you want is to stand on the sidewalk and watch his dented old Ford rattle off into the distance. She pushed herself out of his arms so that she could face him squarely.

"Last night was wonderful. *Wonderful.* But I want you to know that it puts you under no obligation. To me, I mean."

His expression clouded. "Oh, I see. It's just that . . . I was kind of hoping maybe we could try it someplace more comfortable, like a bed . . . ?" He pulled her close and Kathryn melted into him again. He leaned down and kissed her deeply.

When Francine popped into her head, Kathryn sat back and straightened her hair. "What on earth am I doing? My mother could be . . . and I'm sitting here . . . with you." She wanted to walk the rest of the way, to come upon her mother's house alone, so she scrambled out of the truck with her crutches and slammed the door shut with the hip that didn't ache like hell. They waved goodbye.

Kathryn's heart sank when she came to Francine's place. Five-zero-five Temple Street was a set of four Californian bungalows, two on each side of a central garden alive with petunias and poppies, daisies and lilies. The bungalows themselves were a soft peach color and their roofs blanketed with ivy and bougainvillea. The pink-purple flowers burst with color so bright it almost hurt to gaze at them. Kathryn could tell it must have looked like some idyllic scene from a painting before the quake hit. Now the bungalows on the right looked like they'd been tackled by a wrecking ball on rampage. The ones on the left had lopsided front doors; every window in the place was busted.

Kathryn knocked on her mother's door. No one answered, but a loud bang of metal on wood sounded from inside. She called out. "Hello? Is someone there?" and tried the door, scraping it open with the tip of her crutch. Inside, the place was a disaster. The back corner had half collapsed and the kitchen was flooded with two inches of murky water. Kathryn's mother stood in the middle, brandishing a two-foot lead pipe.

"Mom!" Kathryn cried out. "You're okay!"

Francine's hair was matted with plaster dust. Her torn dress hung from her shoulder and blood dotted her forearm. She eyed Kathryn's crutches. "Better than you are, by the look of it."

"Mother, it's been four years. Don't I even get a hug?"

"Of course, dear. I'm sorry." She waded through the kitchen and embraced her daughter limply. "I've had a bit of a shock." She covered a dusty velvet sofa with a newspaper and helped Kathryn sit down.

"I think we all have," Kathryn said. "They're saying over a hundred people have died, and probably thousands left homeless. It sure was a doozie, huh?" Francine nodded but said nothing. Kathryn gazed around at the mess. "Looks like this place of yours was really quite charming."

"This?" Francine barked out a laugh. "*My* place? Oh, good grief no. You don't want to see my place. I only use this as my mailing address after my mail started to get stolen last year. No, no, no, it's my boss who lives here. He's in New York on a buying trip. He's going to have an ever-loving fit when he sees this wreck. Wait. What are you doing here? How did you find me?"

"I kept expecting you to write to me, or call me at the Garden, and tell me where you were. But you never did, so I hired a private eye. It took him a while, but he tracked you to this address."

Kathryn paused to let her mother explain herself, but Francine said nothing. Instead, she just sat on the edge of the sofa looking a little disheveled and dazed. "So," Kathryn said, "this is your boss' place, then? You do have a job?"

Francine's face darkened. "If you call working like a slave in a sweatshop a job. I work twelve hour days, six days a week, making uniforms in a warehouse down by the docks. I freeze in the winter and bake in the summer for a measly ninety-five cents an hour."

Kathryn maintained her smile. Still with the usual dramatics, she thought. Any boss who gave his slave the keys when he was out of town couldn't be Ivan the Terrible of Long Beach. She felt a speech well up inside her like lava. She tried her best to squelch it, but it blurted out anyway. "Mother! How could you do that to me?"

Francine scowled. "Do what?"

"You moved away and didn't tell me."

Her mother's eyes hardened. "May I remind you, missie, that you did exactly the same thing to me?"

Kathryn glowered at her mother. "That's not the same thing, and you know it."

"I most certainly do not."

"You do, too! We stood there yelling at each other for half an hour and then you watched me pack my crummy little suitcase and march out the front door."

"I didn't know where you were marching to."

"But you knew I was leaving the apartment!"

"Yes, and you knew you were throwing me out of your villa."

"I was doing no such thing. That stock market story of yours was ridiculous. Did you really expect me to believe—"

Her mother cut her off. "So, I drew the obvious conclusion that you no longer wanted me around, and I took the best job I could find. I figured that if you cared, you'd come find me."

"Of course I wanted you in my life. I just didn't want you running it anymore. I never wanted to be an actress. I never wanted any of that—you did. You wanted me to be an actress because when you tried it for yourself, you failed."

Kathryn couldn't believe that she finally said out loud what she wanted to say ever since her twelfth birthday, when Francine announced that Kathryn was to become an actress. They'd lived in Los Angeles for five years, and Kathryn had spent her childhood watching her mother doll herself up for auditions in the morning and trudge home in the afternoon, heavy with rejection. Even at twelve, Kathryn couldn't understand why her mother would want to push her own daughter through that sort of endless loop of rejection. What a shame it took a four-year separation and an earthquake for it to come out, but it was out now and there was no way to unsay it.

The air in the crumbling bungalow turned cold as Francine absorbed her daughter's anger in silence. Kathryn studied her mother for the first time. The last four years hadn't been kind to her. Her cheeks had lines that hadn't been there before and her knuckles were starting to swell, but Kathryn didn't feel the triumph she'd expected. Gwendolyn was right; this was still her mother.

"Well, then," Kathryn softened, "how did your own place survive, Mother?"

Francine let out a *puh!* "This is Versailles compared with my dump. It collapsed like a house of cards on a sand bank in a wind storm."

"Are you saying you have nowhere to live now?"

"I can stay here until my boss gets back. Then I'll be out on the street. Again." Francine shook plaster dust from her hair and tried to pat it back into a fraying chignon. "Maybe I'll pitch a tent on the beach. Bet I won't be the only one."

Kathryn took a deep breath. She knew what she had to do, even if it was going to end in kitchen knives at ten paces. "Mother," she said, "I want you to come live with me."

CHAPTER 32

Everyone at the Garden of Allah always made the biggest fuss over Dorothy Parker — Kathryn and Marcus included — but Gwendolyn had never understood why. She'd read enough of Dorothy's stories to know they were sharp and witty and droll, but reading bleak tales about bored New York socialites and suicidal shop girls wasn't Gwendolyn's idea of an afternoon well spent, no matter how many critics applauded.

When Gwendolyn returned to the booze table with one last load of ice, she found Dorothy frowning at the bottles that were lined up like sacrificial virgins. Gwendolyn imagined that this was the happiest day in over a decade for a lush like her. When the morning papers had announced Utah's ratification of the 21st Amendment, putting an end to America's dry spell, word spread around the Garden that 'National Prohibition Repeal Day' had been unofficially declared and a party to put all Garden parties to shame was started. So why was Dorothy so glum?

Gwendolyn dumped the ice into the aluminum tub. "Something wrong?

Dorothy shifted her graying dachshund from her left arm to her right, rolled her large, nutmeg brown eyes, and sighed. "We've waited thirteen years for those clods in Washington to come to their senses, and now that they have, I don't know if plowing through this stuff will be half as much fun." She grunted. "I feel like someone's invited my parents to the party."

By the time Gwendolyn had hauled the fourth bag of ice in from Schwab's drugstore, she regretted volunteering. Ever since the earthquake, her wrists ached when her hands were cold. She rubbed them to warm them up.

"So what's your first legal drink going to be?" Dorothy asked.

Parker was known for drenching herself in a perfume called Chypre by Coty but Gwendolyn had never been close enough to the woman to know if she truly wore it that strongly. It hovered about her like a low-flying cloud scented so overpoweringly that Gwendolyn had to take a step back. "I haven't decided if I'll be partaking yet tonight."

Dorothy groaned. "Don't tell me you're a teetotaler. I simply can't abide people like that."

"I spent my childhood looking after my mother while she drank herself to death." It was the first time Gwendolyn had said those words out loud to anyone but Marcus or Kathryn.

Dorothy sighed. "Drinking yourself to death doesn't sound like such a bad way to go, considering the options."

Gwendolyn looked at the writer's bracelets, large orange beads that Kathryn said she wore to hide her scars. "It's a slow, slow death," she replied.

"So it's not the option for a girl in a hurry." Dorothy still hadn't taken her eyes off the bottles.

The last nine months had been difficult for Gwendolyn. The earthquake had left deep cuts on her legs and arms and bruised her from collarbone to feet, but the wound that Monty opened with his revelation was slower to mend.

About a month after the quake she'd been frying eggs when it occurred to her that she'd always resented her mother for choosing booze over her children. Mama was always too hungover to cook breakfast, and too drunk to cook dinner.

Gwendolyn's eggs burned while she grappled with the fresh understanding that she had come to see Mama's bottles of gin as the enemy when all along her daddy was the villain. He'd whored around and died an awful death before Gwendolyn formed any memories of him. All this time, she'd seen herself and Monty as victims of her mother's weakness when really, they were all victims of Daddy's.

Gwendolyn had avoided liquor because she was afraid she might turn into Mama, and while liquor was illegal, she didn't have to think about it. But now everything had changed. Maybe it was time to give it a go.

Everyone who arrived added a bottle to the "legal table." Soon it was laden with every spirit the stores could now sell. Gwendolyn was watching Dorothy Parker make martinis like she was pouring rainbows into pots of gold when she felt Marcus and Kathryn by her side.

"I declare I feel like a beggar at the feast!" Gwendolyn exclaimed.

"You know the rule," Kathryn said. The afternoon edition of the *L.A. Times* had declared that everyone's first drink on National Repeal Day must be virgin out of respect for the Great Experiment. Gwendolyn smiled at the irony. She was finally ready for her first drink, and it had to be boozeless; she poured them each a seltzer water.

"Does anyone know who that is?" Marcus nodded toward a burly man in black pants and a dark green shirt on the far side of the garden. Gwendolyn and Kathryn looked, and Kathryn swung back around so fast that strands of hair stuck in her lipstick. "Ohmygod! That's Roy." She looked at Gwendolyn.

"Long Beach Roy?"

Kathryn nodded like a frantic chipmunk.

"Who's Long Beach Roy?" Marcus asked.

Kathryn pulled her hair out of her lipstick. "How do I look?" she asked Gwendolyn.

"Just peachy," Gwendolyn said. Kathryn was wearing Gwendolyn's latest rent contribution: a cranberry red linen dress with dainty snowflakes she'd chosen for Kathryn's coloring.

"Who is Long Beach Roy?" Marcus asked again.

"Why do you think he's here?" Gwendolyn asked.

"I never replied to that card he sent me."

"I thought you liked him."

"I did. I do! But when he drove me and Mother home, I saw a stripe of white skin on his ring finger."

"Who is this guy?" Marcus asked.

"No!" Gwendolyn gasped.

"There had to be *something* wrong with him."

"Whoever he is," Marcus said, "he's coming over." Gwendolyn and Marcus discreetly turned their backs as Roy approached the cocktail table.

"Hello, Kathryn," he said.

Gwendolyn glanced down and there it was: a ribbon of pale skin on his wedding finger. He'd had all summer for his tan to even out. What a shame, Gwendolyn thought. He looks like one of those outdoorsy types who can light a fire and fix a radiator and shoot a deer, all at the same time if the situation called for it.

"Roy!" Kathryn exclaimed, perhaps a little too brightly. "What on earth are you doing all the way up this end of town?"

"I was making a delivery at Vendome Café and it occurred to me that I was right near the Garden of Allah."

"The Vendome?" Kathryn asked. "Billy Wilkerson's place? Do you know him?"

He nodded. "Friend of a friend. Have I walked into the middle of a party?"

"Only the biggest party of the century!" Kathryn laughed. Roy had missed the news, but he had a little something to contribute, if Kathryn would help him get it out of the truck.

"Wow," Marcus said. "Lucky girl. I mean, he seems like a nice guy." Marcus was almost as smitten with Roy's sweet, rugged face as Kathryn was.

"A nice *married* guy," Gwendolyn said. "Didn't you notice his ring finger?"

"What about it?" But Marcus didn't hear Gwendolyn's answer. He had spotted a tall, sandy-haired guy who had just joined the party. He was well over six feet, lean with expansive shoulders, and endowed with a smile as wide as the Pacific. "It seems they're crawling out of the woodwork tonight," Marcus said. "Do you know who this one is?"

"Hellman here can answer that question." From the cloud of Chypres, Gwendolyn knew Dorothy was back. She had returned for a refill with a mannish woman who had lived at the Garden since her last divorce. The two looked like they could mow down a hoard of Vandals without stopping to draw breath.

"You all know Lily Hellman, don't you?" Dorothy said vaguely.

"That's a new boy in town," Lillian said. Dorothy grabbed the scotch like it was a life preserver and filled two large tumblers.

Hmmm, Gwendolyn thought. Scotch whiskey seems to be awfully popular. It sounds so terribly grown up and sophisticated. Maybe I'll start with that.

"I'm seeing a life in front of the camera for that boy. Aren't you, Dotty?" Lillian said. "Who cares if he can act or not? With some people, it really doesn't matter."

"Do you know his name?" Gwendolyn asked.

"Earl O'Flynn, I think. Something Irish, at any rate. He won't leave this party alone, that's for goddamned sure. Some men are just born to be the flame, don't you find?" The writers quivered off toward a table, shoulder to shoulder and giggling like a pair of teenaged gargoyles.

"He's very handsome," Gwendolyn admitted, though her eyes were on the bottle of scotch. Do people put ice in their whiskey? I should have been paying more attention all this time.

She could feel Marcus' eyes on her as she puzzled over the bar. "I think you're a flame, Gwennie," he said.

"I'm what?" she asked. Ice, she decided. Definitely ice. Dorothy probably didn't use any because it took up too much space in the glass.

"I think you're a flame, and the rest of us are your moths."

"Marcus!" she exclaimed, looking into his earnest face. His eyes were a little "boozeshot"–a word one of the Garden's writers invented to describe how someone looked when they started drinking early. "Marcus, darling, what a terribly sweet thing to say!"

"Why none of the studios have fallen for you yet is beyond me."

"What a friend you are." Gwendolyn planted a kiss on his cheek.

"What's your poison?" he asked.

"Scotch whiskey," Gwendolyn replied, feeling very sophisticated. "On the rocks please, Mr. Bartender."

Marcus did a double take. "Scotch? Really? I'd have taken you for a brandy stinger kind of girl. All that crème de menthe and such."

As he poured them both a scotch, she scanned the crowd for that Earl O'Flynn fellow. It was always easy to spot the stars. There was something magnetic about the big ones that set them apart: Douglas Fairbanks, Mae West, Gary Cooper. But it was more than good looks. Bela Lugosi was no great looker, but when he came in to the Cocoanut Grove one night, he stopped bystanders in their tracks. Even from across the pool, Gwendolyn could sense that Earl O'Flynn had it.

Gwendolyn clinked her glass against Marcus' and took a sip, letting it swirl around her tongue for a moment before she swallowed. Say, she thought, this stuff isn't half bad.

"Is it okay?" Marcus asked.

"It tastes better when it's legal." She took another sip and soon began to feel slightly blurry at the edges. When her glass was half empty, she drained the rest in one delicious swallow. She was delighted. She marveled at all the time she'd lost thinking she was going to turn into her mama. She could have been drinking scotch for years!

"I do believe I shall have another," she announced. She grabbed the bottle and splashed a generous slug into her tumbler. When she looked up, Marcus was clear across the yard, talking with Dorothy and Lillian and a portly guy Gwendolyn almost recognized. Some sort of director . . . ?

"Do you need some help there?"

Earl O'Flynn was even more attractive up close than he was at a hundred paces, which wasn't usually the case. Her time at the Cocoanut Grove had also taught her that many of the some famous faces owed much to expert make-up and flattering lighting. But this man's aura didn't dim the closer he got; if anything, it expanded until you were choking on it, like Dorothy Parker's perfume.

"I do require some assistance," Gwendolyn said, although it came out more like 'sistince.' She handed him the bottle and he freshened her drink. "My name's Gwendolyn," she slurred. "Gwendolyn Brick, but I don't like it very much. I'm thinking of changing it to Gwendolyn Lawrence. What do you think?"

"I think Gwendolyn is the prettiest name I've heard all year." She couldn't place his accent, but she got the impression that he was cultured and refined, but not stage actory like Leslie Howard.

"You're Earl, aren't you? Earl O'Flynn." Gwendolyn felt glamorous, like an international woman of mystery who held all the answers to all the questions this loverboy could ask.

He did a brief double take. "Close," he said. "The name is Errol Flynn. I'm new in town; hardly met anyone yet. But surely I'd remember meeting you."

She heard herself laugh–almost as though she were watching from a distance–and tell him that he was a smooth one. He chuckled and said he wasn't sure about that.

Oh my goodness, what a rakish smile he has, Gwendolyn thought. She saw him blink like he was surprised. Did I say that out loud? Who cares? I'm a flame. Isn't that what Marcus said? I'm a flame and this Errol Flynn is my moth.

"What did you just say?" Errol asked with a smile. "That I'm a moth?"

"A mo . . . a mo . . ." Gwendolyn stammered and stared, trying to cover her faux pas. She looked down at his patent leather shoes and knew they must have cost a bundle. Then she threw up on them.

CHAPTER 33

It wasn't far from the Garden of Allah to the Sunset Strip, but in her new three-inch patent leather pumps, Kathryn felt like she was walking to Cincinnati. She couldn't go wrong in Gwendolyn's tight violet-black silk and miles of tulle tarting up a deep, wide neckline. Her cleavage had never seen this much moonlight. She wasn't comfortable, but she was fetching, and that's what mattered.

Billy Wilkerson was opening yet another place on the Sunset Strip. The Vendome Café's success had inspired him to venture into nightclubs, and tonight was the Trocadero's debut. She'd been telling herself for months that she needed a new dream; the old one didn't seem to want her. But when she opened Tallulah's invitation, her heart beat hard at the thought of speaking with Wilkerson again. Give it one last shot, she told herself. She slipped it into her purse and never mentioned it to her boss.

A rowdy group of press photographers stood out front of the Trocadero, a long, red-roofed building whose fresh, white paint gleamed in the streetlamps. She approached the door as William Powell and Jean Harlow stepped out of a limousine. Jean's platinum curls caught the flare of the flashbulbs and Powell raised his hand, calling, "Fred! Fred! Wait up!"

Kathryn turned to see Fred Astaire and his wife at the door. *Flying Down to Rio* had been a smash hit, and RKO was talking about giving Fred and Ginger their own film. Ginger often hung around the Garden of Allah, playing tennis with anyone who was game. Kathryn thought herself a halfway decent player until she'd faced Ginger Rogers on the court. Kathryn hoped like hell she'd see her inside; she could do with a friendly face tonight.

Kathryn waited until the Astaires walked in with Powell and Harlow before she approached the doorman and waved her invitation as nonchalantly as possible. She went to pass right by him but he put out his hand. "Your invitation, please." She handed it over.

"You're not Tallulah Bankhead," he growled.

Kathryn dropped her voice into Tallulah's throaty register. "I'm her sister, Evelyn," she told him. Tallulah did have a sister named Evelyn, but Kathryn had no idea if Evelyn was older, younger, or even still alive, so she figured that the bouncer wouldn't know either.

"I've got strict instructions from the boss. The name on the invite has to match the person holding it. Otherwise, no deal."

"But my sister—"

"I don't care if you're Eleanor Roosevelt's sister. You're not Tallulah Bankhead."

Kathryn snatched the invitation out of the bouncer's hand and marched back down the red carpet. She knew she couldn't just stand there like some store window dummy, so she started down the hill, looking for another way in. She stopped at a wooden door painted blood red. Roy had told her about this; the bootleg delivery boys called it the Blood Door.

Kathryn tried the handle—it was unlocked. She walked right into the Trocadero's kitchen. A waiter in a monkey suit called out, "No, ma'am, you're supposed to use the front door, around the corner on Sunset."

"Have you ever worn three-inch heels?" Kathryn asked him.

He smiled. "No, ma'am, I never have."

She pointed her shiny shoe his way. "I've walked up that hill twice now. Once when I realized I forgot my invitation—" she waved the blank side of her invitation at him, "and again when I—well, I won't bore you. The last thing I want to have to do is climb that hill a third time in these heels. Would it be such a terrible thing if I came in the back way?"

The kid cocked his head, thinking, then grinned and pointed to a swinging door. It opened onto a long corridor which led out onto the stage where a band was setting up behind a royal blue curtain. Dick Powell was singing an impromptu version of "You're Getting to Be a Habit with Me" when she appeared beside him. He shot her a *where-did-you-come-from* double take. She blew him a kiss for an answer and climbed down from the stage with as much ladylike daintiness as she could manage in a too-tight dress and too-high heels.

Wilkerson was standing at a long, black-tiled bar, watching Ginger Rogers make a scooping motion with her right hand. This is perfect, Kathryn thought, she's giving him a tennis lesson. They didn't see Kathryn until she was practically close enough to poke her eye out with his imaginary racquet. Ginger's bright blue eyes lit up. "Kathryn!" she exclaimed, throwing her arms out in welcome. "What a gorgeous ensemble! Bill, this is Kathryn Massey."

Wilkerson extended his hand. He clearly had no memory of their last encounter. "We met a few years ago," Kathryn prompted him. "Remember when the *Graf Zeppelin* landed at Mine's Field?"

"You were there?"

"We were chatting when they missed the anchoring mast and the zeppelin swung around over the crowd and everybody started to scatter."

"Excuse my French, but I nearly pissed my pants when that happened. I thought to myself, There's two million tons of hydrogen right above me, and I'm dying for a cigarette. This is not a place I want to be anymore."

It didn't take Kathryn long to realize that chatting with Billy Wilkerson was like scanning the headlines from a newspaper. The three of them chitchatted through a rapid progression of topics: Howard Hughes' thirty-six-hour transcontinental air service, Fox's new star Shirley Temple, and Babe Ruth's recent seven hundredth home run.

Kathryn was still looking for a break where she could insert a reasonably intelligent question when Fred Astaire came up and tweaked Ginger's elbow. She hugged him, then introduced Wilkerson and Kathryn.

"I'm sorry, my dear," Fred apologized, "but everybody is asking us to do a number."

Ginger looked pained. "In these shoes?" She looked down; they were even higher than Kathryn's.

"The Carioca, no less." It was the big dance number in *Flying Down to Rio* that everyone had either loved or hated because they danced with their foreheads pressed together. The scandal had only fanned the flames of fame.

Ginger asked, "I don't suppose the band doesn't know it?" Fred shook his head. "I'll be lucky not to break an ankle in these things. Kathryn, hold my handbag?"

Kathryn watched as Fred and Ginger made their way to the dance floor amid walloping applause. "Miss Rogers," Fred announced, "would like you to know that she'll be passing the hat around to pay for the hospital bill, should she break an ankle tonight."

The band struck the opening chords and the dancers spun into action.

Kathryn spotted her opening. She leaned toward Wilkerson, her eyes still on the dancers. "I've been reading your editorials, and I have to say that I can't agree more about the Catholic Legion of Decency." Hollywood had been under siege recently, censored heavily by the Hays office and prissy busybodies fighting for what they proclaimed to be the purification of cinema. Wilkerson was a vocal opponent. "They're going to ruin film if they get their way."

But she'd lost her chance. Sam Goldwyn had hijacked him. Her eyes followed them across the room, where they greeted a tall guy with broad shoulders and a tennis tan, who had two yes men in tow. They slid around a booth and Wilkerson was locked in. Damn and double damn.

Kathryn hovered for hours hoping for another chance at Wilkerson, but it never came. He was the man of the moment and always surrounded. By eleven o'clock she was tired and her feet were killing her. She squeezed around the curtain at the side of the stage and made her way through the kitchen toward the blood door.

Her hand was on the doorknob when she saw an open door into an office opposite the kitchen. The light was on and she could see an enormous desk, on which a brass nameplate mounted on a block of mahogany read BILLY WILKERSON. A briefcase was open next to it.

Kathryn opened her handbag and pulled out the papers pressed against the middle pocket. She hurried into the office and tried the latches to Wilkerson's briefcase. They flipped open with a click. She unfolded her papers and re-read the headline of her article.

Revolution in Hollywood: Drive-In Movies and How They Will Change America's Movie-Night Rituals.

She smoothed the crease flat and picked up Mr. Wilkerson's chrome-barreled pen. Next to her name and address at the Garden of Allah, she added *Graf Zeppelin.*

CHAPTER 34

Marcus had just changed into street clothes when his boss called out, "Adler! I've got a telegram for you." Marcus let out a groan. Technically, he wasn't off duty until he had left the Western Union building. "Adler!" the boss called out again. "I can see your shadow. Get in here."

Marcus grabbed his hat, hoping it would say "I was just out the door" for him. He poked his head around the doorway. The boss pushed an envelope toward him.

"Aw, come on, boss. I know what the rule is, but I've got my hat on."

Marcus' boss snorted and smiled. "I didn't mean I've got a telegram for you to deliver. I meant I've got a telegram *for you.*"

Marcus murmured a thank you and retreated to the locker room with his telegram.

* * *

He was well into his first bourbon when he heard Kathryn's voice through his door. "Are you there? It's me. I got your note and came straight over!"

He yanked open the door and thrust his telegram in her face. "I got a telegram!"

"Me too!" she told him.

He let her in and poured her a bourbon. "Ladies first," he said.

She held up her crumpled telegram. "From Billy Wilkerson! He finally got around to reading my article on drive-in movies."

"And?"

"And he's asked me to call his secretary to make an appointment!"

Marcus grabbed his friend by the shoulders and pulled her into a hug. "Kathryn, that's just swell! I couldn't be happier for you."

"Thank you! Damn well took long enough, huh? But what about you? Who's your telegram from?"

Marcus pulled it out of his pocket and read it to her.

RECEIVED YOUR STORY SUBWAY PEOPLE STOP

OFFERING SIXTY-FIVE DOLLARS FOR PUBLICATION STOP

PLEASE SEND ACCEPTANCE OF OFFER BY RETURN TELEGRAM STOP

SIGNED SUBMISSIONS EDITOR SATURDAY EVENING POST

She squealed and raised her drink. "Here's to changing fortunes!" They clinked glasses. "Takes the sting out of losing to Hugo, huh?"

"A little," Marcus admitted. That business about the MGM competition still rankled Marcus, but he tried not to feel jealous. He knew his submission would have been better if he'd had more notice but, try as he might, he couldn't hold Hugo completely to blame. He asked himself for the twentieth time, How did you not know that MGM was holding a nationwide screenplay competition? What a numbskull. Maybe that's what Father had said: *And don't come home until you've stopped being such a numbskull.* But there wasn't much he could do about it, and he was pleased for Hugo. At least Bob Benchley was right when he told Marcus one night. "Marcus my boy, I assure you, there's nothing like that thrill which goes down your spine when you receive word that your first story has been accepted for publication." And he was right. This was a moment to savor.

Kathryn asked, "So, 'Subway People.' Which one is that?"

"The one I wrote after I got trapped under Fifth Street."

Kathryn recoiled. "You were trapped under Fifth Street? Downtown? When did *that* happen?"

Marcus looked at his feet, and wished he could eat his words. "The day of the Long Beach earthquake. I was in the Subway Terminal when it hit."

"The Subway Terminal? But don't those trains go out to Pasadena?"

This is getting worse. Think! *Think!* "I had a special-delivery telegram, and I couldn't very well ride my bicycle all the way to Pasadena."

"But couldn't they just re-route it over to the Pasadena office?"

"There was some nutty reason or other. I can't remember." He was getting short of breath. "So I was in the terminal waiting for the train to Pasadena when the earthquake hit. When it finally stopped and the dust started to settle, we found that the doors to the street were blocked, so I went searching for another route. I kept trying doors until I found one that wasn't locked, and it opened onto this rabbit warren of corridors and hidden passages. Dozens of them, in all directions. Later I got to thinking there could be a whole community of people living under the city, and none of us would know they were there. That was my starting point. I thought it was a pretty good idea."

"Apparently, so does the *Saturday Evening Post*."

"To the *Post* and the *Hollywood Reporter*!" he toasted. They clinked their second glasses. The raw edge of the cheap bourbon seemed to have blunted a little.

Kathryn refilled her glass and sat back on his sofa with a thud. "How well do you know Ramon Novarro?" She rubbed a finger around the rim of her glass and arranged her face into a nonchalant smile, but her eyes were unblinking.

Marcus felt his jaw drop and he tried to cover it up by licking his lips. "What makes you think I know him at all?"

"I'm pretty sure I saw you playing blackjack with him on the *Montfalcone*."

That night on the *Montfalcone* was years ago. Marcus didn't like this line of questioning. As far as he could figure, his tendencies belonged behind the midnight bushes of Pershing Square and Griffith Park. Conversations like this led to forced confessions, and confessions like that led to personal rejection, social ostracizing, jail sentences and career death. The last thing he wanted to be was one of those guys whose lives dried up when the rumor mill started about unthinkable bedroom activities. Especially now that he'd just got started. Losing Nazimova was bad enough; he doubted that he could bear to lose Kathryn too. If that happened, he'd have to move out of the Garden of Allah. Where would he go? He pushed a harsh swallow down his throat to calm the panic starting to rise up from somewhere south of his stomach. "I think I was playing blackjack *next* to him, if that's what you mean."

Kathryn sighed. "I don't know what I mean." She drained the last of her booze. They sat in silence for a few moments. Just as Marcus felt his panic subside, Kathryn sat forward again. "It was something he said to me when we were doing the tango at the threes party."

Marcus forced out an "Oh?"

"He asked me if you were my boyfriend. I told him no, you weren't. Then he asked me if you were anyone's boyfriend. And I said, 'No, not to my knowledge.'"

Marcus nodded, but decided that until he knew where Kathryn was going with all this, the best option to say was nothing.

"He's queer, y' know." Her words were starting to slur, but not her gaze.

Marcus stared down into his glass. After the earthquake, Marcus and Ramon scrambled over broken concrete, wrenched girders and shattered glass, and joined the bewildered commuters wondering how they were going to get home. Marcus was still in a daze when Ramon said, "Goodbye and good luck," and disappeared into the crowd. Marcus hadn't heard from him since.

For a year, Marcus had told himself Ramon disappeared because he'd caught his prey; his appetite was sated, and there was nothing else between them. He'd learned to live with the yearning, most of the time, but Kathryn's questions cleaved him down the middle. He let his head flop back onto his headboard and ran through a host of topics to reroute the conversation.

He said, "You should ask Gwendolyn to make you something new for your interview. Something flattering. Green looks good on you. But it needs to be businesslike. Maybe your mother's got something, now that she's practically running the Marmont."

The months Francine had spent in Kathryn and Gwendolyn's villa hadn't been the gunfight at the O.K. Corral Kathryn had predicted. She even admitted that her mother had been a surprisingly considerate houseguest who pitched in with the cooking and cleaning. Apparently there had been tiffs and tenseness, but nothing they couldn't get past, and it turned out that Francine played a hell of a game of cribbage.

Then one day, Robert Benchley mentioned that he knew the bartender at the Chateau Marmont Hotel who'd told him they were looking for a telephone operator; Kathryn suggested to her mother that she apply. In exchange for working twelve hour shifts, the management gave her a tiny bungalow out the back to live in at a vastly reduced rate.

Francine moved out the next day and Kathryn almost came close to missing her. The hotel was just a little further up Sunset Boulevard from the Garden of Allah so everything worked out wonderfully well. It was nice to see Kathryn getting along so well with her mom. He was a little envious of it, too.

"Marcus, honey," Kathryn blurted out, "I only wanted you to know that I really don't care—"

His ruse hadn't worked, damnit. "I thought this was going to be a happy day," he shot back. Hot shame stung his cheeks.

Kathryn got up and grabbed his glass. "Tell me more about your story." She went to his dresser and refreshed their drinks.

Words charged up his throat and he didn't have it in him to hold them down. "I haven't seen him since the earthquake." The words sounded like they came out of someone else's mouth. The vein in his right temple pounded like a tom-tom.

Kathryn went still. "No?" She didn't turn around.

"We climbed over the rubble and out of the subway and he just took off. I don't even know how to contact him."

The last words caught in his throat like thistles. A year's worth of fat, blubbery tears started down his cheeks. Kathryn wrapped her arms around him and he pressed his head into the nape of her neck. Her perfume made him think of something long and sleek, like calla lilies. She made little tsking noises like he used to make when his baby sister, Doris, fell and scraped her knees. The hurt and disappointment flowed out of him from a well deeper than he'd suspected. "I didn't . . . I just wanted . . ."

Kathryn patted his back and he could feel her nodding gently. "I understand," she told him. "Really I do. I know what it's like to be in love and still feel alone."

Marcus pulled his head up and looked at her through tears that distorted her face. "You what?"

"Secret for secret?" she asked. Marcus nodded. "I've been sleeping with a married man for the past two years."

"You haven't!" Marcus straightened up, scandalized and amazed.

"Remember Roy?"

It took a moment, then Marcus exclaimed, "Mr. Long Beach?"

She nodded like a naughty little school girl. It was a look that rather suited her.

"Really? Two years? A married man?"

"I know, *I know*," she sighed. "It's so tacky, isn't it? I can barely believe I'm doing it. But he's such a good man. Honest, he is. A good man caught in a bad situation."

"A situation called 'married.'"

"He says they don't get along at all; barely even talk."

"Are there kids?"

"No."

"So why not get a divorce?"

"Apparently, she's a religious nut; one of those *marriage is forever and ever, regardless* types. Won't even agree to a separation." She attempted a light-hearted shrug that Marcus didn't believe. "If his wife doesn't want him, then I do."

"As long as you know what you're doing." Marcus said.

"Who the hell said I know what I'm doing?" Kathryn looked at him, her chocolate brown eyes suddenly molten.

Her words caught in her throat the same way Marcus' had in his. He pulled her into a hug just as her tears started to soak her cheeks. She wrapped her arms around his back and squeezed him hard.

"Oh, we're a fine pair, aren't we?" she laughed throatily. "You can't get close to yours, and I can't keep away from mine."

They stayed in the hug for a long, wet minute until she mumbled something about needing to clear her nose. As she fished into her handbag, Marcus asked, "Two years, huh? You sly little fox, you. So, where do you meet up? Seedy little out-of-the-way hotels?"

"Please, Marcus, this affair is sordid, but it's not *that* sordid. We meet here, mainly. Gwennie doesn't get home from work until two or three in the morning, so the place is mine. Ours." She sighed. "Aside from the fact that he's married, this whole thing isn't very sordid at all. He's more of a romantic than I am, and I've never had anyone who shows the sort of affection for me that he shows. Oh, Marcus! The way he kisses me! I melt, every time!"

"I know how that feels," Marcus admitted. "Unfortunately, that's all I know."

"So you and Ramon have never, you know, gone all the way?"

Marcus offered Kathryn a smile. "At least one of us is getting satisfaction." He took her hand and squeezed it. "I'm happy for you. That is to say, I'd be happier if he wasn't married."

"We'd all be happier," Kathryn said. "But I want you to know that it's been killing me that I haven't been able to share any of this with you."

"Does anyone else know?"

"Gwennie does," Kathryn admitted, "but she doesn't pry."

"So, why tell me now?"

Kathryn blew her nose and let out a deep sigh. "I spent the first year telling myself I didn't care he was married. Then I spent the second year telling myself that I didn't love him. Not really, really *love* him."

"And then?"

"And then recently he surprised me with flowers and chocolates *and* perfume. When I asked him what the occasion was, he said, 'Our second anniversary.' That's when I realized, Oh, sweet Jesus, I love him. I truly, truly love him and there's nothing I can do about it. Married or not, he's in my life and so I wanted you to know. You're the last person on earth I want to keep secrets from. And I've been wanting to ask you about Ramon since that night he and I tangoed. When he asked about you, I thought about the *Montfalcone* and, I dunno, two plus two seemed to be adding up to four. Now seemed as good a time as any." She hesitated a moment, playing with her handkerchief. "You don't think any less of me, do you? Sleeping with a married man, and all?"

Marcus stared at his best friend, shocked that she would even think that. "Of course not. Are you crazy? Don't forget, I'm the homosexual around here. I have it on good authority that we don't get to have marriages or relationships or love, so I'm going to have to live vicariously through you. The only way I'll think less of you is if you neglect to tell me all the details, all the time. Okay?"

They looked at each other for a moment, and both burst out laughing. Marcus felt like a matching pair of cannon balls had been lifted off his shoulders. That was the first time I've ever said the word 'homosexual' out loud, he thought. Who'd have ever guessed it could feel so freeing?

Kathryn sniffed at the air. "Do you smell anchovies? I've been smelling them all the time. Somebody must be cooking with them around here. It gives me such a craving for them. Do you have any?"

She got up from the bed and opened the cupboard next to the dresser where he kept his crackers and nuts. The edge of the cupboard door clipped Nazimova's toy rocking horse. It wobbled back and forth a few times before it reached the edge of the dresser and fell to the floor with a crunch.

"Oh, Marcus!" Kathryn cried. "I'm so, so sorry!"

Marcus' heart dropped. It was bad enough that Nazimova had walked out of his life without a word, leaving behind a hole in his life the size of the Hollywoodland sign, but now the one thing he had of hers was broken. He wanted to tell Kathryn it was okay but he couldn't get the words out.

He picked up the horse and pinched the wooden tail with his thumb and index finger. When he tried to push it back to its upright position, it resisted, then he felt it move back into place with a distinct click. Suddenly the horse split into halves, one in each hand.

"Well, would you look at that? It's hollow!" Kathryn said.

Inside the right half of the wooden toy horse, someone had taped a key. He pulled it out and turned it over. It was an old iron skeleton key, thick and heavy, with a thin purple ribbon tied to the end. He and Kathryn looked at each other in amazement. "What do you think it's for?" he asked.

Kathryn took the key and weighed it in her hand. "Brophy has one of these in his office."

* * *

The Garden of Allah's manager held the key up to his own. "No," he said. "It's not mine. But it's a safe key, all right. Perhaps it fits the one in Alla's old bedroom."

"She had a safe in her villa?" Kathryn asked.

"No, no, in her original bedroom here in the main house. She was rich back then. She needed someplace to stash her jewels. We can check, but if we find anything, it still belongs to her."

"Of course. And if there is, I'd like to return it to her."

Madame Nazimova's bedroom was on the top floor of the house that she sold for a hotel. The Royal Suite was rarely rented out; anyone who could afford it preferred one of the villas scattered around the gardens. They were sunny and convivial, more private and closer to the Garden's never-ending party.

The sprawling bedroom was shrouded in darkness. Brophy went to a bookshelf against the north wall and pulled on one corner to reveal a safe built into the brickwork. It was about the size of a small portrait, painted gray with a keyhole on the left and a handle at its center.

"May I?" Marcus said, and took the key from Brophy. He inserted it into the slot. *Let this key work. Let me find her.*

He turned the key and heard the tumblers inside the steel door drop as the key made its clockwise revolution. He brought it back home and pushed the handle down. There was a soft clack and the spring-loaded door opened toward Marcus.

Kathryn peered over his shoulder. "There's something there."

Marcus pulled a small book out of the safe and held it in the sunlight that seeped between the heavy drapes. The book was covered in black felt and worn around the edges, maybe a hundred pages long. He opened it and started to flick through pages covered with deliberate, delicate, slanted handwriting in green ink.

"They're poems," Marcus said. Each one was a page or two long, and dated in the early twenties. "Are they Madame's?"

"No," Brophy said. "I'd know her handwriting anywhere. It's big and broad with dramatic loops and what-have-you. This is somebody else's."

Marcus turned to the front page. In the same handwriting it said, *A Book of Poems for Madame Nazimova*. He looked at Brophy. "Who is Rodolfo Alfonzo Guglielmi?"

CHAPTER 35

The clock on the wall behind the doctor's desk sounded like a disapproving headmistress. Tick, tick, tick.

It's okay, Kathryn told herself. Your appointment with Wilkerson isn't until three o'clock—that's more than an hour and his office is only half a dozen blocks away. So stop fidgeting, for crying out loud.

The examination room had been wiped clean with so much hospital-strength antiseptic that Kathryn felt a tad woozy. Would it be so hard if they mixed a little lemon juice in it? The meticulously organized medical supplies made her want to run screaming for the street. She longed to be among the madness of Hollywood Boulevard to pace off these nerves.

The doctor, a middle-aged man as stark as his office, walked in and closed the door with a slow click. He took a seat. "I'm not sure if my news is welcome, Miss Massey, but the rabbit definitely died."

The words hung in the air like wet laundry. It took Kathryn a moment to find her voice. "Are you saying you performed a pregnancy test?"

"It's standard procedure for female patients exhibiting your symptoms. You complained of strong cravings for salty foods, anchovies—"

"I wasn't complaining. I merely mentioned it in passing." Kathryn struggled to control her breathing. She had come in expecting to hear a lecture about blood pressure or roughage. She was not prepared for this. "You must be mistaken. I don't have morning sickness, I haven't gained weight."

"Not all expectant mothers experience morning sickness," he said. "Miss Massey, you are in fact pr—"

Kathryn jumped to her feet. "Even if your suspicions are correct, don't you need a patient's permission to perform a test like that?" She snatched up her handbag and thought about clocking him over the head with it.

"Miss Massey," he said. "We need to talk about prenatal care and nutrition."

Kathryn strode to the door and threw over her shoulder, "No, sir, we do *not*." She ran halfway down the stairs to the lobby, then stopped to steady herself against the cool brick wall. She couldn't be pregnant. That poor rabbit must have died in vain. She hurried out into the street where the din of car horns and construction on Highland Avenue welcomed her.

Half a block away, Max Factor's new makeup studio was a cacophony of jackhammers and truck engines. She headed toward its chain-link perimeter and held on tight until her knees stopped quaking.

Pregnant.

She closed her eyes but the word appeared in ten-foot neon tubes. A baby. She had a baby growing inside of her. No, she told herself, it's not a baby, it's a pregnancy. What in the name of the hot hairy hounds of hell was she going to do?

* * *

The offices of the *Hollywood Reporter* were almost as loud as the Max Factor site outside, but this was a comforting, exciting noise. There was a hum and a throb to it; clattering typewriters, incessant telephones, people yelling out *Hepburn, box office, Paramount, Bride of Frankenstein, DeMille.* It was the kind of din that enfolded Kathryn like a hug from a hundred friends.

The receptionist pointed her toward Wilkerson's office. His secretary's desk was vacant, but the door behind it was open.

"Hello?" she called out.

"Hey," a deep voice from the inner office called out, "What's the name of that god-awful Jeanette MacDonald/Nelson Eddy operetta you made me go see a few months ago? The one about the runaway French princess."

"*Naughty Marietta,*" Kathryn replied, and waited for a response.

Wilkerson filled his doorway, frowning. "Who are you?"

"Kathryn Massey," she replied and offered her hand. He shook it. "We have a three o'clock appointment."

"Oh?"

"You cabled me when you read my article on drive-in movies?"

Wilkerson's eyebrows shot up. "Ah! The *Graf Zeppelin.* Come on in."

Kathryn followed Wilkerson into an expansive, sunny room overlooking Sunset Boulevard. A pair of loveseats faced each other over a low table strewn with magazines and newspapers. A huge bookcase lined the far wall; its dusty contents looked like it had been shelved by Blind Freddie during an earthquake.

Wilkerson led her to an enormous desk, nine feet wide and made of dark, dull wood that badly needed polishing. It was a glorious madhouse of books, papers, magazines, telegrams, pencils, and ink pots. A monkey wrench lay on top of the *Los Angeles Blue Book*, the city's social register. He rounded his monstrous desk and motioned for Kathryn to take a seat. "That article was the damndest thing," he said.

"Thank you . . . I think."

"No, I mean — well, it was good. Very good, in fact. But it appeared in my briefcase halfway across the Atlantic. You weren't sailing on the *Ile de France* last month by any chance, were you?"

"No, sir, I was not, I'm sorry to say."

"So I can't accuse you of breaking into my stateroom and hiding it in my briefcase?

"No," Kathryn replied carefully. "I've never been within a thousand miles of the *Ile de France*."

Wilkerson started to sift through the small mountains on his desk for something. Kathryn let her gaze drift away from him to an oil painting behind him and her breath caught in her throat.

An aristocratic father with a long rifle stood next to a smaller, younger version of himself with a smaller rifle. At their feet was a dead rabbit.

Kathryn felt something crumple inside her. She pressed a hand to her chest. Wilkerson was looking at her expectantly, so she shook herself a little. "I'm sorry," she said, "I was distracted by that painting."

Wilkerson beamed and spun in his chair to face it. "Ah, my Piermont," he said. "Love his work. Have half a dozen now. This one is my favorite, although I suspect my secretary would prefer I burn it. It's called *Child's First Kill*." Wilkerson swung his chair back to her. "A touch gruesome, I know."

"It's very realistic." Kathryn could hardly breathe. She tried not to think of Roy.

"That's why I like it. Writing about Hollywood, it's trying to make something real out of the unreal. That's what I liked about your piece. Everyone's so damned gung-ho about drive-in movies, but you took a stand I wasn't expecting. Drive-ins robbing us of our communal experience. When I saw your address, it made sense."

The painting with the dead rabbit pulled at Kathryn's eyes like a magnet. *Look at me. LOOK AT ME.* Of all things, did it have to be a rabbit hunt? *The rabbit definitely died.*

"Why is that?" Kathryn asked.

"Everyone knows about the Garden of Allah! Talk about your communal experience. Boozy parties day and night. All those people moving to Hollywood and working their way up the ladder, in the meantime they're all running around half-naked because they've convinced themselves nobody will remember what they did before they hit it big."

"That's what people really think about the Garden?"

"Everyone knows it's where you take your current dish for a spicy afternoon."

He made the Garden sound like a flophouse rife with drunken adulterers running around naked every night. The boozy parties were real, yes. And she had spotted more than one or two pairs of whoopee-seeking hedonists scuttling around the hydrangeas after midnight, but it always seemed to be in fun. The Garden of Allah wasn't sleazy or cheap; just open-hearted and open-minded.

"Perhaps you're thinking of the Chateau Marmont," Kathryn said.

Wilkerson shook his head. "The Chateau Marmont is where starlets go to sleep with their directors. The Garden of Allah is where girls who want to be starlets go to sleep with guys who want to be directors."

Then again, Kathryn reflected, I am one of those people sleeping around with someone I'm not married to and look where it's gotten me. What the hell sort of job interview is this, anyway? Is this what people talk about in business meetings?

She decided she'd better say something. "I can't tell if you think it's a good thing or a bad thing that I live at the Garden of Allah."

"Oh, it's a good thing," Wilkerson assured her. "A journalist must protect her sources, and you can't do that without a good poker face. You, my dear, have a very good poker face."

CHAPTER 36

"That's not for George, is it?"

Marcus turned around to find a man dressed all in black. He'd seen a ton of screen vamps dress solely in black — Theda Bara, Pola Negri and the like — but never a man. The guy had a square jaw and was turning gray in a way that Marcus hoped he might someday. He frowned at the potted orchid in Marcus' hands.

"Yes," Marcus replied. "It is."

Marcus didn't know George Cukor well, but he was clearly a man of class and taste. Despite its exorbitant cost, Marcus felt George would appreciate an orchid. His handwritten invitation to Sunday brunch had arrived out of the blue, and Marcus wanted to turn up with something special.

"Bad move," the guy said. "George is ridiculously sensitive to the pollen of all genus Pleurothallis plants. The minute he spots that, he'll have a goddamned fit."

The guy took the plant from Marcus and placed it behind a weeping willow outside Cukor's front gate. "You can pick it up on the way out," he said genially. He stuck his hand out. "I'm Julian Johns."

"Marcus Adler."

"*Suivez-moi*," Johns said, gesturing up the path toward the house. "The first time I came to brunch, I brought two bottles of French champagne. Cost me a bundle, you know, good impression and all that. Oh brother, was I ever wrong!"

"George doesn't like champagne?"

"On the contrary. He considers himself to be quite the authority. He only allows three vintages into the house, and the rest is pig swill, as far as he's concerned. He didn't say a word when I gave it to him; the silence was beyond mortifying. I'd hate to see you make the same mistake."

"I owe you one," Marcus said.

"No, you owe one to the next guy you see trying to bring orchids or the wrong champagne. The truth is, George doesn't expect anyone to bring anything. Except maybe charm, wit, intelligence, culture, perception and any point of view you can back up with a solid argument."

Marcus swallowed hard. "Any other tips?"

Johns thought for a moment. "Yes, I'd avoid praising *Treasure Island* or *Reckless*."

Marcus thought both those movies were fine pieces of work. "Why is that?"

"Victor Fleming. He directed both of them. Let's just say they don't exactly share a table at lunch in the MGM commissary. So unless you want to pick a fight with your host, it's pretty much the only subject you need to avoid."

It had been an exciting time for Marcus. "Subway People" had come out in the *Saturday Evening Post*, generating another Garden party and a great stack of telegrams and letters. He'd hoped to hear from Alla. A congratulatory note, at the very least, would've been welcome; she would know what this meant to him. But nothing like that arrived, which was both disappointing and frustrating.

Sitting in his dresser draw was a notebook filled with poetry written for her by no less than Rudolph Valentino. Who the hell knew his actual name was Rodolfo Alfonzo Guglielmi? A whole book of poetry by Valentino was worth a small fortune–if only he could track her down to tell her.

His disappointment was tempered by a brunch invitation to the home of one of Hollywood's biggest directors. Kathryn had helped him pick out a new suit; even though he couldn't afford it, the dark burgundy was a good complement to his lucky purple tie.

Cukor's house looked like a British oil painting. Its large expanse of deep green lawns and carefully manicured flower beds looked like they'd been lifted whole from a Jane Austen novel. George appeared at the front door, his round wire-rimmed glasses glinting in the sunlight. "Julian Johns! It's going to be in the nineties today! You're going to cook in that black suit."

"And yet, still I wear it," Johns replied. The two men embraced, then Cukor offered Marcus his hand. "It's a pleasure to see you again!" he exclaimed. "Marcus is the author of that wonderful story in the *Saturday Evening Post* I told you about."

Cukor led them through a Spanish-tiled foyer, a long living room papered with yellow chrysanthemums, an oval room lined with dense bookshelves, and an airy conservatory with glass walls. They emerged onto a patio where men mingled in groups of three and four with champagne flutes beside an enormous pool. There wasn't a woman in sight. Cukor clapped his hands together. "Everybody!" he exclaimed, "I want you to meet Mr. Marcus Adler. Marcus, this is . . ." he made a grand sweep of the crowd. "Everybody!"

Compared to the laissez-faire bunch at the Garden of Allah, this was a well-dressed coterie, color-coordinated in summer pastels—lilac, sky blue, pink, and lots of cream. Scattered here and there were young men in sailor suit costumes. Marcus suddenly felt overdressed in his dark suit. He needed a drink.

Cukor disappeared back inside the house and Julian joined a conversation about French abstract painters with a group of intense-looking men. Marcus spotted the bar across the patio, where a tall sailor with dark wavy hair was pouring a glass of champagne. Marcus approached him.

"I hear George really knows his champagne," Marcus said. He picked up a bottle of Dom Perignon. "Is it nice?" he asked, but the sailor was already gone. The champagne flowed down Marcus' throat like liquid velvet. He took another long sip. The way it tingled on his tongue, sharp but sweet, was like drinking melted Alpine snow when all you've ever had is dishwater.

"Marcus!" George Cukor's voice sailed over the chatter and laughter from a knot of theatrical types in colors that made Marcus' tie look staid. Marcus joined them and George clapped him gently on the back and made the introductions. Most of his friends were in the movie business some way or another; a couple of screenwriters, a set decorator, a costumer, an artist who made boulders and marble columns from papier mâché.

Cukor said, "I was just talking about filming *Sylvia Scarlett*. We've only got another week of editing left, although I don't know why we're bothering. The Legion of Decency is going to throw a pink hissy when they see Kate Hepburn in drag."

"If a girl is dressed as a boy, is it still called drag?" asked the set decorator.

The men all laughed.

"Anyway," Cukor continued, "there we were, filming on the beach—you can guess how awful *that* was. Sand and cameras do not a good combination make. And we're in the middle of a scene with Kate and Cary—"

"Kate AND Cary? That's why it's called drag!" someone said. The laughter had a sharper edge to it this time.

"From out of the clear blue comes this airplane. Oh my god, the noise! We're all just standing there, watching the pilot land the plane right there on the beach. Sand flying *everywhere*. The pilot gets out—it's Howard Hughes. Comes marching up the beach and starts on about how he wants to pay Cary a visit. Apparently they're very good pals. But of course it wasn't Cary he'd come to visit. He wanted Kate. Talk about goo-goo eyes."

One of the writers leaned in, "When you say Howard and Cary are very good friends, do you mean that they're *friends?*"

The decorator scoffed. "You think everyone is queer. Howard Hughes is fucking every slice of pussy pie that he can wrap his lips around. There is no way you can convince me that he's dipping his wick in both ends. "

"I met him once," Marcus put in, "at B.B.B.'s Cellar."

The guys gawked. "At B.B.B.'s?" Cukor asked. "You did? When?"

"A few years ago. I was with Tallulah Bankhead. We met up with Joan Crawford, who was there with Billy Haines, and next to him was Howard Hughes."

"Billy Haines? Was at B.B.B.'s? With Howard Hughes?" The set decorator was scandalized. "Why, that withholding little minx! Wait till I see her next. Did it look like Joan Crawford was fucking Howard Hughes?"

"Not right there on the table."

Marcus' reply sent the group into a squall of giggles. When George slipped away to see a new arrival, the costumer turned to Marcus.

"So," he said, "are you at MGM with George?"

Marcus' heart cramped. The moment of truth. He told Kathryn it would come. He couldn't stand there and say 'I'm a messenger boy for Western Union.'

Kathryn's advice had been, "Just tell them that you're a writer. Drop in the *Saturday Evening Post* story and then change the subject by asking if they'd read the latest Sinclair Lewis or John Steinbeck." It sounded a lot easier to do in the fitting room of the May Company's men's department. Marcus heard Kathryn's voice, *Three easy words.*

"I'm a writer," he said.

"Which studio?" one of the screenwriters asked.

"I just had a story published in the *Saturday Evening Post.* 'Subway People.'"

One of the writers snapped his fingers. "Oh, right! You're the Western Union messenger."

Oh crap. Marcus looked toward the house and calculated how fast he could run for the door.

"You're the one who got banned from the studio lot a few years ago, right? Something about Ramon Novarro?"

"You're a messenger?" The set decorator looked like he'd swallowed straight olive juice. "So, what? You delivered a telegram to George Cukor and . . . ? I don't get it. I thought George only liked to fuck the seafood." He nodded toward the sailor suits. The men exchanged significant looks and drifted away, leaving Marcus alone with his empty champagne flute and his cranberry-red cheeks.

He set his glass on a wrought iron table and slunk into the house, crossing the white tiles of the glass conservatory to the dark study. It was the perfect place to sulk. He flopped into a soft leather chair and rested his head against its padded arm.

He caught his reflection in a mirrored curio cabinet between the blue and white Delft china and made a face. Marcus Adler, the messenger boy who thinks he's a writer because he managed to have one story published in the *Saturday Evening Post*. What a joke.

And don't come back here until you've learned not to embarrass everyone who knows you.

"Listen to me!"

Marcus looked around but saw nobody.

"I'm dressed up like a nancy boy sailor inside Cukor's flaming house of faggots."

Marcus followed the low, gruff voice down a short corridor and peeked around the corner. One of the sailors had his back to Marcus and a telephone pressed to his ear. "You should see 'em all," he said. "What a filthy bunch of queers." It was the guy he'd seen at the liquor table.

"Hey," the guy rasped, "I know what I'm doing. You'll get your story. They're all talking about Cukor's new movie, with Hepburn prancing around in drag and Cary Grant panting after her like the deviant pedophile he probably is. . . . It's a Commie plot to pull a fast one over the Catholic Legion of Decency. . . . Yes, they used the word 'plot.' You should see who's here—writers, designers, every one of them has seen his own name up on the screen. . . . Of *course* I have! Direct quotes. The journalistic standards of the Hearst press will not be compromised by Clifford Wardell."

Marcus retreated and peered back up the hall to the library, where the chatter of the party filtered through. It'll serve George Cukor right if I just walk out of here and let this gutter monkey sling all the mud he can. The sooner I get away from this viper's nest, the better.

Marcus snuck across the foyer and let himself out the front door. It wasn't until he'd reached the front gate before his conscience stopped him. He looked back at the perfect picture-postcard house with its Tudor beams, ivy-covered walls and cool green lawns. It was pretty much Marcus' dream home.

Surely Cukor didn't bring you here to be the joke of the party, Marcus told himself. You don't know it was George who told everyone you're a messenger. It could've been anyone.

Marcus followed the fence around the house to a black wooden gate with a large fleur-de-lis stenciled in white. The party roared on the other side. The gate wasn't locked and he let himself in. Julian Johns was on the other side, fixing one of George's miniature roses to his lapel. "Hello again," he said.

"Have you seen George?"

"There was a redhead from the USS *Goldsborough* that seemed to take his fancy."

"You mean they really are sailors?"

"Here? Always."

"No, not always." Marcus set off toward a quartet of sailors standing beneath a fir tree. One of them pointed him toward the guest house, a small version of the mansion at the back of the property. Marcus rushed across the lawn and knocked on the door.

"Go away." It was Cukor's voice.

"I'm sorry, George, but there's something you need to know."

"Go. The fuck. *Away*."

"This is kind of important." Marcus waited for a few moments. "George?"

Cukor yanked the door open. His pristine suit had been pulled in all directions and he was missing a button on his shirt. "You've got five seconds."

"There's a Hearst journalist here."

Cukor's mouth flopped open. "Are you sure?"

"I overheard him on the telephone to what sounded like his editor."

George slammed the door behind him. "What exactly did you hear him say?" he demanded, shoving his shirt tails into his pants.

"I heard the words 'nancy boy sailor' and 'flaming faggots.' And he said your new movie is a big Commie plot to undermine the Catholic Legion of Decency."

"Holy hell!"

"He's got the names of everyone here and direct quotes of what they've been saying."

"God damn it! You're sure he works for Hearst?"

"He told his editor not to worry, because the journalistic standards of the Hearst press will not be compromised."

They started striding toward the main house. For a man verging on portly, George Cukor could work up quite a pace.

"Did anyone else hear this?"

"No, I was alone."

"Which telephone was he on? The front room with the fireplace?"

"Yes."

"Have you told anyone else about this?"

"No, I came straight to you."

"If this got out, I'd be finished socially in this town, which is as good as saying I'm finished professionally. This journalist, was he the tall one in the sailor suit?"

"Uh-huh."

"I knew there was something fishy about that one. Okay. In my library there is a desk. In the bottom drawer, you'll find an envelope. Count out three hundred dollars and meet me at the front door."

Marcus did as he was told. He peeled six fifties from an inch-thick stack and rushed down the corridor. George Cukor was pinning the journalist to the living room wall with the pointy end of a brass fire poker.

Cukor held the eyes of his prey. "Marcus, is that you?"

"Yes."

"Give Mr. Wardell here what's in your hand."

Marcus moved close enough to hear the man's short, breathy panting and pushed the money into his hand.

"What are you going to tell your editor?" George asked.

Wardell hesitated and Cukor pressed the poker a half inch deeper into his throat. "I'm going to tell him I got the whole thing wrong."

"And that . . ."

"And that it wasn't even George Cukor's house I was in. Some other guy, someone nobody cares about."

George released Wardell. "Get the hell out of my house before I change my mind and make you shit pokers for the next two weeks."

They watched the reporter sprint like a panicked hyena down the driveway. "I can't thank you enough," George said to Marcus. He pulled a handkerchief from his pocket and swiped his forehead. "I owe you one."

This was the chance Marcus had been hoping for. "I need to ask you something," he said. "Do you know who Mercedes de Acosta is?"

Cukor blinked. "Vaguely. Why do you ask?"

"Alla Nazimova up and disappeared from the Garden of Allah a little while back. I'm trying to track her down to return something to her. Robert Benchley and Dorothy Parker told me that this Mercedes woman would know where she is. Who is she?"

"She's a bit of everything. Screenwriter, poet, costume designer, socialite. Someone told me she helped Garbo perfect her English. She was in tight with Alla's 8080 Club. Had affairs with all of them, apparently."

"Do you think she'd know where Alla is?"

"She can be a bit of a nomad, but this town isn't all that big. I'd be willing to bet I know someone who knows someone who knows Mercedes."

"That'd be swell," Marcus said. "Thank you."

"No," Cukor replied, solemn. "Thank *you*."

CHAPTER 37

Kathryn alighted from the streetcar and pulled at her jacket. It didn't need straightening, but she needed to tug at something.

"Find me a color that says 'serious reporter,'" had been her only request. Gwendolyn had come up trumps with this dark auburn shot silk and topped it with a beaver collar. It looked–and felt–divine, and now, more than any other time she could remember, Kathryn needed to feel divine.

It had taken her the best part of a week to lull herself into thinking that the quack she'd picked out of the telephone book had been mistaken. She decided that she'd put herself through a Mt. Everest of worry for no reason. Her cravings had petered out and she hadn't had the slightest morning sickness, nor had her stomach started to swell. She was simply cursed with an erratic period. She'd once gone six weeks without one, but she hadn't worried because she was still a virgin. It arrived with the force of a medieval purgative that time, then returned less than three weeks later.

When Billy Wilkerson told her to show up at the *Hollywood Reporter* on Monday, she celebrated the Fourth of July with everyone else at the Garden . . . until she felt the abrupt compulsion to upchuck in the bushes beside the pool. No one thought anything of it; it was simply that Massey girl from villa number twelve doing what virtually everyone else had done at one time or another.

But it wasn't until the following morning, as she bent over the porcelain bowl revisiting her late supper of spaghetti and meatballs that she thought, "Uh-oh." And when she found herself the morning after that bringing up her pork chops, she faced the facts: the quack was right. She was further along the road to unwanted, unwilling, and unwed motherhood.

But asking around for the name of an abortion doctor wasn't the same as asking where you bought your girdle, even at the Garden of Allah where Kathryn knew she couldn't have been the first resident to find herself in this predicament. Her discreet inquiries had gotten her nowhere. It had occurred to Kathryn that Gwendolyn's friend Alice was bound to know someone, but she wasn't exactly Alice Moore's biggest fan and Kathryn hated the thought of being indebted to her.

It was a hell of a way to walk into the *Hollywood Reporter*, but she had until ten-thirty to locate the ladies' room, because with Swiss precision, morning sickness would hit her like a mule kick.

Billy Wilkerson introduced her to his reporters like she was the prodigal daughter, then delivered her to an alcove on the eastern side of the building. It wasn't quite an office, but it was separate enough from the reporting floor's clattering typewriters, jangling telephones and thick smoky haze. He pulled her chair out for her. "I had this reupholstered for you." Kathryn could smell the fresh leather. "You'll need a quiet corner in which to gather your gossip."

Kathryn raised an eyebrow.

"Laura!" he called. A woman about Kathryn's age with her hair pinned up in an elaborate chignon topped with a nest of curls approached with a stiff smile.

"Laura Pettiford," Wilkerson said, "I want you to meet our new columnist, Kathryn Massey. Laura here writes our obits, our photo captions and our *On This Day* historical spot, among other things."

In other words, Kathryn thought, you get to do everything but serious writing more than four sentences long.

Laura somehow managed to keep the smile frozen on her face and open her mouth at the same time. She barely glanced at Kathryn. "I've come up with a possible title for Miss Massey's column," she said to Wilkerson. "What do you think of *Window on Hollywood*?"

Kathryn's heart fluttered. Wilkerson had said nothing about giving her her own column. It was a goal she'd placed on the Maybe One Day shelf, out of reach for now but maybe one day. Kathryn white-knuckled her new handbag behind her back, thinking of the issues she wanted to cover — potential Communist infiltration, the effect of unionism on the industry, casting couch abuses, the monopoly the big studios had on the industry. She couldn't wait to get to her typewriter.

Wilkerson nodded. "I like it. *Window on Hollywood*. What do you think, Kathryn?"

Kathryn pretended to mull the title over in her head. Laura could have come up with *Cow Plop on My Head* and Kathryn would have agreed, if it meant having her own column. *Her own column!* Kathryn couldn't wait to tell Marcus and Gwendolyn. "It's perfect."

"Good work, Laura." Wilkerson said. "Thank you. That's a great title."

Laura bowed her head and gave Kathryn a half-second glance before withdrawing. Kathryn turned toward the new Underwood that shone in the morning sun pouring through her frosted glass window. She took off a glove and ran her finger along the keys. "Is this brand new?" she asked her new boss.

"A new typewriter for a new sort of gossip column."

Kathryn's finger stopped in the middle of the space bar.

"I don't give two figs for the sort of person you are at home," Wilkerson said, "but once you step outside your door in the Garden of Allah, your public persona will now reflect on the *Hollywood Reporter*. What we need to do is find you the right persona. Louella Parsons has 'It's just us folks,' which works well for her because, let's face it, she's about as sophisticated as porridge. Then there's Adela Rogers St. Johns—she's got that 'Hearst World's Greatest Girl Reporter' thing, which is fine because she's a darn good writer, even if she does work for Hearst. So I think it'll be useful for us to find you a persona, too. Any thoughts?"

How about *The Unwed Mother*? Kathryn thought. She eyed the clock at the front of the newsroom. It was ten twenty.

When Kathryn said nothing, Wilkerson continued. "Here's what I think. Hollywood gossip is based on hearsay, rumor, innuendo, and third-hand Chinese whisper, and most of it is bullshit. What I'm thinking we ought to cultivate is the sort of persona that says, 'You can count on Kathryn Massey for the truth.'"

"You make it sound like I'm running for public office."

Ten twenty-two.

"That's exactly right. I'm glad we're thinking along the same lines."

Kathryn thought, If we were thinking along the same lines, this news about a gossip column wouldn't be hitting me so hard. "Go on."

"I see the *Reporter's* resident gossip columnist as straightforward, honest and trustworthy. That's what struck me about you."

"Me and my poker face, huh?" Not to mention my illegitimate child.

"Right again!" Wilkerson said, looking at his watch.

Ten twenty-four. Kathryn's stomach rumbled.

"I have an appointment at ten thirty, so I'm off. Make yourself at home and do what you need to do!"

Kathryn watched him cross the floor and realized she was the only woman in sight. She folded her coat over her chair and headed for the ladies' room, passing reception on the way. Laura Pettiford and Janice the receptionist had their heads together. Kathryn knew a bitch session when she walked into one. At ten twenty-seven, Kathryn entered the last cubicle in the restroom, unhitched and stepped out of her skirt, hung it on the door hook, and bent over the john. Last night's sausages and mashed potatoes saw the light of day. Gossip column, she fumed between heaves. Because I'm a woman? She hurled again. One more ought to do it. A silly little gossip column about which star is possibly sleeping with which star even though he probably isn't at all, and who really cares even if he is. After the final hurl, there was always an instant settling sensation, like sitting down after standing up all day.

She got dressed, smoothed down her hair, and let out a deep sigh. Oh well, it's a start. Maybe when I prove to Wilkerson what I—

She jumped when she saw Laura Pettiford at the basin, a washcloth in her hand. Laura said, "You and I are the only women in the news room. We ought to link arms in solidarity, oughtn't we?" She soaked the towel in cold water and offered it to Kathryn, who pressed it to her forehead. Relief flooded through her.

"You're absolutely right," Kathryn said. "This is the nineteen thirties. They're just going to have to get used to us."

"Good," said Laura, smiling warmly. "Now that we have that settled." She pulled out a small steno pad with a pen inserted through the curled spine. She wrote on one of the pages which she handed to Kathryn. It said, "Hettie Menzies—Hollywood 2-1141."

"Who is Hettie Menzies?"

"You've never heard of Hettie? Oh my goodness, she's a bit of a legend. She's a calligrapher. Whenever you see a woman's hand writing a letter or note on the screen, that's usually Hettie. She can do any sort of handwriting. All the studios use her."

"And you think she's got some good gossip for me?"

Laura's eyes narrowed and she stepped closer to Kathryn. "I'm giving you her number because from what I hear, she knows someone who is . . . sympathetic."

CHAPTER 38

"Do I look like an idiot to you?"

Marcus didn't dare blink. It was important not to blink at a guy whose face got baboon-butt red. "No," he told the guard. "Of course not."

"So what makes you think I've changed my mind? Is it because you're not wearing your Western Union uniform this time? Is that it? You assumed maybe I wouldn't remember you?"

Of course I assumed you wouldn't remember me, Marcus thought. It's been more than four years. I'm not even in my uniform, for God's sake. What sort of circus memory freak are you?

"You were banned from the MGM lot then, and you're banned from it now."

Marcus took the precious telegram from his pocket and held it up. "This is a completely different situation. I have an appointment."

In truth, what Marcus had wasn't so much an appointment, but a deadline. He was due at the reception desk of the writers' building by twelve noon, or the offer he'd been dreaming about for six years would be snatched away.

"I don't care if you have a wedding ring for Mr. Mayer's daughter."

The red-faced guard snatched the telegram from Marcus' hand, ripped it in half, ripped those halves in half, and tossed them up in the air. Marcus watched his dream flutter to the ground in white squares. He knelt down and started collecting them until a hand grabbed him by the collar and yanked him back to his feet.

"You're from Western Union," said the guard. "You could print yourself a forgery in less than a minute. You think I haven't seen that trick a million times? Now scram before I call the Culver City police for trespassing."

"Look," Marcus raised his voice. "All you have to do is place a phone call to the writers' department and ask for Jim Taggert. There is a contract on his desk made out to me. One phone call and all this gets cleared up."

Marcus held his breath while Captain Hoolihan glowered at him for a very long moment, then disappeared inside his booth and placed a call. He didn't draw in air again until Hoolihan came back outside.

"Taggert's in a story conference for the rest of the day and cannot be disturbed."

"Did you ask whoever answered the phone if there was a contract there for me to sign?"

"Listen, squirt, you're lucky I placed that call at all. There's nobody to confirm your story, so scram."

"Hugo Marr!" Marcus blurted out. For the very first time, Marcus was sincerely glad that Hugo worked at MGM. "Do you know who he is?

"I do. But–"

"Then please, call him and confirm with him that I am who I say I am–"

"You're lucky I made that first call. I'm not going to go wasting my time–"

"Better you waste the time of Hugo Marr than George Cukor, because if I have to find a public telephone and bother George with this, he won't be a very happy person."

Marcus copped another pump-action stare, but the bluff worked. Marcus knew that George was in the midst of crisis-editing his Hepburn picture–the Legion of Decency had erupted over what was supposed to be a sneak preview–and would shoot on sight anyone interrupting him, even for something like this–and Hoolihan retreated to his booth. When he returned, his face was even redder.

"Mr. Marr is off work this entire week."

"He is? Why?"

Hoolihan took a step closer. "Get the hell off my lot before I call the cops."

The two stared at each other unblinkingly until Marcus faced the fact that this was not something he was going to win, and returned to the sidewalk on Washington Boulevard. The ten ornate columns at the official front gate of the Metro-Goldwyn-Mayer studios were at the center of a ten-foot-tall wall that stretched a couple of blocks in each direction. There was no getting over it without a pole vault.

He looked down to see a square of white paper pressed against his shoe. The sole word printed on it was 'noon.' He had read the telegram a hundred times and knew exactly where that word was.

Less than a week ago, that telegram had come from MGM, informing Marcus of the studio's wish to buy the screen rights of "Subway People" for a stupefying one thousand dollars. Would he be interested in a one-year contract with MGM as a junior screenwriter for a hundred dollars a week? Marcus was astounded. He was being offered his dream job at seven times his Western Union salary, and they were asking if he would be interested?

REPORT TO MGM WRITERS BLDG ON JULY 15 TO SIGN CONTRACT STOP
OUR OFFER WILL BE RESCINDED IF YOU HAVE NOT ARRIVED BY NOON STOP
SINCERELY JIM TAGGART WRITING DEPT SUPERVISOR STOP

Of course, Kathryn's response was, "Careful what you wish for. I thought I got my dream job, and look at what they've got me doing. Ugh!" Marcus didn't blame her for being just a little bitter, but at least she got in the door. And Hugo had assured him that it was standard procedure to give offers like this a specific time by which the contract had to be signed. He said they did it when they really didn't care if you signed or not; all the studios did it that way. It was the same when he won the screenwriting contest–so, ". . . don't think it'll be waiting for you at twelve-oh-one. Noon means noon."

Marcus looked up and down Washington Boulevard until he spotted the Coffee Cup Café across the street. Maybe they had a payphone.

* * *

From the south side of Culver Boulevard, Marcus watched MGM's employee entrance. From what he could see, there was just one guard on duty. There had to be thousands of people employed at MGM—could that guard know every single one of them? He could if he was like Buttface Hoolihan around the corner at the front gate.

It was now going on ten-thirty. Getting through to the receptionist in the writers' department on the Coffee Cup Café's payphone wasn't hard. Yes, she had his paperwork. Yes, she had instructions to tear the contract up at one minute past twelve. No, she couldn't put him on the gate list; that had to come from the supervisor, Mr. Taggart. No, she couldn't put Marcus through because Mr. Taggart was in a meeting for the rest of the day. No, she couldn't interrupt it. But did he know about the other gate into the studio?

Marcus crossed Culver Boulevard at the light and broke into a run. As he approached the booth, the guard looked up and stared at him. "I'M SO LATE! I'M SO GODDAMNED LATE!" he yelled, and shot his arms out as if to say "Gangway!" "Thalberg's gonna be wearing my guts for garters!"

Marcus almost made it past the guard, but at the last moment he caught Marcus by the elbow. "Are you saying you work here?"

Marcus felt a convenient sweat break out across his forehead and he made a big play of wiping it away. "I'm already an hour late. I gotta get—"

"What's your name?"

"Hugo Marr."

"If we go in the time-clock office here, there'll be a timecard with your name on it?"

Marcus nodded.

The guard squinted at Marcus. "Let's go inside, then."

A series of metal slots filled with timecards were mounted on three walls. A clock on the center wall divided them into two zones, with the slots to the right mostly filled. A few unclaimed cards filled slots to the left. It wasn't hard to find the one marked "Marr, Hugo."

* * *

Marcus roamed the studio looking for a building marked "Writers." He passed a flat, broad building marked "Rehearsal Halls," a tall, narrow one labeled "Film Vaults," and a boxy one whose sign said "Plaster Shop." He stopped a quartet of tuxedoed violists who happened by, but all they knew were the rehearsal rooms and recording studios. An efficient-looking secretary type holding a stack of papers was more helpful.

"Oh, sure," she told him. "You want to go past Stage Nine, then past Eighteen, past Seventeen and you'll see a building marked "Advertising" and another one marked "Commissary." Go past them and you'll see another building, the Scenario Department. That's the one you want."

But Marcus only got as far as Stage Eighteen when he saw Buttface Hoolihan heading toward him, schmoozing a tall brunette in a coat with a huge fur collar. Marcus looked around and saw a pair of guys in overalls walking out of Stage Eighteen. He glanced back at Hoolihan—big mistake. Their eyes met. After only a second's delay, recognition burst onto the guard's face.

"HEY!"

Marcus ran toward the door to Stage Eighteen, yanked it open and pitched his body onto the set of a vaudeville hall. Scores of extras in turn-of-the-century costumes milled around tables and chairs, cooling themselves with feathered fans and newspapers. More extras filled a balcony off to the left, and the stage to Marcus' right had a formal British garden painted on its background. An eight-piece band had gathered in front of the stage.

A flash of sunlight glinted behind him as the soundstage door opened, and Marcus melted into a rack of fur coats. Buttface Hoolihan called out to one of the stagehands, "Hey, you! Did you see someone run in here? Mid-twenties, dark suit, white shirt, purple tie and shiny new black shoes?"

Christ almighty, was there no detail that escaped this guy's attention?

"Nope."

Hoolihan let fly a few choice swear words. "I'll search this whole place my goddamned self."

"I don't know, Hooley. We start filming in fifteen minutes. We're doing one of the big sequences today. We only got one take to get it right, and everybody's tense, especially Van Dyke. He won't appreciate anybody getting in the way."

Marcus listened to Buttface Hoolihan stomp away before he dared peek around the mink he was clutching. As he turned to leave through the same door, Woody Van Dyke entered with Clark Gable and stopped in the doorway. Gable, dressed in a sharply tailored black tailcoat, towered over the slim graying director as he watched him explain something with his hands as much as with his words. Marcus backed away and spotted a clipboard and pen on a stack of fake bricks. Figuring it'd make him look like he belonged, he grabbed it and started looking for another exit.

The set towered nearly two stories high, almost as far as the spotlights threaded across the ceiling. Marcus drew closer, puzzling over a jagged line in the floor. He realized it had been made in two separate sections, and this was where they met. He looked at the clipboard in his hand:

Production number: 18103
Production name: "San Francisco"
Director: W.S. Van Dyke
Start date: June 30th, 1935
Today's production day number is: 6

Marcus had been reading about this picture in one of Kathryn's first *Window on Hollywood* columns. Clark Gable and Jeannette MacDonald were going to star in what the MGM publicity machine claimed would reconstruct the entire 1906 earthquake.

"Okay, people," a voice boomed out over a megaphone, "you need to finish up what you're doing in three minutes. Don't be overly fussy. It's all going to come tumbling down into a heap of rubble anyways."

Buttface Hoolihan was standing at the door, his arms crossed over his chest and his feet spread apart as if to say, *Just try and get past me, punk.* Marcus headed in the opposite direction. Surely a soundstage this big had a second exit. Pretending to check items off a list on his clipboard, Marcus picked his way past wooden ladders, extras, cameras, and buckets and buckets of dirt.

Around the back of the vaudeville set he caught sight of another door. He'd managed to get about ten feet closer to it when he spotted Hoolihan approaching it from the other direction. A couple of stagehands loading papier mâché bricks into a net slung from the roof blocked his retreat. He made a left hand turn and walked through a doorway . . . and onto the set. It was the last place he should have gone, but he had run out of options.

Right at that moment, someone yelled, "LIGHTS!" and the rows of overhead spotlights flooded the set with the intensity of a half-dozen California August suns.

Over a megaphone, a deep voice said, "Extras, please take your positions. I'm sure I don't have to remind you people that this is a one-take shot today. All other personnel, clear the set immediately."

Marcus shielded his eyes from the unrelenting light and looked around for another escape route. He spotted a door at the end of the long wooden bar. If he could get there and wind his way around the back, he could reach the exit. He headed for it, keeping up his checklist charade as stagehands cleared the set and extras found their marks. As he reached the door, the megaphone blared again.

"Let's go through this one more time. I will call 'Action!' and we'll all wait a full five seconds. Then, strictly in this order: walls, chandeliers, dust, bricks, and windows."

Marcus made it through the door. He looked to his right—the exit was in sight. Just then, a hand clamped onto his upper arm so tight it cut off his circulation.

"Gotcha!"

"ROLL CAMERAS!"

"You wouldn't believe me, so I had to do something," Marcus said. He tried to pull away from Buttface Hoolihan's monstrous grip but the guard had five inches and forty pounds on him. Squirming only made Hoolihan's grip hurt more.

"We're going to stay here until they've shot this scene."

"I've got paperwork—"

"Shut the hell up. I am going to have you arrested."

"Fine! Do what you have to do," Marcus whispered. "But can we just swing by the scenario building? If I don't sign those papers by noon—"

"AND . . . ACTION!"

Marcus' hand began to throb. He looked down at it and saw veins begin to pop out. He and Hoolihan stood with their backs against the soundproofing mattresses as the stagehands began to shake the set's walls. The chandeliers started to tinkle, and grew louder and louder until an almighty crash filled the air. The extras screamed and shrieked as they fell about the bar, pretending the whole thing was being ripped apart. It reminded Marcus of being caught underground with Ramon during the Long Beach earthquake. That hadn't worked out so great, either.

Hundreds of papier mâché bricks fell to the floor with a rumble, and suddenly the air was thick with dust. Marcus looked around and spotted a loose wooden banister within easy reach. He curled his fingers around the end, and swung it as hard as he could around his body in one smooth arc. When it hit Hoolihan across the stomach, the guard let out an "Oooph!" and released Marcus' arm. Marcus sprang to his left. He had his hands on the exit door when he realized he couldn't open it without setting off the alarm and spoiling the entire one-take scene. All that time, effort and money—he just couldn't do it.

A grinding, wrenching noise erupted, and the two walls on either side of him started to twist and moan. He looked back at Hoolihan; the guy was clambering to his feet. The wall next to him started to bend toward breaking, and pushed a stack of wooden barrels back toward the stage wall. The grinding noise became almost deafening and the floorboards started to buckle and splinter. Dust choked the air. It was hard to see much of anything. When the barrels closed in on Hoolihan, the space between them and the soundproof mattresses narrowed to a handspan.

Just give me a few more seconds, Marcus prayed. This can't go on for much longer. Through the haze of whirling dust, Marcus could make out Hoolihan clearing the barrels like a gymnast.

"AND . . . CUT!"

Hoolihan made a grab for Marcus' sleeve and missed, but caught the strap of his wristwatch with a fingertip and pulled it off. Marcus heard it clatter to the concrete floor as he threw himself against the door and sprinted out into the sunshine. He narrowly dodged a huge pair of horses pulling a covered wagon. One of the horses reared up and brayed. Marcus skirted the wagon and dashed down an alleyway.

"GET THIS DAMN THING OUT OF MY WAY!" echoed after him.

Marcus wasn't sure which way the writers' building lay, but he kept running. He brushed the dust from his suit as he sped past a row of soundstages. Just as he was starting to run out of breath, he spotted some signposts: Research . . . Camera Department . . . Advertising . . .

Marcus rounded the corner and spotted the Scenario Department sign over a set of double glass doors at the end of a long building that looked more like a sawmill than the birthplace of the most glamorous motion pictures in the world. He ran to the doors, pulled them open and dashed inside.

The woman behind the desk let out a little yelp and looked at Marcus like he was the long-lost Yeti.

"You're Dierdre, right? I'm . . . Marcus Adler," he gasped. "We spoke . . . on the phone. You . . . have paperwork . . . for me."

"Oh, Mr. Adler, I'm so sorry."

Marcus gripped the edge of the reception desk so tight it hurt. "What?"

Dierdre was a rather nice-looking girl with a long reddish braid down her back. She pointed to the wall behind him and he turned around. A clock big enough for a railway station read four minutes past twelve.

* * *

244

Marcus stepped out into the sunshine. Earlier, that same sunshine had infused his every step with optimism and buoyancy. Now it seemed liable to give a guy sunburn. He sat on the steps of the scenario department and rested his chin on his hands. What a difference four minutes could make.

He felt a shadow fall across his face. "It's all right, Hoolihan," he said, "I was too late by four lousy minutes, so nothing matters anymore."

Marcus heard a soft chuckle, then, "My dear boy, what *are* you doing?"

CHAPTER 39

"You don't have to come if you don't want to. I'll be fine."

Gwendolyn looked from the approaching streetcar to her friend. Kathryn had been so pale all morning; more pale than usual. Gwendolyn couldn't imagine how she must be feeling. "Really honey, I doubt this is something you want to do on your own."

The streetcar rattled to a halt. They climbed aboard and took a seat. Gwendolyn let a couple of stops go past before she stole a glance at Kathryn. Her eyes were glazed; Gwendolyn let her be for the moment. The twelve o'clock appointment loomed, and it was easier to think about business. She'd been rethinking her strategy lately, after she overheard Myrna Loy say to the Cocoanut Grove photographer something that Alice had been saying for years: an actress' real job is to attract a talent agent. That was the only surefire way into the studios.

The streetcar dropped them off at First Street and they headed into Chinatown, a part of Los Angeles Gwendolyn hadn't been to before. They turned onto Dragon Road where a rusting iron dragon nearly five feet high was welded to the street light with its tail wrapped around the base. The dowdy late-Victorian buildings here were overlaid with red-tiled roofs hipped up at the ends, and neon signs in Chinese lettering: CHOP SUEY and SOO HOO IMPORT CO. The street was disconcertingly silent and empty of all but a few people.

This Chinatown's days were numbered. The city fathers had decided L.A. needed a new railway station that housed all three lines in one building, and the best place for that was on the spot where Chinatown had stood for decades. The neighborhood was relocating a mile or two to the north and, Gwendolyn thought, they were probably glad to. The buildings here were so rundown and dingy, and the streets strewn with deep potholes and covered in filth. Where they were going had to be better than this. Not that they'd been given any choice in the matter.

"This is a heck of a way to spend your birthday," Kathryn said. Gwendolyn shrugged it off. She hadn't given much thought to her birthday; it was the lesser of the day's happenings. "I'll make it up to you," Kathryn insisted. "Let's go out to a really nice place for dinner afterwards. Maybe Victor Hugo's."

Victor Hugo's was a swanky new spot on Wilshire with white linen tablecloths, real palm trees, and an indoor fountain. Gwendolyn didn't know which was more astounding — that they could extort two dollars for their fixed price menu, or that there were so many people willing to pay two whole bucks that you had to wait for a table.

"You think you'll be up for a swell meal . . . afterwards?" Gwendolyn asked.

Kathryn smiled weakly. "Maybe in a couple of days."

They stopped to let a line of Chinese men jog by, their long black braids bouncing over enormous copper bowls slung on their backs. As the last one hurried past them, Gwendolyn caught Kathryn by the arm.

"Are you sure this is what you want?"

Kathryn's face was like stone. "What I want is for this never to have happened."

Gwendolyn tried to think of another way out. She was panicked at the thought of delivering her best friend to a back-alley butcher with tuna-stained clothes and spittle in the corner of his puckered mouth. "Well," she said gently, "it has happened. So your options are to go ahead with today's appointment or to — "

"Or to what? Conjure up some invented husband that I've neglected to mention at the *Hollywood Reporter* for the past three weeks?"

Gwendolyn took Kathryn by the hand. "I just want you to be sure that this isn't something you're going to regret later."

"GOD DAMN IT ALL TO GODDAMN HELL!"

Kathryn's outburst echoed off the ratty buildings. She lifted her handbag and whacked it against the brickwork as hard as she could. The force was enough to snap the ends off one of the handles. When she saw what she'd done, she let out a raspy grunt and slammed the bag into the dirt, then spun around to face Gwendolyn, her cheeks red with fury.

"This!" she pressed a hand against her stomach, "is what I regret. I'm like you, Gwennie. I have *no* wish to be married or to be a mother. NONE! I want a career! I want stature! I want to talk about Hemingway and Edna St. Vincent Millay with painters and poets, to go shopping in London, and to learn to speak French. It was such a struggle to get out from under my mother. And it's been a struggle to land a good job. And even though Wilkerson thinks all I'm fit for is a silly little gossip column, the timing of *this*," she poked herself in the stomach again, "could not have been worse."

Tears glazed Kathryn's eyes as she struggled to maintain what little composure she had left. She took a deep, shuddering breath. "Look honey, I love that you want to be here for me, and I very much appreciate your support. But if this isn't something you're comfortable with, then that's okay. I'll see you back at home."

* * *

Dr. Walter Harrison's office was across the street from Wong's, the biggest Chinese laundry in Los Angeles. Six enormous frosted glass windows took up most of the block. At any other time it would have been a steaming hive with dozens of workers washing and pressing the linens of half the hotels downtown, but they had already moved to a big new warehouse half a mile north.

Hettie had warned Kathryn that there was no sign for the office. They looked for a blue stained-glass window with *122 San Pedro Street* painted in white lettering. Gwendolyn opened the door and motioned for Kathryn to go in. They took the staircase to the second floor; there was only one door at the top. A nurse with dyed black hair and a starched cap looked up and smiled. A lush painting of three figures stretched out at the edge of a pond hung on the wall behind her. Kathryn introduced herself as Lorelei Boothe.

"Ah, yes, of course," the nurse said in a soothing tone. She excused herself and disappeared behind a closed door. The clanging of Chinese drums started up in the street, beating a somber rhythm punctuated by the occasional clash of cymbals.

Kathryn's brown eyes darted back and forth across the nurse's desk, never resting for more than a half second on any one place. Gwendolyn pointed to the painting on the wall. "Isn't that gorgeous?" she said. Neither of them had said anything since Kathryn's outburst on the street but her breathing was still jagged and shallow. "Look at those colors." The scene was lush with dark apricot and soft rouge. The pond in front of the reclining figures was mirror smooth. "It's so restful, isn't it?"

Kathryn's eyes quit their manic wandering and rose to look at the painting. Her face broke into a smile. "Well now, isn't that something? It's a Maxfield Parrish."

"Oh?"

"Tallulah has one. You know what this one is called?"

"Tell me."

"Would you believe *The Garden of Allah*?"

The nurse reappeared. "The doctor is ready to see you now. May I suggest you put your jewelry and your wristwatch into your handbag and leave it with your friend?"

Kathryn took off her jewelry, grabbed Gwendolyn's hand for an encouraging squeeze and crossed the threshold into the doctor's office.

The nurse had a kind face, wide and open, and a gentle smile. Gwendolyn looked at the name plate pinned to her chest. "Your name is Guinevere Brykk?"

The nurse nodded.

"Mine is Gwendolyn Brick! That's almost close enough to make us cousins, or something."

"At least you spell 'Brick' the normal way," Guinevere said.

Gwendolyn pulled a face. "But 'Brick'? Ugh! It sounds so clunky. What do you think of the name 'Gwendolyn Barrett'? Can you see it on a marquee?"

Guinevere assured her that she could, and poured them each a cup of coffee. They stood before the window while the Chinese paraded down San Pedro Street. A long dragon of green cloth and a carved wooden head zigzagged from one side of the street to the other.

"They've been holding parades like this all week," Nurse Brykk said. "Something about bestowing luck on those who will occupy the land after they leave. Damned decent of them, I think, seeing as how they're being tossed out on their skinny little behinds."

Gwendolyn nodded but her mind was with Kathryn in the consulting room and wished she'd offered to go in with her.

"Dr. Harrison is a fine doctor," the nurse said, keeping her eyes on the scene below them. "He's very gentle, and he believes in what he's doing. Your friend is fortunate that she's in such good hands. He went to Yale Medical School, so he's not just some back-alley hack."

Gwendolyn felt her shoulders relax. "Where are you moving to?"

"We haven't found a new place yet." Guinevere returned to her desk and wrote something on a piece of paper. Back at the window, she handed it to Gwendolyn. *Dr. Clarence Yale.* "The doctor uses a pseudonym for when he places a notice in the personals to announce that we've found new premises." She gave a quiet little laugh. "We call it his stage name."

Gwendolyn put it into the pocket of her jacket and wondered if the good doctor knew of any talent agents.

CHAPTER 40

Kathryn changed her outfit three times before settling on her burgundy suit with the new cream blouse she'd bought with her first paycheck. It was a good investment–a cream blouse goes with just about every color–as was the hat she'd found at Kress department store. She knew she was taking a chance wearing anything from Kress–the place was barely a step up from Woolworth's five-and-dime–but it was a darling little hat with black trim and the cutest little pom-pom on top that matched her suit exactly. It was just what she needed to impress Louella Parsons. Thank heavens she was finally starting to feel like herself again.

The weeks following her appointment had been rough and, for the longest time, seemed to be without end. The nausea, the night sweats, the stomach cramps, the bleeding, the insomnia. The doctor had told her to expect some of these symptoms, but she hadn't been prepared for all of them. If this was what it was like to get a relatively safe abortion, what must it be like for the poor girls who had their unwanteds extracted by medical school drop-outs crouched over grimy beds in dreary back rooms?

What a kind man Dr. Harrison turned out to be. His clinic had been clean and organized — what more could she reasonably expect from an abortionist?

But even so, he couldn't tell her how to alleviate herself of the guilt that racked her. Not from having the operation performed, but keeping it from Marcus. It kept her awake as much as the cramps and the sweats.

That night when he confessed that he was a queer and she admitted she was an adulterer, she felt the bond between them strengthen and tighten. They later made a pact–"No more secrets, ever."–and Kathryn had meant it. But an abortion? That was different. Too painful. Too shameful. So she decided not to tell him and prayed that he understood.

But now that the whole sordid episode was behind her, she was free to make the best of the meager plate she'd been handed at work. Gossip column, indeed. It had the words "women's work" stamped all over it. The meaty stuff — mergers, takeovers, box office analysis, censorship, unionization — was all done by men. Kathryn did her level best to ensure that she'd never be called a sob sister; she'd break another handbag over the head of the first guy who called her that.

Laura Pettiford helped her track down Dr. Harrison, but there was something about the woman that Kathryn didn't trust. When Wilkerson called Kathryn into his office, Laura stood silently in the corner with her arms crossed over her chest.

"Laura here has wrangled you an invite to the Hollywood Women's Press Club's monthly luncheon at the Brown Derby. This'll be your chance to meet Louella Parsons. You only get to make a first impression once so wear something extra nice when you come in on Thursday."

It was a mystery to Kathryn how a frumpy, dumpy, bitchy, snitchy, ignorant, illiterate heifer like Louella Parsons had become the unassailable gossip queen of Hollywood and the most powerful woman in town. Between her newspaper columns, her magazine articles and interviews, and her *Hollywood Hotel* radio show, the woman was everywhere. If a cross-town bus hit Walter Winchell tomorrow, she'd be the most famous journalist in America.

In fact, Louella's success wasn't much of a mystery. It could be explained in three words: William Randolph Hearst. To fall foul of Louella Parsons was to square off with the most powerful media tycoon in the country. It was important that Kathryn pass muster.

Kathryn was blotting her lipstick when Wilkerson buzzed. He closed his door behind her. "I just wanted to check that everything was okay." He used a gentle side of his voice that she'd never heard before, or suspected he possessed.

"Yes," Kathryn replied, "everything's fine."

He blinked slowly, deliberately. "I mean everything . . . healthwise . . ."

Kathryn felt a blush spread up from her cream collar like a grease fire; she was relieved when he looked away. "Everything is fine," she repeated evenly.

"I just want you to know that I'd choose practicality over dogma every damned day of the week. You can come to me with any problem, of any sort."

Kathryn nodded and fumed.

"Good," he said, returning to his desk. "Enjoy your lunch."

* * *

The taxi pulled away from the curb and entered the traffic heading east on Hollywood Boulevard. Laura stared out at the pedestrians with a stone jaw.

"Laura?" Kathryn asked.

"Mmmm?" Laura didn't shift her gaze.

"Did you mention anything to Mr. Wilkerson about my appointment?"

"Appointment?"

"With Hettie's doctor."

"No, of course not. What a thing to ask me. How would Bill even know?"

Kathryn glanced at Laura. Oh, so it's 'Bill,' is it? "He asked after my health."

Laura turned to look at Kathryn. "One's boss asking after one's health does not mean he knows about your so-called appointment."

"General inquiries into one's health do not usually make mention of choosing practicality over dogma." Laura snorted and turned back to watch the sidewalks.

So much for linking arms in solidarity.

* * *

A large table had been set for twenty on the left side of the Vine Street Brown Derby. Not yet half the seats were filled, but there was no mistaking the woman around whom the Hollywood Women's Press Club orbited.

Louella Parsons wasn't plump, but she was headed in that direction. Her bosom was starting to swell in that matronly sort of way. She had a horsey face, heavy and jowly with a vacant but permanent smile, which was unfortunate because her teeth were brown and ragged. As Kathryn and Laura approached, Louella stuck out her hand rather like the Queen Mother expecting it to be kissed. Laura shook it like a man.

"How lovely to see you," Parsons said. "Mr. Wilkerson has been rattling the cups of anti-communism, I see." That week, the front page of the *Hollywood Reporter* had screamed that Hollywood was rife with Reds. "Worked himself into quite a rage over those submissives — no, no, that's not the word I meant, is it?"

"Subversives?" Kathryn suggested.

"Yes, of course. Subversives. Thank you, my dear." Louella frowned at Kathryn. "I don't believe we've had the pleasure."

Louella thrust forward her Queen Mother hand. It felt to Kathryn as clammy as last week's cod. When Laura introduced them, Louella's eyebrows flew up. "Ah, yes, I heard that the *Hollywood Reporter* was starting a new column. The title . . . something about a window?"

"*Window on Hollywood*," Kathryn said.

"Ah, yes. When does it start?"

"Last week," Laura put in with a smile that Kathryn couldn't decipher. Their exchange in the taxi had rattled Kathryn. She thought she knew where she stood with the only other female in the *Reporter*'s newsroom but now it appeared she didn't.

"I must make an effort to read it," Louella said, as though the thought of reading Kathryn's column required more exertion than she was prepared to expend.

At one o'clock, Louella called the women to the table. All twenty seats were filled with indistinguishable variations of Laura Pettiford, plus or minus ten years. Every one of them was color-coordinated—hat, suit, gloves, handbag, and shoes all exactly the same shade from head to toe. Each hairdo was every bit as complicated as Laura's. Kathryn and Louella were the most cheaply dressed women at the table; Kathryn's dimestore hat felt like a rhinestone brooch at Tiffany's.

Everyone around the table quickly settled into chatting with her neighbor. Laura seated herself on the other side from Kathryn and down five places, and launched herself into a conversation with the heavily freckled woman next to her. Kathryn didn't mind being left alone; she needed to think.

What did Laura hope to gain from making the *Hollywood Reporter*'s new columnist look like an immoral slut who got caught with a bun in the oven? Did Laura want her job? Or was it the boss Laura had her eye on? *How would Bill even know?* Kathryn decided she'd be damned if she was going to let Laura Pettiford get her job, but she would let her know that as far as Mr. Wilkerson was concerned, the field was wide open.

The waiter cleared his throat as he lowered a glass of iced water in front of her. "Thank you," she said, absently.

"You're welcome, Kathryn. It's nice to see you again."

She looked up to see the skinny fellow who helped Gwendolyn get in front of the camera that day of the *Graf Zeppelin*. "Oh, hello! Ritchie, isn't it?"

"Yes, that's right," Ritchie smiled warmly. "How's Gwendolyn? Did anything come of that day down at Mine's Field?"

"No." Kathryn smiled. "Not for want of trying, though."

"Please tell her I said hello."

Louella rose at the head of the table and announced that they were honored to welcome the latest female addition to the Hollywood press, Miss Kathleen Massey from the *Hollywood Reporter*, whose new column, *Hollywood Window*, would begin next week. A round of applause, more rote than welcoming, followed. Parsons invited the women to ask Kathryn any questions they liked. "It's sort of our getting-to-know-you initiation," Louella explained, and sat down.

"I have a question." It was the freckled lady next to Laura. There was something unsettling and smug about her smile. "Where do you stand on your boss' accusations that Communists have infiltrated the studios?"

Kathryn took a moment to organize her thoughts.

Wilkerson's recent editorial had caused an uproar in the industry. The studio bosses worked up a rabid froth thinking he was accusing them of personally allowing Communists to take over the movie business. They got him all wrong, though. Wilkerson's point was that if these alleged Communists actually did manage to work their message into Hollywood films, then the ninety million Americans who went to the movies each week were being subtly brainwashed. But his point sunk under the torrents of abuse the bosses had poured into print.

Wilkerson was uncharacteristically floored by the backlash; he played high-stakes poker with these guys every week, and claimed he hadn't seen it coming. Kathryn had to wonder if this was all just some silly brouhaha they'd concocted around the card table to give themselves more column space.

She looked around the table and tried to read the women's faces. Would they respect loyalty over personal feelings? Or moral conviction, regardless of the company line? But this was an unreadable crowd of pleasant smiles and perfect make up.

"I've only been with the *Reporter* a short while," she said, "but I'm no stranger to the ways of Hollywood. Mr. Wilkerson hasn't told me where he got his information." She said the name of her boss deliberately for Laura's sake. "I don't enjoy the strictest confidence of my boss, nor do I ever expect to. You'll have to ask him about his editorial."

Laura's shoulders relaxed.

"Yes, but do you believe him when he says the studios are rife with Communists and they ought to be routed out?" Freckles persisted.

"I don't know that 'rife' would be the word I'd use."

"So you disagree with your own boss?"

Kathryn glanced around the table again, desperate to discern what they expected of her, but nobody gave an inch. All right then, she decided, I might as well just be myself and hang the consequences. "I think Hollywood is in the business of making all kinds of pictures about all kinds of stories for all kinds of people. The greater the range of perspectives contributing to the output, the better it is for the industry as a whole."

The women sucked in a quiet collective gasp.

An older woman with wispy gray hair said, "Personally, I'm not convinced that Communists have infiltrated our industry. But if they have, it almost sounds as though you don't mind."

"It's not illegal to be a member of the Communist party," Kathryn pointed out.

"Are you a Communist, Kathleen?" Louella Parsons asked.

"No, I am not. But the last time I looked at the Constitution, it said that people are entitled to their opinions. It's called freedom of speech. All I'm saying is that a variety of opinions and viewpoints can only make motion pictures more interesting. And surely, more interesting pictures can only be good for the industry."

Kathryn looked around for someone willing to take up the argument for or against, but nobody would look her in the eye. She mumbled, "Thank you," and sat down.

The conversation around the table resuscitated in fits and starts, but Kathryn was left to stare into space. By the time the main course was served –a filet of Colorado rainbow trout in Amandine sauce, with French fried eggplant–she wished she'd never come. She ate her fish in silence and focused on the caricatures on the walls.

They were becoming as famous as the Brown Derby itself; you knew you'd made it when you were asked to sit for your portrait. Something told Kathryn that "Kathleen Massey" wasn't likely to attend any more of these dreadful affairs. Oh well, she decided, at the very least, I hope I've let Laura know that if she wants "Bill" in her claws, she'll get no competition from me.

Once the main course was cleared, Ritchie circled the table with dessert menus. Kathryn shook her head. The last thing she wanted to force down her throat was a slice of black bottom pie.

"You're going to want to see this menu," he told her.

"Thank you, Ritchie, but coffee will be fine."

Ritchie set the menu down in front of her. "No," he said. "Really."

She opened the menu and found a handwritten note inside.

Kathryn,
We have a friend in common.

Kathryn looked around and spotted a portly man in glasses sipping coffee in the corner, watching her read the note. He shot her a shy smile and nodded subtly.

WRH & LP hate Commies. LP thinks you're Red now. The man in gray is Clark Gable's agent. MGM wants CG to wait 'til after Call of the Wild is released to announce his divorce. This is gold — tell LP & you'll be o.k.

Kathryn looked over to see a stern gentleman in a gun metal suit with a permanent squint and a wide moustache. He pulled his wallet from his jacket pocket and thumbed through the wad of bills inside. He looked up and met Kathryn's eyes, hesitated and smiled. Kathryn returned his smile. It would have been rude to brush off the guy whose big mouth was going to save her ass.

* * *

As it turned out, the black bottom pie was delicious. It was a shame to gulp it down but she wanted to get the whole luncheon over and done with. She left the table without saying goodbye and headed straight to George Cukor's booth. His companion was a rigid woman with porcelain skin even paler than her ivory muslin dress. Her smile was genuine, though, and she studied Kathryn with intelligent eyes. "Thank you so much," Kathryn said to George. "I don't know how to repay you."

George waved away the rest of her speech. "Don't mention it," he told her. "Kathryn, may I introduce you to Mercedes de Acosta?"

"Ah!" Kathryn said. "Nice to meet you."

"Marcus wondered if Mercedes might know where Alla is."

Kathryn sought the woman's eyes. "Do you?" Kathryn asked Mercedes. "We all miss her at the Garden."

The woman's smile widened. "You should have stuck closer to home."

"To home?" Kathryn was puzzled.

"The best person to ask that sort of thing is the one who knows everything about everyone: Tallulah Bankhead."

CHAPTER 41

The collar of Marcus' shirt rubbed against his neck. A quarter to nine in the morning, and it had to be at least ninety degrees. He pulled at his purple necktie and wiped away the dribble of sweat rolling over his Adam's apple. You're not sweating because it's hot out, he told himself. You're sweating because you're afraid Buttface Hoolihan isn't going to let you in.

He pulled an envelope from his jacket pocket and extracted a single sheet of paper, which he unfolded and held so that Leo the Lion and the *Ars Gratis Artis* motto embossed at the top was clearly visible. Let Buttface Hoolihan accuse him of forgery now. He took a breath and rounded the corner. Hoolihan stood in the middle of the driveway, staring straight at him.

"Mr. Adler," Hoolihan said. "Welcome to MGM."

Marcus blinked. "Thank you."

Hoolihan raised his clipboard and turned the New Arrivals page toward Marcus. "See? You're on the list . . . *today*. You understand, last time we met I was only doing my job, right?" Marcus nodded. "Do you know which building to report to?"

"Scenario building," Marcus said, "same as last time."

Hoolihan ignored the jab. "I hope your time here is fruitful." He sounded genuine.

"Thank you, Mr. Hoolihan."

"Everyone calls me Hooley."

* * *

Hooley's voice was still ringing in Marcus' ears when he reached reception in the scenario department. Dierdre didn't recognize him.

"Adler . . . Adler . . ." She rifled through the papers on her desk. "Ah yes, Marcus Adler. You've been assigned to building twenty-three." She pulled out a map of the studio lot. "It's right near the reservoir. Just take that main street under the big Metro-Goldwyn-Mayer sign and keep going until you see a giant pool with a pier and a pirate ship. Just look for the big numbers painted on the doors."

Back outside, the sunshine seemed a little harsher, the heat a little more concentrated. He walked past the commissary where the strong aroma of coffee filled the air, past the research building and the dance school, where a jaunty piano number wafted out with hand-claps and foot-stomps. He was passing under the huge studio sign at the middle of the lot when someone called his name.

George Cukor was striding toward him with his hand extended. "Hello, dear boy! First day on the job! Pretty exciting, eh?"

"This is going to take some getting used to."

"By day three you'll be as jaded as the rest of us."

Marcus dropped his voice to a whisper. "Can I assume it's thanks to you that I'm here at all?"

Marcus had been feeling more dejected than an orphan on Christmas when George found him sitting on the steps of the scenario department, four lousy minutes too late. Worry not, Cukor had told him. There is always a remedy. When a miraculous letter emblazoned with MGM's letterhead announced that his screenwriter's contract would take effect at his earliest convenience, Marcus' glum telegram delivery routine was a thing of the blessed past.

Cukor smiled. "I owed you one." He rubbed his hands together. "I'm due for a meeting with Thalberg. He's all worked up over *Romeo and Juliet.* I fear he wants his wife for Juliet."

"But isn't Norma Shearer a little . . . mature?"

Cukor rolled his eyes. "Hence my trepidation. Can I walk you to your new home?"

"You're going my way?" Marcus pointed toward the reservoir.

"No, no, Thalberg's office is across from the scenario building. This way."

"I think twenty-three is across the pond."

Cukor frowned. "Twenty-three? Are you sure?"

"That's what the girl said."

"Hmmm," Cukor said.

Marcus fought a sinking feeling. "What's wrong with building twenty-three?"

"I thought my recommendation carried more weight. Twenty-three is the production office for Cosmopolitan Pictures." He gave Marcus an encouraging slap on the shoulder. "I wish you lots and lots of the best luck," he said, and walked away.

Marcus stared at the reservoir and sighed. Cosmopolitan Pictures was a vanity production house established by William Randolph Hearst to satisfy his mistress, Marion Davies, and his libidinous ego. Marcus' dreams of his family gazing at his name on the screen credits of an MGM picture evaporated. So much for *And don't come back here until you've made it big in Hollywood.*

He checked his watch, composed himself, and hurried along the street to a brick building with a large 23 painted over the door. He opened it onto a long, comfortable room with desks spread throughout. Light poured through the windows onto potted ferns and philodendrons. The creamy white walls were hung with framed posters of Marion Davies in *The Five O'Clock Girl, Not So Dumb, Polly of the Circus* and *Blondie of the Follies.*

Marcus, Kathryn and Gwendolyn had gone to see Billie Dove, Marion's co-star in the last one. Billie had been floating around the Garden of Allah for years, and the inside story was that Hearst had ordered extensive editing after she outshone Marion. At least, that was how Billie told it.

There was only one person in the whole place. He stopped pounding away at his typewriter when Marcus walked in. "You must be Adler."

"Yes. Marcus Adler, reporting for duty."

"Terrific," the guy said flatly. "Welcome." He waved a hand over the five empty desks. "Pick a desk, any desk."

Marcus chose one against the wall in the far corner. He hung his jacket and hat on the nearby coat rack and sat down as the guy approached with a thin stack of papers. "The name's McNulty, you can call me Bub. I'm the script supervisor. I'm also in the middle of an emergency rewrite, because Hearst doesn't like — ah, skip it. You'll learn. I don't have time to give you the full tour. I want you to read this and start sketching out a screenplay."

Marcus nodded and picked up a short story titled "Ursula Goes Underground." It was about a girl called Ursula who spots an old flame — the one who got away — on the New York subway and follows him. It took all of four paragraphs before it dawned on Marcus that he was reading a version of his own story, "Subway People." Roscoe the journalist had been changed to secretary Ursula, the L.A. subway had been changed to New York, and instead of discovering a whole community underground, Ursula discovered her one true love, a neighbor she'd never worked up the courage to talk to.

Marcus looked up at Bub. The guy had a cigarette drooping from his mouth, another in a conch shell ashtray, and a bottle of pills as large as his coffee cup. Marcus picked up "Ursula Goes Underground" and approached Bub's desk. "I know you're busy, but I need to have a word with you about this story."

Bub yanked a sheet of paper from his typewriter and studied it. "Which name sounds better for a wise-cracking sidekick: Rhonda or Rosemarie?"

"Rhonda. Look, about this story —"

"You're right. Rosemaries bake cakes, but Rhondas chew gum."

"This "Ursula Goes Underground" story. It was originally — "

Bub's chair scraped over the mottled linoleum as he stood up. "I've got to get this over for approval, but pronto. This Ursula thing, I know it's a piece of shit."

"I wouldn't say that."

"I just need you to turn it into a script. Can you do that?" Bub looked at him with eyes bleary from fatigue.

"Yes, sure, but this is my story."

Bub was halfway to the door. "Absolutely. All yours. I'm more than happy to give you credit for it. By the way, the coffee is probably old by now; you might want to make a fresh pot." The door slammed behind him, leaving Marcus alone in an empty room.

CHAPTER 42

Gwendolyn's eyes widened in the flickering torchlight. Enormous red and black zombie masks gaped at her. "Where in heaven's name are we?"

"It's called the Zulu Hut," Kathryn replied.

"They don't actually serve Zulu food here, do they?" Gwendolyn asked. "If the menu is all fried bugs and goat gizzard stew, then I vote we give Tallulah one hour or three drinks, whichever comes first. If she doesn't show, let's go to the Tick Tock Tea Room for meat loaf."

Kathryn laughed and shook her head. "Don't worry. It'll be fine."

The Zulu Hut's bar ran the length of the place, ending at a small stage where a dusky-skinned man quietly played Polynesian music in a jazz style on a ukulele. The floor under the tables was a layer of sand. Gwendolyn regretted her spiked heels.

The hostess seated them in the middle of the room and a Negro waiter handed them menus and recommended the Zulu Warrior. As he leaned in to confide that it was just rum punch with extra coconut, Gwendolyn saw a bead of perspiration running a white line in front of his ears. He was a white guy in blackface.

"What are the chances Tallulah will actually show?" Gwendolyn asked. "She's a hootful of fun, but punctuality isn't exactly her strong suit."

"Mercedes said Tallulah was our best chance of tracking down Alla," Marcus insisted. "I know she's not reliable, but let's give her a chance. If there's no sign of her, you can take off. I don't mind waiting around, fried bugs or no fried bugs."

Poor Marcus, Gwendolyn thought. He still seemed so lost without Alla around. She once spotted him through Madame's window while the two of them were having one of their Saturday afternoon visits; it looked for all the world like a doting mother taking tea with her favorite son.

A rowdy *just-a-coupla-drinkies-before-dinner* foursome burst through the door and headed for the bar. They took up residence next to a fair-haired guy in a navy blue pinstripe who was drinking alone. The guy took a sip of his drink and swung his bamboo seat around to survey his new neighbors. Gwendolyn let out a sudden "Oh!" It was one of her new regulars. Or, more accurately, one of her new non-regulars.

He'd been hanging around since the Cocoanut Grove's Fourth of July party. Even in a room full of people born with a congenital case of the charms, this guy stood out. He was imposingly tall, with thick, wavy fair hair and broad shoulders that needed no padding in his expensive suits. His movie star teeth suggested that he took the practice of dentistry very seriously. Not only did he have movie star teeth, but he had movie star everything, except perhaps the overweening urge toward self-promotion. He chose the booths which favored seeing over being seen; more often than not the same one Anderson McRae used to occupy.

Whenever Gwendolyn walked past this new guy, he'd flash her a knowing smile, but he never beckoned her over. Not once, not ever, and that made him stand out more conspicuously than a roll of hundred dollar bills and a statuesque blonde with a forty-inch bust. And now here he was in a Valley joint called the Zulu Hut?

The waiter with the dissolving blackface returned with their drinks. "The specialty of the house is squab," he announced, "It comes fried with a spicy black bean sauce, potatoes, zucchini and corn pone."

Gwendolyn pointed toward the bar. "That guy in the blue suit—who is he?"

"Mr. Laird? He's one of the owners."

"Is he a good boss?"

The waiter shrugged. "He's pretty hands-off. You want I should send him over?"

"That won't be necessary," Gwendolyn replied.

They told the waiter they were waiting for a fourth. As he walked away, Gwendolyn commented, "He's a new face at the Grove. I thought he was one of those fat cat studio types." She took a long sip of her virgin Zulu Warrior. They made it with lots of coconut and pineapple. Boy, it was good.

"Well now, there's a funny coincidence," Marcus said.

"I'll say," Gwendolyn said. "I never figured he'd go to a joint like this, let alone own it."

"That's not what I mean," Marcus said with a lopsided smile. "Look who just met him at the bar."

Gwendolyn looked over to see a barrel-chested hunk of a man in shirt sleeves approach Laird. They shook hands coolly.

"I don't believe it," Kathryn whispered hoarsely.

"That's Mr. Long Beach, isn't it?" Marcus asked. Kathryn nodded silently. "They're not happy. Look at all that finger pointing."

Gwendolyn watched Kathryn go pale.

A few weeks after Kathryn's appointment, Gwendolyn had found a telegram in the kitchen trash can. It had been from Roy asking why she wasn't returning his calls. The following week she'd found two more. Different wording, same desperate tone. Gwendolyn didn't blame Kathryn for avoiding him. He sounded like a great guy, and all, but he was married. *Married.* With her column in the *Hollywood Reporter*, Kathryn was becoming a public figure; she had a reputation to think of. No, it was better she ended it. The sensible thing to do. But Gwendolyn knew the look lingering in Kathryn's eyes now. She missed Roy something fierce.

"Pity we weren't seated nearer the bar," Marcus said.

"This is near enough, thank you very much," Kathryn muttered. "In fact, this is about seventeen miles too close."

"Still, you have to wonder what they're talking about," Marcus said.

"Christ almighty! Where the hell am I?"

Tallulah Bankhead appeared at the table wearing a sleek dark orange satin suit and a huge onyx scarab brooch. She raked her eyes over the restaurant, looking bewildered.

"This is the Zulu Hut," Kathryn replied. "It's where you asked us to meet you."

"I thought this was the Hula Hut. With the barbequed pig and the ham steaks and the grilled pineapple." She flopped into a bamboo chair and threw her patent leather handbag onto the table. "How disappointing." Her face lit up when she spotted their drinks. She called the waiter over to order a Zulu Warrior–"Heavy on the rum, darling, and light on the coconut."–and lit up a long pink cigarette.

Gwendolyn couldn't keep her eyes off Laird. He and Roy were deep in conversation and it didn't look like they got on well. There was lots of finger pointing and chin jutting. She had to get closer. "Excuse me," she said, "I'll be right back."

She took the long way around to the bar, making sure not to catch Laird's eye. She and Roy never actually met that night of the End-of-Prohibition party at the Garden. The party was over for her the moment she threw up on that good looking actor's shoes. As long as Laird didn't turn around she was just some girl waiting to catch the bartender's attention.

"Yes, but you told me you'd help me make the move from stunt man to actor," Roy said to Laird. "You promised we could do it by the end of last year. It's September now, and all I've got from you is a great big pile of bupkis."

Laird scoffed. "I'm an agent, not Mandrake the Magician."

"Dammit!" Roy said, hitting the bar with his fist. "I gave up that cowboy picture because you led me to believe you had something better lined up."

The bartender approached Gwendolyn. "What can I get you?"

"A book of matches, thanks."

He grabbed one from a bowl sitting on the bar not two feet from where she stood and dropped them into her hand. "Your waiter would have been more than happy to get you all the matches you need. Is he not providing you with excellent service?"

"Oh no, nothing like that. It's just that he's very busy and I didn't want to—"

"Don't even—!" Roy was on his feet now. "You're fired, you miserable, deceitful bastard." He picked up his Bloody Mary and threw it into Laird's face. He was out the door by the time Laird could open his eyes.

Gwendolyn teetered on sand and stilettos back to the table. Mr. Mystery was a talent agent! The words were music to Gwendolyn's ears. The Anderson McCrae connection was dead in the water. She could tell that when he next came into the Cocoanut Grove, his face a frozen mask.

"You'll be pleased to know that Hank only spent four days recovering in the hospital."

She'd seen neither Broochie nor McRae since. So, no murder rap, but no screen test at RKO. However, this Mr. Laird was something better: a talent agent!

Tallulah had worked her way into a melodramatic fever. "You should have heard their tale of woe. It was positively *endless*. First the famine, then some plague that killed what was left of their crops, then they had a fire that burned down the barn, then the sister-in-law needed some sort of women's operation. I swear on a bowl of cocaine, compared to them, Anna Karenina had it easy."

"So did Madame send them any money?" Marcus asked.

"I really have no idea. Remember, this was all told to me third-hand at some cocktail party. DeMille's, I think. I remember him being there. At least, I think I do. At any rate, for what it's worth, whoever it was who told me all this seemed to think she'd returned to Russia."

270

Gwendolyn looked at Marcus. His sweet, round face was deflated.

"Well, my darlings, I'm off." Tallulah sprang to her feet. "I had my heart set on roasted pig, so squabs just aren't going to do for me. If you do track down Madame, please give her my love. Ta-ta!"

The three of them watched her dodder across the sand toward the door. Marcus cleared his throat. "She was sort of my last hope."

Gwendolyn reached out and laid her hand on top of his. "We'll track her down," she told him, although she really didn't know how.

"So?" Kathryn nodded toward Laird, who was starting his third Zulu Warrior. "Did you find anything out?"

"Oh, yes," Gwendolyn said. "I most certainly did."

CHAPTER 43

Warner Brothers' press release announced their new motion picture, *Captain Blood*, in the usual hyperbole. The name of their magnificent new action hero, the dashing Mr. Errol Flynn, rang a bell. Where had she heard that name before?

This was the life of a gossip columnist. Sort through an endless cavalcade of words like "heroic" and "magnificent" and overworked turns of phrase like "capture the hearts of audiences everywhere" and "unforgettable performance," and turn them into news fit for consumption on a more human scale. She was still puzzling over that Errol Flynn name when her boss approached her desk.

"Praise from Caesar is praise indeed," he said. "I just got off the telephone with Louella. She tells me I've got a sharp knife in that Kathryn Massey girl."

"She actually got my name right?"

Thank God for George Cukor, or she'd still be on the dark side of Louella Parsons. Since that awful luncheon there had been rumors that Clark Gable got Loretta Young pregnant on the set of their latest movie, *The Call of the Wild*, and MGM was killing itself to squash the news until after the premiere. Louella hadn't made any sensational announcements about the Gable divorce, so Kathryn had assumed her gesture was for nothing.

"What else did she have to say?"

"Isn't that enough? It's not often that Parsons goes out of her way to praise the competition. So, I'd like you to write a movie review for me, please."

Write something that wasn't a regurgitation of some PR hack job? Kathryn marveled. Well now, that was more like it.

"Do you have a particular movie in mind?" Kathryn asked.

"What was the last one you saw?"

She thought for a moment. "Last weekend I went to see *Stranded*."

"Kay Francis? Great. Write me a review of that. Three hundred words. You've got one hour."

Stranded. What a woeful pile of trash. Writing a review wouldn't take an hour. She wound a sheet of paper into her typewriter and began.

STRANDED, starring Kay Francis and George Brent

Warner's latest Kay Francis offering is perfectly titled — it leaves any moviegoer expecting a coherent plot utterly stranded by the ten minute mark. A San Francisco Traveler's Aid Society dogooder meets up with a Golden Gate Bridge builder —

Her telephone jangled. After that luncheon at the Brown Derby, Kathryn had got to thinking. If George overheard what Clark Gable's agent was cooking up, surely waiters and waitresses did, too. And if they did, then so did hotel bell boys, bootblacks, shop girls, elevator operators, porters, valets, and maids. If these people knew they could get a silver dollar for calling Kathryn Massey about who'd checked in to which hotels and with whom, who was shopping where and what they were buying, who was seen getting into whose car, that would put her smack dab in the middle of the gossip game. Her telephone hadn't stopped ringing since. "This is Kathryn Massey."

"Katey-Potatey."

It was Roy. She used to like the way he said that, especially after making love to her.

"Hello, Roy."

"I need to see you. Today." His words came out slurry. Not counting that night at the Zulu Hut, they hadn't seen each other since before her appointment three months ago. She'd been half-expecting this call and half-hoping it'd never come.

"Perhaps I can meet you for a drink after work."

"No. I need to see you now. Right now."

"Roy, I'm working. I'm in the middle of something important and I'm battling a deadline. My time isn't my own like when I worked for Tallulah."

"I'm at the Top Hat. If you don't come down, I'm coming up."

"Don't do that. I won't have you making a scene. The best I can do is meet you in an hour."

There was some heavy breathing at the other end of the line. "Fine. One hour. If you don't show, I'm coming for you." He hung up.

Kathryn returned to her typewriter and read over what she had written. She poised her fingers over the keys but her scorn hung in the air like a parachute caught in the trees. She stared at the telephone. She'd seen him drunk before, but he was a happy drunk, a tender one. He'd never sounded like this.

She hacked her way through a draft, using every synonym for *trash* she could muster, but she could've worked until midnight and it wouldn't have made one bit of difference. Until she saw Roy, nothing coherent was coming out of her. At 12:45, she grabbed her hat, handbag, and gloves and went to Wilkerson.

"This is the first review I've ever written. You only gave me an hour, so there wasn't much time to polish."

"This business is all about deadlines, Miss Massey," Wilkerson said, scanning the headline. "And sometimes they're impossible."

* * *

Roy sat alone in a booth along the eastern wall of the Top Hat. Kathryn slid in across from him. "Have you ordered anything to eat yet?"

His eyes were as blurry as his words. "Not really in the eating mood."

Kathryn realized she wasn't either. "Just a cup of coffee, thanks," she told the waitress. She was going to ask him how he'd been, but his stained shirt and greasy hair pretty much answered that question.

"I saw you, you know," he said, abruptly.

"Where?"

"I got this buddy, he owns a warehouse where they're moving Chinatown to. He's got this new tenant, some sort of Chinese herbalist. They needed an extra pair of arms to help move them. Anyways, I saw you standing on a corner with a real good-looking girl, bit of a knockout. That's your roommate, isn't it? I started to go over to say hi but the closer I got, the more upset you looked. Then you both turned and walked into a building so I followed you. Dr. Harrison, right?"

Kathryn stirred her coffee without looking at it, and maintained her famous poker face. Oh Jesus, she thought, he even knows the doctor's name. She nodded but said nothing.

"So here's my question: What kind of gynecologist keeps an office in Chinatown?"

Kathryn felt a deep breath leave her body. Thank you, kind Nurse Brykk. "When a woman finds the right gynecologist," she said, "she'll go wherever his office is. Dr. Harrison is wonderful. He . . . he . . ."

They stared into each other's eyes. Roy's were bleary with hurt. He crumpled a napkin in his fist until the skin across the back of his hand stretched tight. "Are you going to keep it?"

A part of Kathryn breathed a tiny sigh of relief. She'd had the abortion for practical reasons–this simply wasn't the right time to have a child–but she hadn't told Roy for selfish ones: it was easier to leave him out of the decision process. But the guy deserved to know. And now he did. The silence was heavier than a bag of boulders.

"Roy," she said softly. "You're married."

He forced a gulp down his throat. "Yes," he said. He was barely audible. "But not happily. If it was up to me we'd get divorced tomorrow, but she's so Catholic she goes to Mass every single lousy day. Divorce is out of the question. Katey, my life was misery until the moment the Long Beach earthquake hit. You changed everything. And now you're having our baby and I can't . . . I can't even . . ." He pressed the napkin to his face and breathed into it with staccato breaths. His body sagged over the edge of the table, his head slumped onto his chest.

She desperately wanted to touch him, but she kept her hands grasped around each other in her lap. For chrissakes, put the poor dope out of his misery. "I lost the baby."

Roy's face shot up. "What?"

"I was jaywalking across Wilshire, not looking where I was going. I got myself knocked over by a streetcar."

"Jesus!" He sat upright, his torso now straight and pressed against the back of his seat.

Kathryn continued. "I pretty much got up and walked away. But the next day I knew something was wrong. And the day after that . . ." She gave an *oh-well-what-can-you-do* shrug. She reached out and grabbed Roy's meaty hand. "Listen to me. We dodged a bullet, you and I. Leastways, that's how I'm looking at it. So let's quit while we're ahead, huh?"

* * *

One of the advantages of working for Tallulah or Bob Benchley was that Kathryn could take an afternoon off and get drunk if she felt like it. Not that she often felt like it, but there was freedom in knowing she could. No such luck working for the *Hollywood Reporter*.

She dropped her handbag on her desk, peeled off her gloves and looked at her watch; it wasn't yet three o'clock. Could she ever do with a drink. Her review for *Stranded* lay on her desk. A slash of red pencil ran diagonally across the page. Wilkerson had scrawled SEE ME over the whole thing.

She picked up her review and walked down the corridor to his office. "I told you it was just a first draft."

"There was nothing wrong with what you wrote," Wilkerson said.

"So what's with this big red slash?"

"It seems I neglected to tell you our company policy about movie reviews."

"There's a policy?"

"We only write bad reviews when we're feuding with the studio who made it. If we're not feuding, we write a glowing review."

"Even if the picture's a stinker?"

"Sixty-nine percent of our revenue comes from advertising, and eighty-nine percent of our advertising comes from the studios. If we write scathing reviews of their movies, they'll pull their advertising. Then where would we be?"

"Your policy is to trade good reviews for advertisement revenue?"

Wilkerson shrugged his shoulders. "We're not called a 'trade paper' for nothing."

"In other words, all movie reviews in the *Hollywood Reporter* are meaningless.

"Not to those who aren't aware of our policy."

Roy's face still haunted Kathryn. She really didn't have the strength to deal with this right now. All she wanted was a good slug of whiskey with a second one already lined up. Why did she have to go and lie about getting hit by a streetcar? Couldn't she just have said she miscarried and left it at that? God, what she wouldn't give for the chance to play that scene down at the Top Hat over again.

Kathryn nodded slowly and considered the pointlessness of punching holes in her boss' logic. She picked up her review. "You want me to write a glowing review for the worst picture I've seen all year?"

"What I want is for you to follow company policy."

She stood up and told him she'd start right away. At his doorway, she couldn't resist asking one more thing. "But doesn't this company policy make a mockery of that 'You can count on Kathryn Massey for the truth' persona you thought we ought to create?"

"Your column and this review are two completely different animals."

Back at her desk, Kathryn inserted a fresh sheet into her typewriter and typed "STRANDED, starring Kay Francis and George Brent." She stared at the word *stranded* and thought, Good thing the last movie I went to see wasn't called *Noose*.

CHAPTER 44

Long before he typed the words THE END on the final draft of *Ursula Goes Underground*, Marcus decided that if nobody who saw it connected it with "Subway People," then he was lucky.

God knows he had done his best to salvage his own story and make it into something approaching a halfway decent picture. However the result was a turgid and improbable piece of crap that had only one thing going for it: William Randolph Hearst liked it. And that meant *Ursula Goes Underground* would be Marion Davies' next picture. He tapped out THE END just as Bud was putting on his jacket.

"The only thing I want you to do while I'm having lunch is come up with a name."

"What sort of name?"

"Do you really want this picture on your résumé?" Bud asked. Marcus let out an involuntary groan. "If you get stuck, think about the two teachers you most hated in high school."

By and large, Marcus' high school years were a pleasant time. His outstanding ability to slice through the water of any swimming pool had made him McKeesport High's star swimmer, and filled his father's eyes with pride. But the teachers he hated the most? Mr. Jacobs in chemistry and Miss Pratley in French. Make a mistake in either class and they'd scream at you like you'd personally kidnapped the Lindbergh baby.

Marcus tossed his original title page into the trash can. He inserted a new sheet and typed,

Ursula Goes Underground
Original screenplay by Jacob Pratley
He pulled out the paper and laid it on top of the manuscript as the telephone rang.

"Cosmopolitan Pictures, writing department," Marcus said.

"Hello there. I need to speak to the chap who's writing *Ursula Goes Underground.*" It was a woman with a light, airy voice.

"I can probably help you there."

"Your name?"

Marcus looked at the manuscript. "Jacob Pratley."

"Mr. Pratley," said the woman, "I've been asked to send for you by Miss Davies."

"In that case, you probably want —"

"Immediately," the woman cut in. "Can I assume you are acquainted with the whereabouts of Miss Davies' dressing room?"

William Randolph Hearst had built his mistress a two-story, eleven-room bungalow on the lot after he signed a distribution deal between Cosmopolitan Pictures and MGM. Everyone knew where The Dressing Room was.

"Yes, Ma'am," Marcus said.

"I'll see you momentarily." The woman hung up.

Marcus grabbed his jacket and straightened his tie. It wasn't his lucky purple tie today; not a good omen. He grabbed *Ursula Goes Underground* and hurried across the lot to Miss Davies' Spanish Mission bungalow, with its curved doorways and thick stucco painted a pastel shade of terracotta. He knocked on the heavy wooden door.

A short, pixie-like woman with a wild mass of blonde hair opened the door. "Pratley, I presume?" It was Marion Davies herself, in a jade-green silk robe and, from what Marcus could see, not much else.

"I'm from the writing department."

Davies waved Marcus into a huge living room decorated with oil paintings in ornate gilded frames and masses of carpets in swirling turquoise and scarlet. A spray of peacock feathers sprang from an antique Chinese vase at the end of a marble fireplace that looked like it had never been used.

"Sit, sit, please, by all means," Marion said. "I've just brewed myself up a pot of tea. Some limey concoction I've started to drink by the absolute gallon."

Marcus looked around. Hearst was notoriously jealous of any man who even glanced at Marion, but Marcus saw no evidence of him — no hat, no cane, no lingering cigar smell. "Tea? That would be nice."

"Lovely!" Marion exclaimed with a clap of the hands. "We haven't met yet, but I am Marion Davies." They shook hands. She had a warm and surprisingly firm grip. She bustled into the kitchen. "Won't be long!"

Marcus looked around the living room with its Tiffany lamps and crystal chandeliers, its enormous brass birdcage and its zebra pelt hung on the wall. It was just one of eleven rooms, but was twice the size of his whole space at the Garden of Allah.

"Here we go," Marion singsonged a few minutes later. She set a tray down on the mahogany coffee table next to a gold letter opener studded with small rubies along the handle. It sat on top of a copy of *BUtterfield 8*, a recent bestseller that seemed out of place.

"Honestly," she said, "I have so many people doing so many things for me these days, I can't tell you the simple joy I get from making my own tea. It's such an individual thing, don't you find? Nobody makes it exactly right unless you do it yourself. Cream? Sugar? Lemon?" She giggled. "Call me greedy, but I like all three, which I'm sure simply horrifies my British pals."

She poured the tea from an exquisite porcelain teapot with scarlet Chinese dragons painted on the side and handed a cup to him. She dumped four teaspoons of sugar into hers and sat back in her chair, crossing her legs. It divided the panels of her silk robe and they fell apart, revealing a creamy white leg all the way up to the top of her thigh.

"Now, about this *Ursula Goes Underground* drivel. Let's be honest, it *is* the most terrible drivel, isn't it?"

Marcus' teacup hovered halfway toward his open mouth. On his very first day, Bud had impressed upon him that the steadfast rule was: *William Randolph Hearst is always right.* Whatever Hearst wants, likes or needs, Hearst gets.

"I wouldn't say *terrible* drivel . . ." Marcus ventured.

"Oh, pish-posh!" Marion's gold and diamond bracelets jangled as she fluttered her hand and then slapped the next-to-last version of the manuscript on the table in front of them. "Who but the most soft-headed simpleton is going to believe any of this?" She leaned forward and her pert breasts peeked out. "You look like an intelligent chap, Mr. Pratley. You can't possibly be proud of this thing."

Marcus looked at Marion Davies, repeating the mantra to himself: *Hearst is always right. Nobody else's opinion matters in the goddamned slightest.*

Most people preferred to write Davies off as a gold-digger rather than see her screen work on its own merits. Long before he came to Cosmopolitan Pictures, Marcus had thought Hearst was hindering her career. She was a far better comedienne than she got credit for, and was nearly always better than the movies Hearst saddled her with. I can't let her think I like this movie, Marcus thought.

"Miss Davies, it's my personal belief that you deserve better material than what you've been given."

Marion laughed. It was a tinkling sound, like children on a playground. "W.R. keeps insisting it would make a terrific picture and I keep telling him no, no, no. It's ludicrous what this woman goes through. Nobody's going to buy it for a second. Now we're getting somewhere."

She put down her teacup, pulled Marcus' out of his hands, and set it down next to hers. She leaned back and stretched out her legs, then landed her feet in his lap. "Would you mind rubbing my feet?" she asked. "I've been in the most diabolical heels since seven this morning."

Marcus looked down at Marion's feet. They were dainty, manicured in a jade green nail polish that matched her silk robe. He had never rubbed anyone's feet before and wasn't sure how to start—or, frankly, whether he should. If Hearst's mistress complained about some writer on the Cosmopolitan Pictures payroll, that writer would be out of a job before he could say "pish-posh." I have to get out of this job, he told himself. This can only take me down a dead end. Or worse. He grabbed a foot and started kneading it.

"Oh, that's good!" She let her head fall back onto a quilted pillow. "W.R. has no feel for this sort of thing. But you do, don't you, Mr. Pratley?"

Marcus looked up. She had pulled open her robe. Marcus had never seen a woman's naked breasts before. From purely an objective standpoint, he was curious to see what the fuss was all about. They were lovely breasts, as far as he could tell, full and round and not the least bit lopsided, as he'd heard some were.

"Make love to me, Pratley," she whispered. She whipped her feet out of Marcus' lap. Before he could stop her, she loomed over him like a determined moth.

"Miss Davies!" Marcus exclaimed. He pulled back and felt the end of the sofa. "This isn't appropriate."

"Oh, never mind about ol' W.R. He can't get it up much these days. He doesn't mind this sort of thing in the least! You like my breasts, don't you, Pratley? I've been told they're irresistible." She pushed them closer to his face.

He grabbed Marion by her shoulders and pushed her back. "They're lovely, to be sure, but they're not irresistible."

"Well, thank God for that!" Marion exclaimed, and suddenly backed off, rewrapping the robe around herself.

"Excuse me?"

"I had you pegged as queer from the moment you walked in, but I had to be sure."

"What, just because I knocked back—"

"Oh relax, lovie. Your secret is safe with me. But I just had to be sure you weren't going to jump me."

"What made you think I was going to?" Marcus asked.

"Because you're a *man*, lovie. Men have been jumping on top of me virtually my whole life. Not that I've minded most of the time, but I'm in a different situation nowadays. I need to be sure who and what I'm dealing with. You wouldn't believe the number of people who sidle up to me, all cozy-like, when all they really want is to climb over me like I'm nothing but a footstool just to get to W.R."

She patted his arm. "I hope you understand, my sweet. If you had tried to jump me, I'd have knocked you flat with a left hook you wouldn't have seen coming. And that would've been a shame, because I like you. You have the personal fortitude to be honest about this claptrap they keep shoveling at me. I'd have felt dreadfully let down if you'd grabbed at my girls. But you didn't, because you're queer as a duck, and that's terrific news. More tea?"

She lifted the teapot and filled his cup before he could answer.

"So," Marion said, "if we're going to throw out this *Ursula Goes Underground* trash, we'd damned well better have something solid to replace it with. You must have a dozen stories bouncing around inside that queer little head of yours. Why don't you pick me out the best one and tell it to me?"

Ordinarily, Marcus' head was filled with a handful of stories colliding around inside his skull, and choosing one was as easy as picking a grape in a vineyard. But he was just now catching up with what had happened. Someone in this room made a pass at someone. Someone saw someone else's breasts. Just who saw what and who did what was simply a matter of who is sleeping with the boss. You'd better come up with something, Marcus told himself, but panic had canonballed every story idea out of his head.

His eyes fell on the letter opener. "I do have one story I like," he said slowly.

"I knew you would! Tell me!"

"It's about a boy and a girl." It was a safe start; that's pretty much what most movies were about. He kept his eyes on the letter opener. "And they live in the same building. They keep getting each other's letters because they have the same name. Samuel and Samantha, perhaps. Sam and Sam. Of course, they don't know they've got the wrong mail until they open it and read each other's letters." He took an extra long sip of tea.

"Samantha keeps getting love letters from a potential beau she doesn't like, but who is trying to woo her with bad poetry, which Samuel keeps reading and laughing at. In the meanwhile, Samuel is getting mysterious notes from a secret admirer who doesn't want to reveal her identity."

Marcus set his cup down in the saucer and looked up at Marion. "The story goes on a lot further, of course, but I'm a writer, not a public speaker. I'd rather type it up and bring it back sometime, if that's okay with you."

"I love what I've heard so far!" Marion enthused. "I'd like you to run back to your office and start working on it immediately."

When Marcus stepped out of the bungalow, the first dry Santa Ana wind of the fall hit him in the face. He let out a long breath and stared up at the enormous Metro-Goldwyn-Mayer Studios sign that stretched across four soundstages. Atop it sat a picture of Leo the Lion. The sight of Marion Davies' breasts flashed before his eyes. "Oh, God, Leo," he muttered, "you gotta get me away from Cosmopolitan Pictures."

CHAPTER 45

Several months passed before Gwendolyn saw Eldon Laird
again. He resurfaced at the Cocoanut Grove for the party
Max Factor threw to celebrate the opening of his new salon
around the corner from the Hollywood Hotel. The joke that
night was that only Max himself knew the real hair color of
every woman in the place. It probably wasn't far from the
truth.

As usual, Eldon arrived in a sleek suit that fit beautifully.
This one was a midnight blue that he'd teamed with a stark
white shirt and an impeccable burgundy silk necktie. But
what was most striking was the company he kept. It was
unusual to see him in the company of anyone, but when he
walked in with three oddballs in cheap suits, it was like
watching King George V arrive with the court jesters. They'd
had a decent shave and haircut, but squirmed inside their
tight collars. When Jean Harlow swept past in a white fox
coat, they gawked and nudged each other like teenagers in a
whorehouse.

What on earth, Gwendolyn had to wonder, was a class
act like Laird doing with these three bumpkins? She
straightened the cigarettes in her tray. Sooner or later
everybody at the Cocoanut Grove got around to flagging
down the cigarette girl, but not Eldon Laird. Not once, not
ever. Does he smoke some rare brand I don't carry?

She watched as they took a table much closer to the dance floor than Laird usually preferred. Then she made a long, visible circuit of the room, making sure her boss saw her, and cut back to the hat check. Terry had been working the booth for about a year. She was a nice girl with a cheeky smile that earned her more tips than any predecessors. "You know that party of four guys who just came in?" Gwendolyn asked her.

"You mean Silent Sam and his silly sidekicks?"

"Yes. Did Silent Sam come in with an overcoat?"

"He sure did. Beautiful cashmere."

"Could you do me a favor and check his pockets?"

Terry looked at her warily. Going through pockets was a big no-no on Grainger's long list of no-no's.

"I'll stand guard," Gwendolyn implored. "Please? I'll owe you."

Terry disappeared into the coat room for a moment. "I found this." She handed over an empty, flattened box of Viceroys.

"So much for that theory," Gwendolyn said. "I stock Viceroy."

"Those are the new ones with the cork tips." Terry pointed out. "They filter out all the bad stuff. Much better for you."

Gwendolyn turned the pack over, wondering what the odds were that Bobo carried them. She headed out to the hotel's tobacconist, but Terry called her back. "You might want to take a look at this." Terry placed a coaster from the Vine Street Brown Derby next to the Viceroys.

"I don't need to know about that," Gwendolyn said, and tapped the cigarette pack. "This is all I care about."

"I wouldn't be too sure of that," Terry told her. "Turn it over."

Gwendolyn flipped the cardboard coaster over and saw, stamped in faded black ink, the words *Gwendolyn Was Here*.

* * *

"Marcus? Marcus Adler? Is that you?" The voice was a hoarse whisper.

Marcus glanced at the clock over the check-in desk; it read two minutes to two. "Yes," he said into the telephone. "Who's this?"

"Marcus, it's George Cukor."

"George? What's wrong?"

"Holy crap, where do I start?" George croaked.

"Are you in trouble?"

"Is there any way anybody could overhear this conversation?"

Marcus looked at the night clerk, who had roused him from sleep for an urgent phone call. He was already nodding off. "What's happened?"

"I've been arrested."

"What for?"

George let out a groan. "For lewd behavior."

"What did you do?"

"I got caught approaching a young sailor at Pershing Square."

"I thought the sailors came to you."

"Sometimes a man needs the excitement of the hunt. Anyway, we got to talking, and I could have sworn he knew what was going on." Cukor let out a breathy groan. "But he didn't. When he cottoned on, he started yelling. It caught the attention of a cop and now I've been arrested. I need your help, Marcus."

"What can I do?"

"I need you to come down here and get me out."

"Sure thing. I can do that," Marcus replied. "Is there a bail?"

"It's two thousand dollars."

Cukor may as well have said two hundred thousand dollars. "George, I don't have that sort of money laying around."

"Normally, I have it at the house, but I just bought a set of French silver, and the seller wanted cash. At best there's a couple hundred. Marcus, I need to impress upon you how urgent this is. Reporters come to the jail every morning to sniff out any story-worthy detainees. I need to be out of here before seven."

Marcus was flattered that someone like George Cukor would turn to him in such a dire hour, but was he really the best person for this? "Aren't there people at MGM who do this sort of thing? People with pull?"

"Of course, but my contract is up for renegotiation soon. I don't want MGM or Louis B. Asshole to hold something like this over me."

"But what about your lawyer? Or Billy Haines?"

"My lawyer just had a heart attack and his partners wouldn't understand. Billy's back east on decorating business, and the others don't have your sensible head. Please do this for me. I'm begging you."

"Okay, George, I'll try to think of something."

"It goes without saying that you cannot tell a soul about any of this. Really, Marcus, not one word."

Marcus hung up the telephone, but not before he heard a whimper crawl down the line to him. He stared into the dark. "Two grand?" he muttered, and ran his fingers through his hair. "How on earth am I to dig up that kind of dough?"

Return to Sender, the romantic comedy he penned for Marion Davies, was about to go into production. Even if it got released, it probably wouldn't make the small-time picture show circuit like McKeesport, and so his family would never know that he wrote it.

I need to get out of Cosmopolitan Pictures and into MGM, Marcus told himself. I need to write a hit picture so that all of McKeesport–my father included–will be sitting in the orchestra seats of the Bijou when my name fills the screen. The only way that was likely to happen was with the help of someone like George Cukor. But Jesus Christ. Two grand…?

* * *

Kathryn was dreaming about hitting Louella Parsons over the head with a half-inflated beach ball when the knock at her front door punched her awake. She raised her head off the pillow, still hearing Louella grunt.

"Kathryn, are you in there?"

She pulled on her robe on the way to the door. "Marcus?"

"Open up."

She glanced at the mantle clock. He didn't sound drunk. She opened the door. "Marcus? What the hell . . . ?"

Marcus stepped inside Kathryn and Gwendolyn's villa. His shirt was buttoned wrong and his hair was flattened on one side. "I'm so sorry to wake you, but there's been some trouble and I'm out of ideas."

"What sort of trouble?"

Marcus curled his face up into a wince. "You don't happen to have two thousand dollars on you, do you?"

Kathryn couldn't help the laughter-gasp that popped out of her mouth. "Marcus, honey, if you're in trouble you know you can tell me anything."

She watched her friend stare at her in the moonlight slanting through the living room window. Clearly something was up. She took him by the hand and sat next to him on the sofa.

"It's not me who's in trouble," he said.

"But somebody is, and they need your help. At two o'clock in the morning? It must be a sensitive matter."

He nodded.

Kathryn thought, And he's not telling me because I'm a gossip monger. It had to happen sooner or later, that people would see me as a gossip columnist first and a friend second. But I never thought it would be Marcus at the front of that particular line. "I can't help you if you won't tell me what's going on," she said.

Even in the dim light, she could see the vacillation in his eyes. He shifted his gaze from Kathryn's face to the clock and seemed to study it for longer than necessary. The moments dragged by. Eventually he said, "You have to promise me that you won't breathe a word of this to anyone."

Kathryn nodded, but he made her swear it out loud. Then he spilled out his telephone conversation with George Cukor.

"Two thousand dollar bail?" she asked. "That's outrageous."

"And somehow he expects me to come up with it. We don't know anyone who has that kind of cash lying around . . . do we?"

The cogs started clicking inside Kathryn's mind. Maybe this was how she could repay that favor. Kathryn had always wanted to pay George Cukor back for the way he'd saved her bacon that day of the hideous Hollywood Women's Press Club luncheon. After MGM had opened that Clark Gable/Loretta Young picture, Louella had eventually used the tip Kathryn handed her, and even remembered her name when she called Wilkerson.

"Cash, no," she said, "but we do know someone with something worth three thousand bucks."

Hope shined out of Marcus' eyes. "We do?"

She grabbed a kitchen chair and led Marcus into the bedroom. She placed the chair in front of the closet door and climbed up.

"What are you doing?" he whispered.

"Gwendolyn's diamond brooch." She reached up and pushed aside the cover of an air vent built into the ceiling. "It's the only hockable thing any of us have."

"Oh, Kathryn, I don't know . . ."

She reached up into the hole in the ceiling and felt around. "Of course, we'll have to ask her first, which probably means she'll want to know why, but unless you've got some other big idea—" She pulled a striped pillow case out of the hole. "Gwennie showed me this, just in case something happened to her."

But the pillow case felt far too light and far too empty. "Uh-oh."

* * *

Knowing that Eldon Laird had a *Gwendolyn Was Here* coaster in his coat pocket cast the man in an entirely different light, and gave Gwendolyn a new thrust of courage. She approached his table and lingered long enough for the Three Stooges to get an eyeful before she sang out, "Cigars, cigarettes . . ." She caught Laird's eye. "I have the new cork-filtered Viceroys, in case you're running out."

His eyes flickered with a subtle double take; his lips parted slightly.

"Why, yes, I do need a couple of packets, Miss Gwendolyn," he said.

Thank God for Bobo and his stock of every tobacco product known to mankind. "Never fear," she told him, "Gwendolyn is here." Laird's eyes narrowed. He had the look of a man not accustomed to being caught off guard.

She turned around when Chuck tapped on her shoulder. "You have a couple of visitors," he said. His face was more solemn than she'd ever seen it. She raised her eyebrows. "Grainger knows they're here. It's okay. He told me to come get you."

Gwendolyn found Kathryn and Marcus in the alcove by the Grove's front door. They looked unsettled. "What the heck are you two doing here?" she asked. "No!" she gasped. "It's Monty, isn't it? He's been killed!"

"No, no," Kathryn assured her, "it's nothing like that."

"Gwennie, honey, we're so sorry to pull you away from your work," Marcus said. "But I have a friend in trouble and we need to come up with some cash, real quick."

"Okay . . ."

"And I wanted to know if I could borrow your diamond brooch in order to hock it. I'd get it back in a day or two, plus interest for the trouble."

Gwendolyn's big green eyes darted between her friends' gloomy faces. "Sure you can," she said.

Marcus shot Kathryn a curious look of surrender.

"Sweetie," Kathryn's whisper was hoarse. "We looked inside the pillow case. It's not there. I think we've—you've been robbed."

Gwendolyn hoped she wouldn't have to own up to the silly boo-boo she'd made but who knew that someone would need her diamond brooch so badly? This week, of all weeks! "No, we haven't," she said.

"Gwendolyn, it's gone. Nothing's up there in the ceiling, just the pillowcase."

"That's because Alice has it. Something about a big date with some director she's desperate to impress."

"No honey," Marcus fought to keep the disappointment from his voice. "I mean the real one."

"She's got the real one."

"You lent Alice—?"

"Last week I took them down to be cleaned. Somehow I got them mixed up and I ended up lending her the real one."

Marcus and Kathryn exchanged a completely different look. "Where's her date?"

* * *

The Biltmore Bowl was one of those places Marcus had always wanted to go to but had never seen. It wasn't outrageously expensive—you could have a night of dinner and dancing in the World's Largest Ballroom for less than five dollars.

But as good a dancer as Kathryn was, and as much as he'd be the envy of every man there if he took Gwendolyn out for a samba, it wasn't the sort of dinner-and-dancing date he longed for. Nice places where nobody would drop their highball in horror at two gentlemen waltzing around the floor simply didn't exist. Men like him could only have clandestine gropings behind bushes and sand dunes, or at best, half-decent hotel rooms. Like that Zachary guy said at Pershing Square, *We don't get to have dates any more than we get to have marriages or relationships or love. This is it, so learn to like it the way I have.*

It was nearly four o'clock in the morning by the time Marcus and Kathryn got to the Biltmore Bowl, but the Central Casting goon out front wouldn't let them in unless they paid. "You want in, you pay in." They did, but it didn't leave much for cab fare.

The Biltmore Bowl was a cavernous room two stories high and decorated with enough gold to choke King Tut. A surprisingly healthy number of dancers filled the floor. Even in a vast, classy joint like the Biltmore Bowl, Alice Moore wasn't hard to spot.

She was smoking a cigarette at the bar in an atrocious crimson dress with a sparkly silver neckline. As Gwendolyn and Marcus got closer, the dress began to shimmer like mercurochrome. The diamond sunburst only made it look cheaper.

There was something about this girl that Marcus never quite trusted. It went all the way back to that night she and Gwendolyn were part of that crazy human billboard. He'd been watching Gwendolyn the moment she lost her balance and toppled off like a Raggedy Ann doll. It was hard to say for sure but it looked to him like Alice had nudged poor Gwendolyn off their perch. But she did it in such a way that it could have just as easily been the accident Alice swore it was afterwards. Everyone had given her the benefit of the doubt but Marcus had never been as convinced as he'd have liked.

Marcus forced a smile. "Alice, we've been looking for you."

"Do me a favor." She jabbed her cigarette into a Biltmore ashtray. "Give me a minute to get back to my table then come ask me to dance. I've been playing cutesy pie with that dyke director Dorothy Arzner all night. I've been angling for a role in a Rosalind Russell picture she's doing at Columbia and I think I've got her hooked. But I don't want this crowd thinking that I'm her actual date or nothin'. Thanks a bunch!"

"I really need to . . ." But Alice had already started back to her table to join a mannish woman whose dark hair was slicked back like Clark Gable. She wore a dark brown suit, a cream blouse and a copper necktie, and leered like she was about to get lucky. Alice plopped herself down on the vacant seat and started making ridiculously big arm gestures.

"This is the girl Gwendolyn gives a three thousand dollar brooch to?" Kathryn asked.

"I'm going to have to dance with her now, aren't I?" Marcus said. Kathryn offered him a *better-you-than-me* nod. He counted out ten seconds and approached the table.

"Miss Moore." He bowed stiffly toward her. "I would so enjoy the pleasure of this dance."

"Why, Mr. Adler!" she exclaimed in the over-the-top way that only actresses of negligible talent can summon. "How lovely to see you." She turned to her dinner partner. "You don't mind, do you?" She didn't wait for a response and jumped to her feet.

They were still within earshot when she said, "Honestly, would it kill that woman to put on a little lipstick?"

"Alice," Marcus broke in. "I need Gwendolyn's brooch."

"My brooch?"

"Gwendolyn's brooch. I need to borrow it. And I mean right now."

"At four o'clock in the morning?"

"I'll see to it that Gwendolyn gets it back."

"Sorry, chum. Gwendolyn lent me this brooch for a whole week, and that week doesn't end until Monday. I have a date with a new gentleman friend who's connected to Fox. He's taking me dancing at the Palomar tomorrow evening and I intend to wear it."

"You planning on wearing the same dress?" Marcus asked her.

"What's wrong with this dress?"

"I'm not saying there's anything wrong with it." He shook his head solemnly. "A silver neckline with a gold brooch . . . ?"

Alice's hand pulled free of Marcus' and flew to cover the brooch. "It's the nicest piece of jewelry I could lay my hands on!"

"But that doesn't mean it matches. Haven't you heard that old saying? Silver and gold leave me cold."

* * *

Kathryn thought the pawnbroker Alice directed them to was remarkably well groomed, considering he'd been open all night. She'd expected some seedy character, all tired and sad from dealing with people teetering at the bottom rung of life's ladder. He was dressed neatly in a pressed suit and a cinnamon necktie. The only unsurprising thing about this setup was that Alice knew an all-night pawnbroker at the south end of downtown. He took his time studying Gwendolyn's brooch.

"So?" Kathryn pressed. "How much for it?"

"Eighteen fifty."

"Don't jack us around, buddy," Kathryn shot back. Her voice was harsher than she suspected possible. "We'll accept twenty-one hundred."

"Nineteen twenty-five."

"Two thousand," Marcus cut in. "I guarantee you I'll be back within forty-eight hours and I'll buy it back from you for twenty-two hundred."

Kathryn was dying to wipe her clammy palms on her skirt, but she didn't dare show how desperate they were. "That's a two hundred dollar profit in two days," she pointed out. "Is that really a deal you want to knock back?

The pawnbroker looked at them unblinkingly. "I don't know that I'll see you again any time in the next forty-eight *months*, but I'll make it two thousand if you tell me who you're bailing out."

Kathryn kept her eyes trained on the pawnbroker and heard Marcus push a laugh out of his throat.

"Listen," the guy said. "I'm the only twenty-four hour pawnbroker in L.A. I'm ten blocks from the city lockup. Two thousand is steep. The only people whose bail is more than a couple hundred are movie people in a hell of a jam, but movie people usually have fancy lawyers and studio heavies calling police chiefs and D.A.s for them. Let's just say you've got my curiosity up."

Baloney, Kathryn thought. As soon as we leave here, you'll be on the phone to some yellow journalist for your big fat tip about who's been locked up. She looked outside. The taxi driver was still waiting for the big fat tip Marcus had promised him.

"Okay," said Marcus, "it's a deal."

Kathryn spun toward Marcus and glared at him until he couldn't ignore her cobra stare anymore. His expression said, What else can we do?

"Okay then," the pawnbroker said. He opened a drawer and pulled out two wads of twenties and counted them out loud. He started to push them across the counter toward Marcus, then stopped and raised his eyebrows.

Marcus cleared his throat. "Victor Fleming."

Oh lord, Marcus, Kathryn thought, you're a genius.

Victor Fleming was a hard-drinking, hard-living, wildlife-hunting, ex-stuntman-turned-director that man's-man actors like Gary Cooper and Clark Gable liked to work with. He was everything George Cukor wasn't and never wanted to be, and George couldn't stand him.

"Fleming, huh?" The pawn broker rolled the name around his mouth. "You mean the director?"

Marcus took the money, folded it in and pushed it into his pocket. He pointed a threatening finger at the guy. "But you didn't fucking hear it from me."

* * *

It was nearly closing time when Eldon Laird and his pals gathered the strength to lift themselves up from their table. Despite their succession of Manhattans, Laird was the model of sobriety, but the Three Stooges looked like they'd been run over by the J&B Scotch truck.

It had been a busy night–the Max Factor crowd had all been a hard-drinking and hard-smoking bunch–but things had tapered off now. When she saw Laird and his pals get up, Gwendolyn positioned herself between the hat check and the front door and struck a casual pose. But when the men collected their coats and strode past her without a glance, her shoulders slumped.

Then a man cleared his throat behind her. She turned around to find Eldon Laird standing with his overcoat folded over one arm.

"Do you have much call for filter-tipped Viceroys?" he asked.

"Only from my more discerning clients."

"I'm having a hell of a time finding them. Could you get more in?"

Well now, that was more like it. "Of course," she said. "Next time you're in here I'll be sure to have some in stock."

"I'm nearly out of them. If you are able to get your hands on them, I'd appreciate it if you could drop by my office." He flipped a business card into her tray. "A carton, maybe?"

She picked up the business card and glanced at it. "Eldon Laird, is it?" she said, as coolly as she could.

"Yes, that's right. I'm a talent agent. But I'm guessing you knew that already."

* * *

The taxi lurched to the curb. "Tell you what I'll do," the cabby said. "I'll turn off the meter this time and wait for you to come out. I can take you and your buddy home."

Marcus sighed to himself. Did all these people really think we don't know what they're up to? "No, that's okay," he said, feigning nonchalance. "This could take a while." He handed over a ten dollar bill. "Keep the change." That meant a three dollar tip — the best one he'd get all year. They didn't wait for the driver's response and climbed out.

It was six forty. Nobody was about but surely that was going to change any minute. Marcus headed toward the terrazzo steps, but Kathryn pulled him back.

"This is as far as I go," she said. "Tell him it's payback for the Brown Derby and that I won't breathe a word of it in my column." She gave him a shove. "Now, you go in and get him while I skedaddle."

Marcus took the marble stairs two by two and hurried through the revolving door into the city jail's waiting room. A dozen of society's rejects slouched over the scarred wooden benches as the desk sergeant smirked at Marcus and directed him to the cashier's window. "Come back here with a receipt for two grand, and he's all yours."

It was five to seven when one of MGM's most respected directors, currently guiding Greta Garbo through a high-profile version of *Camille*, appeared before Marcus looking like a skid row bum after a three-day bender. He was in his shirt sleeves and his rolled-up necktie was poking out of a pants pocket which had been ripped several inches at the seam. His shoes, always so immaculately polished, were scuffed and dull.

"Oh, thank God!" George exclaimed hoarsely, and grabbed Marcus by the forearms. "The night I've had. You're my savior. Twice! I'll never forget this. *Never!*"

"You and me both, Georgie. Come on, let's get out of here before–"

Marcus stopped short of the revolving door. The taxi driver was on the front steps talking to a couple of guys holding large cameras.

"Is there a side entrance?" Marcus asked the guard.

"Nope. Everyone goes in and out the same door."

"Where's the men's room?"

The guard pointed off to his right. Marcus pulled George in and locked the door. "We need to swap clothes."

"Look at your waist!" George said. "I'll never fit inside those pants."

"Then you'll need to suck in your stomach and keep it sucked in until we're clear of the building. Let's just be thankful that we're about the same height."

The two men stripped down to their underwear and exchanged clothes. George, a doughy man at best, managed to squeeze into Marcus' trousers. "I feel like a Victorian lady in her tightest corset." They checked themselves in the mirror and left the bathroom.

They crossed the waiting room and threw themselves through the revolving doors, striding into the sunlight with their heads turned away from the knot of photographers and reporters gathering on the granite forecourt.

"Got a minute?" called a reporter. "Either of you guys know Victor Fleming?"

George stopped and turned around. "Victor Fleming?"

"Yeah," the reporter said. "The director at MGM. Some dame told me a big-time movie director got himself hauled into lockup last night. She said it was Victor Fleming. You see him in there?"

Cukor flashed Marcus a sideways glance. Marcus smiled. "You're welcome."

CHAPTER 46

"NO!" Gwendolyn exclaimed around a mouthful of a onion bagel. They'd come to Schwab's Drugstore at the end of their sleepless night for the best bagels in all of Los Angeles. "It *wasn't!*" Marcus nodded his head. "I hope he was grateful," she said.

"Oh, don't you worry, he was. But don't breathe a word about this to a soul."

Kathryn stifled a yawn. The poor thing still hadn't gone to bed yet. Neither had Marcus. After such a dramatic night, it was no wonder they were still all keyed up and devouring toasted bagels like they were cotton candy. "Marcus made sure he knew who you were and that the brooch belonged to you. Mr. George Cukor owes you one."

Gwendolyn watched Jack and Leon Schwab hang the same silver and white tinsel they used every Christmas across the magazine rack at the back of the store. Gosh, and to think my little ol' diamond brooch helped save the reputation of one of MGM's most important directors. She picked up her coffee and blew on the steam. "I'm glad I knew where Alice was going, or you'd still be peeking inside every nightclub between here and Long Beach."

"Good lord, Gwennie!" Kathryn exclaimed. "You should have seen who she was there with."

"I don't need to. I've seen enough of those movie studio guys that Alice dates to know they're all the same."

"Not this one," Marcus said. "I mean, she *looked* like a man and she dressed like a man . . ."

"Some director," Kathryn added.

"A woman director?" Gwendolyn leaned forward. "What was her name?"

Marcus and Kathryn looked at each other. "I think she mentioned the name Dorothy," Marcus said.

"Oznow . . . ?" Kathryn guessed. "Arznow . . . ?"

"Arzner?" Gwendolyn asked.

"Yes, I think so. Do you know her? Very manly, huh?"

Gwendolyn turned to Marcus. "Do you remember when I told you about a conversation I had once with Alla? About how important it was to have a close friend I can confide in? I told her I had the two of you, and she told me about her friend."

Marcus nodded.

"Alla's friend was someone called Arzner. She was in Alla's 8080 Club when the Garden was all hers. And you know how those gals were all hot to trot for each other. Maybe she knows where Alla is."

* * *

Marcus took deep breaths to calm himself as he, Kathryn and Gwendolyn walked up the driveway of Arzner's house in the Hollywood Hills. It hadn't taken long to track down the only Dorothy Arzner in the telephone book; they were there within the hour. Her front door was made of cherry wood and had a round stained-glass window with a Roman goddess holding a long, arched bow.

A woman built like a fire plug answered the door. "Can I help you? — Wait!" Arzner frowned as her gaze flickered between Marcus and Kathryn. "You two were at the Biltmore Bowl last night, weren't you? Alice's friends." When she caught sight of Gwendolyn standing behind them, her eyes widened. "Well, what can I do for *you?*"

"We've come about Alla Nazimova," Marcus said.

The woman's eyes darted back to Marcus. "How did you know she's here?" Marcus' heart gave a jolt.

"She is?" Kathryn blurted out. She leaned to one side and peered past Arzner. "Can we see her?"

"Best I can do is pass on a message." Arzner was stony-eyed again.

"Please," Marcus said. He could feel a rising tide of panic fill his chest. "Could you tell her it's Marcus Adler? I'd really love to see her."

"It's okay, Dorothy." Alla's voice was unmistakable. "Let them in."

Alla stepped into the bright foyer. Three years ago, she was a handsome woman who'd waltzed beyond the height of her beauty but still carried it with her. Now her hair was thinner and grayer, the lines on her face deeper. Even her magnificent violet eyes had dimmed a watt or two. Instead of wise and worldly, they looked worn and weary. But her smile, soft and warm, was all that mattered to Marcus.

"Madame!" he exclaimed. He stepped past Arzner and embraced the friend he thought he'd lost. She smelled as she always did: tart blackberries, sweet honey. He couldn't speak. He held her tightly and swam in the pool of relief that drenched him.

She let him hug her for a few moments before grabbing him by the shoulders and pushing him back to arm's length. She stared into his eyes. "What an enterprising young man you proved yourself to be."

Marcus nodded. "You add two and two together long enough, you can track anyone down."

Madame widened her smile. "No, no. You achieved your goal. You're a professional screenwriter now. Marion Davies, eh? Well done."

Marcus couldn't help but smile at the encouragement from Madame he'd longed for. The fact that she knew about his job at Cosmopolitan Pictures showed that she hadn't forgotten him completely.

Madame led them into Arzner's spacious livingroom; the walls were covered with gilt-framed oil paintings of female nudes. As she motioned for them all to take a seat, Dorothy murmured something about making orange blossom tea and left the room.

Marcus took Madame by the hand. It felt dry, like an autumn leaf. "I've missed you," he told her. "Very much."

"We all have," Gwendolyn put in.

"You're very dear. All of you. It is heartening to see your faces once more." She turned back to Marcus, her expression a veneer of Russian stoicism. "I am sorry that I left without saying goodbye. That was remiss of me. But I . . ." she lowered her eyes. "I was at my weakest."

"We heard about your family back in Russia," Kathryn said.

Alla nodded.

"We thought that's where you'd gone." Marcus said.

Madame Nazimova looked up, her eyes wide with horror. "Back to Russia? Never!" She sighed. "My family are wheat farmers. A terrible plague swept through Yalta and destroyed everything. There was terrible, terrible famine everywhere, everyone starving. Then my sister-in-law, she had trouble with her kidneys. She was about to die. I sent them everything I had." She shrugged.

Marcus was aghast. "But Madame, where did that leave you?"

She shot Marcus a severe stare. "They saved Irina's life and bought seed to sow their fields. Now they have acres full of ripe wheat, they have bread upon their table, money in their pockets, Irina is healthy, and they smile once more."

"But what about you?"

She shrugged. "I've been poor before in my life. But when the last of my savings had gone, I looked around the Garden of Allah and found it too painful to remain. Every time I looked across the pool and around my gardens, I thought of the time when I earned thirteen thousand dollars every week. That's more than my family has earned in their entire lives. I was foolish, and now it is gone. I could stay no longer. My darling Dorothy took me in."

"We want you back," Kathryn said.

Madame smiled sadly. "I cannot afford pickles for my lunch, let alone a room at my Garden of Allah."

"Maybe you can," Kathryn said. She reached into her purse, pulled out a small book covered in black felt and handed it to Marcus.

"Madame," he said, handing it to her like it was a newborn baby. "In your haste to disappear, you left this behind."

Madame Nazimova took the book, turned it over in her hands and then opened it at a random page. Her lips moved as she read the lines of poetry inscribed in green ink. Her violet eyes lit up. "I remember this."

"These poems," Marcus said. "Were they really written by Rudolph Valentino?"

Alla nodded and turned the page. "He was a beautiful man."

"Madame," Marcus said, but she was lost in memory. He laid a hand on her arm and pressed it gently. She looked up into his face. "Madame, you own a book of poetry written by Rudolph Valentino in his own hand. Do you realize how much that is worth?"

CHAPTER 47

Gwendolyn had just finished hanging the last of the fire engine red tinsel on the darling little two-foot Christmas tree Kathryn had brought home that morning when Marcus tapped on the door and walked in. "How does it look?" she asked him.

"I haven't even begun to think of Christmas yet," he said. He dropped two tickets on the kitchen table where the morning light was starting to inch across from the window sill. Marlene Dietrich's new picture was called *The Garden of Allah* and Paramount's PR department thought it would be keen to have residents from Hollywood's Garden of Allah attend the premiere at Grauman's. "I keep expecting the weather to turn cold," Marcus said, "but it never does."

Kathryn appeared in the bedroom doorway brushing her hair. "Has anyone seen Madame around the Garden yet?" she asked. "I want to invite her to join us for Christmas dinner."

The president of the Valentino fan club turned out to be a very good friend of Madame Nazimova's. She knew Ramon Novarro's collector friend in New York and put the two of them in contact. The collector offered Madame an obscene amount of money for the book. Gwendolyn hoped, if only for Marcus' sake, that Madame would accept the offer and move back into the Garden, but they hadn't heard her answer yet.

"She should get herself an agent," Kathryn continued. "There's no reason she shouldn't be working. The lines on her face only make her more interesting. She could get all sorts of character roles." She turned to Gwendolyn. "Speaking of getting an agent, I've been meaning to ask you: what about that one you had an eye on? The one from the Zulu Hut."

"Oh!" With all the Cukor drama happening that night, she hadn't shared her latest career development with them. "He popped up at the Grove, so I got the hat check girl to go through his coat pockets."

Marcus hung the last of the painted wooden holly leaves on the tree. "Isn't that against the rules?"

"Completely! But I was utterly desperate to find out why he never bought tobacco from me. You wouldn't believe what he had in his pocket. Remember my loopy *Gwendolyn Was Here* plan? Gosh darn it if Mister Eldon Laird didn't have a *Gwendolyn Was Here* coaster from the Brown Derby right there in his pocket!"

"So it worked?" Kathryn asked. Although Kathryn had never said as much, Gwendolyn knew that Kathryn had thought her plan was ridiculously far-fetched.

Gwendolyn reached into her purse and pulled out a business card. "He gave me this and asked me to stop by his office."

Kathryn took the card and read it. "Gwendolyn!"

Gwendolyn nodded. "All I've been hearing since I moved here was that a smart girl gets herself an agent. They're the way in. Easier said than done. And now I find this guy's had one of my coasters all along."

Kathryn gave her hand a squeeze. "That's terrific. Congratulations, my dear." She drained the last of her coffee. "I'd better move my behind. Just as I was leaving the office yesterday, Wilkerson called me in and told me there's a book he wants me to read and summarize for him."

"Is that part of your job?" Marcus asked.

"Until I get what I want at the *Hollywood Reporter*, everything is part of my job."

"So which book does he want you to read?"

"That new one everyone's going nuts over. *Gone with the Wind.*"

"The one about the Civil War?" Gwendolyn asked. She felt like she'd spent half her childhood listening to Mama's stories of the tragedies suffered by the Boyington family at the hands of those despicable Yankees. The last thing she wanted to do was wade through a slab of a book about the same thing. She had better things to do now that she'd piqued the interest of an honest-to-goodness talent agent. "But isn't that thing over a thousand pages long?"

Kathryn nodded. "He wants the first part by Monday morning, and if we're due at Grauman's at six, I'm going to need every minute I can squeeze out of today. And a lot of coffee." She picked up her handbag and headed out the door. "See you later!"

Gwendolyn and Marcus bagelled in silence for a moment. "Do you think Madame Nazimova will come back here?" she asked him.

He sighed. "I sure hope so. I've missed her. Why? Don't you think she will?"

Gwendolyn shrugged but kept her eyes on Marcus. There was a look in his eyes that she saw from time to time and it filled his face now. It was a quiet sadness, like a longing for something he'd lost. He'd never said anything, but she felt she knew what he was thinking. She often thought the same thing.

"Once you've left a place," she ventured, "I don't think there's really any going back. Not really. You'd be expecting to return to the same place you left, but you can't. It couldn't be the same place. Life has gone on. There's no going back, and I think Madame is wise enough to know that."

Gwendolyn silently begged Marcus not to look away. Come on, she thought, you know I'm not just talking about Alla. Marcus' lips fell slightly apart and his shoulders relaxed as tears filled his eyes so subtly that she might have missed it. She was glad to see them.

The slightest of smiles broke out on Marcus' face.

"Yeah," he said quietly, "you're right. There is no 'until you've . . . blah-blah-blah.'"

She shook her head and looked down at her bagel. She'd made her point; there was no need to linger on it.

They sat in silence until Marcus got up from the table.

"Well," he announced, "I've got some reading of my own to do. Yesterday I picked up a copy of that book they reviewed in the *L. A. Times* last week, *How to Win Friends and Influence People*. I've decided not to count on anyone else–George Cukor included–to get me out of this Cosmopolitan-Hearst-Davies hole I've fallen into."

"Is it really that bad?"

"You know what they call it around the studio lot? The yoke of the joke. I want to get somewhere, make something of myself. I want to write real movies, and I'm not going to do it while I'm fluffing up these cotton candy pictures for Hearst's mistress. I need to get out of there and I figure it might help if I can charm my way out. Wish me luck."

"You don't need luck," Gwendolyn told him. "You've got talent. And us."

He smiled again. "Actually, I meant luck in staying awake. If I'm not going to sleep through this picture tonight, I've got to get me some shut eye." He kissed her on the cheek, whispered his thanks and was out the door.

Gwendolyn spotted Eldon Laird's business card on the kitchen table. The sight of it made her smile. Of all the things she'd had to endure since she got to Hollywood — falling off billboards, kneeing drunks in the groin, hocking diamond brooches–how funny that everything she wanted could all come down to a little piece of cardboard.

She looked around the villa. It wasn't often that she had the place to herself. Everyone seemed to be always popping in for a chat or a drink or to borrow a newspaper. She rarely got to enjoy the early peace of a Saturday morning alone. She sat at the kitchen table and watched as the edge of the morning light sidled its way toward her. When it hit the edge of the table she smiled, closed her eyes and tilted her face toward the sun.

THE END

Did you enjoy this book? You can make a big difference.

As an independent author, I don't have the financial muscle of a New York publisher supporting me. But I do have something much more powerful and effective, and it's something those publishers would kill to get their hands on: a committed and loyal bunch of readers.

Honest reviews of my books help bring them to the notice of other readers. If you've enjoyed this book, I would be so grateful if you could spend just a couple of minutes leaving a review on the website where you bought it.

Thank you very much,
Martin Turnbull

ALSO BY MARTIN TURNBULL

Hollywood's Garden of Allah novels:

Book 1 – *The Garden on Sunset*
Book 2 – *The Trouble with Scarlett*
Book 3 – *Citizen Hollywood*
Book 4 – *Searchlights and Shadows*
Book 5 – *Reds in the Beds*
Book 6 – *Twisted Boulevard*
Book 7 – *Tinseltown Confidential*
Book 8 – *City of Myths*
Book 9 – *Closing Credits*

Chasing Salomé: a novel of 1920s Hollywood

The Heart of the Lion: a novel of Irving Thalberg's Hollywood

Sign up for Martin's no-spam-ever mailing list, be the first to hear the latest news, and receive *Subway People* - a 1930s short story exclusively available to subscribers.
Go to: **http://bit.ly/turnbullsignup**

ACKNOWLEDGEMENTS

Heartfelt thanks to the following, who helped shaped this book:

My editor: Meghan Pinson, for her invaluable guidance, expert eye, and unfailing nitpickery.

My cover designer: Dan Yeager at Nu-Image Design who totally got what I was going for from the first email.

My Proof Reader Dream Team: Bob Molinari, Vince Hans, and Bryan Jossart, for their objective feedback and keen eyeballs.

My beta readers: Caitlin Crowley and Linda Sunshine who generously guided me through earlier incarnations of this book.

My go-to guys for everything Hollywood: James Parish and Woolsey Ackerman.

CONNECT WITH MARTIN TURNBULL

www.MartinTurnbull.com

Facebook.com/gardenofallahnovels

Twitter @TurnbullMartin

Blog: martinturnbull.wordpress.com

Goodreads: bit.ly/martingoodreads

Made in the USA
Las Vegas, NV
01 May 2021